CRUX

ALSO BY GABRIEL TALLENT

My Absolute Darling

CRUX

Gabriel Tallent

FIG TREE
an imprint of
PENGUIN BOOKS

FIG TREE

UK | USA | Canada | Ireland | Australia
India | New Zealand | South Africa

Fig Tree is part of the Penguin Random House group of companies
whose addresses can be found at global.penguinrandomhouse.com

Penguin Random House UK,
One Embassy Gardens, 8 Viaduct Gardens, London SW11 7BW

penguin.co.uk

First published in the United States of America by Riverhead Books,
an imprint of Penguin Random House LLC 2026
First published in Great Britain by Fig Tree 2026
001

Copyright © Gabriel Tallent, 2026

The moral right of the author has been asserted

On p. v, photograph © Adobe Stock

Penguin Random House values and supports copyright.
Copyright fuels creativity, encourages diverse voices, promotes freedom
of expression and supports a vibrant culture. Thank you for purchasing
an authorized edition of this book and for respecting intellectual property
laws by not reproducing, scanning or distributing any part of it by any
means without permission. You are supporting authors and enabling
Penguin Random House to continue to publish books for everyone.
No part of this book may be used or reproduced in any manner for the
purpose of training artificial intelligence technologies or systems. In accordance
with Article 4(3) of the DSM Directive 2019/790, Penguin Random House
expressly reserves this work from the text and data mining exception

Printed and bound in Great Britain by Clays Ltd, Elcograf S.p.A.

The authorized representative in the EEA is Penguin Random House Ireland,
Morrison Chambers, 32 Nassau Street, Dublin D02 YH68

A CIP catalogue record for this book is available from the British Library

HARDBACK ISBN: 978-0-241-76731-3
TRADE PAPERBACK ISBN: 978-0-241-76732-0

Penguin Random House is committed to a sustainable future
for our business, our readers and our planet. This book is made from
Forest Stewardship Council® certified paper.

For Hattie

I.
THE PRINCESS

One

He heard her crunching through the sand and then she dropped into the wash and came swaggering toward him in cutoffs, baggy white muscle shirt, and chuck taylors, carrying climbing shoes and an oversized hardbound lab notebook. The shiteatingest girl you ever saw.

"Hello, numbnuts!" she said.

"Hey there, Tams," he said, rising to a stand. Together they followed the wash, two seventeen-year-old kids on the evening of the first day of their last year of high school. After a couple of miles, they passed through a break in low hills to a kind of parking lot full of discarded tires, shell casings, and used condoms, with plastic bags snaggled in the grickle-grass. Nearby, the ruin of some strange purple house. Fridays and weekends, Dan and Tamma stayed away. This place could be a scene. It could feel not entirely safe. Once a guy had asked Tamma for "just a little dicksucking," and she'd said, "Little in what way?" Weeknights, they had the parking lot to themselves.

The boulders lay singly or in huddles, forming alleys through which they walked, kicking aside cans and red solo cups, until they came to the last and greatest of the rocks. She was thirty-five feet high, chai-colored, glinting with mica and quartz, the edges outlined in chalk. The route was Fingerbang Princess, put up by Jane Sasaki before they were born, and graded V4. The wind stirred sand from about their feet.

Tamma said, "Fuck me, dude."

"Every time," Dan said.

"I could puke. Could you puke?"

Joshua trees stood limned against the whiskey-gold horizon. The clouds were tangles of cotton-candy pink. The desert otherwise sere in the grayness, going to hills banded blue, pale green, and pewter, looped with ATV tracks, the gravel like shattered pottery. Though it was not yet quite dark, some few satellites showed in the bruisy vault. She dredged her cutoffs with witchy fingers, played a quarter into her hand, showed him one side, the other.

"Tails," he said.

Tamma lofted the coin into the air, caught it on her forearm, and uncapped it: tails. Grinned snaggletoothed and cattywampus, big ears peeking out through tangled hair.

"Are you *scurred*?" she said.

"I ain't scurred."

"It's not dangerous if you don't fall."

"I think about that all the time."

Daniel Redburn set up in the dust, shaking his head, loosening the laces on an old pair of la sportiva mythos. He'd found these shoes in the dumpster at the Intersection Rock parking lot on some long-ago family venture into Joshua Tree National Park. In places, the rubber was worn down to the leather. They were stained brown inside with somebody else's blood. Dan drew the slack up eyelet by eyelet. He had a patient way about him. Careful, tall, broad shouldered, and lean, with tousled blond hair, shorn close on the sides. His old man cut it every Sunday night, and knew only the one style, which he had learned by studying the brochure that had come with the clippers.

The Princess loomed above. She was a boulder problem: a short, difficult climb, usually protected with crash pads. But Dan and Tamma had no pads and so spotted one another as best they could. The route started in an overhang, climbed to a roof at fifteen feet, and then it was twenty feet of slab to the summit. He scooched forward on his butt. Feet on lego-block starting holds. He chalked his hands, clapped them off on his thighs, pulled onto the rock, and—first move—greased back off into the sand and sat laughing. He twisted around to look at her.

"I can confirm," he said. "It's still hard."

"Isn't that your dad's catchphrase?"

"Such a bitch."

She angled the flashlight down into the grotto. He pulled onto the rock, timed his breathing to the moves. There were edges he hit so hard that his vision dimmed when he caught them. Then he'd adjust with a hitching motion that started at the feet—kipping up to slack and reposition on incut fifteen- and twenty-mil patina rims, digging his fingertips into the deepest cranny of each. He threw desperate move after desperate move, with a gathering sense of wonder that he was still on the wall. His feet slipped off and he tucked his chin and fought for it, muscles cabling up out of his forearms. He groaned with effort, sure that he was off, but hung the move anyway, brought his right foot back to its edge, set it gently, and pivoted the heel right, then left, finding the angle.

He climbed to his high point beneath the roof, a crusty, full-pad patina rail they called the Last Homely House, because it was the best hold on the overhang, and a sort-of rest before the first crux. He took a few breaths, getting his left foot high, sinking down to the full extension of his arms. Then he pounced up for the roof, coming entirely off the wall, hands extended. His left was going for a teacup pocket just over the lip that Tamma called Tinkerbell's Bandersnatch.

He struck the pocket one-handed, sank two fingers, and willed them to hold. Then his legs swung out in a pendulum that ripped the pocket from his grasp and he was off, cartwheeling sideways. He had a wild flash of the Princess Boulder, the cobalt horizon, the desert, and then Tamma clawed her hands into his shirt and he cratered her to the ground.

Sprawled out beneath him, she started to laugh. He palmed down into the sand and she army-crawled away, cackling, and then stood herself up, knock-kneed, pigeon-toed, patting herself all over. Adjusted the straps of her bralette. Hitched up her cutoffs. Checked her teeth with her tongue. Hocked and spat. Examined it for blood. Tamarisk Callahan: figure of grace.

"You okay?" he said.

"I think . . . ?"

"Yeah?"

"I think . . . I'm okay."

"Dang," he said. Sitting in the dirt.

"Dang, what?"

"Dang, dude, we really need a bouldering pad."

"You know what Ray Jardine used to say?"

"Fuck Ray Jardine."

"A stone master, a total visionary, and what he used to say was—"

"I fucking hate this saying."

"He had this mystical insight, which was: Whatever you don't have, you don't need."

"Goddamnit," Dan said, laughing.

"He called it the Ray Way," Tamma said. "Which is just *great branding*, you know?"

Tamma went lurching over to her shoes. They were old TC pros restrung with indestructible pink hockey laces. She started clawing them loose.

"I tell you what," he said. "A bouldering pad sure would be *nice*."

"Yeah, well, we don't fucking have one, do we!"

"Jeepers, I didn't mean to rile you."

"I'm not riled," she yelled. Then pitched her chuck taylors away into the dark and pulled one climbing shoe on.

"What is it?"

"I almost dropped you."

"You didn't drop me though."

"I fumbled you and you almost swan dived into the dirt. I could feel it happening. I had this thought, like: I'm losing him!"

"You caught me," he said. "It's fine. What about Ray Jardine?"

"Fuck Ray Jardine," she said, pulling on her other shoe ferociously, seething beneath Fingerbang Princess. "You're right! We need a pad. *Dude*."

"Yeah, dude?"

"What if one day I don't catch you? I blow it and you take a header into the sand and you're lying there all crumpled up and you can't, like, move. And it's my fault. What do I do then?"

"Dang."

"And you're just like, 'Help me, Tamma, I can't feel anything.' But I can't help you. What happens to us?"

"Pick up a rock, tell me you love me, and crush my face in."

"No, thanks."

"Just don't let me suffer. Make the first hit really count."

"And what would I do without you?"

"You'd be fine."

"I'd never be fine again."

"You'd be okay," Dan said. "You spend one night astraddle your best friend, mortaring his face into chef boyardee with a granite pestle, and the rest of your life wondering why you can't come any way but cowgirl."

"You asshole!"

The maglite lay where she'd dropped it. The beam askew. From out the dark came glittering green flares and brief, smeary, holographic glimmerings: reflections off the iridescent eyes of spiders hunting the sand.

"Besides, it would add secret darkness to your backstory. Two children go out into the desert and only one comes out. You go on to become a professional climber. Travel the world with your black diamond sponsorship. At night you cuddle hard-sending offwidth babes in the back of your toyota, drinking whiskey, telling them about how, once upon a time, you were best friends with this guy and he didn't make it. You shed a single tear. 'He was so beautiful and so young,' you say. 'So mysteriously close with my mom. How she wept at the funeral!'"

"You motherfucker!" Tamma said, laughing, wrenching at her hair. "You dickhole! You can't go ker-splatting yourself. All we gotta do is make it through this year. It's one school year that stands between us and a life of freedom and sendage and seeing Alex Puccio at the crag and asking for her number and getting shut down, but *gloriously* shut down. So don't joke about that: because you don't *get* to die. I won't let you."

"Oh yeah?" he said. "Are you worried about me?"

"Shut up!"

"Are you having feelings right now?"

"No!"

"Oh man I think you're having *hella* feelings."

"Fuck you I'm not!" she said. She'd gotten her foot into her climbing shoe, and now she stretched it out before her, took up the laces, and yarded them till they creaked.

"Dude," he said.

"Dude," she said back.

"*Dude!*" he said.

"DUDE," she cried. "I was! I was so scared for you!"

They sat in the dark together. Tamma underneath the boulder. One close to the other.

Two

Every day after school, Dan gave Tamma a ride back to his place. He'd strike north on a side street from the school parking lot, blaze down the highway, then turn onto unsigned double track through creosote and smoketree desert. To the west, there was a historic, tourist-trap type of a town, which Tamma liked to call Lone Coyote as a sort of joke, and to the east, a larger town she called 73 Coyotes. But Dan and Tamma weren't from any town. They were just from out in the desert, though the desert here was really a kind of vast, dispersed warren of properties slowly turning into vacation rentals. There were mansions, survivalist compounds, movie star bungalows, curated midcentury trailer homes, a twenty-million-dollar art installation, and a six-story aluminum pyramid. Dan's place was a single-story cottage where whip scorpions lived in the siding and a horny toad waited on the concrete porch. He'd go inside, carrying his boots by the laces, and speak to his mother, Alexandra Redburn, through the bedroom door. Danny, is that you? Yes, Mom, it's me. Remember to do your homework, Danny. I will, Mom.

Tamma'd come sauntering in after him in run-down jeans and a scissored-out Puscifer muscle tee and stand at the kitchen island, menacing the leftovers. From his mother's door Dan would turn around and catch Tamma eating orange peels. Chewing steak bones from the night before. She'd nab butter off the stick. Side-eyeing him as his mother spoke. "Dude," he'd whisper, meaning, *That bread is moldy*, and "Dude," she'd say back, meaning, *Don't worry, I scraped the mold off.*

Dan liked to get his homework done before they took off, if he could, because after, his hands would hurt too much to hold a pencil. The two of them would work in his room, Dan at his desk while Tamma basked on the bed, clashing her heels together, making use of Dan's laptop and the extravagantly expensive dish internet to watch videos of Sasha DiGiulian, of Akiyo Noguchi, of Alex Johnson, perhaps women's #2 at the IFSC Vail World Cup, pausing the video, closing her eyes, imagining herself climbing it just how Angie Payne had climbed it, laying back double bowling-ball slopers with a high left foot, flagging her right, powering left to a third sloper, then standing up to double crimps.

When he was done, he'd again speak to Alexandra through the door. Are you going out with Tamarisk, Danny? Yes, Mom. Well, be careful. I will, of course. Watch out for rattlesnakes. Yes, Mom. Absolutely.

They spent the first nine weeks of senior year getting utterly shut down. There were nights where they fell lower and lower down on the problem until Tamma was just rage-sobbing and looking at her pink, weeping, traitorous fingertips in disbelief. They shambled from class to class like car crash survivors. At lunch, Dan brought her into the bathroom to watch him piss. "What do you think?" he said.

"Do you have insurance?"

"No?"

"Don't think of it as blood, then."

"How should I think about it?"

"Your kidneys are girls no longer," Tamma said, throwing out jazz hands. "They're women now."

Their finger pads were raw and forearms bruised black and Tamma's tailbone hurt. What she'd said was, "My tailbone hurts, can you take a look?" and then she'd hooked her thumbs under her jeans and pulled them down without unbuttoning them. Dan, seeing her do it, had said, "Owow!" and she'd said, "Shut up and look at this," and quartered to show her butt cheek, deep ugly green marbled with black, the bruise running from the dimples above her hip girdle down her left thigh, and he'd said, "What am I looking for here?" and she'd said, "Does it look bruised?" and he'd said, "A little."

After their night climbing sessions, she would walk back home to her family's trailer, grasp the bedroom window, beach herself over the sill, and lie in her dirty laundry, hurting all over, saying to herself that she'd never make it as a climber, that it was time to prepare for a life of taking margaritas from one place to another while slowly, inexorably, margarita-by-margarita, nacho-plate-by-nacho-plate, becoming her mother.

She'd crawl across the floor, mount up into her bunk bed, and in the morning, she'd wake, turn over, and scream her excitement into her pillow, because any day you were going to go climb granite was the best day in the world, her brother, Colin, saying, "Tammmmmmmm-mma!" and Tamma swinging up off the pillow and saying "What up, asswipe?" saying it full of joy and sisterly affection, and rolling off the bed and coming down the hallway to the kitchen, picking her underwear from her butt cheeks, and finding the cheerios farther back in the cabinets than usual and making a short hop for them, and another, and a third, pulling the box out, catching it in her cradled arms, and stopping with her mother's boyfriend watching her from the couch, the girl smiling for him, putting her fist up in the air, and slowly, oh so slowly raising her middle finger, looking at him with the smile plastered on her face, and the boyfriend pursing his lips and looking back down at his phone and shifting side to side on the couch in contained amusement.

School let out at three thirty, it was a forty-five-minute drive home, a forty-five-minute walk out, and sunset was just before six. Each night was colder than the last, counting down until it would be too bitter for night climbing and too much of a scene for weekend climbing. If they had free use of the car, they could drive out into the park and climb weekends and breaks, but they only had permission to drive to and from school. The moment when night climbing season would close, and they would have to give up on Fingerbang Princess, was fast approaching. The two of them walked out to the parking lot in early November, Tamma thinking goddamn she was sexy, striding out through the cold Mojave night like Washington crossing the Delaware; that was about how majestic she felt, and about how cold it was; and GODDAMN she was hot, you wouldn't know it to look at her, but goddamn she was, she was secretly hot, she was George Washington hot; her enormous dick barely fit into her golden knee breeches; and they walked again through the notch in the hills, Tamma saying, "Dude!—duuuuuuuuuude. Do you ever think, if we were, like, walking out here some night, and we, like, met the devil, do you ever imagine what you'd ask for? If you could give up your soul and have anything?"

"I'd ask for Mom to get up out of bed and be all right," Dan said.

"Does she literally not get out of bed, or what?"

"I mean, she gets up and walks around during the day. I find things she left out. Like she'll make ramen and leave the pot on the stove. She'll eat dinner with us sometimes. And she'll be all like, 'Sorry I was absent, Danny, but I'm here now, we're gonna get this all worked out, I'm gonna help you with your college applications, you can count on me.' She'll make all these promises. And you can be like, Okay, wow, maybe it'll be different this time. And then she'll disappear again."

"Well, now, I'm gonna sound like an asshole," Tamma said. "But I'd ask to be the best climber that ever lived. Because, think about it. You and me, we're out here trying to make it work! But we're FAH-BLAMMED!"

"We're what?"

"We don't have good climbing shoes, we don't have bouldering pads, a rope, gear, harnesses, access to climbing gyms, mentors, help, or anything that we need. Paisley Cuthers is out there in the world, crushing V10 at Hueco and the Buttermilks."

"Has she actually sent V10 in the Buttermilks?"

"Don't nitpick my numbers! Alex Johnson is the first American to win two World Cup golds. Puccio is sending everything in a globe-trotting, jaw-dropping, panty-soaking orgy of sendage that will go down in history. Angie Payne is Angie Payne. And meanwhile, we're stuck here, in Buttfuck, California, working this one chossy V4 nobody has ever heard of. Which—speaking of different lives, dude. Can you believe this: My big sis Sierra is giving birth tonight."

"Wait, what?"

"Yeah, dude! They're all there! My mom, her boyfriend, Sierra's husband, my little brother, everybody! At the hospital! But she's already got two kids. And Samantha is only ten months old. Can you imagine? Like, she's just stuck at home forever, taking care of babies, right? Except of course she also has a job? Like: Kill me."

"Should you be there?"

"Nah, fuck her. I want to be out here, with you, in the teeth of glory! And if we met the devil, standing there with cloven hooves and a bowler hat, we could make it happen."

"Because if you were famous and sponsored you could go places," Dan said. "Red Rocks. Yosemite. Vedauwoo. Indian Creek. Squamish. Be the opposite of your sister, Sierra. You could escape your circumstances. Never see your mom again."

"That's just the start!" Tamma said. "I don't just want to go places, Dan, I want to be the best trad climber that has ever lived. The sendiest, thirstiest, baddest motherfucker in the history of motherfuckers. I want to be legend. I want to send Cobra. I want to send Belly Full of Bad Berries and Century Crack. I want John Long to write a story about me called 'The Snatchiest Bandersnatch That Ever Snatched.' I want Cedar Wright to look directly into the camera and adjust those 'fuck me' glasses of his and say, 'Unsponsored and unknown, this acne-ravaged, emotionally stunted fry cook has been quietly ticking off some of the hardest and most dangerous trad climbs in the world,' I want Andrew Burr to shoot me climbing Primrose Dihedrals with a stogie in my teeth like an even dykier Clint Eastwood, and I want every human being who sees that film to go, 'Holy fuck, is that what the world looks like, when it isn't all strip malls and sadness?' I want them to toss and turn at night, electric with a yearning they forgot was even possible, dreaming of an America that is, just a little bit, still out there.

We will show them that there are things yet in this country for which to strive, and there will be a chance to save this nation before it's all just miles and miles of denny's and walmarts. Do you know what I mean?"

"Jesus Christ," he said. "You're saying you want to crush so hard you change the world."

"Yes! It doesn't look possible. But yes! That's what I want!"

Three

The Redburns sat at the dinner table beneath a hanging lamp. Lawrence, Alexandra, and Dan. The edge of the light lay upon the concrete floor. Alexandra cradled a wineglass with violet fingertips. On the plates, meatloaf and potatoes. It was the thirteenth of November, 2011. Fingerbang Princess still unsent. Storms hovering on the edge of the ten-day forecast. Storms that, if they were real, would close out the season. Tamma's big sister, Sierra, had given birth to River McCulluch only days before.

"How are classes going?" Alexandra asked.

"Pretty good."

"And your grades?"

"Good."

"And the applications?"

"I've been talking to the counselor," Dan said. "He likes the application. The deadline is January fifteenth for Reed and Whitman. A few are earlier. Willamette is February first. So we're in good shape."

"Letters of rec?"

"They're in. I do need your help with FAFSA. There's a bunch of stuff on there I don't know how to do."

"Okay, when is that?"

"Earlier is better, but it's due when I turn in applications."

"I will work on that with you this week," Alexandra said. "I'm sorry I've been gone. But we're gonna get this all done. I'll help you. What about the personal statement?"

"I'm still going over it."

"We will go over it together. I actually had to do a lot of writing of that kind when I was touring my first book. Pieces for journalists, magazines, interviews. We can do this."

"I'd like that."

"You'll be the first in the family to go to college," Lawrence said. Broad shouldered, rawboned, his ancient blue work shirt rolled up, his forearms the color of old leather boots, with fine, papery wrinkles and scattered brown sun-stains.

Alexandra pressed her mouth into her cupped shoulder, coughed, and then spoke. "To that end, we have thirteen thousand dollars set aside in a savings account."

This was not news. Alexandra did this from time to time—got up out of bed and came to dinner, as if she were going to start writing again, as if she were going to be around from here on out. And when she did, she brought up the money, always as if she had not brought it up before. Dan thought maybe that was because if you were making a heroic, last-ditch effort to save your own life, you had to pretend as if you hadn't tried and failed a hundred times already, and not because you didn't remember, and not because you didn't hate yourself for that, but because it would be impossible to get out of bed at all without rendering yourself this little grace. She had set the money aside at great personal hardship, was what he understood. Dan never knew what to say when she told him this. He wished they would keep it. He did not know if they had anything set aside for themselves and he could not ask.

"You're spending," Alexandra said. She coughed into her arm again. Small, dry throat-clearings. "You're spending a lot of time with Tamma."

"Are you two . . . ?" Lawrence said.

"Ew, Dad," he said. "Gross."

"Well, I'm just asking, Danny."

"She's like my sister."

"Well, that's true."

"And she's gay," Dan said, with great self-assurance, though Tamma had once told him that her New Year's resolution was to do a one-arm pull-up off Ryan Reynolds's erection while he did the Van Damme splits in a bathroom stall of the YMCA.

"So, you're not dating her?" Alexandra said.

"We're friends."

"I don't know if men and women *can* be friends."

"Why not?"

"Because of who they are to one another."

"Peers?"

"Don't feign naivete, Dan. It wouldn't be okay with us, for you to date her."

"Why?"

"She's not like you."

"Not like me, how?"

"She's self-destructive and oppositionally defiant. I hear her talking. She is a nasty little girl, which she can get away with for now. But when she's an adult? And besides, if she aims any higher than being a hostess at wing stop, her mother, Kendra, will pull her right back down again. Kendra can't stand to see anyone succeed. I feel badly for Tamma. I do. But you can't help people who won't help themselves."

"Are you seeing any other young ladies?" Lawrence asked.

"I'm sort of busy, Dad."

Dan didn't spend time with anyone except Tamma. He'd had crushes from time to time but they came to nothing. What Dan did was he worked. He did all the climbing Tamma did, plus a morning workout, his own reading, the homework Tamma did not do, additional homework for honors and AP courses, prepping for the SAT, and college applications. He got around five hours of sleep most nights. Sometimes he lay in bed, going over everything in his mind. If his personal statement would be stronger if he took another tack. If he'd picked the wrong letters of rec. If he and Tamma could really make it as climbers. If moving to a higher, worse, intermediate hold before Tinkerbell's Bandersnatch would be better than the dyno from the Last Homely House. If he had already destroyed his application by having too few extracurriculars. If his life would be livable at all without climbing.

There was this question Dan had about himself. He wondered, sometimes, if something wasn't wrong with him, the way it had been wrong with Alexandra. Sitting at his desk at night, if Tamma wasn't there, he'd feel this growing tightness in the pit of his stomach. Tamma kept all that at bay; she was surrounded by an aura of brightness and swagger. But with her gone, that tight feeling would suck away everything else, like a bathtub slowly draining, leaving him in this cold, bereft world-that-was-not-the-world, where each thing—the desk, the walls, the chair, his golden #2 pencil, the ashtray full of shavings—was a clever facsimile of itself. His room was not *his room*. The pencil in his hand was not *his pencil*. It was all ticky-tacky stage dressing. Like he had died and gone to hell, and hell was a perfect recreation of his childhood bedroom, in which he did his homework, alone, pretending everything was okay, when nothing was okay: The pencil, the bed, the walls, the concrete floor, all of it manufactured to deceive him, and beyond the paper-thin walls, it was a godless abyss into which he had been sunk, a hundred thousand miles from Tamma, and if he crossed the room and opened the door, the living room would be created from out of nothingness, a lie, about which he could feel nothing, because it was not real, and he knew it was not real, without being able to say exactly how.

When this happened, he'd sit, sharpening his pencil as if nothing were wrong. Even alone in his room, he had to do everything right. He was going to be the *first in his family*. His parents didn't have savings. They didn't have insurance or pensions or 401(k)s. It all depended on him. He was too smart, too hardworking, too high performing to dick around with whatever this was. And so, he'd wait for it to pass, calmly sharpening his pencil like an actor playing the part of the Straight-A Student, the American Golden Child. He'd keep doing his homework and repeat, to himself, silently, as if auditioning the statement, I need help. I need someone to help me. I'm thinking about killing myself. Giving no sign. His handwriting fontlike.

Maybe he was working too hard, but not doing well, or not getting into college, those weren't options, and he couldn't stop going out with Tamma, either. Out in the desert, things felt luminous with meaning.

Every crunching footstep was real. And when you were up on the rock, then every crystal, crack, and rimple was endowed with indissoluble, life-saving importance, each dike and chickenhead inalienably itself. He sometimes felt this hope, that out there in the great American emptiness he could find himself. It was a stupid idea, but he could catch himself thinking that he might live a life in such close and sustained contact with the implacable reality of things that the sickness couldn't take it from him.

So, he hoped someday to date girls. He wanted that for himself. He wanted to find a hard-sending deep-reading art girl, a girl so straight, so desperately into guys, that Tamma would regard it as an outrage against feminism; he wanted that, but mostly what he felt was that everything was fine, everything was doable, as long as he did not make a mistake, never stumbled, hesitated, or flinched, as long as he spent his nights with Tamma and his days doing what his parents needed him to do. He could not miss a single question on his math homework, nor a single move on the Princess's intricate and sequential overhang, and he didn't have time to double-check his calculations, so he had to get every question right, every time, and he had to do it quickly, and when he did that, it was merely what everyone expected. So when his old man asked if he was seeing any young ladies, what he felt, really, was a kind of rage. With what *time*, Dad? Aren't you living here? Haven't you seen me? Aren't you paying attention? Don't you have any idea, any idea at all?

"I just thought . . ." Lawrence said, "a handsome kid like you."

"No, Dad."

"I don't want you," Alexandra said, "to talk to Tamma about this. She will object to seeing you succeed where she cannot. She will try and hold you back. But you are possessed of opportunities she has foreclosed, and in your life you will have very many friends brighter and more promising, deserving of your company, alike to you in prospects. When you're my age, Tamma will just be a girl you used to know a long time ago."

"I understand that," Dan said.

After Alexandra excused herself, Dan and his old man stayed up. Dan sat in a dining room chair, under a nylon cape. His father stood behind him. Lawrence had a can of beer on the kitchen island. He brushed the clippers with a spare toothbrush. Dabbed them with rem oil. Turned them on.

"We don't mean," Lawrence said, "to be hard on you. You know that, don't you, Danny?"

"I don't feel you're hard on me."

"Good, good. It's tricky."

His old man walked to the side and took a drink and sighed and set the can back down. He was silent for a long time. Here and there were columns, which were pinyons he had carved down with a drawknife and darkened with castor oil. Dan still had the levi's his old man had worn to do it, stained at the thighs, and gone at the knees to white yarns. Dan looked on, reflected in the murky window, waiting to hear what was tricky. Beyond that dark reflection, distant and scattered light. Other houses, out there on the plain.

"It's tricky," Lawrence said again. "On the one hand, she worries about pushing you. On the other hand, she has regrets about things not done."

"What things?"

Lawrence drank, held the can to his breast. You could ask him a question and he might say nothing in return. Fifteen minutes of silence as he worked. At last, he said, "Well, you know, Danny. She had to leave home so young, she was just your age. She'd been writing stories in secret, and when she got them published, her parents turned her out. Well, she'd been working at the diner with your buddy Tamma's mom, Kendra. So Kendra took her in, when she needed a place to stay, and Alexandra kept on writing. But I think she wishes she'd just left, gone to college. She'd been so sheltered, you know? Kendra taught her everything about life, I think. Taught her how to put on lipstick. How to talk to boys. How to balance a checkbook. How to dress. They used to cut up lines in the back of the diner together."

"Dad!"

"They were best, *best* friends then. Her and Kendra. I think that's why she stayed. Funny how that is, you know. That you can be so close to somebody. And you think they want the best for you, but it turns out that's not what they want at all."

Dan was listening as hard as he could. This was more than he'd ever heard about his parents. There were entire years where you could add up all the things his old man said to him and it wouldn't be this much.

"That's when you met?" Dan asked.

"Just out in front of the diner. Her and Kendra, leaning against the wall. Kendra was this great beauty. Famous for it. But there was just something in your mother's eyes. I couldn't stop looking. And right off, she was the smartest person I ever met. You could just feel it, Danny. Brilliant. Brilliant from the very first words that fell out of her mouth. It was love if there was ever love. I used to drive her out into the desert and we'd lie out there on a wool blanket and try and count the stars. I bought this little plot of land right next to Kendra. Cost two hundred dollars. I started building the house, and Alex, she wrote her book right out there in the backyard. Well, we were desperate poor and hardworking, but we had this dream. Of our future. She was going to be the voice of a generation. I was going to do fine carpentry—desks and armoires and such. We had these close, close friends in Kendra and Patrick, Tamma's dad, right next door to us, we'd spend every evening out in front of the firepit. Alexandra and Kendra used to bathe you and Tamma together in the same pink bathtub. We had everything, it seemed like. The world was in our hands. It doesn't really seem fair, does it, us coming down on you like this. But that's what I'm telling you. We thought it would all work out. We thought we had the American dream. But when your old lady had her accident, they took everything. They took all the money she'd made and we had to mortgage the house."

Lawrence stepped back to make a study of his work. To see if it was even. It wasn't. When he started again, Dan could hear the hair alighting on the nylon cape. Alexandra had not had an accident. It had been a congenital heart defect, a bicuspid aortic valve. Dan had very many memories of that time. Or maybe the same memory, over and over again. Of walking down a long, vinyl-tiled hallway with his father, toward a room at the end of the hall. Walking. His old man cut off at the chest. Just jeans and a flannel shirt. Holding his hand. Hospital beds and carts left against the walls. And the smell. The distinctive smell. The tile, the lights, the room ahead of them. Just that. Passing doorways, each, in Dan's remembrance, a rectangle of black, as if they windowed into a profound outer darkness. He had been nine years old, but it felt strange and distant, as if he had been much younger.

Lawrence turned off the clippers and riffled Dan's hair.

"So, I think the thing your mom is trying to get you to understand," he said, "is that it's not enough to follow a dream at the cost of stability. I think the thing is, for all her promise, she wishes she had gone to school, gotten a paycheck, had health insurance and a pension. Wishes she'd been able to leave Kendra, and this desert, behind. Go somewhere else. Somewhere better. That's the thing about dreams, Danny, they come and go, you can't keep hold of them, you can't build a life on them. Your mom was brilliant, gifted, she worked as hard as she could, every day, she made a million dollars, and it wasn't enough. Do things the right way, Danny. Go to college. Be a doctor or a lawyer or something. Have some security. A paycheck, health insurance, a 401(k). Don't ever mistake this for a country in which you can set off on your own. It's not a place dreams come true. At least not anymore. Because we really tried, Danny. That is why your mom is putting the screws to you. So you won't be young, dumb, and hopeful the way we were."

Four

They went to school; they did school-kid things, opened their lockers, put books away, took notes; Tamma sketched climbs in her lab notebook; Dan did homework; Tamma downloaded videos of Alex Johnson; Dan stooped over his textbook; they sat in brightly colored, molded-plastic chairs; they walked vinyl-tiled hallways, full of the feeling that life was somewhere, elsewhere; and on Monday, the fourteenth of November, Tamma was crimping up the overhang of Fingerbang Princess, her breath falling in evanescent plumes, sinking down into the last good hold, skittering her feet about on matchbook edges until she found the high, left, dice-sized nub, and then she leapt. Going up on pointe like a dancer and then leaving her stage behind, out into the dark.

She caught Tinkerbell's Bandersnatch and her feet caromed left in an enormous swing, her shoulder packed, her hair fanning, and sneering with effort, she held it. For the first time ever. She was so surprised that she just dangled there, waiting to fall, holding the roof with one hand, nothing else. When she didn't fall, she kicked her heel up over the lip and, in one smooth, clean, desperate movement, boosted herself up onto the slab above.

Standing in the dust, Dan was thinking, Fuck me, but she is good. On the ground, Tamma was the clumsiest person he had ever met, but on the wall, she was breathtaking. People who didn't climb tended to imagine climbing as a series of *Cliffhanger*-style pull-ups, and indeed, that's how Dan climbed. Dan could solve entire boulder problems with his feet nowhere except in the way. But Tamma—Tamma set each hold gently, and rather than cranking with her arms, she stepped through the move, turning her hip to the wall, driving with her legs, extending for the next edge, so that it appeared effortless, tiptoeing up climbs with body english and devious footwork. If there was a big, pull-up-style move, she'd sling a heel above her head and pull through with her hamstrings. Watching her, he felt himself to be in the company of grace and courage such as most people went their entire lives without ever seeing. Everyone he knew seemed to think Tamma was trash, but he thought she was some kind of genius.

He waited, holding the flashlight, and in him moved the twinned, scissoring-apart, scissoring-together wantings, wanting to see her succeed, and a peeling-back from her, a fear that she would do the boulder before him, and that with her having done it, the pressure would be on for him to do it too. Since his fall, he had been holding back, more concerned with not dying than topping out; he wasn't committing from one move to the next with the send-or-splatter intensity that Fingerbang Princess required. But if Tamma climbed this thing, then he'd have to put on his big-girl panties and climb it next. And yet, he wanted that; he watched her, brimming with hope, and not sure what he hoped, maybe for something bigger, scarier, riskier, more wide open, for whatever came next if Tamma proved that they could actually, for real, finish this thing.

The slab above the roof was crossed by three slanting crystal dikes: outsloped rails like the crimped edges of a piecrust. The wall was otherwise featureless save for the subtle dishing of the rock, about as deep and positive as paper plates. Tamma climbed with hand-foot matches going to intricate, balancy sequences, until she came to a blank place more than twenty-five feet above the deck, her stance as high as she could get it on the last piecrust dike. Dan could see no footholds except a crystal shaped like a domino pasted onto the rock. It was high up by her hip. She had to leave the security of the dike behind, step left to a terrifying friction-smear in a paper-plate dish, and then right to the domino, which would be level with her groin. Her only handhold was a molar-sized crystal, high and left, angled the wrong direction, which she would pry against with the pad of her left thumb.

She was blowing with panic. In the flashlight's beam, he could see gooseflesh on the backs of her arms. She dipped one hand into her chalk bag, clapped it clean on the butt of her jeans. The slab was so steep that her cheek was up against the rock.

He watched as she planted her pointer finger on the domino hold by her hip. Then she backed off.

"Dude!"

"Yeah?"

"That's a bad hold, dude."

"Tamma, there's no other choice. It's go, and *maybe* fall. Or stand there, and *definitely* fall."

"I just want to go home!"

"You have to try, Tamma!"

"I'm too scared, dude!"

She planted her finger again on the domino hold. A centimeter deep. Four centimeters wide. She started bringing her right foot up to it, and then, once again, retreated to the stance at the dike. Put her face to the wall, making scared and miserable noises.

"Commit or crater, slutcake."

"How's the fall?'

"Not good!"

"I can't do it!"

"You *can*!"

"Dan?"

"Yes?"

"If I die?"

"Yeah?"

"At the funeral? Like, during the speech? I want you to say I was the best lay you ever had."

"What?"

"I don't want people to think I died a virgin, dude."

"You *are* a virgin," Dan said.

"But it's so embarrassing, Dan! I want people to think I lived a rad life of adventure and blossoming sexuality. A kind of slutty, swashbuckling pirate princess!"

"Why?"

"Just say I was better than Madison."

"What? At the funeral? Won't it seem inappropriate and apropos of nothing?"

"Nah, dude, it'll be fine."

"But I barely know Madison, won't she find that confusing? Won't her mom be alarmed?"

"I'm sure she's amazing. She's, like, the third hottest girl in school. Just stand at the head of the casket, weeping, and say, 'Ah, Tamma. The best lay I ever had. Even better than Madison Van Der Meer.' Then point her out in the crowd. So everyone can see how hot she is."

"Tamma, don't make me do that!"

"Promise me!"

"I promise!"

She began drawing her right foot up to the hold, hooking her leg around the back of her arm, aiming to share space with her fingertip in a hand-foot match. She was trembling all over, canting her hips, engaging every muscle. Then her left foot greased out from beneath her and she came cheesegrating down the slab, and at the last moment her foot snagged an edge and she flipped over backward. Dan reached up to catch her and she came on toward him headfirst, her hands extended in a backward somersault. She put her thumb into his eye and he twisted away with her thumb pad catching in the socket, bringing his chin down and reaching to catch her nonetheless, and she squirted out from his grasp and took a header into the dirt.

She lay in the sand for a time and then rolled over and tried to prop herself up and then she puked and put her face right back down into it and lay breathing. Dan crouched beside her, not wanting to say anything, covering his eye with his hand. Then he let himself down into the sand, staring up at the stars with one eye, holding a hand over the other, unwilling and afraid to open it. She crawled over to him. Her face crusted with gravel.

"I'm sorry, sorry, sorry," she said. She started to cry, leaning over him, bracing her head with both hands, as if to hold it together at the temples.

"*I'm* sorry," Dan said. He spoke to the stars. Andromeda lay there above him, the chained daughter of Cassiopeia swathed across the starscape.

"No it's me."

"I should've caught you."

"I shouldn't've fallen."

"It's my job to catch you, Tams."

"It's my job not to fall."

He could feel sludge beneath his fingers. He did not yet have the guts to lift his hand. Tamma was crying and snotting into the downy peach fuzz of her upper lip. Jupiter was enormously bright.

"You okay?" he said.

"I'm great," she said.

With a single effort he sat up and tore away his hand. He could see out of his injured eye. He began palming away a thick clear mucus. The world was strange, webbed and distorted, but it was there. She was crying but when she saw him, she lit with smirking amusement. Her lips worked delicately from crying to smirking and back to crying, her chin quivering, and she said, "*Dude.*"

"Sorry."

"Your eye is gooing."

"I know."

"It's glue-gunning."

"Yeah, I feel it."

"Your eye is doing just what I do when I think about Paisley Cuthers."

"She's a person," he said. "Not just a famous climber, she's a real person, you can't make those jokes."

"A real *sexy* person."

"Can I say something?"

"I love how *boldly* she climbs."

"Tamma."

"She climbs like she can't fall, you know? She throws for holds like she *can't miss*. Like she's never slipped. Never fucked up. Never been hurt. Never, ever fallen. Total self-belief."

"Tamma—"

"But in interviews? She's humble and kind of *flustered*. I like that too. On the wall: a bitch. On the mats: a damsel."

"Tamma," he said, again.

"Yeah?"

"Can we be serious for a moment?"

"Sorry, yes. Yes."

"I think you do lead a rad life."

"I think *you* lead a rad life," she said. She fell on him and beat upon his breast with the heel of her hand.

"You lead an amazing life," he said. "It's just not a life of adventure and blossoming sexuality."

"Not *yet*," she said.

Five

When she came back into sight of her house she hunkered down, prized off her beanie, and beat it thoughtfully against her thigh. Dan stood beside her. It was a faded pink trailer built up with additions, encircled by collapsed privacy fencing, run-down outbuildings, a galvanized-steel water tank, dying cottonwoods. There was a chicken coop that had once held iguanas and an outhouse that now held filing cabinets, a fax machine, and a fish tank. The seventeenth of November. Several days after her fall. Her eye blacked, her face mottled green and blue. Dusk, with roadrunners stalking the banks. The girl in hoodie, barn coat, and borrowed redlines.

"You want me to come in with you?"

"Nah."

"You sure?"

"Yeah, go on."

Dan stood for a beat. Then he turned and went crunching away through the blue dusk. Tamma seated her beanie and adjusted it a little side to side and spat and rose and crossed the yard and took the steps in a single bound and came in through the sliding glass doors. Kendra was at the microwave with a soup can. She said, "God fucking damnit, where have you been? Why can't you come home ever, don't you want to see your family for a change, can't you answer your phone, which we pay for?, are you out there trying to kill yourself?, do you know how stupid and reckless and *dumb* that is?, don't you remember we said we'd see your sister?, don't you have any sense of other people?, or is it all just about Tamma?, is it all just Tamma in your head?, is your own snotty little self the only thing that means anything to you?" The microwave door stood open, the interior plastered with exploded gore, the light shining out upon her.

Tamma came swaggering across the room, thinking, *Shauna Coxsey, give me strength!* and fell upon a chair, her mother shaking her head, decanting soup into a pyrex dish, helping it along with a spatula, rattling the utensil around in the can. "Well," she said, "well, we're gonna go and visit your sister, Sierra."

"Oh, Mom, *whyyyyyyy*?"

"Because she has a little baby and needs help, is why."

Tamma turned around in her chair and looked at her mom's boyfriend sitting on the couch with his feet up on a coffee table covered in beer cans.

"Is *he* coming?" she said. His name was Hyrum. He hated to be called Hyrum. "Hyrum?" she said. "Is Hyrum coming? Hyrum, are you coming, Hyrum?"

"Uh . . . yeah," Hyrum said from the couch.

"Does he *have to*?" Tamma said. "Hyrum, Hyrum, *do you have to*?"

"Yeah," Hyrum said. "Your sis needs our ahhhhh . . . support."

"Mom, where's Colin?"

"Your brother is getting dressed," Kendra said, and started the microwave going. She stood square-on in the galley kitchen, her hands on her hips, the microwave humming as the tray revolved, the great and famous beauty of her high school, completely unlike her big-eared, snaggletoothed, acne-scarred daughter.

"Great," Tamma said.

"Oh don't say that," Kendra said. "You love your sister. You love Sierra and you want to help."

"Is there anything to eat? Other than soup?" Tamma said.

"Yeah," Hyrum said. "Because ahhhhh . . . your mother loves you."

"Hyrum—thank you," Tamma said. "Ahhhhh . . . hmmmmm, thank you for that, ahhhhh . . . Hyrum."

Kendra took a plate of grilled cheese sandwiches out of the oven, went back for the soup, and set that too in front of her daughter. The sandwiches were wonder bread and american cheese fried in margarine. She said, "Why do you do this to yourself? It *hurts* just to see you like this."

Tamma selected a sandwich. She ate with difficulty, dipping the sandwiches in soup until they were falling apart. Her jaw made creaking, ricekrispieish noises. Had ever since she was a little girl.

"Where *were* you?"

"Out with Dan."

"I hope you weren't climbing."

"No, Mom, we were shooting black tar heroin." A better idea occurred to her. "Oxy, Mom! We do oxy in shacks out in the desert! With Baphomet-worshiping Obama liberals! And *Hillary Clinton*! And Maynard James Keenan was there! He sang 'The Humbling River'; and Bill Clinton was standing on a rock, in the middle of the desert, wearing an iridescent pantsuit, playing the saxophone solo in the beam of light cast down by a UFO, because aliens are real, Mom."

"That sounds like quite a party," Hyrum said.

Her mother sighed and came to the table, drew out a chair, sat down. Packed her cigarettes and lit one. Sat smoking, making a study of her daughter.

"Tamma," she said. "Whenever you're out, I can barely breathe. When I think of the danger you put yourself in. It's like a weight on me, baby girl. A weight right here." She touched her breast with two fingers. "A suffocating weight that I can't get out from under because you won't listen."

Tamma was holding a half-eaten grilled cheese, staring at it, unwilling to look up.

Kendra ashed into the glass tray. "Don't eat all those sandwiches."

"Did other people not get any?"

"No, it's just you'll get fat."

"Thanks, Mom. Wonderful."

"I'm just saying. You're seventeen. If you can't stay skinny now."

Tamma pitched her sandwich down onto the plate and frowned at it.

Colin came down the hallway with his hair slicked to the side, wearing a baggy white collared shirt, acid-washed jeans with embroidered flourishes at the pockets, and white basketball shoes.

"Great," Kendra said. "Colin, can you move some stuff from the fridge to the car?"

"Oh, Mom," he said. "Can't Tamma do it?"

"Tamma's changing," Kendra said, with a glance at her daughter.

Tamma rose and sauntered away down the hall.

"Something pretty!" Kendra yelled after her. "Like a girl!"

"I hate you!" Tamma yelled back.

She tramped around her bedroom, throwing off her barn coat, pulling her shirt up over her head, raking through her drawers, clawing her hands down her cheeks. Soon she was hunched in the backseat of a ford taurus driving almost an hour to her sister's place, her face buried into the seat back, her brother singing along to the Nickelback album *All the Right Reasons*. He knew every song. His voice was pretty good. He and Hyrum did a duet with the song "Rockstar." Hyrum took the part that went, "*I'll have the quesadilla, haha.*" Tamma breathed into the upholstery, trying, through pure force of will, to surrender herself to the sweet release of death.

"Aren't we gonna be there really late?" Colin said, at a break in the music.

"Well *somebody* doesn't answer their phone."

"I was *out of service*!" somebody screamed into the seat back.

Her sister's place was a green vinyl portable, fenced in chain link and razor wire. Kendra parked and popped the trunk and handed frozen casseroles to Tamma and Colin, who stood with their arms out, accepting them in attitudes of misery like the burghers of Calais.

They waited at the gate, with the pit bulls snarling and throwing themselves against the chain link, and Brad kicked the door open and said, "Stupid fucking dogs! Shut up! Shut the fuck up! Goddamnit!" He beat back the dogs and latched them to an eyebolt set into a truck tire filled with concrete. "Dumb fucking dogs!" he said, coming to the gate and opening it. "You came late, didn't you?"

"Somebody didn't answer her phone."

"Oh well the babies are all up now, aren't they?"

Everyone crowded into the living room, Tamma and Colin stacked chin high with casserole dishes. The baby monitor on the coffee table showed the ten-month-old, Samantha, wallowing around in her crib, screaming. They could hear her through the walls. And they could hear River, the newborn. Sierra's five-year-old, Hunter, sat on the couch watching *Critters* and playing with his big toe through his ratty white athletic sock.

"Jeepers that's a shiner," Brad said. "What's the deal, Hyrum, are you entering her in cage fights?"

"That girl couldn't win a cage fight with a squirrel."

"How is the little rug muncher, anyway?"

"Me?" Tamma said, wheeling around, looking for a place to set down the casserole dishes. The living room was newly laid ceramic tile strewn with drop cloths. The ceiling had been stripped to exposed insulation with white wiring tacked up among the joists. There were ladders and paint cans everywhere. "I mean—but—what I mean is—if I'm a rug muncher—I mean, you're a rug muncher!"

"Gross," Brad said. "That's disgusting."

"Tamma," Kendra said. "What a horrible thing to say to someone!"

Sierra came in from the other room holding River. She hissed, "Brad! Samantha is up!"

"Right," Brad said, and left.

Tamma followed her sister into the kitchen. The linoleum had a large bubble that moved as Sierra paced the floor. The cabinets had been torn out. There was a gas hookup but no range. Instead, there was a propane expedition stove with a five-gallon tank.

Tamma set the casseroles on the counter and looked at her sister, holding the baby and rocking side to side. Sierra was the pretty sister, five foot six, narrow waisted and 32DD even before breastfeeding. She smiled with dimples and straight white teeth and after she shot tequila she swung her hand up in the air and yelled "Whooooo!" and exposed an armpit smooth of either hair or razor burn. When Tamma had been just a kid, her pretty big sister used to call her ugly and told everyone that she hated her and wished she had died. She'd said it at dinner once. They'd been at a Mexican restaurant with Tamma telling a story and her sister had looked across the table and just said, "I hope you die, I wish you were dead." Then she had tilted her head to the side and dimpled up in a fake sort of smile, which Tamma had found both charismatic and devastating. Her mother had said, "Honey, you don't wish that," and Sierra'd said, "No, I do. I hate her. I wish Tamma was dead. Everything would be good without Tamma. She is ugly and mean and dirty and she has weird ears and I hate her."

Tamma's dad had slapped the tabletop and laughed, and Kendra had looked at her husband and he said, "What? It was a joke. Tidbit, it was a joke." No one ever talked about it again and everyone acted like it was done. Tamma thought about it every day.

Rocking the baby, standing underneath the bare kitchen lights, with deep black circles beneath her eyes and her face rawboned with exhaustion, sashaying back and forth, Sierra said, "Mom, it's after nine. I told you. Samantha goes to sleep at seven thirty, you can't be coming out here like this. And what happened to Tamma's face?"

"I'm right here," Tamma said.

Kendra put her hands up. "Take it up with your sister," she said. "It's not me who didn't get the memo."

"I didn't know!" Tamma said.

"I don't care," Sierra said. "I don't care whose fault it is. If you're not going to help, you can at the very least not hurt."

"I'm here to help, honey. That's why I just drove out here. Doesn't that mean anything to you?"

"No, Mom, what means something to me is that you woke up the baby."

"Oh so my love means nothing. My love isn't support. That's not the kind of help you want, to know anyone loves you."

"Mom! Everyone should be in bed!"

"Well, I want to help, and now you're saying it doesn't matter that we love you, doesn't matter that you have a fridge full of casserole I spent all day making."

"Can you hold the baby so I can get some sleep?"

"Well, honey," Kendra said, "we have to get Tamma and Colin back to bed. They have class tomorrow and Colin has practice. You're not the only one with kids or things to do."

"Oh, right, great then," Sierra said.

"They do," Kendra said. "I have to get them back."

"I know," Sierra said. "It's just we're dying."

"Oh come on," Kendra said. "I didn't have my parents coming around with casseroles telling me they loved me and everything would be all right and being there to help. You think you have it hard? You don't have it hard. You're fine."

Brad came into the kitchen. He said, "I can't get Samantha back to sleep."

"Oh for christsake," Sierra said and passed River into Tamma's arms. Then she went down the hall into the nursery, where they could hear Samantha screaming.

"She's great with her," Brad said. "I can't put her down. I have this trick elbow. I rock her to sleep and when I try and put her down into the crib my trick elbow goes *pop* and wakes her right up and starts her screaming."

Tamma wasn't listening. She stared down into River's shriveled bright red face with its mop of greasy disordered hair and a tiny person stared back at her. His eyes were like the deep centers of storm clouds combing the desert at evening. She could not believe the size of him. He weighed less than a coil of rope. He was a tiny, heart-throbbing, rib-flaring, lung-pumping intelligence, and he looked back at her with an expression utterly passive and wondrous. For a long moment Tamma stood swaying side to side, gazing at him.

Her mom came in close and said, "Welcome to the world, little guy."

Tamma said nothing and Kendra said, "He's beautiful, isn't he?" and Tamma still could not speak. She went groping around inside herself for what she was feeling and she could not parse it. She walked out into the living room, leaving everyone in the kitchen, and she wandered back and forth on the tile floor strewn with drop cloths and paint buckets, the baby cradled in her arms with his hand drawn up out of his swaddles and against his face. She wanted to hold him in her arms forever and keep him safe. At last her sister came out from the nursery and found Tamma in the living room, pacing with the lights turned off.

"He's amazing," Tamma said, and Sierra laughed. Not in contradiction. It was a laugh of seeing the same thing in someone else that you'd felt in yourself and Tamma looked at her and smiled falteringly, a little hopefully.

"I'm surprised you feel that way," Sierra said, opening her arms and accepting the baby back.

"Why?" Tamma said.

"Well you're such a little dyke, you know?"

"Oh," Tamma said. "Yeah," she said, "that is funny," and she laughed and walked back into the kitchen, dusting her hands off on the thighs of her pants.

Six

Dan labored over his calculus homework, stretched at length on the floor. From time to time he sharpened his pencil, letting the long curling gold cedar shavings fall into an ashtray. Then there came a tap tap tapping on the glass and Tamma boosted herself out of the darkness into the window well, grinning molar to molar. She put the heel of her hand to the rail, slid the lower sash up from the outside, and slung her scabby shanks across the sill. It was bright in the room and dark behind her. Dan put his finger to his lips and Tamma gave him a look like—*Please, I am a slab climber; I move through my life like a prima ballerina across her stage*. Then she slung herself off the sill into the laundry hamper, overturned it, went hard down against the dresser, knocked everything off, recoiled against the wall, and there caught herself and shook out her hair to regain some dignity, mouthing, *Sorry, sorry*. Dan put his finger to his mouth again to shush her and she seated herself beside him. "My mom's humiliating herself again," she whispered. She took a film canister out of her bralette, shook the buds out into her palm. "I had to get out of there. It sounds, dude, like he's just, like, pounding the, like, living good goddamn god almighty out of her."

"Jeepers!"

Tamma spanned rolling papers around one fingertip and with the other broke apart the bud. Her nails were electric pink, close-trimmed and chipped. She licked the paper, rolled it on her thigh, played it up between index and middle.

"What is this?" he whispered. He blew it out all in a wash. "It has a strange taste."

"Guess where I got it!"

"I can't guess."

"Just, like?, hazard a theory."

"I have no idea."

"Under my mom's bed, dude."

"For real?"

"She has several thirty-gallon bags of dank purple nuts and an AK-47."

"Why an AK-47?"

"So when the charges come, she can make a clean sweep of it."

"Where'd she get it?"

"It's all her boyfriend's, dude! He's dealing weed now as well as oxy and flunitrazepam."

"Roofies?"

"Yeah, dude, he's a sweetie pie."

"Well anyway, that's very nice of her. To let him keep all the stuff at her place."

"She like, looks out for her guys, my mom."

"And her having children and everything."

She rolled over, propped on her elbow, combed her fingers through her sweaty hair, swinging her feet. One ankle enormous, purple and yellow.

"My parents are after me about college again," he said.

"Haven't you told them you're not going?"

"I don't square off with them like you do."

"Don't tell them! Come June first, after graduation, you just go: 'I'm not going to college! PSYCH! I'm going to Canyonlands with Tamma! Later, bitches!' Then spike your diploma to the floor and walk out."

"That does sound like me."

"You could do it, dude."

"I *couldn't* though. I'm sort of everything they have."

"Well they're gonna find out sooner or later."

"They put aside thirteen thousand dollars for me to go. And it's like the proudest thing my mom ever did. But it's totally heartbreaking because for college, it's not even that much money."

"You can't live for someone else, you know? They're afraid. But you don't need to be afraid. We're going to go to Indian Creek, in Canyonlands. The last place on earth you can still dirtbag, the way the old-school climbers did. Yosemite is all done out—regulated and controlled by the curry company. You can't even sleep in the valley. But out there in southern Utah, it's hundreds of thousands of miles of canyons, cliffs, and glades, with not enough rangers to keep track of it. You can sleep in washes, search out Anasazi ruins, bathe naked in the Colorado with hard-sending Moab girls. Some of the very last wild country in America. No one trying to tell you what to do, except Andrew Bisharat. There are sandstone towers six hundred feet tall and hidden in those canyons are some of the wildest, most epic trad climbs in the world—thin, overhanging finger cracks, roof cracks two hundred feet long, chimney climbs that go up between two side-by-side towers. The bravest deeds, wildest campfire parties, strongest whiskeys, and most brazen runouts will be ours. Tales of our misadventures will race across the nation, going crag to crag, sprinter van to sprinter van, campfire to campfire. Damsels will throw their bras through the open windows of our toyota as we drive through the dusty streets of Moab. You're the real thing. There isn't anything to be scared of. We totally have this."

"Hey," he said. "Should we have a benchmark?"

"What do you mean?"

"Like, I think we both feel this way: If we can't send Fingerbang Princess, then we're probably not really climbers."

She lay on her belly, swinging her heels. "What you have to remember," she said, "is that Fingerbang Princess is a highball. This isn't the sort of climb where you can make twelve attempts in a row. Once you take a twenty-foot screamer to the deck you have to sit down and weep silently into the crook of your arm for a while. It takes time."

"Goddamn, climbing is a great sport."

"Gosh, isn't it?"

"But if we get shut out on V4, then I think you and I both know we're not the real thing. And we probably shouldn't bet our lives on a sport at which we're not even really that good."

"It doesn't matter because we're going to send Fingerbang Princess just as hard as Hyrum is sending my mom right now."

"But what's the climb that, if we could pull it off, you would think—Okay, we have a real shot at this."

"Dude! I have it. Perhaps the finest route in the park. The first pitch is a hundred feet long, with seven bolts crisscrossing a spectacular, heart-shaped patina shield on the side North Astrodome, put up by Randy Vogel and Dave Evans in 1978. It's the one, the only, the infamous—Figures on a Landscape!"

"Yeah," Dan said. "Runout, technical, five-star 10b face climbing on edges as small and sharp as babies' teeth, all of it deep in the Wonderland!"

The Wonderland was a part of Joshua Tree National Park, a vast sprawl of pinyon pine, beavertail cactus, desert tortoises, decaying rockpiles, microdosing hippies, and lost climbers from Denver. John Long had once gone out into the Wonderland to make garlands of cactus flowers and search for tortoises, and some said, through the time-warp magic of place, he was there yet; at once out in the world, adventuring and writing books, sitting patiently at signing tables, and at the same time still there, clambering from rock dome to rock dome, draped in sacred datura and opuntia blooms, petting an ancient tortoise named Good King Wenceslas; and if you went out into that desert, who knows but that you might come across the Eternal Stone Master. Dan and Tamma had stayed up many nights, hunched over the laptop, poring over route descriptions, imagining being high up on Solid Gold, a rope hanging slack from your harness to a bolt thirty feet below. A bolt possibly placed in 1977 by a man wearing tiny red track shorts and out of his mind on acid. They had studied photographs until routes like Mental Physics, Dangling Woo Li Master, and Figures on a Landscape were graven on the insides of their eyelids. Just the word *Astrodome* could make the hair on Tamma's arms stand up. If you lived where Dan and Tamma lived, and you hadn't climbed in the Wonderland, then you weren't a real climber. But to do it, they would need a rope and a rack of gear, and they didn't have those things. They'd also need free use of the car, which they only had permission to drive to and from school.

"Okay," he said. "I like it. It's ambitious. But it's not Spiderline. It's not some gnarbawls 5.12 that we will never, ever actually send."

"They set aside thirteen grand?" she said.

"Thirteen grand," he said.

"And it's yours?"

"It's mine."

"We could buy a van with that. That's enough money to get started. We could really do this."

She levered herself up onto one arm and looked at him, chewing on her lip as she thought about it. He loved everything about her. Everything about her was dear to him. This girl: graceless, frolicsome, and indestructible, like you'd imagine a newborn moose might be. She was just full of hope. Her hope was a thing you could feel. It was a fire in the dark, breathing with the flaring open of her ribs.

Seven

Struggling through the tea-colored evening side by side, hands drawn up into sleeves, reefs of ocher dust rolling past, tumbleweeds bounding out of the brush, crossing the wash, then vaulting the far side and crashing away through the creosote. The day before Thanksgiving. Conditions suboptimal.

"You know, there's this comp in the spring," Tamma yelled.

"Yeah?"

"In Los Angeles! It's a national cup. So anyone can walk in off the street. I mean—no sane person *would*!" Hollering over the wind. "But they're not gonna stop you. If you place high enough, you get a national ranking and can start competing more seriously. A lot of climbers get their start that way. Like Tommy Caldwell. When he was sixteen years old, he entered the citizens' division of the climbing comp at Snowbird, one of the very first competitions in the States. He takes first and so gets a wild card entry into the main event, competing against the best climbers of his time. And he sweeps the whole thing. This kid who came out of nowhere. All the great climbers have stories like that, Dan. That could be us."

"You should go."

"But, the Princess, dude."

They came through the break and found the sand before the boulder stained black. Torn nitrile gloves and gauze packages were blowing in the wind and there were boot prints in the sand and a women's la sportiva miura resting in the dirt. Tamma rubbered her eyes from Dan, to the rock, to the stains, and then looked down and found a hank of hair fastened to her shoe and went hopping backward, trying to scrape it free.

"Did you see anything about this on mountain project?"

"I did not."

"Did she live?"

"Fuck, man, I don't know. But it doesn't *look* good."

They dragged out an old tire. Dan sat at the edge of the wet sand. He could see the tracks of kangaroo rats. They had left lickmarks in the blood like the marks of a knife on cake frosting. He laced his shoes, looking up at the monolith, seeing every chalked hold. Freckled blood from the backsplatter. He thought, If you take the pitch from the top, Tamma can't catch you. She will stand between you and the ground, but you will crater her into the sand like a cartoon anvil and then she will hold your face and crack desperate jokes while you die in her arms.

He splayed his fingers before himself and watched them tremble. Then he stepped from the dry sand onto the tire, and there he cleaned his shoes off on the calves of his jeans, sat on the tire's far edge, and toed onto the boulder. Tamma fired up the flashlight in order to bring the holds into relief, casting his shadow before him on the rock. All about him the Princess Boulder was overhung, golden, streaked with chalk.

He made the throw for Tinkerbell's Bandersnatch, coming entirely off the wall, sank his fingers in the pocket, middle stacked over the pointer. His legs cut beneath him, but he held the move, steadied himself with a left foot on the wall, and kicked his right foot up to heel-hook a sandy pocket.

"Yar!" Tamma said.

Dan started the mantle, transitioning from a pull-up to a palm-down press with the left hand, creeping his right hand up the slab, his left foot dangling free beneath him. Panic started to back up from his guts. It rose sickeningly through his throat.

"Yar!" Tamma said, again. "You got this!"

And inside, Dan was going *Fuck fuck fuck fuck*. He thought—Just fall here, fall where the falling is safe, and you won't have to face what comes next. But a life where you surrendered every hard move was no less a risk, so Dan muscled through the press, breath smoking into the spotlight, almost exactly like getting out of a swimming pool, if the pool were empty and fifteen feet deep, the wall was right up in your face, and the sandy bottom was stained with gore from the last person who'd tried to get out. Grimacing, baring his teeth, the boy rose to a stand, his cheek flush to the slab.

Tamma had once said that climbing the slab was like having sex with sketchy guys you met on the internet. It was great fun as long as you did not decide, halfway through, that you would like to stop and go home. Then it became horrifying. Neither of them had ever hooked up with anybody, but he knew what she meant.

He began to pad his way up, digging inside himself for the courage to trust his weight to shoe rubber and friction. With each step, he did not believe it would hold, and then he committed his weight to the stance, and it held. It felt impossible every time. Like stepping out of a boat onto thin ice.

Knit into the fear was the cold, painful feeling of the rock, the way the cold got into your toes so that every step was nauseous, the way it got into your fingers so that they felt stiff and weak, so that your skin blanched waxen and breakable, so that the sharpness of the holds grew cruelly razorous. He knew he was close to his limit but did not know where it lay exactly. He expected to find it with every move and with each move it did not come.

From the last piecrust dike, he stepped left into the insecure paper-plate dish. The summit was close. For the left hand, a crystal like a molar budding obliquely out of the slab, the crown at two o'clock. He latched his thumb over it in a kind of thumbhook-gaston-press.

He looked down to the domino-sized hold at his hip. He could see a chalk tick mark left by the fallen climber. This is where she fell. At the psychological crux of the climb. The place where everything inside yourself told you to wait, to stall, to cling to safety, and yet where, if you wanted to live, you had to take the risk.

He set his pointer finger down onto the edge of the domino. He cleaned his right foot on the left calf of his jeans: a firm, smooth, careful movement. Then brought his foot back up and matched it beside his finger, sharing space on an edge a centimeter deep and five centimeters wide, his right arm threaded through the inside of his knee. All the tension ran between his left thumb pad and his right foot. The move felt impossible. It felt like to try it would be death. And yet that was wrong. Waiting was death, and total commitment his only chance. He closed his eyes, exhaled, and then opened his eyes and stood up—stood up cleanly, sickeningly, boldly—captured the top, and summited into the full force of the wind. He stood up there, atop the Princess Boulder, with his shirt flapping against his stomach and his hair blustering about and his breath sucked away.

He'd sent Fingerbang Princess. November the twenty-third. All that remained was for Tamma to send it too. Maybe, he thought. Maybe, just maybe, it's all possible, maybe it's all within reach, and all these ruined and failed people, that need not be you. He was thinking, This is it. This is what I want to do with my life. I don't want to do anything else. I want to spend my life climbing. He didn't know if he had what it took, or if he would be sucked back up into the geary bowels of the great capitalist machine, but it was the first time Dan felt entirely clear to himself, the first time he had looked into his soul and knew for a certainty who he was. His purpose was out here, at the world's numinous edge.

Eight

Dan left Tamma at her place and walked down the wash alone, his sweat-sodden shoes hooked in his fingers. Tamma hadn't sent. She'd made nine attempts, and never even stuck the dyno. She seemed to be getting worse. He had the first feeling of a rift, a disparity in their possible futures. What if people were right about Tamma, and she was just a burnout? What if he was wrong? He was the only person who thought anything of her. Was it courage, to trust that judgment, or was it idiocy? He didn't know. If she still dreamed of being a climber, she could not afford to leave Fingerbang Princess unsent. He boosted open his bedroom window, sitting on the sill, unlacing his boots, beating the sand off his pants, and then slinging one leg after another into the room. She wouldn't have that many more chances, either.

He let himself out into the kitchen for a glass of water and found Alexandra at the island, stooped, wearing gray terry sweatpants and a stained white tee. Before her, a box of chocolate chip cookies, a cup of milk. He opened the fridge, took out a pitcher of water, and poured a glass. She set her hand upon the open white box and slid it across the counter to him. He selected a cookie.

They sat in silence. The only light from the stove.

"How goes the personal statement?"

"Good."

"I'll take a look sometime."

"Mom?"

"Yes?"

"How did you know you wanted to be a writer?"

She passed her tongue along the inside of her lip, like someone who'd been struck. "My father," she said, "your grandfather, read me *The Hobbit* when I was seven or eight. Of course, he never read Smaug as 'the dragon' but rather as 'the giant, red, fire-breathing chuckwalla lizard.'"

"What? Why?"

"Oh well. You know—there are dragons in the bible. He thought they were unholy, dragons. He did not approve of fiction, but he loved *The Hobbit* despite himself. I'd lay awake all night, thinking of Bilbo Baggins riddling in the dark with Gollum."

"Were they really that religious?"

"Oh, yes."

"What was it like? Coming up like that?"

"About like any childhood I guess."

She took a softened bite of cookie. Chewed thoughtfully.

"Are you happy that you did it?"

"Did what?"

"Became a writer?"

She sat there, staring fixedly through the wall out into the night, her irises blown to narrow blue shores. "Happy?" she said. "Well. I wanted to tell a story that would keep some other little girl up all night with excitement. I used to imagine what it would be like when I was a famous author; in my head, I'd practice all the interviews I'd do with *Rolling Stone* magazine. I haven't thought of that in a long time. I'd almost forgotten that was the start of it all."

She dunked her cookie, her attention far away. He waited for ten minutes. After a while, he asked, "Was it the right thing to do?"

"Well," she said. "I was a little more than a year older than you are, when I published that book. Much was made of that—of my age, my promise, the fact that I had come from nowhere. But there are wolves out there, waiting for any young artist."

She seemed to consider that. They each ate a cookie in silence. After she dunked hers, he could hear the drip drip drip of the milk back into the glass. "A person needs help. And what did I have? A bowling alley waitress and a carpenter. Although—"

"Although what?"

"Once upon a time, Kendra was kind of brilliant. Probably difficult to imagine now. She was terrifically, *terrifically* talkative. The greatest beauty I ever saw, she could suck all the air out of the room, and it wasn't just her looks, it was her wild, voluble, unpredictable mind— she had charisma, real charisma, and guts of iron, the way they say great beauties are supposed to. She could drink all night and work all day and it wouldn't show on her. And she was besides that quite funny when she got on a tear. A great mimic. I suppose that is some kind of intelligence; the capacity to see any gesture, any facial expression, and reproduce it exactly."

Tamma had that too, Dan thought; she could watch Alex Johnson throw for some bullshit hold and Tamma, sitting on the bed, blazing a joint, so stoned she could barely see, could throw the same move exactly.

"Why did you fall out with her?" he said. "If she was so bright? If she was so beautiful and charismatic and brilliant and you were so close?"

"A story for another time."

"Mom."

"Yeah?"

"I love you."

"I love you too," she said. She reached out. She set a cold, shapeless hand upon his own and said, "If I had it to do again, I'd go to college, and leave Kendra to stay here; she stayed anyway. You can't save people, Danny. They are always, in the end, themselves."

Afterward, Dan went into his room and shut the door behind himself and crossed to his desk and opened his computer. He stood, stooping forward to read, planting his hands on the desktop. He keyed open a forum and looked at the string of subjects and there it was, at the top. *FATALITY ON PRINCESS BOULDER (11/23/2011)*. He read through the comments, stopping sometimes to pace. She had been an accomplished climber. She had sent V10 in Joe's Valley. She'd sent a V8 called Round Room in Little Cottonwood. Other boulders, unknown to him, in Font and the Buttermilks. She was climbing with her fiancé, two ER doctors just out of residency. Another climber had witnessed the fall. She'd blown the highball crux and struck her head on the slab. Had come back to consciousness just long enough to talk to her fiancé. She'd been coughing up blood. He'd coached her to keep breathing. They'd had a satellite emergency signal device and had used that to text out to EMS, which had flown in with a helicopter.

She'd been intubated on site, packaged up, and taken to the medical center. Then sent on to a trauma one and she'd died on the table.

Someone had written:

Stay safe out there, everyone.

Dan stood there, his hands on the desktop, reading comment after comment. Am I right about Tamma? he thought. Or is my mom right? How should I conduct my life? Do you trust yourself, or do you not? And in all this. You have to take seriously. That there is blood in this sand. Where you hope to make it, others have not made it.

Nine

Two figures side by side in a vast prospect of desert, the clouds like wasp nests caulked up into the eaves: low, swollen, sashy, striate, and gray; the light, dishwater; the sun, a bed of coals embanked in ash. They followed the wash with their maglites crisscrossing the rippled sand, starting hares and roadrunners from out the creosote. It was eight days since Dan had ticked Fingerbang Princess, and they both had a bad feeling about Tamma not sending. They came to the boulder and stood, the flashlights askew in the dark.

Her session was disastrous. She'd pitch back into his arms and go staggering away, standing on one foot and then the other, taking off her TC pros, hurling them out into the desert, hinging at the waist to shriek after them. Then she'd hobble about barefoot, wrenching at her hair. Dan would wordlessly bring her shoes back, soaked with fear-sweat. Finally, she was pressing herself up from the roof, her right heel hooked in a pocket, her left foot dangling, when Tinkerbell's Bandersnatch greased out from under her. Tamma's face went down into the rock so hard he saw her head bounce. He caught her by the hips and lowered her to the ground and she went reeling backward, holding her mouth, blood running from chinks in her fingers.

She seated herself on a tire and began to roll a spliff, hunched, goblinish, leering, resplendent in her slouchy dishabille, her hands chalk white to the wrist, her eye blackening, her cheek raw, her lip pulpy as a split mandarin, blood painted ghoulishly down her chin as she tested each tooth with a pink tongue, nodding to find them set fast, smiling with an injurious delight all her own, intent upon rolling papers. About her, every rock and discarded can and shell casing, each crushed plastic bottle, glass shard, sprawling club of prickly pear, and tapering ivory spine, every single thing that stood up from the ground flung its shadow eastward and the light among those shadows stained the sand to amberous sienna.

"Dude!" she said. "*Duuuuuude*: It's fucked if you think about it."

"What is?"

"Fucked, dude."

"This boulder?"

"Your mom and mine."

"What?"

"Think about it. Best friends: inseparable, tanned, leggy desert bitches in cutoff jeans. Crusty attitude on the outside; gushing sexual submission on the inside. Your mom a blond mormon chick with a cheap notebook in her apron. My mom this ravishing, high-desert heartbreaker with that super special sexy sauce women have when they're moms, but *terrible*, slutty moms. You know, my dad once told me that Kendra used to give guys HJs on the bus to school?"

"What! Weren't you like four or five when he left?"

"Well, this is later, when he was visiting, back when he still cared. Anyway, it seemed like a normal thing to tell me at the time, but it's weird in retrospect. Like—Why, Dad, why? Her maiden name was Stockwell. They called her Suckscockwell, apparently. Which is just an amazing, amazing nickname, but what was wrong with her? What demon torments her, that these are things she does, what is she running away from, when she flees into that diner, into friendship with Alex, into early marriage with an alcoholic sculptor fifteen years older? She is beautiful and wild, maybe she has high hopes that she has finally HJ'd the guy who is gonna wife her and keep away all her demons. Alex and Kendra! Two young women just full of fucking hope! They're desperate and they're poor, but they have each other."

Tamma brought the spliff to her lips with a shaking hand and it took her four tries upon the knurled wheel to spark the lighter. Her finger pads were raw pink with blood blisters within.

"Alex is living with Patrick and Kendra. She's writing her novel. Kendra is raising her first baby girl. Patrick is welding up sculptures in the yard. Lawrence comes into the diner. It's love at first sight, says my mom, Kendra Callahandjob née Suckscockwell. He sees her and he's all, like: 'Oh, lovely Alexandra, splendiferous as an eagle, golden as the dawn! Be my maiden fair and I shall build-eth you a cottage in which to lay-eth your beautiferous head, and I will do-eth odd and sundry-eth jobs, and you shall write-eth the great American novel and everything shall be totally fine, because you seem-eth normal, and not ravaged-eth with mental illness!'"

"You sound just like him," Dan said. He knew all this, but this was a thing she did, from time to time. Thinking out loud, making sense of the world, sifting through their long and varied prehistory of failure like going move by move through some attempt on a boulder, trying to parse if it could be done, if it were even possible.

"And it works! They get married. Sexy, broad-shouldered, narrow-hipped blond mormon cowboy, born in a log cabin in Sevier County, Utah, and come out to the old Iron Mission to find love with an apostate novelist! He follows her out of the church. Isn't that sexy? He forsakes *god* for the woman he loves. He has a mustache and wears tight blue jeans. He works all day in Palm Springs putting up parking garages and best buys and walmarts and other things we totally want and which are absolutely worth paving over the Mojave for, and at night he comes back to their empty campsite at the end of a dirt road they call Lifted Lorax Lane and he fires up a skilsaw and builds her a house, working by lantern light, smoking cigars, his jeans incredibly tight, his mustache virile, his work shirts unbuttoned. So many scorpions in the lumber, my mom told me, that he carried tongs in his belt and he would tong them up into a five-gallon bucket he had around.

"Alexandra Redburn gets back from the diner late at night. She's young and she's thin and she's blond and she nips through her T-shirts and she is *stunningly gifted*, however gifted you have to be, to be born *here* and then eighteen years later they're profiling you in magazines with your literary smile and great big dick-sucking eyes."

"You're an inappropriate person, you know that?"

"I am a deeply fucked-up sort of a person! The damage goes all the way down, Dan. All the way to the core. I am just a scared girl begging the world for love and the world doesn't love me back!—but you have to understand, it's not *my* fault that your mom has such enormous dick-sucking eyes! I saw the profile in Kendra's sock drawer! I just call it like I see it! Anyway: Alexandra comes back to her campsite at night, she puts her typewriter on a chopping block, takes an enormous fucking drag on her cigarette, pours some black velvet whiskey into a tin cup, and she does what she has been wanting to do all her life: She writes a novel! *Ephedra*! A nine-hundred-page epic about the desert! Mormons and massacres and polygamy! Prophets, white salamanders, and true love! She shows the novel to my mom, and my mom is all like, 'More bodice-ripping! More skirt-hoisting!' and you know what? She's right! Eight months later they're toasting *Ephedra* in New York! In Paris! In Los Angeles! In Salt Lake City, they're excommunicating her. She walks a red carpet in Milan; goes to Hollywood and shoots with *Vogue*; in Iowa City, she does orgies with Jonathan Franzen."

"I never heard that?"

"It just *feels* true!"

"Does Franzen attend a lot of orgies?"

"I've seen you reading *The Corrections* with that steamy little smoke-show smoldering from the back cover. You *know* he does, Dan! And the whole time he's like, 'Where are my glasses? I lost my glasses!' And that's because Margaret Atwood keeps stealing them, isn't it?"

"Who hurt you?"

"Oh, you know who hurt me! Anyway, your old man is like, 'My Alexandra, maiden fair! I always knew-eth you could perforce do-eth this thing!' and she goes, 'Put a baby inside me!' and he goes, 'Forthwith and posthaste!' And they get pregnant and they have this beautiful baby boy with a gigantic ween!"

"Strange thing to say about a baby."

"A *stunningly* sexy baby with piercing blue eyes and blond hair and chiseled jawline and shy smile. Just this—god, the *handsomest* toddler!"

"Tammmmmmmmmmmmma!"

"Everything golden! It's the American dream! Do you see what I'm saying?"

"No," Dan said. "What are you saying?"

"*Ephedra* was her Tinkerbell's Bandersnatch. A crux move, right off the deck, that proved homegirl could pull hard. It made her famous. And everybody thinks that's the test. But the real test comes later. Because the question isn't: *Can you do it?* Lots of girls can pull hard, Dan. The question is: *Can you do it again, high above the deck, with consequences this time? Can you do it when you have something to lose?*"

She sat, smoking, dabbing fragments of tobacco off her tongue with her fingertips.

"Then Kendra has her second daughter. She isn't worried; the first one was this *delightful*, peaceful little cherub. Babies are easy, my mom thinks. You just love them, and they love you back, and when you need a little break, you set them down on the bed and go out for a smoke. It's just not that hard, babies. But whatever dreams she has about how easy kids are, about the sacred bond between infant and mother, it turns out that this second baby is an *asshole*."

"Will you cut that out?"

"An ugly, vile, scrunched-up, bright red eczema goblin that will not sleep, will not stop spitting up, just keeps crying."

"Don't talk like this."

"You know my mom told me that when I was born she was shocked because my vulva was enormous?"

"Did she really say that?"

"She was like, 'Well it's a thing that can happen to babies but at first I thought, is my girl some kind of freak?'"

"Oh, Tamma."

"And little did she know—*it's still enormous!*"

"Tammmmmmmmmmmmaaaaa!"

Tamma held the spliff between thumb and forefinger, leaned over, and spat blood out into the sand. Much too much blood, like someone spitting tobacco juice.

"Is it really that big?"

"I have no idea. Nobody has time for that *Vagina Monologues* hand-mirror stuff. Let's just say it's an enormous vulva *spiritually*. Anyway. Kendra spends years of her life trying to make ends meet, nursing the car along, trying to keep us in diapers and formula and then later, cereal and milk. All Patrick does is eat beans, drink beer, and weld scrap metal. His art doesn't sell. Actually, now it does."

"I didn't know that?"

"Several years ago he married a twenty-two-year-old. He has a daughter named Ceinwyn. We're Celts, I guess. Who knew? He lives in a bungalow in Los Angeles with an infinity pool. He's been on *Oprah*."

"Really?"

"Fuck him! For my entire childhood he made no money. They're desperate poor and Kendra, who does a hundred percent of all the working, childcare, house stuff, and also suffering, is watching Alexandra's meteoric rise to fame, and then, one day, Patrick Callahan breaks his daughter's jaw. And she leaves him. Bravest thing she has ever done. A twenty-eight-year-old high school dropout, living in a trailer, eight months pregnant, with a ten-year-old, a four-year-old with a broken face, an unreliable car, no health insurance, no savings, and a job slinging tacos for two dollars and thirty cents an hour plus tips. Meanwhile, her best friend tours the world, because my mom, unlike your mom, does not have a way to make hundreds of thousands of dollars by just basically noodling about things. That person goes: I will try and make it on my own. Think about the *fucking* radioactive goddamn heavy-metal ovaries on this bitch. I mean think about the guts it would take to do that. And do you know what happens to her? Do you know how this brave deed is rewarded?"

"How?" Dan said. He knew what came next, of course, but he wanted to hear it from her, because Tamma could make a story of all these facts, and he could not.

"Daddy Capitalism comes into the bathroom behind her and locks the door. Hangs his cane from the handle. Sets his top hat on the counter. And he buttfucks her for the next decade of her miserable, overworked, *humiliating* life. America's answer to Kendra Callahan's leap of faith. I'm talking: blood in the shower drains. I'm talking: welcome to the land of opportunity! And, about this time—your mom and mine?—they fall out. It's some *terrible* betrayal and nobody will say what. And whatever *horrible thing* it is that happens—they never talk to each other again. So, my mom, Kendra? This was a girl who was so afraid of being alone that she HJs any guy who so much as looks at her, and now she is *totally* alone. No Patrick, no Alex, and absolutely *no way* of making ends meet. Meanwhile, your mom sits down to write her third novel. All she has to do is go tippety-tappety on her typewriter. But she can't do it."

"She went into heart failure," Dan said. "She had a bicuspid aortic valve. It's supposed to have three little wings, or flaps, called cusps, that seal shut after the heart beats, to keep blood from flowing backward into the heart. She couldn't push out enough oxygenated blood to her body. She had to have the valve replaced."

Tamma shrugged. "That was like ten years ago. She goes to San Bernardino, she has an itty-bitty, teeny-weeny minor little open-heart surgery, and she comes back here, and, what? Lies in bed for the next decade of her life? 'Oh, woe is me, I had a health problem!' And what is she even doing? Is she just in there watching youtube? And is it that she *can't* get out of bed or is it that she *won't* get out of bed? It's like she's frozen on the last good stance, looking at the horrifying slab move that comes next, saying 'I can't do it,' but for *ten years*. And these two once-upon-a-time beauties, these two inseparable, tanned desert bitches who started out with nothing except each other, they end up with not even that, dude. They cruxed out and failed. All their dreams. Ker-splat."

She reached deep into the pocket of her hoodie and took out her superglue and, passing the spliff back to thumb and forefinger, caught the glue top between her eyeteeth and cracked it open. She began superglueing closed the cracks in her pads, dusting the wet adhesive with chalk so it wouldn't cure slick. He understood now what she was getting at. It was not lost on her, that Dan had opportunities she did not, that he could go to college, and that they were both watching her life's ambition come to an end in a parking lot full of meth spoons and windshield glass. She did not want him to abandon her, and this was her oblique, slabclimberish way of coming at the chains of that particular conversation.

"That's why Kendra is terrified for me," she said. "And that's why Alex wants you to go to college. She thinks—Go to college, get a degree, find a good job with healthcare. She thinks if you own a two-door refrigerator and tweed jackets, if you sit up late at night finishing a bottle of white zinfandel with your Scandinavian wife Helga while your children sit beside you in bow ties and short pants eating wilted spinach with nutmeg and playing chess with one another, then you'll be safe from whatever it was that happened to her."

"You're right," he said.

"But I've seen into your heart, dude. Your mom, she doesn't know who you are. But I do. You're not that guy. You don't want to be safe. Safety is the latex between you and what's real—it's about always keeping away from the jaws of death. So what if Alexandra couldn't hack it? You're not her! You're not some wilting literary damsel. You're a highball boulderer who toiled under the most heinous conditions to send Fingerbang Princess. You're a fucking *climber*, and climbing isn't about being safe your whole entire life, it isn't about the layers of tweed and latex and zinfandel and health insurance between you and the implacable reality of the world; climbing is about wrapping your hands about the grim reaper's slopery skull and nutting deep into the jaws of death. So let's not try and be safe. Let's not run away from this. Let's do it, together. You hold my rope and I'll hold yours. And whatever comes, we will face it down together. I'm not saying there aren't risks, I'm just saying we've sent highballs before. We can do it again."

"Dude," he said. "You're crying."

"I'm not crying, *you're crying*," she said, tears cutting down the dust on her freckled cheeks. "Dude. I'm so fucking afraid I'm gonna die on this boulder tonight. I mean, don't get me wrong. I'm gonna grab my enormous adventure taco in one hand and the start hold in the other and give it my all, but whatever happens, you should not give up on me. I know I look like I'm choking. But this is our destiny, dude, and if you wimp out on it, you will always regret it. You'll never, ever be happy going that scared, safe way your parents want you to go. I don't care that they failed. You're not her. And I'm not Kendra."

She flicked the spliff away into the dark, then stepped up beneath the project and got down slowly, careful of her bruised tailbone, lowering herself onto the tire to keep out of the crusty sand. She drew her shoes out of her barn coat where she'd been keeping them warm and she pulled them on and laced them tight and then she flung the coat away into the sand. She drew the inside edge of each shoe against the opposite calf like a chef sharpening a knife upon a steel, one smooth swift movement down, and then the other side, down again.

She pulled onto the wall. She looked unstoppable. Hung Tinkerbell's Bandersnatch effortlessly and tiptoed up the slab to the exit-move crux. Her right hand went to the domino crystal, and she bore down with one finger pad, brought her right foot up, trembling, and set the edge of it down beside her pointer finger, in a hand-foot match. Calmly, with no sign of effort, she pressed herself up, caught the top, and floated onto the summit and out of sight. And just like that, Fingerbang Princess was done. The cleanest send of a boulder he'd ever seen.

Then she reappeared, standing at the edge, up there on the rock, and screamed. She put her hands between her thighs, bent forward at the waist, and screamed until she ran down out of breath and then she took a great suck of air and kept on screaming, veins standing out on her forehead. She scrambled down the backside and came around the side of the boulder and ran right into him, holding him and shaking all over. It was as if all the shaking had been stored up and now she let it go. The shivering came in racking episodes and then it would fall away and she would be still and then it would come back. She was hiccuping with joy. A cold wind blustered her hair and it stuck to her wet face in hanks. "I am a goddess of sex and slab climbing," she said, and with the pad of her thumb she wiped snot out of her mustache.

"What?" she said, taking great sobbing snorts of air. "What is it?"

"I was just thinking how goddamn amazing you look right now."

"I know, right?"

"You're ineffable."

"Dude," she said. "Not cool: I feel myself to be deeply F—able."

She clucked her disappointment with him, shaking her head. I did it, she thought. She was delirious with it. She was so happy she could've donkey-punched Fred Beckey. She was thinking, Now I know how I can do any of the big things. Now I have the recipe. It is hard work and attention to detail and one thing after another. The whole world goes this way. It seems impossible but the moves are there, you just have to find them and you have to have a little hope. It took me ninety-seven days but that doesn't matter, what matters is I know how to do it now, and it's all guts and work and belief, that's all it is, and if you're willing to give it everything, day after day, week after week, month after month, then you can do the sorts of things no one believes a girl like you can do. You have done it before, you can do it again.

II.

INTERSECTION

One

Dan sat on the edge of his bed, wringing his hands to warm them. What light there was came from the pine-framed window set in plaster. A frisbee overturned on the dresser, an old brass shaving canister, a lighter, a clasp knife, these things all cast their own particular shadows. Books were stacked against the wall. Tamma had sorted them by who would win a fight. Emily Brontë and Marcel Proust. Whitman and Melville.

Alone now, Dan waited, his elbows on his knees, a great hood of muscle laid down over his back, smiling despite himself, every rib showing with his slow and careful breathing, just the memory of his friend warmth in a cold, dark room. He pulled his shorts on, then vaulted for the pipe bar and started on pull-ups. A set of thirty. Walked to the wall and grasped the thirty-six-kilo kettlebell and carried it to the middle of the room. Waiter-hold kettlebell get-ups. Pause at the top, standing, the bell cradled aloft in his open hand.

If we're going to chase this dream, he thought, then we have to go into the park. You've been afraid of its reputation, its storied rocks, its many ghosts. But worthy or not, the real thing or not, you've strived out your backyard boulders and now you have to go to where the climbing is.

Lie down on the concrete floor. The bell cradled in his open palm. Rise up to a sitting position. The bell at full extension. Rise to a kneeling position, sweat dripping down his hair. Seeing the palimpsests of it on the concrete. Then stand all the way up.

After, he pulled on his jeans, shrugged into his shirt, and went out for breakfast. There, laying back against the interior wall with the sliding glass door cracked open, smoking a cigarette and working out sums on an envelope across her thigh, pale as if cut from marble, was Alexandra Redburn. Beside her, floor-to-ceiling windows lit an eerie blue. She exhaled smoke through the gap in the door and then leaned back against the plaster, the white tee slack on her thin shoulders, showing the scar raised like a bead of weld down her breastbone.

Dan started the toaster and opened the fridge, poured himself a glass of iced coffee. She stubbed out the cigarette among the others on the concrete skirt. Dan carried his plate and his glass across the room and seated himself on the rug. She set the envelope on the floor, slid it across the concrete. Dan peeled it up. She had their bank account balance with everything subtracted out for the month. He recognized the dish internet bill, the waste disposal bill, a figure for their electricity, the water bill. They had their water delivered and pumped into a tank that sat on the north side of the house.

"Dad'll get paid," he said.

She took a sip of her coffee and her lips peeled back and showed her teeth. "I hear you come out in the morning."

"Ah, well—sorry. I always mean to be quiet."

"It's okay. You don't wake me up. I'm not sleeping. I'm never sleeping anymore. You're working hard."

"I try."

"You've had a chance at things."

"I think so."

"There's something you should know, Danny."

"What?"

"The pig valve. It's no good anymore."

"What does that mean?"

She raised her hands and let them fall.

"How do you know?"

"I know the symptoms. I lie in bed, propped up against the headboard, trying to keep from drowning. Afraid that if I go to sleep, I won't wake up."

"Can't you get it replaced?"

"No."

"Why not?"

"I promised myself. Never again. They crack your sternum with a wedge and a hammer. Clamps to spread you open. Shine a light where god never meant light to be. There're only so many times they can do it before the sternotomy doesn't heal and nobody knows what that number is. They stitch in the pig valve and from the moment they put it in, it's in you, deteriorating. They sew your chest up like a spiral notebook and every time you cough it feels like you're going to split open along the front, like your heart is going to fall out into your lap."

"What does Dad think?"

"We've fought about it. But I don't guess it matters. We don't have insurance. Lawrence wants me to do it, but he doesn't say how. We'll find a way, he says. And I have to be the one who says, *'Find a way—Lawrence—what way?'* Because the only money we have is the money I set aside for your education."

"Use the thirteen thousand, Mom."

"It is not about the money, Danny. The only thing about the money is—I don't want to end up in surgery somehow and lose everything I set aside for you. That's what scares me most. That is why I am here, holding on. So that we can get that money safely to you, and you can go and have the life I never could. A life with some hope to it. But even if we had the money, I would not do this thing. It is a step out into darkness I cannot face again."

"So, there's nothing to do?"

She lay against the wall, the skin above her collar bones retracting with each breath. "When you turn eighteen, you can have your own checking account. We need to go to the bank, set that up, and we can transfer you the money we set aside for your education. Then it won't much matter what happens to me. It's not perfect. If it comes to bankruptcy, they might go through our financial records and claw it back from you. Otherwise, it'll be all yours, and you can go to school and leave this place behind forever." She grimaced. "Soon. In two weeks, we'll go. I'll take you. Maybe in the morning. I usually feel better in the mornings."

"Okay," he said.

Dan set his plate on the kitchen island. He picked up his boots and his bag and carried them out to the front door and thought, When I open this door, let Tamma be out there. He knew she would not be there. It was much too early. But he thought: *Let her be there.* He opened the door and walked out onto the porch. And there, walking heel to toe across the split rail fence, was Tamma Callahan. The rails were loose in their notches and squirrely under foot. She hinged forward and cartwheeled over the post, hesitated at the apex of the handstand. Then she kicked forward and alighted once more on her feet and, seeing him, flashed a smile. He crossed the yard to her, and she clasped one hand over her eyes, pirouetted about, swooned backward off the post, and Dan said, "Oh fuck!" stepping forward to catch her, dropping his things.

Two

Some other morning, on the way to school, Tamma was lying kicked back in the seat, feet up on the dash, lab notebook on her thighs, when she looked out the window and saw climbers at the pump of the 76. She beached onto the sill, her hair sucked out in the wind, thinking, *Climbers!* The one chick was leaning back against her truck, letting the pump run. Thumbs hooked into the waistband of double-paneled carhartts ragged from kneebarring. Rock rash on her shoulders, dirty-blond hair in a messy bun. Not a sport climber. *A chick trad climber!* With big orange sunglasses. Purple lenses. The rig a rusted toyota. A tough-looking Asian chick with a trucker's cap was sauntering out of the convenience store, ripping open a bag of chips.

"Avast!" Tamma said. "Chicks to starboard! Climber chicks!"

The girl with the bag of chips turned. They looked right at one another. The girl's hat said I ♥ BEAVER. Then Tamma snaked back in through the window and crushed her face to the dash. That was the person she wanted to be: a rad climber chick! Sauntering out of a gas station! Ripping open a bag of cool ranch doritos with the magnetic physical presence of Pete Whittaker tearing open a magnum condom!

Dirtbag climber chick: the only possible life worth living. Close your eyes and find your own private hell just redblack with rage. Put your fist into your mouth and bite down savagely, ready to scream; rage, rage at your life; rage, and hope, and seethe—your guts a moiling cauldron of impossible dreams. "Dan!" she said, heaving up, clawing the flesh down from around her eyes—"Dan! We have to go into the park and *climb something*. The next thing, Dan! The next project!"

After she'd sent Fingerbang Princess, she had felt that the whole world was hers for the (friendly, consensual) ravishing, so she had signed up for the bouldering competition in Los Angeles. And immediately, all the confidence had gone out of her, and she'd realized that she'd just doomed herself to compete against girls who climbed six grades harder.

"Yes!" he said. "What should we do?"

"Figures on a Landscape, here we *fucking* come!"

"Sure but—"

"Fuck!"

"Figures is a route," he said. "It's two hundred and fifty feet long! We need a rope, harnesses, belay devices, gear, shoes without holes in them. And we don't have the money for that stuff—do you have money?"

"What about the thirteen thousand?"

"It's socked away in some separate account. It's not in my name."

"You know what Lynn Hill used to say?"

"It goes, boys!"

"Sure—but no, the other thing—?"

"I do, it's just—"

"Footholds exist wherever they are needed, Dan, that's what she used to say!"

"It's just——" Dan continued, "I worry she was talking about climbing, and not about poverty."

"*Footholds*," Tamma said, more slowly, and more emphatically, "exist. Wherever. They. Are. Needed. It's self-explanatory, Dan."

Later that morning, walking classroom to classroom, she passed the teacher's lounge and from inside she could hear Mr. Jeremiah talking to Mr. Cruiser, Mr. Jeremiah saying, "I don't get it, I had her sister, and Sierra was a joy, a model student, and then Tamma comes along, and why even show up if you're going to be spaced out and high the entire time? I was trying to explain metaphor versus simile to her and it was just: *nobody home*. Not a very bright little girl, you know?"

Tamma stood there, for a beat, and then kept walking. She could probably get a job, but it wouldn't leave much time for climbing. There was cash under her mom's bed, plus oxy, flunitrazepam, weed, a ten-gauge pump, and an AK. But taking cash felt like a line too far.

She wondered what would happen if you just showed up in the park and started going campsite to campsite and explaining that you thirsted for glory and hand jams and that you just needed someone to teach you and that in exchange you would bring the mega-stoke because that's all you had? Would some ancient, leathery climber god take them under their wing? Perhaps a campsite full of French girls, with thick accents, out from Fontainebleau to see America? But she couldn't imagine anyone helping them. No one helped anyone and everything was fucked and they were doomed and if they were gonna do it, they were going to do it alone, just the two of them. She couldn't even imagine asking. What would you do, just walk up to someone, and talk to them, as if you deserved help, as if you deserved to be there, as if you weren't poor, illiterate, trash living in a trailer, with your fat, miserable, diner waitress mom and her creepy, psychopathic drug dealer slampiece? They'd take one look her and shoo her out of the park. Climbers were supposed to be like Paisley Cuthers—gorgeous, beloved, errant golden children of nurturing, middle-class families, carrying their liberal philosophical principles out into the wilds on a journey of self-discovery. Fucking Paisley.

They needed a rope, maybe $250. Twelve quickdraws, $13 apiece. Alpine slings would be better but were more expensive. A rack of nuts, $120. Anchor slings and carabiners, $50. A rack of cams. Cams were essential trad climbing gear and would run you $80 a piece plus a $9 carabiner. Six or seven cams made a single rack, but a double rack was standard. She didn't know the figure exactly, but she did know that it was an unreachable amount of money. Plus gas in and out of the park, and free use of the car. Or buying a car. Preferably a van.

After class she walked out into the hallway, unpocketed her cell phone, and discovered that she had sixty-five missed calls, twelve voicemails, and hundreds of unread text messages. As she watched, her phone lit up. It was a call from her brother, Colin. She swiped it open.

"Tamma!" he said. "Where are you?"

"Isn't your girlfriend named Katie?"

"Yeah?"

"I'm fingerbanging Katie right now."

"Tamma," he said.

"She's a delight. Feminine, but desperate with passion."

"Tamma!"

"Yeah?"

"We're at the hospital in LA."

"What? *Why are you at the hospital?*"

"Tamma! Listen: Brad fell asleep in a rocking chair with the baby on his chest and River rolled out of his arms onto the tile floor."

Other kids were issuing out past her. Tamma did not move.

"Sierra and Mom are here, so you need to watch the kids."

"Wait—what? Who is with them?"

"Brad was with them, but he left."

"He *left?*"

"We don't know where he is. But Mom and Sierra are already here. Mom says you need to get over to the house and watch those kids."

"Okay," Tamma said. "I'm there."

She hung up and stood in the hallway with everyone slamming their lockers and filing into the classroom she had just left. Dan was coming on down the hall toward her.

"Borrow your keys?" she said.

"Don't get pulled over, right?"

"Right."

"I don't know what happens if you get pulled over without a license."

"You end up sucking dick in the back of a cop car, I think."

"Hopefully not though, right?"

"Yeah, *ideally*."

He pitched her the keys and she caught them, already turning. She blazed down an empty, sun-scorched highway going twenty over and hit the turnoff so hard the car fishtailed. She roared down dirt roads, towing a plume of dust, and found the dogs gone and Brad's truck gone, and she went in through the gate. She could hear Samantha crying. She knocked on the door until the blinds swung to the side. Hunter looked out at her, chewing.

"Hunter!" Tamma said. "Can you, like, let me in, dude?"

He was eating a handful of froot loops.

"Please let me in."

He just watched her, paying froot loops into his mouth one at a time. Samantha was screaming behind him. The screaming rose and fell. Hunter chewed thoughtfully.

"Hunter buddy," she said. "Do you remember me?"

"Are you a boy or a girl?"

"I'm your mom's sister, Tamma."

"Oh," he said, his little blond eyebrows knitting together. He paid another froot loop up between thumb and forefinger and put it between his front teeth and cracked it apart and stood staring at her.

"Open up, buddy, it's just me," she said.

Hunter opened the door and Tamma walked through the living room and down the hall, treading over discarded leggings, jeans, tees, scrubs. She crossed to the nursery and swung the door open. Samantha was in her crib with her arms outflung, shaking her head side to side and screaming, red-faced, with tears running down her temples. You could see her tongue fluttering when she broke to quavering ululations.

Tamma picked her up and the baby opened her tearstained eyes and fixed Tamma with a look of horror, then tilted her head back and wailed.

Tamma said, "It's okay, baby! It's okay! I'm your aunt! You're okay! I'm here to take care of you!"

Hunter stood in the doorway eating froot loops. He said, "She doesn't know who you are."

Tamma opened her mouth to say something saucy, and then she thought: What would Akiyo Noguchi do? Would the legend of comp climbing stand around snarking a kindergartener? No. She'd take this problem with discipline, patience, and sustained attention, which was how Tamma would take it.

"When did she last eat?"

The baby was thrashing and heaving at Tamma with both hands. Hunter knotted his fingers together and knocked one socked foot against the other.

"That's okay, honey," she said. "You don't know. That's okay! Can you show me—is there formula, or is there—?"

Hunter wrinkled his nose. "She eats *food*," he said. "She's almost *one*."

"Right," Tamma said. "Of course. When does she eat, usually?"

Hunter looked at her, looked all about the room, made his face up into an expression of doubt and lifted his hands, palms up—*I don't know?*

"You don't know and that's okay," Tamma said. "Can you tell me *what* she usually eats for lunch?"

Hunter said, "I'll show you!" and then he bent at the waist and charged out of the room with his arms outflung behind him. Samantha was still screaming. At the ragged end of each scream her little fists trembled and shook. Then she would suck air, opening her eyes on the inhale, fix Tamma with a look, and then scream for the entirety of the exhale with her face bright red and her mouth going to a tiny, terrible, chin-quivering frown. Tamma followed Hunter down the hall into the kitchen, with its bubbled-up linoleum, torn-out ceiling, and missing stove. She found Hunter on the countertop, opening one of the cabinets. He had taken out a sippy cup and now brandished it in triumph.

"That's good! A sippy cup!" Tamma said. "We're doing great! We're figuring things out! You're my very helpful little dude." She hitched the baby up onto her hip again and opened the fridge and slung out the gallon of milk and uncapped the sippy cup.

"She takes *whole* milk!" Hunter said, sitting on the counter, swinging his legs.

"Right," Tamma said. "Should've known that."

"Yeah *duh*," Hunter said.

Tamma took a breath. Be more Akiyo, she thought. She brought out the whole milk and poured and passed the sippy cup to Samantha, who took it in her chubby little hands.

Three

A hard day, full of uncertainty. At noon, Tamma made mac and cheese from a box, microwaved a packet of broccoli, and fed Samantha in her high chair, the baby looking at Tamma with a worried expression, her eyebrows a little raised, bringing one cheese-covered hand to her chest and wringing her fingers together before going back, somewhat doubtfully, to eating.

After lunch Tamma went through the house, the baby on one hip, picking up dirty clothes. She carried the trash can into the living room and swept everything off the coffee table into it. Then she walked to the dumpster and slung the bag inside and when she came back into the house, Hunter said, "What are you doing?"

"Picking up some clothes and trash and things, kiddo."

"Why?"

"Just trying to help."

"Why?"

"I thought I could."

"Why?"

"Seemed like the right thing to do."

"Why?"

"Because I'm here to help, kiddo."

"You're weird."

"That's true."

"You're not pretty."

"Everyone gets to have an opinion!"

"Why are you so skinny?"

"I'm average weight for my height. I just have big shoulders, and don't carry a lot of fat, so I look leaner than I am."

"You're real short though."

"I'm five feet tall."

"Are you a stunted midget?"

"Nope! That's my normal height. My grandmother, your great-grandmother, was only four foot nine, and she once shot a charging grizzly from horseback with a lever action 30-06."

"But my mom is tall."

"Your mom is five-six."

"My dad says you're a stunted midget."

"Well, people come in all kinds of different heights and also personalities."

Later, Tamma made snack—thawing frozen blueberries under tap water, cutting up slices of cheese, putting out cheerios in a bowl, and frying a quesadilla for Hunter. Afterward, she changed Samantha's diaper and put the baby down for a nap. She moved the dishes to the washer and ran it. She swept the floor while Hunter watched from the couch. Sam slept for forty minutes and then she was up, crying. All day like that. Make it to dinnertime and come out into the living room, holding the baby on her hip, to find Hunter still on the couch.

"Now, bud, what do you like to eat?"

"Oreos."

"How about breakfast for dinner?"

"How about . . . oreos?"

Tamma found hash browns and sausages in the freezer and knocked the ice off the bags. She cranked on the propane canister and started the burner and holding the baby on her hip she struck a match and fried it all in a cheap nonstick skillet, hash browns and bacon and sausage and over-easy eggs, and plated it all up with sunny D for Hunter and Hunter looked at it and said, "I don't eat eggs."

"Try them," Tamma said.

"No."

"Have some hash browns."

"They're touching the eggs."

"Hunter, kiddo, you got to eat something."

"No."

"Cut me some slack here, tiger."

"No."

"Will you *try* the eggs?"

"I want ramen. My mom makes me ramen."

Be more Akiyo!

"I'm sorry, I didn't know that, I understand your disappointment, I've made eggs, will you please try them?"

"I hate you!" Hunter said. The baby startled and jerked, planted her tiny hands on Tamma's chest, opened her eyes wide, and then sealed them down to unhappy crescents and started to cry.

"You scared the baby!" Tamma yelled.

Hunter threw the orange juice at her. Tamma turned and caught it on her shoulder. Then he started screaming. His screaming was high-pitched, continuous, breaking for breaths. In her arms, the baby shook her head from side to side and screamed back.

Tamma said, "You little dick!"

He got up, bending forward, hands clenched, veins standing out on his forehead, and he said, "Go away! Go away! Go! *Away!*"

Tamma retreated down the hallway, holding the baby, Hunter coming after, brows drawn, saying, "We don't want you here! We wish you were dead! We're going to kill you!"

Tamma backed herself into the laundry room, pulled the door shut, and locked it. Hunter tried the knob, then put his shoulder to the door.

"I hate you!" he screamed. "*I hate you!*"

"I hate you too, you selfish little shit!" Tamma said.

The baby was shaking all over, and her sucking gasps came at the ragged end of her screams, when she seemed to have emptied herself entirely.

"I'm going to kill you with—!" Hunter seemed to search for the word. He was kicking the door. "With a—with a—with a backhoe!"

Tamma thought—With a backhoe?

"Or a—a—a—" He searched for the word. "A dinosaur!" he said. "No one will ever find your corpse!"

Tamma was rocking the baby, trying to compose herself. This may not, she thought, really be about the eggs. Samantha's fists quivered at the racking end of the sobs. Tamma held her close, whispering to her, and Samantha leaned forward and puked onto Tamma's shirt.

"Holy ballsack!" Tamma said, but the baby bucked and screamed harder and so Tamma stooped forward, rocking side to side, saying, "Shhhhhhhh, baby, it's all right," trying to quiet her. She was not handling this situation with calm Noguchi-ness. Tamma wanted to climb Moses Tower and Lighthouse and Washer Woman; she wanted to compete internationally; she could not let herself be the sort of person who fell apart under pressure.

"Go away!" Hunter said. "I don't want you here! I want my dad!"

"I want your dad here too, but he's not here, because he's a cowardly dickhole!"

Tamma began opening drawers, looking for a towel. Hunter was beating on the door. She found a white tee and started to mop the baby's face. The baby recoiled and cried harder, her lower lip curling, her cheeks streaked with tears. Hunter said, "Go away! I hate you! I want my dad back!"

Tamma looked Samantha in the eye, and took a deep, calming breath to show her how. The situation, she thought, is getting out of hand. Tamma had mantras for her fear and this was one. She didn't know why it helped but it did. Saying it filled her with a secret joy. She said: The situation is out of hand. You're a rad climber and people like you. Don't worry about your next project. You'll get to that. Right here, right now: this. These kids, this house, dinner. Deep, calming breaths: The situation has become fucked up. That's okay. You're going to learn your craft here on the cryptic rocks in this kitty-litter desert and you'll take those skills to the cliffs of France and those French girls will teach you how to climb limestone. She was taking calming breaths and looking at the baby with her calm eyes and her calm face and she was ignoring the beating on the door and the baby was staring at her like—*What are you doing?*

Tamma took another deep, persuasive breath and let it out and the baby's eyebrows went up. "You're a rad baby, Samantha," she said. "You're a rad baby and people like you."

Samantha considered Tamma with a speculative frown, her lower lip still pouting, tiny expressions of attention, interest, and worry flickering across her face.

Tamma took another big, conspicuous, easy breath. And the baby took a breath back and sighed it out. Tamma smiled at the sigh and the baby smiled back.

"I understand you're upset," she said to the door.

"I hate you!" he said. "I'm going to kill you! I hate you and I'm going to kill you and no one will ever find your corpse!"

"Don't mind him," Tamma said to Samantha. "He's allowed to get upset. He's had a hard day. People get the heebie-jeebies sometimes. Even Beth Rodden got afraid when she was putting up Meltdown. Very desperate gear on Meltdown you know, and it was the hardest trad climb in the world at the time, I think. People tried to take that away from her, saying that it was finger-size dependent, and you could only climb it if you had porcelain-doll hands, but really it was a magnificent, pioneering accomplishment. In order to place the gear, they say she pre-clipped it to her rope and duct taped it to her harness. I always thought that was a great solve. All she had to do was reach down and tear it free and stuff into the crack. You see, she was afraid, but she found a solution. This is a very scary situation for everyone. But we're gonna get through it."

Hunter was throwing himself against the door.

"I hear that you are upset," Tamma said. Raising her voice. Trying to keep it calm. "But I am pretty sure that we can find something to eat for dinner!" Then to the baby: "We're gonna figure this out, baby girl." She put her face right into the baby's neck and Samantha giggled and shrugged up her shoulder and Tamma kissed her. "I promise you," Tamma said. "I'm going to get everyone fed and dressed and cleaned and then I'm going to put everyone to bed and everyone will be safe and tomorrow, we'll get better. And the next day, better yet."

She came out of the laundry room wearing one of Brad's shirts. The shirt said FISH FEAR ME WOMEN WANT ME. Hunter stood in the hallway: upset, astonished, and crushed all at once. Tamma knelt down, holding the baby on her hip, put one hand on his shoulder, looked him in the eye, and said, "I'm sorry I said those things. I didn't mean them. I was upset. This is stressful and new for all of us, and I got a little stressed out too. We're gonna figure this out, little dude. And you were right. Let's make ramen. Why don't you pick out the flavor you would like?"

She fed everyone ramen with fried sausage and hash browns. Herself, she ate four eggs. She got through the day. She put the baby down and then put Hunter to bed. She messaged Dan. Dan didn't have a phone and so messaged back from his computer.

> I'd come help . . .

> > yeah yeah
> > but some slutcake took ur car
> > is alex okay with that

> she hasn't noticed

> > lol we were always like
> > we cant take the car!
> > living in terror

CRUX

> bc Alex said we could
> only take it to school
> but maybe
> it turns out
> no one
> is paying attention
> to where we go
> actually

Goddamn
Do you know what that means?

> yes

Do you though?

> it means
> we can drive into
> the park
> climbing season doesnt
> have to end

It means
We can just drive into
The Park!
Climbing season doesn't
Have to end!
Weekends!
Winter Break!
Climb during the day!
When it's warm!
And sunny!
And you can feel your fingers!
This opens a whole new world
A whole new can of worms
How are you doing

> im not good at this
> im not this kind of girl

> Loving? Determined? Hardworking?
> You're this kind of girl

>> you don't think that

> Of course I think that
> I believe in you

>> lol you dont really

> No of course I do

>> but me?
>> with kids?
>> nobody thinks
>> this is ideal

> why

>> just nobody does
>> because I'm
>> .... me

> I do!
> I think you'd be great with kids

>> lol no you totally dont

> Yes I totally do
> You have this.

She slept on the couch with the baby monitor beside her. She got a three-hour stretch after she put the baby down and then Samantha was up every two hours and each time it was forty minutes of rocking and walking around the darkened nursery singing to get her back to sleep. Then Hunter came out and stood in the living room and said, "I'm scared," and Tamma said, "Come here, my dude," and she lay on the couch with Hunter sleeping on her breast, sick with exhaustion. That was how it was when Sierra called.

"Sis," Tamma said, whispering into the phone. "How's River?" She backed up onto the arm of the couch and let herself down one leg at time so as not to wake Hunter, skulking away through the kitchen.

"This is hell, Tams. He's in the ICU. And it's hell."

"Ah."

"I wish I was dead."

"Sorry, sis."

"You should see the stitches. They have him in an isolette, this little see-through plastic box with a ventilator, and he's lying in there and you can reach through the side to touch him, and you should see his little head with its stitches."

Tamma did not know what to say. She was holding the baby monitor, watching the screen of Samantha lying in her crib and what she wanted was that no baby, anywhere, should come to any harm.

"Are you okay there, Tams?"

"Yeah, I'm fine." Whispering.

"How are the kids?"

"A little upset." Tamma boosted herself up onto the counter in the dark kitchen. "But we're all making it through together."

Sierra breathed out, raggedly.

"Is Brad really not there?"

"He's really not here."

"I thought he might come back."

"Yeah."

"What am I going to do, Tams?"

"You'll get through it, sis."

"I can't do this. I can't bear it."

"You *can* do this. We're gonna be okay."

"You don't get it. Nothing is going to be okay ever again, Tamma. They're saying brains are plastic. That's what everyone keeps saying. Brains are plastic. They mean—*Who knows how he might adapt?* But there is a lot of damage. There will be developmental delays, and could be other effects: seizures, blindness, we may not know for years." Sierra was crying on the other end.

"Listen, sis. Whatever it is, we'll figure it out."

"It would be better if he had died," she said, and after she said it, she made an awful, wet, shuddering, sucking sound. "Oh god. Oh god. I'm a horrible mother."

"No," Tamma said. "No no no no. You're a mom who's hit a tough spot but we'll dig deep and we'll get focused and we'll put this together."

"I wish he had died."

"I hear that," Tamma whispered. "But I don't think you'll feel that way forever. We don't know what tomorrow brings. We don't know what's possible, we don't even know what's happened."

"You don't get it, Tams. I wish my baby had died. He might never grow up and I could be changing diapers for the rest of my life. Alone. With no husband and no help. How will we live? I want him to grow up so I can meet him. I want him to love somebody and have a life."

"I can't promise that any of that will happen. But I can promise that I'm gonna be there for you."

"I can't do this, Tams. Did Brad really leave?"

"All I know is, he's not here. Maybe he's having a thinky-thought and a can of beer and a curry pizza and he'll be back. People get gripped sometimes but they can still rally."

"He's gone, Tamma. Every man in your fucking life is going to leave."

"I hear you." Not mine, Tamma thought. Not Dan.

"Oh, god. We're alone. We're all alone. We're so fucking desperately goddamn *alone*."

"What does Hunter eat for breakfast? Sierra, can you tell me what to make for breakfast?"

"Oh god," Sierra said. She was gasping into the phone and she started to calm then. And she talked about what they had for breakfast. Waffles. Those little toaster waffles and a glass of orange juice and Samantha has oatmeal. You make it unsweetened on the stove top. Hunter will want two waffles with margarine and syrup. He won't eat butter. He won't eat the waffles if you put butter on them. If you say anything about butter he will freak out. And he won't drink water, but he will drink orange juice or dr pepper so make sure he gets a glass. Don't even mention butter. Hunter can take the bus to kindergarten, but you have to pick him up. I'll call and make sure they know it'll be you, otherwise you can't take him. After he's gone, Samantha watches an hour of television while I clean up. She went on like that, with Tamma listening and afterward they said good night and Tamma thumbed off her phone and crept back into the living room and laid herself down on the floor and was asleep and ten minutes later the baby monitor was sounding and she left Hunter sleeping and walked into the nursery and opened the door already shushing and cooing.

In the morning, she made breakfast with Samantha on her hip, waffles for Hunter and oatmeal for Samantha. While Hunter ate, she fed Samantha in her lap.

"So buddy, you take the bus to school?" she said.

"I go to kindergarten," Hunter said. He was delighted to say it. He said it smiling and beaming at her silliness not to know this kind of thing.

"And you can catch the bus?"

"I can—uh—I can take the bus, yeah," he said, and then had to catch his breath for some reason, looking all around. "But you walk me to the bus stop and then you have to pick me up, yeah."

"Okay," Tamma said, and she made him another toaster waffle, and spread it with margarine. She packed him lunch and walked him out to the bus stop and stood and watched him get on the bus. She walked back along the long empty lane through white hardpan with joshua trees growing crooked by the roadside, holding Samantha on her hip. Passing a house, she looked and saw a dumpster with the gate open, and she backpedaled.

A long loop of climbing rope was hanging out the closed and locked dumpster lid. There was no municipal trash service, and some people here locked their dumpsters to keep others from dumping in their bin. Trash service could be one of the bigger household bills. Tamma walked over and dragged on the line. It was heavy cord, the sheath fuzzy with age, the nylon gone frangible and crispy in places. Holding the baby on her hip, she started paying the rope out, one-handed, spooling it onto the ground. She paid sixty meters into the dust and scooped it up and carried it back with the baby sucking on her thumb and making sudden pivoting turns in Tamma's arms to look forward or back. Tamma opened the car and dumped the rope in the back and then carried the baby up into the house. When she got Samantha down for her nap, Tamma let herself into the workshop out back. It was a shipping container full of tools. Miter saw, skilsaw, stacked lumber, table saw, bins of drills and hand tools. She found a chisel and an eight-pound sledge and walked back out to the dumpster and knocked the lock right off.

Inside, there was a purple cordura backpack. Tamma hoisted it up and pitched it over the side. Then she dropped out and zipped it open. It was full of ancient climbing gear. She collapsed onto her butt in the gravel. There was a rack of old-school hexes, steel hexagons placed by climbers in cracks to protect against falls. Obsolete now, but once standard. They were slung on lengths of cords so old they were crunchy. My god, Tamma was thinking. This could change my life. She gaped the bag open. There were SMC carabiners clipped together into knots. There was a rack of steel nuts slung on cables. Two different helmets. It was a full rack of climbing gear from the seventies and eighties. Tamma sat with her legs out before her, thinking, This is my break. She planted her hands and boosted herself back into the dumpster. She pitched aside trash bags and found an old expedition duffel. The nylon was rotting with age and the zipper was stuck so she ripped it open and poured the contents over the side. Holy god, she was saying to herself. Holy mother of god. It was full of danskin tights and leotards. Bright orange and electric pink tiger print. She climbed back out carrying the expedition duffel, shouldered the backpack, and walked on toward the house with it all. She was halfway there when she stopped and pitched everything down and walked back. She climbed back into the dumpster and fought her way down through the bags. There at the bottom was an ancient wooden hangboard, a training tool used by climbers. It had a series of fingerpockets in varying depths from fifty-five-mil shelves to barely there fifteen-mil edges. Work on a hangboard could build devastating finger strength. She blew trash and dirt off it and held it up. Famous, these wooden beastmaker hangboards. She tilted it over her shoulder and walked back to grab the old backpack and the duffel. Approaching the house, she could already hear the baby crying. She was with the kids for five days.

Four

Tamma woke facedown in the sheets to the muted cricketing of her alarm. She thumbed it off and lay in the dark, slowly opening her cramped hands, straightening her toes and letting her ankle pop, rolling first one wrist, and then the other, the right making a crackly sound. She spread her fingers as straight and wide as they would go, feeling the tension run through her forearms and into her elbows. She could hear Colin breathing. Kendra had dropped the little kids off with their mom at a hotel room near the hospital, and here Tamma was, at the weekend. Below the bunk bed, leaning up against her dresser, the pack of gear. Back up the wash, Dan would be waiting for her with the car. She'd been having twinges in her right ring finger and she pinned the place between thumb and forefinger of her left hand, searching out the connective tissues beneath the skin and bearing down on them. Then she rolled to the edge of the bed and dropped quietly to the floor. She slid the window open and from the other side of the room Colin said, "Tamma?"

She stood beside the window in the dark.

"What're you doing?"

"None of your business, dickweed."

"I'm telling Mom."

She walked over and punched his arm.

"Ow, Tamma!"

"Don't you dare tell Mom, you little donkeydick."

"Okay okay! I won't!"

"Why would you, you fucknut?"

"Mom's really worried about you!"

"I promise you, she isn't."

"She's scared for you, dude."

"Fuck her."

"What if something happens to you? Like, I love you, Tams."

"Nothing is gonna happen, you little buttsucker. Besides, Mom would just think of all the money she'd save on milk and cereal and then she'd be fine."

"Tamma?"

"Yeah, dude?"

"Do you want to see a picture of the girl who sucked my dick behind the ball shed?"

"*What?*"

"Jenny Armstrong. She's dick-crazy."

"Dude!" She felt around under the covers for his arm and punched him again.

"Ow! What?"

"Don't say that. Don't say she's dick-crazy."

"But she *is*, Tamma."

Tamma punched him in the back.

"Ow! Fuck! Cut it out!"

"I don't care. Don't say it."

"What do I say?"

"Say she's romantic."

"Do you want to see pictures?"

"No!" She hit him again.

"Ow! Tamma! Stop hitting me!"

"Don't show anyone pictures! Delete the fucking pictures! Don't take pictures! What about Katie?"

"Well, yeah," he said, the smile in his voice. "Katie's cool, I guess."

"You asshole! Delete those photos. Never pull that shit again. And take better care of your girlfriend, you prick!"

"Tamma?"

"Yeah?"

"Do you think Brad's coming back? For serious. Do you think so?"

"I don't know, buddy. What do you think?"

"I was at the hospital with Mom when he showed up."

"What?"

"Yeah I was there in the NICU when Brad just all of a sudden comes into the room. Like, they aren't supposed to let kids in. But they let me in, because I think they thought River was gonna die. So they were being—you know, nice."

"What happened?"

"Well, Sierra, she started to breathe really fast. And Mom started talking at him and she was just saying all these things like how it was good that he was there now, and they have the baby in this little plastic box so you can't pick him up because he's on this breathing tube thingy, and his little head is all stitched up, which you mostly can't see because he has on this little stocking cap, and Brad comes over to the box and they're both—Mom and sis—they're, like, talking at him and you could kinda tell he wasn't listening, he was just sort of standing there with this really weird, like, *look*, and Sierra was all, like, 'Hold his hand, Bradley,' and Brad, he doesn't like, *move*, he's just, like, looking at the baby, and the baby, River, he opens his eyes and the one on the left kind of shakes, which was freaky?, and under the stocking cap you can see the like, bandages and stuff, and the stocking cap is kind of stained like this orange color, and River, he's, like, so small and red, and he's moving in like, a kind of a jerky-shaky way, and Brad, he puts up his hands and he's all, '*I can't, I just can't*' and the baby is, like, trying to look at him, like, trying to look toward his voice or whatever, but his left eye shakes and keeps rolling up, and Sierra is like, 'Hold his hand, Bradley, please will you just hold his hand, even if only just this once,' but Brad, he goes, 'I can't do it, SieSie, I just *can't*,' and then he goes back out the door, and then out through the doors of the NICU, which you have to get buzzed out of, and then there's this long hallway to the elevators and Sierra runs out after him and she's screaming, it was like really scary because she's *screaming* screaming, you know?, she's going, 'Go back in there and hold his hand, Bradley, just hold his hand, you're *his father*,' but Brad won't do it, he's just, like, walking away shaking his head, saying, 'I don't need this shit,' and Sierra is just going, like, full total fucking apeshit, but he won't look at her or anything, and she keeps grabbing his shoulder but he just, like, shrugs her off and he doesn't, like, say anything back, he just gets in the elevator and clicks the button to close the doors over and over and Sierra stands there just, like, *shrieking* at him, and that's how he left, Tamma."

"Fuck."

"Do you think he's coming back?"

She came over to the bed and swept his hair off his forehead and kissed him and said, "I don't know, kiddo. And by the by, don't you worry about me. When I fall off things, I just climb back up out of the crater and change my underwear. You're not gonna get rid of me that easy."

She picked up her bag and went out the window and walked down the wash toward Dan's place. She kept thinking of Brad walking away down the hallway, shrugging off Sierra's hand. Then she thought: Forget it. The sand in the wash was icy and broke underfoot like she was walking across a great crusty pie. The sprawl of desert ran before her to hills nacreous by moonlight. Islands of creosote and dead opuntia swamped in windblown chaff. Tumbleweeds eddying in the bends and lees. There was a way that the small decisions you made every day became big decisions. You picked the person you spent time with and that became the person you were depending on when something went wrong.

She climbed out the side of the wash and Dan was there, leaning against the old subaru. She quietly popped the shift release with a screwdriver and dropped it into neutral.

"Wait," Dan said, leaning in through the window.

She waited.

"You really think they won't notice?"

"I think," Tamma whispered, her elbow on the open window frame, leaning her head into his conspiratorially, "that Alexandra said once that we could only take the car into school. And we listened, because the park feels like something that maybe shitheads like you and me don't deserve. So, we've been stuck going grool-for-glory on heinous death-rocks in a place where we know *for sure* other climbers have died. And while we're still shitheads, I think we should try."

"Okay," he said, and walked around the front of the car, braced against the hood, and casually pushed the subaru backward down the drive. Once out on the lane, and well away from the house, Tamma started the engine and they headed south.

"Dude," Tamma said. "Are you scared?"

"I'm scared," Dan said.

She hit the highway and took it east, then turned down through side roads and past the shut-up ranger station. It was Saturday, December 10, 5:19 a.m., and thirty-one degrees by the dashboard. The headlights spooled out gray tarmac and lit upon joshua trees overhanging the road, and beyond all that lay the vast and empty desert strewn with rock piles.

"Do you ever think about Paisley Cuthers?" she said.

"No?"

"What do you think happens if she comes to this comp in the spring?"

"What do you mean, what happens?"

"I mean, what do I do?"

"What do you do? You try your hardest and you get crushed."

"You think?"

"*Yeah*. We suck. Paisley is *famously* strong."

"That makes me so angry!"

"Why?"

"What do you mean, *why*? She's been climbing in a gym since before she could walk. They vacation in Font and Hueco. She has a power rack and moonboard in her home gym. Everything we want in life, she has just been given."

"None of that is her fault though."

"The legends of climbing, dude, lived in caves. They survived on wine and dumpster food. They risked their lives to do things that only like nine other guys understood. They were mystics, dude: vagabonds. But now they've been replaced by glossy, anorexic, pampered trust-fund bitches with nine-step skincare routines like *Paisley Cuthers*! That's not *fair*. That's not *American*. Money and privilege can't just pick some barbie doll and anoint her queen bitch of *our sport*. This isn't tennis. This is *climbing*. It is about facing death and pain and darkness and your own demons to do something cool; to climb is to be almost shitting yourself with fear and yet to make the next move anyway, and what does Paisley Cuthers know about any of that? I don't want to lose to Paisley Fucking Cuthers, Dan. I want to come out of this empty godforsaken litter box and walk out onto those competition mats and stand under bright lights and *wreck* her, wreck her and her flawless, *beckoning* armpits. I want to prove that grit and passion matter more than money and privilege. Because this is *our* sport! It should belong to *us*—to reckless dipshits who thirst for adventure."

"I know you want that," Dan said.

Tamma took the road slowly. They were both full of the restrained, excited feeling of what lay before them. There was nothing else like it, knowing that you were headed on toward it, but for one long, quiet, good moment you were shut up in a car with your climbing partner, taking it in before you had to face it down. The feel of her close beside him was intense and reassuring. It was dark in the car and she radiated Tammaness like an open potbelly stove put out heat. They'd been into the park before. They'd found Dan's shoes in a dumpster there. But this was the first time that they were headed into the park to climb a route with a rope and a rack.

"Do you want to hear something fucked up?"

"What?"

"It's going bad. Alexandra's bioprosthetic valve, I mean. And we don't have the money to do the surgery."

"But if she needs the surgery, they will do it, money or no."

"The thing is, she's decided not to."

"What?"

"Yeah."

"Dan, that's awful!"

"What she says is, it's too painful, it's too scary."

"Well, fuck, dude!"

They pulled into the Intersection Rock parking lot and she cut the engine and jerked the parking brake tight with a squelch. Dan was leaning over the dash, looking at the buttress in the crepuscular light. The steep western front slashed with left-leaning cracks running to the top of the dome, the low, overhung places worked to honeycombs. They both sat in the car, the engine ticking as it cooled.

"All I can say is," Tamma said, "she's making a mistake. But very well, she's making a mistake. All this is, is the thing we've always known: We have nothing and nobody except each other. But that, we have in spades. Now, let's go climb rocks."

Tamma kicked the door open and got out. All about them, hulks cut against the horizon, and beyond, the shoulders of still more rock. Storied rocks, rocks to which Tamma could put names. John Long had been here. Lynn Hill, John Bachar, Tobin Sorenson, Dean Fidelman, Yabo, all those and more.

They walked along the side of Intersection Rock. It was a hundred-and-fifty-foot granite dome mired in sand and dust, its flanks water-stained desert granite, pleated with cracks that ran from the foot of the dome, up through terraces, and tapered closed short of the crown. It looked awful lonely and cold with the dawn just touching the summit. Climbers had worn faint paths through the patina to the paler stone beneath. Dan and Tamma threaded through mormon tea and joshua trees, among brooms, rock goldenbush, grass tussocks quivering and pale, the breadcrumb gravel crunching underfoot. A coyote passed an open place in the sand before them and turned and looked and then trotted on, fox-small, with huge, upright ears. This was not very remote climbing, nor very glorious. These rocks were gumby central, a gumby being a species of beginner: a clueless, blundering, dangerous shitshow. But for Tamma, it was the wildest and most exciting moment of her life.

When they came to the route, Tamma hooked her thumbs in her waistband and nodded to it. Dan looked after. An ugly squeeze chimney hatcheted into the foot of the dome. Above, the chimney tapered from offwidth to hands, then gained a flake on the right. That flake was a curtain of stone that had started to break free along its left-hand edge, a cleavage weathered out by water, rippled, podding open and closed. There would be a place where you were climbing both cracks—on the left, the tail end of the chimney, now narrowed to a hand crack, and on the right, the beginning of the flake. Then you would commit to the flake, which ran up the side of the wall for something like fifty or sixty feet. The end of the flake curled around and formed a shallow ledge. That stance had a bolt. From there it was blank low-angle slab to the top, with a second bolt before the summit. Dan and Tamma had climbed cracks in boulders, but they had never climbed above the ground on a rope. They had never placed gear, though they had read about how to do it.

"Fuck, Tams, look at it."

"I am looking at it."

"*Look* at it."

"I *am*."

Tamma dredged through her pocket, laid a quarter out on her palm. She held the quarter up, turned it, capped it onto her fist, lofted it into the air and brought it down, covered, atop her forearm. She looked at Dan.

"Hell," Dan said.

"Are you *scurred*?"

"I ain't scurred!"

"Call it!"

"Tails!"

Tamma uncapped the coin. "Heads," she said. "My lead."

They walked to the base of the dome. Dan pitched the bag to the sand and they stood in the gray directionless dawn light, both of them shifting foot to foot, exhaling into their cupped hands. They had the shared joy of taking part, for the very first time, in the rituals that defined their vocation.

Tamma hunkered down and gaped open the bag. She found the old nylon harness, stepped into it, pulled it up over her hips to her waist. The nylon had a smell, chemical and musty and wet. It felt greasy to the touch. She slung the rack of chocks onto her shoulder and sorted through it. The steel was so cold, she had to stop to warm her hands. She riffled through her gear to see if she had everything: hexes, nuts, slings, ATC, personal anchor.

She picked up the top of the rope stack and tied a figure eight a yard back from the end, passed the end up through her harness hardpoints, and retraced the knot. Then she knelt, pulled on her shoes, laced them tight.

"On belay?"

"Belay is on."

"Climbing."

"Climb on, Tams."

Tamma boosted herself up into the chimney. The walls were chalk-stained and the chalk had formed a slick, limelike concretion. In places the holds were greasy with shoe rubber and rat piss. She put her back to the wall, braced her hands, and walked her feet up beneath her, one foot on the wall before her, the other heeled behind. This was chimney climbing. There was a pattern to the work—walk her feet up, then hitch her hips up, then her feet again.

The tips of her shoes were blown out and she could see the pink-painted nails of her right foot. As she climbed, the chimney narrowed. On the inhale, her ribs pressed against the walls. She found a heel in a wind-hollowed pocket and rested, her own ragged outbreaths pluming against the stone and coming back to her. She felt like she was in the jaws of a vise. The cold was getting into her hands, her fingers blanched of blood, the rock painful to the touch. The inside of the chimney was water-smooth but the outside was coarse, like when sticky dough adheres to an unfloured rolling pin and a tacky grain rises off the surface. It was awful close, claustrophobic work, squeezed between the two walls, with the cold seeping into her guts.

Her right side in, the steel hexes dragging, her harness and jeans raking against the stone, she thrutched and humped her way up the chimney to a diagonal gash that broke away on the left. There she stopped and groped among the carabiners on her shoulder sling for her #10 hexentric. It was the size of her fist, an irregular hexagon slung on yellow-and-red cord. She slotted it into the crack, and then reached down, past her hip, for the rope, and dropped the lead rope through the carabiner's gate. Her first piece of gear.

She latched a patina crimp on the left-hand wall and dragged herself up. To her right, there was a column like the wax drippings that build up along the flank of a candle. Tamma bridged her foot out to it and stemmed her way up past the difficult offwidth sections.

Above, the crack narrowed to good hand jams. It was a method familiar to all trad climbers, and strange to everyone else. She slid her relaxed hand deep into the crack and then cupped it closed, pressing her finger pads and the base of the palm against one side of the crack, and the back of her hand against the other. Tamma had seen chuckwallas—the huge, basking desert lizards—crawl into cracks and then inflate their guts, wedging themselves so tight that they couldn't be pulled out. And the hand jam was very much like that—sliding your relaxed hand deep into the crack, and then expanding it, locking it in place. That way, she could hang off it.

Above her and to the right, lay the flake, an overlap of granite, its wavering left-facing edge worn white from the traffic of other climbers. It started only wide enough for fingers and thin hands. She reached out for it and caught it and climbed using both cracks—the tapering hand crack on the left, the flake on the right. She placed a #8 stopper, slotting it in where the crack podded open and dragging it down to where the crack bottlenecked. Tamma had read about this technique in the books *Climbing Anchors* by John Long and Bob Gaines and *Basic Rockcraft* by Royal Robbins.

With every move, the flake leaned away from the crack, and Tamma finally committed to the flake, climbing on tight, left-facing hand jams. With each move, she swam her arm up and sank her jam. Then there came a moment of suspended doubt, when she had to commit to it, and each time the jam held, she grimaced to herself, full of determined joy. She wasn't just some not-very-bright little girl. She was a not-very-bright little *climber* girl.

The crack shallowed and leaned right and began to taper closed and Tamma grunged and fought her way up to a pedestal stance at the crown of the flake, something like eighty feet above the ground. She had four pieces of gear below her. Here there was a horizontal gash in the wall and just above that was a single bolt.

She boosted up and clipped the bolt with a sling. Then she reached down, grasped the rope, paid it up, and clipped it to the sling's second carabiner. This was the first of two bolts on the route.

Above her lay the slab: a less-than-vertical desert of granite rucked into dunes and basins, without any crack or feature, no weakness in which to place gear, just friction stances, slopey handholds, and delicate climbing.

The foundation of route climbing is the rope team—two people holding each other's lives in their hands: the climber and the belayer. The belayer, Dan, stands below, in gravel and dust. He wears a climbing harness. Clipped to his belay loop is an air traffic controller. The

ATC is a belay tube, about the size of a shot glass. The rope threads down through the mouth of the ATC, wraps around the locking carabiner, and threads back out. The end running from the ATC to the climber is called the lead strand. The side running from the ATC into the belayer's hand and then to the rope stack is called the brake strand or belay strand. The angle of the brake strand controls the friction in the system. Hold the brake strand up, in line with the lead strand, and rope passes freely through the device as if it were a pulley. Bring the brake strand down to your hip, and the line tensions across the lip of the ATC and locks off.

So, Dan stood in the dust, paying up slack, feeding it up from the rope stack with his right hand and drawing it out of the ATC with his left. Tamma was out of sight, so he stood alone, shivering in the cold, somehow ready for his entire ballsack to crawl back up into his abdomen, and at the same time, to shit himself with fear, but he was also a little bored. Trad climbing was replete with such moments. You undertook the climb together, but for long stretches, you were out of sight of each other, alone, each on your own separate journey. You had to trust the other person. That was the pattern: Each climbed out into uncertainty and solitude and then, finally, was returned to the company of the other. The rope snaked away up the wall, clipped at twenty-foot intervals to her gear. He monitored her progress by how it paid out. Slow work or fast. And when it yarded up, that would be her clipping more gear. The rope was ancient and hairy, the sheath decaying. Climbing ropes are very strong. But nylon goods decay in time, and the common wisdom was that ropes survived five years of use or ten years on the shelf. This rope was from 1989, and on that day, it was older than either of them.

Tamma stood, lonely and high up on the side of Intersection Rock, underclinging a horizontal gash, looking up at the slab, trying to calm her breathing, trying to keep from panicking. Somewhere up there, out of view, there was a second bolt before the summit. The sun was slivered upon the distant horizon and the light touched the dome above her with a golden blush. She took a deep breath, reached back, dipped her hands into her chalk bag, and swatted them off on her pants. Then she started up onto the slab: holds, holds everywhere; everywhere, holds, all of them bad, like water for ancient mariners, or online dates for contemporary ladies. She worked left, tiptoeing up on slopers. The bolt drew farther and farther away below her; she climbed, aching with cold, her hands bloodless, sweat dripping off her nose and tangled in her eyelashes and slick upon the flaring rack of her ribs. When she looked down, she could see the rope slanting away from her harness to the bolt ten feet below her, and beyond that, down the flank of the dome and out of sight. With a hundred feet of rope out, and the bolt ten feet below, it would be a twenty-foot fall, plus slack, plus rope stretch. The rope could split at any hidden weakness along its length, but ropes are weakest at the bends of knots and where they pass over carabiners. Breathing hard, sucking air, she climbed high on friction stances, a hundred, a hundred and ten feet above the ground. The second bolt came on closer and closer. The final bolt on the route. She climbed toward it, reached back, unclipped a quickdraw from her harness.

As she hooked the carabiner through the bolt, she goosed the steel hanger and the hanger pivoted. It was loose.

Huh, she thought.

Curiously, she gripped the bolt and tested it and the whole thing came free from the stone; a hanger threaded with the long steel shank in its corroding steel cage. It wasn't supposed to do that. That bolt was supposed to be firmly seated in its bolthole. She stood toed onto friction, shaking all over.

The summit was close. But there remained a few moves of slab between her and the top. This bolt would not catch her. And that left only the first bolt, a long way below. She put her face to the wall, poised on outsloped granite edges, and nothing for it but to climb to the summit. She was deep in the runout now.

Five

There is a photo that shows the two of them as children. Tamma is standing next to a joshua tree. She is shirtless, with ratty, colorless underwear. Dan is beside her wearing a dish towel cape, holding a hammer across his chest, his chin up. The joshua tree is not impressive, the desert is washed out, and the sky is burned to dingy white. It was one of the earliest things Tamma could remember, that wash, and Tamma could remember early things; she could remember wearing diapers, she could remember breaking into a bottle of flintstones vitamins, and the delight of eating them all at once, one after another, sick, unable to stop herself, and her dad finding her and getting so angry that he picked her up and threw her against the wall. And she could remember another time, breaking out through the door of the trailer and running through the sand of the wash, the stinkbugs going up onto the points of their legs in alarm, the long whips of creosote swinging in the breeze, the coarse, heavy sand underfoot, the headlong feeling of walking at that time, the way the ground seemed to come up to meet you or swing down away from you, the sense of wonder Dan held for her, her friend, her buddy, and then the feeling of her mother coming up behind her, grabbing her by the heel and swinging her into the air, Tamma hanging inverted with her hair tangling to the ground. But nothing much seemed to touch her. Tamma did not remember being deterred by anything, really, until one particular day. Four years old, sitting on a rubber-slatted lawn chair out in the front yard, the sun bright upon the trailer, upon the sand, and upon the white aluminum of the chair frame, hot to the touch, as her dad split wood, repeatedly clipping the same log. Each time he clipped it, the log cartwheeled away, uncut. Each time, he walked unsteady to where it lay to pick it up. Tamma was laughing at how he walked and laughing at how he hung down to pick it up and laughing at how he set it up on the block, just laughing, meaning nothing by it, watching her da line up to cut the log and clipping it again, and her da saying shut up, which was a joke, and walking back to the chopping block, and clipping the log again. He picked up the log and extended it to her and said, "Don't you listen, girl," and Tamma was full of this safe, delighted, hilarious feeling. She can remember saying something but cannot remember what, just remembers her own high-pitched voice, her da unsteady, her da plucking up a piece of kindling and walking toward her huge-eyed, and she was laughing in the beach chair, sharing her grin with him, and he drew back with the shank of wood and swung forward. She could have leaned back from it. But the thought did not cross her mind. She just looked on, her dad putting the full length of his arm into the swing, Tamma smiling, her mouth open, her whole expression one of puzzled delight. Then came the sudden, sharp shock of darkness.

Sometime in fourth grade a teacher took Tamma aside and said to her, "Listen, Tamma, I want you to have friends, and if you keep acting like this, you won't. You are much too loud and much too talkative. I am telling you this to help you. Just, you know, try and be a little bit more normal. Don't talk so much. You pick up a lot of words from Dan. He can get away with that. You can't. Stick to the kinds of words other kids use."

Then, in tenth grade, the class was reading *Tess of the d'Urbervilles* and Tamma was unable to help herself but to talk; for all that she was a terrible student, she had opinions. She had not read the novel but from the discussion she got the gist and she had thoughts. Todd, in the back, whispered to his friend, "*Dyke*," and Tamma mantled up off the desk ahead of her and turned around in her seat, opening her mouth and speaking in that headlong rush, which she could not help about herself, "What was that, Todd? The class didn't, like, *hear* you, Todd?"

TODD: Midget freak—

TAMMA: Cast down your buckets from where you stand, Todd!

TODD: What?

TAMMA: Todd, my love! Set yourself free! No need for lurking in men's bathrooms, tapping your shoes, waiting upon a stranger's response from one stall over with bated, foreskin-smelling breath!

TODD: Huh

MS. JORDAN: Tamma!

TAMMA: *[Standing on the chair with one foot on the desktop, gesturing to the class, thinking, Why isn't she stopping me? Can't she see I can't help myself?]*

Todd—I understand. *I see you.* You are afraid! You are afraid that it will stay secret forever! You lie in bed at night, afraid that you will have to go on with this awful playacting all your life. That you will never get to run down Haight Street during Pride wearing rainbow suspenders and rainbow banana hammock while carrying a streaming rainbow flag—!

And I agree, Todd. How fine you would look!

But worry not! THE TRUTH WILL OUT. And its outing will not be so painful as you think. You thirst for dick! You *thiiiiiiiirrrrrrrrrrrsssssssst* for it, Todd.

I *know* it. Sarah Jo knows it. Connor knows it.

[Gesturing to Sarah Jo, who, singled out this way, draws back, stunned, in her desk, shaking her head, wide-eyed, like, Oh my god leave me out of this, and to the rest of the class, this stunned, singled-out denial is a confirmation. Then Tamma flings her hand to Connor, his expression so surprised that it appears that Tamma has hit upon the truth of his thoughts through witchy, lesbianish powers.]

TAMMA: *[Continuing, in terror, because Todd is going to kill her. Her fellows look on with awe. Doesn't this girl know that Todd is going to kill her? She does. She very much does, but she cannot be some other, more careful girl. She cannot be quiet. She cannot sit down. She cannot be sensible. All her life she has been thus: harnessed to a giddy and unstoppable enthusiasm she cannot curb.]*

I, a fellow of your LGBTQ tribe, can see it, *and I understand.*

[Tamma cannot see it. Nor is this appropriate. But by god she is having fun.]

Give up the masquerade, Todd! *We all know.* You fool no one but yourself! And Aaron—you fooled Aaron.

[Flinging her hand out to Aaron, who indeed gives the class a vacantly uncomprehending expression.]

Alas, poor Todd: I don't hate you for being cruel to me! You want dick so powerfully you feel the need in your puckering and willing SOUL! And that's okay. Just say it out loud. Sing it from the rooftops. The hills are alive with the sound of your homosexuality! With the song of thyself! You could contain multitudes, Todd, if only you would let them inside!

[Tamma has never in her life seen such a look of horror on someone's face.]

TODD: [*desperately*] No—! That's not—

TAMMA: Shhhhhhhhhhhhh. We all know.

TODD: I am going to—

TAMMA: Hush now, honey bear.

Then, later, Tamma, flushed with victory, walking down the hall, looked at Dan ahead of her, there by the lockers, beaming at him, and he looked at something close beside her, and somebody said, "Hey, *freak*!" and she could have moved, but she did not move, she just stood there, gaping, useless, smiling, and watched it come.

Todd hit her and she went back into the lockers and then down, and Todd's friend Aaron kicked her in the cheek and her head jarred back and the world grayed out and she thought, Please god, just not in the jaw.

Everyone in the hall retreated in a widening circle. A crowd of kids all standing back. There she was, the laughing, hotheaded, unlovable girl, sitting in the dust, waiting with that stupidly, hateably hopeful expression on her face.

Todd got down and said, "Thirst for this, bitch," and Tamma looked back at him, mustering a blood-tasting fishhook sneer, trying to stare her reply back down into his very soul: *That's not even a good line.*

Todd had her pinned to the locker with one hand and his other arm cocked back and this one was going to be the end of her jaw, maybe the end of her entire face, and then his expression transformed to one of gathering surprise and he was sucked backward. He and Tamma looked at one another, united in their mutual, uncomprehending astonishment. Todd simply raptured up into the air like god decided Tamma Jonesy Callahan had finally had enough and was vacuuming Todd up off the floor with his divine shop-vac. Then Todd swung to the side and Dan, holding him by collar and belt, battering-rammed him into the lockers, and all the locks jumped on their hasps and the doors set in their frames, and Dan should've done it again, but he was so shocked at the noise that he dropped Todd to the floor and stood, looking around, and everyone in that hallway knew that Dan was about to take the beating of a lifetime. Except for Tamma, who lay against the lockers and just beamed unicorns and rainbows and kittens at him. When you're hurt, when you've been knocked down, then everyone in the world backs away from you and you find out just how alone a person can be. And if there's just one buddy that's coming after you, then you're lucky. And Tamma had that, had this guy who was wading into the fray after her.

There is a term in climbing: exposure. It's a little slippery, a feeling or idea more than a definitive thing, and it's one of those words that some people use differently than others. But what it gets at is the vertiginous feeling of depth that can overcome a climber on the wall. For Dan and Tamma, *exposure* was a term independent of safety, not a measure of risk, but of their own perceived smallness, of what it felt like to be cast out upon a prospect of stone, amazed, as if for the first time, by the world's grandeur, its inhuman vastness and towering depth.

CRUX

There are places where exposure can be epic—it is said that climbers on El Cap can step upon some crystal edge and see, beyond their shoe rubber, fir trees thousands of feet below. In the park, there are no such grand walls. These are short, sandbagged little routes on ancient and inglorious little rocks. But Tamma and Dan had no experience of big walls, and for them, when they said *exposure*, they meant something like this: standing on the side of some rock, your belayer out of sight, the slab stretching in all directions, your life fragile and precarious.

Think about this moment. From out the starry black, the world welling up pale and gray like water backing up from the drain—the desert askew, the horizon line aslant, the trailer looming up above her, and joshua trees queerly tilted. Tamma facedown in the sand. Her father has just hit with a shank of kindling. And something is wrong. Her mouth is seized open. The muscles of her face are cramping. Her jaw will not close. There is sand in her mouth, sand on her tongue. She props herself up off the dirt. She hears footsteps and she thinks with relief, He's coming to pick me up. She is bloody, gape-mouthed, wide-eyed. Propped on one hand, reaching with the other to feel her face, she can hear him walking, but the moment of his arrival is delayed, the moment of him scooping her up stalls, and its stalling takes on an uncanny feeling first of wrongness, and then of horror.

She turns to look, expecting to see him almost upon her, and instead he is walking away from her, backstepping, dropping the kindling: backstep and backstep away. And she sees that look and understands. He is never going to scoop her up off the ground. No one is coming for her. She will forever be that same dumb, smiling, hopeful little girl, but with a forever difference: That childhood feeling of safety, that you were loved, that everything was going to be okay, that there would be someone to catch you if you fell—that feeling was gone. She inhabits the widening, sickening, gyring province of her own solitude and vulnerability. That too is exposure.

And now, however many years later, she stood in the cold dawn, a hundred and something feet off the ground, holding the useless bolt in her hand, her brain coming apart at the seams, the ground receding, the sky lifting away above her, so that she hung poised between two retreating horizons, readying herself for the next move, and she held no childish illusions about what could come next.

She slotted the bolt back into its hole like slotting a sword into a scabbard. The bolt was not going to catch her. The last bolt was maybe twelve or fifteen feet below. You had to think it would be a thirty-foot fall. Her every exhalation was sucked away in the wind. She put her helmet to the stone. Whispering her mantras. Cuffing snot off her nose and smiling when she did it. Things, she thought, have gotten out of hand.

From the second, useless bolt, she stepped up and right to a clamshell bulge. The granite crunched underfoot. Slowly she committed to this right foothold, transferring all her weight, and matching her feet side by side. She looked down and saw her shoes, wallowing around on her feet with sweat, her toes peeking out through the leather.

It felt like a strange and awful perfidy, standing there. Her father saw her and hated what he saw. You are nothing. Her mother too. Her peers at school. Everyone. They wanted her to sit down and shut up. She was a trailer-trash leftover, a dumb burnout with no hope and no prospects. It was blasphemy, this fundamental, outrageous belief in her own competence. It was hearing all those things that the whole world said about you, and never believing them.

With her feet matched on the clamshell hold, Tamma had to step up and right to a cluster of crystals at thigh height. It was like a scab on the rock, a place where crusty granite offered greater friction. She stood, and looked at the move for a long time, feeling the distance to the bolt below her.

The granite was sand-colored, with streaks of mocha and henna and graham-cracker gold. Her heel was jittering with nerves. She had begun to breathe up a bitter, coppery-tasting mucus. She lifted her trembling shoe from her matched stance and stepped right to the scaly patch of granite. She began to transfer her weight to it. She had her palms flat on the wall for balance. Her jaw was cold, her mouth was dry, her guts were trying to galumph their way out her throat, and the granite was taking on a queasy, disassociated look, becoming less and less like stone, more and more like the naked golden flesh of the world.

Above her, there was a crescent-moon pocket, the scar where a flake of granite has broken away. It made an incut micro-crimp. Once Tamma committed right, she would be able to reach up and latch that crimp and the climb would be done. It was very close now.

Slowly, slowly she stood up off the right foot on its scab of granite. See the girl—see her in her jeans and ratty sweatshirt, baring her teeth, her crooked nose bright red at the tip, her lips chapped, acne in the crease of her chin, big ears sticking out of her tangled hair, see her straightening up off the right leg, and the half-moon crimp is above her, and she is reaching, reaching. She thinks: *I can do this—I can really do this*—and witness: The bottom drops out of her world.

Her right foot greased off the wall. Her entire weight came onto her left hand, which was cupped in a shallow, sandy dish, and there was no holding it. She fell, still reaching for the half-moon crimp. Her hair rose up around her. Her gear went weightless on her harness. A plume of standing rope reeled up beside her. It did not feel like falling so much as it felt like the world about her was sucked up into the sky. Her right foot was still toed onto a hold that was no longer there.

For a moment she went skating down the slab, patting at the rock as it went by. The second bolt sprang backward out of the rock and came sailing toward her, spiraling helically around the rope. Then she was off the edge of the slab and flung out into the open. She had a dizzying view of the pale sky, and then she heard the dreadful slurping noise of her knot cinching tight and she was plucked out of the air and whipped into the wall backward and upside down. Her helmet crunched and her breath left her. She rebounded back into the air, grabbed her rope, flipped herself over, and came to rest upright, with her feet braced on the wall. Dan was thirty feet below her, lifted just off the ground and sitting in his harness.

She reached up and felt about her head. The back of the helmet was crushed in. She unbuckled the chinstrap and pitched it to the ground. Her hands were bloody and raw. The bolt that she ripped off the slab was hanging off the rope. She unclipped it from the rope, clipped it to her harness.

"Tamma!" Dan said.

"Yeeeeeeeeeehaw!" she said, looking down past her hip at him.

"You're okay?" he said.

"I'm going to keep climbing!"

"Really?"

"Yar!"

She climbed it all again, reached the bolthole beneath the summit, unclipped the bolt from her harness, and fitted it back down into the hole. It was illegal to take antiques out of the park. She pulled the next moves effortlessly and boosted herself over the edge and walked across the top of Intersection Rock among potholes filled with water and brine shrimp. It was windy there at the summit and she walked hunched over toward the chain anchors, and when she reached them, she sat on the rock and cried. Crying, she built the anchor, and called, "Off belay!"

Dan climbed the route on top rope, coming up slowly, and she took in the scaly rope inch by inch, watching it slide up over the edge and come across the top to where she sat at the anchors. A white patch in the rope appeared at the far edge of the dome. Tamma watched it, drawing in slack. It paid up to just beside her.

The spiraling strands of the sheath were gashed open, exposing the long white bundled strands of the core. The rope was coreshot.

She almost died, is what she was looking at. She almost went all the way to the ground. Tamma drew the coreshot through her ATC, careful not to tear the sheath any further, and laid it down on the rope stack and kept pulling in rope until Dan came up over the side of the dome, wide-eyed. He walked among the brine shrimp tanks to her. They hunkered down together against the wind.

"That was close," he said.

Tamma was digging in the center pocket of her hoodie; she seemed to be about some complex operation deep within.

"What are you doing?"

"Fuck."

"What?"

"I fucked it."

"Fucked what?"

And with this, she pulled free, in one hand, a lighter, and, in the other, a crushed and misbegotten cupcake with a single candle stuck into it. She started striking the lighter but the wind was blustering, so Dan sheltered it, the candle flared briefly, and he leaned in and blew it out.

"Happy birthday!"

"How long was that in your pocket?"

"Too long."

"That's love."

"What'd you wish for?"

"I think you know."

"Yeah, I think so too. Dan, take a look at where we are."

"We're on the top of Intersection Rock."

"We're *on the top of Intersection Rock*," she said. "We've read about it. We've heard stories. We've looked at it from the ground. We've dreamed about it. It's a fucking famous piece of stone. And now, we're here."

"Holy shit you're right," he said, standing up into the wind and looking around.

"All those things are gonna come true," Tamma said again. "You and me, we're gonna do some epic shit together."

They sat on the edge, shoulder to shoulder, eating the cupcake with dirty fingers, watching cars go by on the road below.

Six

After that, Dan did not see Tamma for more than a week. She was watching Sam and Hunter so her sister could be with River in the NICU. The house was cold and silent. The door to the master bedroom closed. He'd open the fridge and stand framed in golden light, holding his boots by the laces. He'd sit at his desk, sharpening a pencil into an ashtray, stooped over the personal statement, the drafts neatly labeled in the upper right-hand corner: #204, #205.

Lawrence would come home and eat at the kitchen table, sighing to himself, the ice in his glass clattering. Then he'd lie on the couch, reading a Dean Koontz novel, turning pages with a pulpy rasp. Dan would go out and his old man would say, "Well, Danny, how was your day?"

"Good," Dan would say, seating himself on the arm of the couch. "You?"

Lawrence would shake his head. "I tell you what, Danny, knocking together these concrete molds—it's a young man's game." Then he'd say, "Well, I better let you get back to your homework."

Dan kept the overhead light off and worked by the desk lamp. He was so lonely he could've died. He'd text Tamma.

> Colorado Crack looks good
> It takes nuts the whole way
> And it's in Conan's Corridor
> Where we've never been

Lawrence would groan as he got up from the couch and Dan could hear his knees popping as he made his way to the fridge to pour himself another glass of water. Without Tamma, there was nothing that staved off his thinking and the more he thought, the worse it got. Alexandra's there, he thought, locked in that bedroom, propped up against the headboard.

Wake before his alarm. Pull on shorts and leap for the black pipe bar set into the rafter. Single arm pull-ups, sets of three. One-arm push-ups, sets of twenty. Pistol squats, sets of eight. Open his computer and find texts from Tamma.

> i was thinking
> white lightning, mikes books, sail away
> double cross, dogleg

Her texts were timestamped 2:28 a.m. He wrote:

> people die on double cross
> Colorado Crack is harder
> But it's safe

> nah dude no bc
> we can keep the lead climber

> off the coreshot
> but the follower has to climb
> on bad rope
> so we have to think old school
> the leader must not fall
> but really
> no one can fall

He sat there, smiling to see the texts from her come in.

> Tamma!
> you're right
> instead of falling
> we will have to
> hold on

> climbing is so easy
> when you think about it
> bruh im gonna try and get
> 20 minutes of sleep

> Sweet dreams
> Slutcake

Toast in the toaster, coffee from the carafe in the fridge, homework at his desk. Then out the front door thinking, Please let her be there: the sun coming up colorless and gray, the yuccas dusty, the clouds thin and far away, and Tamma not there.

He let himself back into the room carrying a plate of his old man's green chile enchiladas and read from the textbook, stopping sometimes to take a bite off his plate, turning around in his chair, looking about the room. Lawrence came home. Dan went out and sat on the arm of the couch. His old man set his book open and facedown. "Well, Danny," he said. "I sorta missed your birthday, there."

"That's all right, Dad."

They both raked about for anything to say. Lawrence picked back up his book. "Well, Danny," he said. "I better let you go."

Dan went back into his room and keyed open the browser and navigated to a wikipedia page. The page was rambling and footnoted to dead links or else to print articles. He wasn't the only person wondering. Born October 19, 1973, Alexandra Josephine Lavinia Tingey. Child of Orson Tingey and Sophia Tanner Tingey. She had impressed her language arts teacher by extemporizing sonnets. Quit high school her senior year. Married Lawrence Redburn at city hall. Wrote her nine-hundred-page novel over the course of eight months, unhoused in the southern Mojave desert. Her only reader another waitress at the diner where she worked. The novel arrived at her agent's office with centipedes crushed between the pages. Her agent had flown to California to meet her. Alexandra had come in late, wearing cutoff jeans and cowboy boots, and he had thought he was being pranked. *Ephedra* was published in September of '92. Alexandra almost nineteen. Dan would be born a year later, in December of '93.

He sat there, the light of the screen thrown back on him. She must've believed. He drummed his fingers on the desktop.

The next day, Dan waited in a kind of windowless dropceilinged closet with the guidance counselor. The counselor was a big guy. He lay very deep back in his ergonomic chair, spanning it side to side. He had a trick of spinning a pen around his thumb. There was something in him a little kingly. He seemed to listen with a ferocious attention, his forehead canted forward and his chin pulled back into his neck and his eyes very bright. He gave off the air of holding back his judgment. He read Dan's college application from beginning to end and he picked up the personal statement and read that too, the first page, and then turning it over for the second. He heaved a sigh and raised his eyebrows and looked at Dan, sitting his chair as if melted into it. He seemed reluctant to say it but spoke at last. "It's brilliant." He tossed it to the desktop. Shook his head. "It's the best application I've ever read."

"Uh-huh."

"I have just one observation, which is that your personal statement cannot, and I emphasize this: *cannot* be titled 'Fingerbang Princess.' In fact it would be good if we could change the name of the climb altogether to something more politically correct."

"Why?"

"Well, it's not polite conversation, Dan."

"Fingerbanging is safe sex," Dan said. "I read that in the early eighteenth century, petting was a much more common and accepted practice—that later, the cultural hegemony of penile-vaginal intercourse and an attendant emphasis on avoiding sex until marriage arose as a way to structure intimacy so as to preserve the generational wealth of the elites, creating a hierarchy of relationships, a framework in which romantic love was valorized, and other relationships—like friendships, or homosocial relations, which may or may not have had a sexual element—were devalued, framed as inconsequential, even suspect or profane; maybe fingerbanging exists outside that regimented order, encouraging safe, ephemeral, queer, free, nonstandard, and lateral romantic encounters; maybe it is anti-patriarchal and anti-capitalist, which is why it's offensive."

The counselor held his brow with his hand. His stooping, exhausted demeanor suggested that he admired Dan for his academic successes, but also that he—the counselor—was not the enemy, and that Dan could either work with him here or tiresomely stand in the way of his own success.

"I don't think that's coming through, Dan," he said. "The utopian subtext is pretty subtle, I'd say."

"Okay, we can change it. What would you like to change it to?"

"Something avant-garde, but inoffensive. Something political, but not problematic. Something that suggests that you're an ally."

"That's quite a needle to thread."

"What about Girl Power?"

"It feels condescending, considering that we're literally censoring the courageous and pioneering adult woman who named the route."

"Male Feminist?"

"Why would Jane Sasaki name *her own route* Male Feminist? Besides, climbers like Jane often *weren't* feminists—they clashed with feminists during the culture wars because feminism was striving to be part of the establishment and these were anti-establishment punks. Dave Bingham says that after Jay Goodwin put up routes like Adolescent Homo on the Decadent Wall in City of Rocks and gave other, already climbed lines on the wall names like Preteen Sex and Dimples and Tits, the National Organization for Women lobbied his university to deny him a degree; in response, Aimee Barnes put up a route called Feminist Activists That Can't Understand Normal Thought. Calling Jane's route Male Feminist is off base. I think there is something weird about effacing the work of a pioneering first ascensionist by renaming her route Male Feminist so that some white guy should have a better chance of getting into college. Am I wrong?"

"Mission Accomplished. That's political, but subtle."

"What's the deal—fingerbanging is verboten but American imperialism is funny? I believe we need to think more seriously about how language constructs political truth and maybe question what people tell us is profane."

"But it's such an inconvenient name, Dan! I get what you're saying, that there is actually some sort of punk-rock, hippie-dippie subversive politics involved here that I do not fully understand, and there is some free-love climber-babe folk hero you think highly of, but *come on*, all that is sure to offend. This is your future we're talking about here. And listen to yourself: This is why you need to go to college—you are brilliant, passionate, voluble, eloquent. I'm guessing that this is a side of yourself you don't get to indulge among your peers."

"Look. We can call it Better Bold Than Pretty or something, I guess. But I strongly feel that this is an injustice done in subservience to a propriety which exists to silence the margins for the despicable comfort of the privileged center, thereby preserving the cultural capital of the hegemonic elite."

"Great! That's excellent! I'm glad we've got here, I'm glad you're on board! That's so good! Just amazing. And otherwise: It's perfect. This is your life, you have to take this seriously."

"These schools cost eighty thousand dollars a year. I think that's repugnant. You think fingerbanging is repugnant. We're at opposite ends, here, about what seriousness entails."

"Huh, well, that's very interesting. Anyway, Dan, I think this is totally brilliant. There is one other thing I'd like to change—I think we should add in that you have a bouldering pad, so the climbing isn't dangerous, just athletic."

"Fine."

"Good! Everybody understands excellence in sports. But this thing of risking your life is a bit much. Otherwise, it's the best essay I've ever read. I just want to make sure we're clear, that it's morally wrong, to take these risks, and that we need to present a certain image, the image of a responsible, committed young man with leadership skills, if you're going to get into these schools."

"Yeah, okay."

The counselor sat, cueing up his pen in his hand and giving it a flick so that it pirouetted around his thumb and came back to rest on his fingertips. These applications were due after Dan got back from winter break.

Seven

Dan walked out of the last class of fall semester and found Tamma leaning against his locker, green at the gills. River had come home five days before and Sierra had gone back to work. It was less than a year since Samantha had been born, so Sierra couldn't again take FMLA leave. She'd been offered unpaid leave but couldn't afford to take it. She could not place River, who was one month old and just out of the ICU, in daycare, because she had been warned by her doctor not to, and even if she wanted to, the daycare wouldn't take him, and even if they would take him, there was no daycare that could cover her twelve-hour shift, and even if there was, she couldn't afford it at nearly half her take-home pay. So Tamma had been five nights with the kids, nights she spent singing to River and bouncing him and holding him to her breast. Nights she had spent walking back and forth on the sticky linoleum of the kitchen, shushing and humming. Nights she spent heating up pop-tarts in the toaster oven and cooing to the baby and breaking the pastries apart on the counter and eating them crumb by exhausted crumb, nights when it was so dark beyond the windows that the outside world seemed not to exist, seemed to be emptied of people and of hope, nights that the baby, nestled in her arms, had for her a profound, urgent reality beside which all else paled, nights that seemed to make of all her hopes so much nonsense and so much vanity, because she needed no very great successes for this little guy, she didn't need him to be smart, or unblemished, or handsome, or famous. She didn't need to him to stand on podiums, she just wanted him to be alive, and so what did it mean, to face down gut-coiling runouts in pursuit of a dream? And yet—walking back and forth in that dark kitchen—Tamma wanted that he should strive at things too, that he too should have dreams, that he should have the privilege of being himself. It was just that she didn't care if he succeeded, because success touched not at all on the love she bore for this tiny, slumbering, drooling, farting little life.

"Dude," Tamma said. "You want to go into the park?"

It was Friday, December 16, and winter break lay before them, seventeen days during which they had a sketchy rope, a rack, the shirts on their backs, and, as long as Alexandra didn't notice, free use of a car. This thing of the car, it was still an astonishment to Dan. They had risked their lives, climbing at the Princess Boulder, when they could've been going into the park and climbing safe, classic lowballs this whole time, all because of what they had supposed to be an ironclad proscription on where they could drive. Were there other things like that—? Rules by which they abided, but which were not really rules at all?

Dan drove, Tamma asleep in the passenger seat, her chucks up on the dash. They parked at the Hemingway lot and Dan shouldered the bag and the rope and they walked out together.

"Dan, buddy," Tamma said. "Help me on this."

"Okay."

"Let's say you take someone climbing and they pull the roof on the Princess. They come to the highstep crux. But they can't bring themselves to make that dicey highstep to the domino. They don't have the guts, dude, just simply . . . don't have it."

"Uh-huh."

"Is it morally wrong of them not to try?"

"They *can't* try; they're too scared."

"But let's say they have kids at home. And let's say they're a V8 gym climber, so if they attempt the highstep, they'll live. Only instead, they just stand there saying 'I can't do it! I can't do it!' until a charley horse slaps them off the wall and they crater. You're holding them in your arms, they're blowing bubbles out of lungblood, and with their last gasp they're all, like, 'I just *couldn't* do it.' Is that wrong of them?"

"Nobody can make scary moves above the deck without experience, Tams. Courage is more like a skill than a virtue. It's something you have to practice."

"Well, would you say it's *impossible*? You could still choose to try the move. I did. You did. Jane Sasaki did."

"That highstep is hard to face, even for a seasoned climber. It's not something you can expect of a person."

"Okay. So. Let's say you drop a baby."

"Fuck, Tams!"

"I know, I know dude. Heart-wrenching. But this is my life. You go to the hospital and there the baby has his little head all stitched up because they had to take away part of the skull to suck out the hematoma. He's in a little plastic box, with a ventilator, and his mom is like, 'Take his hand,' but you can't take his hand. You can't face it. You just stand there going, 'I can't, I can't, I just can't.'"

"Jesus Christ, Tamma!"

"Is that like, *morally* wrong, dude?"

"Fuck, dude!"

"Is it wrong, yes or no."

"I'm not sure! If courage is a skill, like playing the piano, or pulling a dicey highstep, then sometimes you don't have it, no matter how high the stakes. So maybe, it's sad, but it's sad for Brad too, and that situation is hell, but nobody is the bad guy."

"On the other hand," Tamma said, the path wending through creosote and beavertail. "Courage is *not* like a dicey highstep; you get to practice courage every day of your life. Just doing the dishes when you're tired. Making the beds and folding laundry when you've got nothing left. These are situations where you think, I just can't, but then you do, anyway. Speaking gently to a baby when you've been awake for thirty-six hours and you're dying. Being nice to your sister when she's a bitch. All of those are difficult acts of kindness and taking care, they're on some continuum with taking a dying child's hand, when you don't want to face what's happened. Sure, maybe Brad didn't have the guts. Sure, maybe Alexandra *couldn't* face her typewriter. My dad *couldn't* hold his temper. But when a comp climber arrives on the mat and can't solve the problem, we don't say, 'Oh, well, they couldn't do it.' We say, 'They didn't train hard enough.' So do you say of that person, who arrives at the darkest hour of their life without the courage to face it down, 'Oh well, we could never expect more of a person,' or do you say that they had a thousand chances, it is not something that just happened to them. Day in and day out, they have been ungenerous assholes, they have not asked enough of themselves, they have not held their tempers against the hundred thousand small provocations any toddler will give you over the course of an afternoon, they had six thousand days to be more than they are, and they let each day pass them by, snapping at their children, not doing the dishes, not making the beds, not folding the laundry, not being kind or patient with those around them, never asking more from themselves than the bare minimum; a thousand small acts of cowardice have culminated, finally, in a life-ruining act of cowardice, for which we can hold them responsible, and so do we say, 'Fuck them, fuck the weak?' Like, the weak have allowed themselves to be weak."

"That's it," Dan said teasingly. "We've solved moral philosophy, Tams: 'Fuck the weak.' There are two sorts of people in life: The *cans* and the *cannots*, and the world belongs to those who can."

"But maybe it does, Dan: Maybe the world belongs to those with courage and purpose."

"I think you're a savagely hard person, Tams. And I admire it very much. But I am not that way."

They'd climb all day and then Dan would drop Tamma off just in time for Sierra to get out the door for night shift and there was always a frenzied debrief with Tamma holding River cradled to her breast with one arm and Samantha on her hip with the other arm while Sierra, still wearing her makeup from the night before, pulled on her compression stockings; toed into her clogs; shoveled through her bag for her ID, stethoscope, water bottle, and tums; raked her hair into a ponytail, patted her wrists for hair ties, and punched yellow caffeine pills out of their foil backing; all while telling Tamma, "Samantha still hasn't pooped; she's had two pears today, so I don't know what to do, maybe prune puree with breakfast?" And Tamma would say, "Where's Kendra?" and Sierra would say, "That's cute, Tams. Where's Kendra?

That's hilarious. Kendra is nowhere. Is where Kendra is. Kendra is home watching TV and jerking off her boyfriend. Or maybe Kendra is at work, I don't know. I dare you to call her and ask though, because you would not believe the things she would say to a person who might suggest that she could help more. Or maybe you would. I don't know. The point is that if Kendra wanted to be here, she'd be here; so, that's where Kendra is. Listen, Tams. River's diaper rash is looking better but he still has three open sores and he's had six hunter-green diapers today, almost black, pretty sure it's the iron supplement that makes them that color, but it could be occult blood, so we need to keep an eye on that, be careful, you know, not to miss a poop, and make sure to use plenty of butt paste, and keep an eye out for mucus or any change in color," and then she was out the door and the kids were all Tamma's.

After dropping Tamma off, Dan drove home. He unlaced his boots, carried them into the house, and found Alexandra at the counter. Unshouldered the bag and rope coil. "Dinner?" he said, and crossed to the fridge, opened it, stood looking inside. "Tacos all right?" He cast a glance over his shoulder, lit a burner, shook out the match, started pinto beans, grated cheese, cut avocado, poured salsa, fried tortillas in a skillet, and then lidded it to melt the cheese. Dished up two plates and set one in front of her and stood at the island opposite.

"How was your day?" he asked.

"I'm not going to talk about this with you."

"All right."

There were days like this, when she seemed full of rage, when she seemed to hate the world, to hate him for his very presence in the house. He knew that there was more coming; he could feel it from her.

After a while she set down the fork. "Look, when I was your age, I wanted to leave."

"I can understand that."

"No. You have no capacity to imagine it. You are a spoiled, reckless, selfish child who takes everything for granted. You have been handed everything. You do not understand what it means to want anything." She held her temple with one hand, closed her eyes, and sat that way with her forehead flexing delicately.

"When I was your age," she said, "I wrote a *New York Times* bestselling novel while working full time as a waitress. Whereas you seem to think eking out a two-page personal statement is more than anybody ought to expect from you." She stopped to catch her breath. Her head in her hands. Her fingers splayed into her blond hair. Sucking air.

"Maybe you should rest."

"Rest? For what—for what reason—to see you grow up and piss away opportunities for which I would've given anything, literally *anything*?" When she could go on, she said, "No, I want you to know, Danny. I never wanted kids. I wanted to be a writer. Well, what your father thought was that a child might be good for me. Was he going to care for this child? I made two hundred and eighty thousand dollars the year before you were born, and your old man made sixteen thousand dollars, and there was no discussion that maybe he ought to be the one to stay home and take care of you. Your dad was off building strip malls and—and I was stuck here, raising a child I didn't want to raise, when all I wanted was to be writing."

She sucked air, propped on the counter, her neck slender, her hair curtaining in blond hanks that pooled on the countertop, her lips curling back from her teeth. Dan could see it, that she was a great artist, hard done by the world, and the keenness with which she felt it, and the hostility with which she now spoke, was apiece with her genius. And yet, Dan recoiled against himself. He was filled with an inward-turning rage, for feeling so convinced. His most profound experience of her was of her absence, her locked-away-ness, her depression, and so there was a nauseous dissonance in this idea, that her career had been squandered away raising him. And yet, he still believed, and hated himself for believing.

"Mom."

"No, I can talk."

"Are you sure?"

"And so there I was—with a screaming baby in a half-built house, my agent calling me and saying, 'Where is the new book, Alexandra?' I never pretended to be a person of inexhaustible resources, who could write a book under any circumstances. I wanted to be a writer and only a writer. I wanted to have the opportunity to give my art the room it deserved in my life. Well, I pulled that second book from out the depths of hell, carrying it page by page from out of depression and childcare and poverty, like Sisyphus, pushing my dream up the hill, a dream that would always roll back down, which everybody knew but me. After such a debut, every writer gets buried beneath the flood of newer, younger, sexier debuts, full of promise. And here you are—with opportunities for which I would have given anything. But none of that matters to you. All you do is waste your time with glue-huffing trash. They're crabs in a bucket, those people. Anyone who tries to crawl out gets pulled back down."

Dan just barely held on to the counter. He had the old familiar feeling, that he was standing invisibly behind a cardboard cutout of himself. The Dan that those around him were forever talking about was a person unrecognizable to him, because what Dan really was, was suffering and afraid, privately laboring through a depression about which he could not speak, if depression might even be the word for the blank disinterest he felt for the life to which he was supposed to aspire, and the profound interior emptiness and feelinglessness that only ever broke when he was out on the rocks. Dan was not the person she was describing; he was not the lucky kid, with opportunities for which she would given anything; no, he was her, and he was seeing in her now his own future, his own looming collapse.

"I'm sorry, Mom."

She had to stop and breathe again, leaning forward, forming some expression of grimacing hostility, her jaw clenching and unclenching.

"After a year of touring the book I had tried so hard to write, a book I and everyone else knew was a failure, after living through the slow collapse of all my dreams for thirteen months, I came back here, and I was at this bar with Kendra. And you know what she said to me?"

"What?"

"She said, '*I could've been a writer if I'd had the chance.*'"

Alexandra shook her head.

Dan sat watching her. Of course, he thought. Friendships are messy.

"My best friend in the world, and she didn't see what I'd done. *I could've been a writer if I'd had the chance.* I thought, She doesn't believe in me; I am alone; I have always been alone. Everything—my entire life—depended on writing the third book, and I could barely *breathe* let alone write. And, well, you know what happened next. I waited in that hospital room for her to come, with my chest stitched closed over my new pig-meat heart. And she never came. My best friend. The dearest person of my life. I understood something, then. Lying there in that hospital bed. I saw the world for the first time, clearly, and seeing it, I could not believe I'd wasted years of my life trying to make sense of it on the page, when the truth was that people are nothing to one another, and the world in which they live is finally meaningless and empty."

While Dan spoke with his mother, Tamma was putting the children to bed. She put Samantha to bed at seven thirty, sitting in a rocking chair in the nursery with Samantha and River in her lap, reading *Oh, The Places You'll Go!* And when they got to the part about the Hakken-Kraks, Sam would smile and make a kind of a monsterish howling noise like *rawr!* and then Tamma would put her down in the crib, and after her it was Hunter, and then she would be up for a while with River, who most often slept from nine until just after midnight, or maybe until one or two in the morning. Then Tamma would be up with him, walking him back and forth in the bedroom, holding his tiny, warm body close to hers, finding her way from one side of the room to the other, and if she could not get him back to sleep in the bassinet, she would cosleep in the bed with him, holding him close, and never sleeping deeply. He was at an elevated risk for SIDS, but poor sleep was a complication of his injury, and sometimes he just would not sleep in the bassinet, so they resorted to this, this dangerous, desperate half solution: Tamma holding him on the mattress, and never sleeping long. She would wake to feel the flaring rise of his chest in the dark, to feel his tiny hands made up into tiny fists, and how beautiful it was to let her eyes adjust to the chinks of moonlight coming in through the blinds and see him there with his head turned toward her, his little hands outflung, his potbelly rising and falling. Tamma would touch the top of his stocking cap with her chin and put her lips to him, feeling the crinkling bandages beneath the cotton, and take in the smell. He smelled like milk, like honey, and like the sticky yellow antiseptic that was painted on beneath the gauze. She'd think about those Hakken-Kraks, feeling this grand piano of nihilism and despair that always waited out there for her, suspended in the dark, ready to drop. River was coming up on two months and it did not seem like he was going to meet his milestones. They had been told, by the pediatrician, that he might start cooing, that he might begin to hold his head up during tummy time, that he might begin to smile, and look at their faces, and appear happy when he saw them, that he might track them as they walked across the room, that he might begin to look at toys and open his hands briefly. That grand piano hung out there, waiting. Tamma couldn't say that she'd never despair. All she could do was think, Not today. All her hope felt terribly insecure. And she could get to where she had this feeling of rage. I don't want to be strong. I don't want to have to try and find joy when it all feels so scary. And then she'd think: You can do this. You are a rad climber and people like you. You can show up every day and be an indomitable force for joy and hope and you can let everyone else fall apart without falling apart yourself. Sure, hope is the big, scary, dangerous thing. But does Shauna Coxsey give up when the clock is ticking down and she's hurt her knee and the slab doesn't look like it will go? No. Shauna Coxsey digs in. So does Akiyo. All those girls you admire, you admire them not because they did the easy things, but because they did the hard things.

Eight

She lay in bed with the baby beside her and waited for his deep blue eyes to blink open and when they did she dabbed the tears out with her shirt and whispered, "Good morning, Button," or "Squishy McSquishertons," or "Toots McFartypants," or "Mr. Littlest-Booty-in-the-Household," and she carried on with things, making bottles and getting Hunter ready for school, making breakfast—pancakes or toaster waffles or oatmeal or little cheese and spinach cornmeal muffins, and they ate all together with Hunter at the counter and Samantha in her high chair, Tamma toting River about in a wrap, animated, full of life, digging deep for her best, warmest, most enthusiastic self, and Dan would come in and pick up around the living room and do the dishes while Tamma brandished a spatula and told Hunter stories of brave deeds done high above gear, miming every finger jam and half-pad crimp, letting the pancakes fry. Then the door would swing open and in would come Sierra, tripping through the entryway off her twelve-hour shift, shucking off her scrub top, kicking off her clogs, unpeeling her sweaty compression stockings, staggering to the counter in a pit-stained undershirt. Tamma would pour her coffee from the carafe and Sierra would put her head down in her hands and say, "Go, it's okay, just go," and Tamma was out the door with Dan. She'd lay her seat back, put her dirty feet up on the dash, drop an ancient cowboy hat over her face, and sleep through the trip. Then, three minutes out, she'd wake and begin to change, taking shots of coffee out of the thermos, hooking her heels on the dash and bridging to pull on her jeans. She'd kick open the door and sprawl out onto the tarmac, still sliding her hands down inside the waist of her jeans to adjust the lay of her bagged-out, secondhand American flag hip-huggers while Dan shouldered the backpack, the rope draped over his shoulders.

During that holiday break, there were days when they put up fourteen pitches, running between routes. Hard, cold, sunlit, backbreaking, skin-destroying, mind-altering days, joyful days of clipping chains, setting nuts, and calling belay commands into the wind, days of danger and friendship; Tamma climbing Taxman with laybacky finger stacks up an offset corner like a buckling contraction joint in the sidewalk, turning to look back at him when she sent the crux and yelling, "SUCK MY DICK!"; Dan sketching up through Overseer, high above the ground in a blustering wind, calling out "Watch me!" and knowing for sure that she would; Tamma hip thrusting Dan to the ground and falling upon him in a cackling heap; Dan swimming beautifully up a hand crack, turning his hip into the wall to make plunging, muscular, sun-soaked reaches; and moments of stillness when one checked the other's knot. Dan thrutched his way up White Lightning with six pieces of gear. Tamma got gripped on the first move of Mike's Books—a flared hand jam to a water-grooved apron—and so sat in the sand and cried while passing climbers looked away in embarrassment. They climbed Double Cross and Dogleg beside it, Dan making a thin, mantling bid from crimpy edges into a tight dihedral with greasy pockets in the back, savoring that rare, perfect feeling of making committing moves and being sure of them. They climbed Mental Physics, Tamma in crack-ravaged boyfriend jeans over electric pink leopard-print tights and clashing yellow tiger-striped bodysuit, somehow, on the second pitch, stepping on her laces, accidentally untying her own shoe, and so climbing to the summit half barefoot, her sweaty TC pro in her teeth. They climbed Sexy Grandma, Toe Jam, Dandelion, and something called A Dog in the Ass, and after that last, everyone they met kept asking them what they'd done that day. They climbed out the Dairy Queen Wall, with Dan swashbuckling up line after line, blue-eyed, broad shouldered, big jawed, and ferociously strong. They climbed Touch and Go, Sail Away, Wild Wind, Sphincter Quits, and Clean and Jerk, and Tamma onsighted Illusion Dweller with three pieces of gear. Walking back they were stopped by an Englishwoman who asked, "Is this the way to Skull Rock?" and Tamma, delighted to be of use, started spraying directions and then interrupted herself to ask where the woman was from and whether there was gritstone or if she was from Sheffield and wasn't Shauna Coxsey also from Sheffield and did she know Pete Whittaker or Tom Randall, because you wouldn't (like) run into Tom Randall and (like?) *not recognize him*, right?, no, you'd be all "Hail fellow well met, sir! Might I chew upon your puka shell necklace with my teeth?"—and had Tamma actually seen Tom wear a puka shell necklace, or did a puka shell necklace just feel right for him, spiritually?—and didn't she think Shauna Coxsey should play Thor in the next movie?—and wasn't Coxsey just magnetic to watch?—wouldn't you watch Coxsey just stand on the mats?—wasn't that how much presence Shauna Coxsey had?—and the woman looked at Dan and said, "Is she speaking English?" and Dan said she was, and the woman said, "Ahhhh," and then took two steps back and knelt down and took a photograph of Tamma with a disposable camera and smiled and nodded in a reassuring way while advancing the little knurled dial.

They finished the walk out and drove farther on into the park and Dan took the lead on Rubicon and found the granite as coarse as spalling concrete, striking his fingers down into the tight and toothy gap, camming them in place so that they blanched white with tension, toeing onto footholds like the scales of pinecones, shaking and blowing with effort. He clipped the chains and lowered, walking backward down the rock, holding his hands clamped in his armpits with Tamma letting the rope pay up through the ATC, and when he alighted on the ground, he found his hands fastened to his shirt with blood and Tamma, seeing it, cracked a grin so full of wonder that Dan smiled back.

At the end of the day, he would drive her to Sierra's house and she would drop the cowboy hat over her face and be once again asleep. Her hands were so crushed that they would curl up on her chest, cocked forward at the wrist with the tension of the finger tendons. If he tightened his hands on the steering wheel, he could feel an ache in the outsides of his elbows. If he lifted anything so heavy as a coffee cup, he felt it along the back of his upper arm. He would park before Sierra's house, darkness already coming on, and Tamma would lurch up out of her seat with a great drooly suck of air. In that confused moment, surfacing from sleep, she always felt around in a panic for River, so often did she dream of holding him and so wake with the feeling of having lost him, and Dan would put his hands on her and say, "Tamma, River's safe, he's inside, you're in the car, you're all right," and there was always some mix of confusion and trust, both, with wakefulness coming to her even as he watched. Then she would give him a half-cocked smile and pop the latch on her seatbelt and kick the door open, scrubbing at her eye sockets with the heels of her hands, sauntering across the yard like a gunslinger. After ten hours out on the rocks, she'd spend her evening with the babies, holding River in her lap and singing songs to a constipated eleven-month-old in the bath:

> *Poo, poo, poo your poops*
> *Gently out your colon!*
> *Merrily, merrily, merrily, merrily*
> *Let's get these guts a rollin'!*

Samantha gazing up at her with limpid blue amazement.

Nine

On Christmas Eve they lay in bed side by side and talked. It was a rare night off. Tamma passed the joint to her mouth and drew on it so that a faint circle of emberous illumination expanded until it encompassed them both. "Fuck it," she said. Talking off the top of her lungs. "Let's do it! Tomorrow—Christmas day, dude!" She exhaled a plume of smoke. Drew again, the joint crackling. "I gotta do presents with my family but then, afterward, everyone splits. You and I can hike into the Wonderland and get Figures. Sixty-something degrees in the afternoon. It's north facing so the morning would be cold. But around two or three?"

She passed him the joint and as its light subsided, the room grew dark and he could just see her, faint and gray.

"Okay. And if we send it, what then?"

"Then we start planning where to go, what to climb, how we'll live, and what to say to Brittany Goris, when we see her at the crag."

"I think we should say nothing."

"We should definitely say *something*."

"What if, instead, we were just . . . cool."

"But what if she doesn't know that we know who she is?"

"What if we just, like, nod to her?"

"That doesn't seem like enough. Like what if I say something to her, and it becomes the start of an amazing, lifelong friendship?"

"Okay, what would you say?"

"'How YOU doin'?'"

"Definitely don't do that. Regardless. We'll sort this out later. In the meantime—Figures on a Landscape!"

"What will you do?" Tamma said, taking the joint back. "For Christmas I mean?"

"Coffee and toast with my old man. If I get lucky he might tell me again how knocking together concrete molds is a young man's game. If Alexandra comes out, he'll make French toast. He usually gets me a book. He's gotten me *Far from the Madding Crowd* twice. At least I got to read two different prefaces. Alexandra is supposed to take me to the bank any day now to put that money in my account but that's not gonna happen tomorrow."

"Did you get him anything?" Speaking off the top of her lungs.

"*Dark Rivers of the Heart.*"

"It's truly a very exciting life, here at the Redburn family home."

She let the smoke out in a great wash and it swept across the room and fell off the sides of the bed and across the floor and purled up into the slant of moonlight from the window.

"I can't feel my lips."

"Yeah?"

"Touch them."

"I don't know."

"Touch them."

She touched them.

"I can't feel that."

"Daniel, by god but do you have a glass of water?"

"Hell."

"Is that a no?"

"I do, but it looks pretty far away."

"Away yonder?" She rose up onto her knees and gestured out into the dark with her arm outflung like Lewis sighting a mountain to Clark. He climbed out of bed and crawled across the floor and went along the wall so as to approach the glass from a lateral and unexpected direction, gained the desk, worked hand over hand toward it, and Tamma said, "Avast!" for no reason, and then he encountered his desk chair and went over it and down onto the concrete floor and got up, propping himself on the overturned chair, a little proud of how gracefully he'd done it all.

"Dude," she whispered. "Are you okay?"

"I see what you were saying," he said. "I just didn't understand *avast* in time."

Through the glass and through the window, he could see the Milky Way spanning the horizon and he could see the scale where the water had been. He held the glass out for her to see it was empty.

She leaned forward and squinted and fired on the joint to make as much light she could and still couldn't seem to see it.

"Is it half empty?"

"It's totally empty, dude."

"Damn!"

"I have this," he said, rising up to a stand.

"Abort!" she said from the bed. "Abort! You don't have this!"

"I can do it, sarge!" he said, bracing himself on the desk and looking sideways at the door, choosing his moment like a sailor crossing the decks of a storm-tossed ship. He reeled backward and then tilted forward and went staggering across the open space, Tamma whispering, "Send it! Sennnnnnnd it!" and he fetched up against the jamb, quietly withdrew the tongue, tilted forward, and this way was flung out into the living room. It was very dark. He could make out the windows and there was faint light on the counters and on the side of the fridge. He came to the edge of the kitchen island and labored along it toward the sink until he came to where the rag rug was folded over, and there he tripped and spilled off the counter onto the floor. Slowly he heeled himself about in the dark, passed his hands across the concrete, and touched, with one forefinger, an eye: open, gelid, wet.

"Tams," he yelled. "Tamma!"

He grasped the kitchen island, pulled himself to stand, crossed the open space between island and counter, and turned on the light. Alexandra lay against the cupboards. Sitting on the edge of the island was the glass of water she had been drinking. Her mouth was open, her eyes staring, fixed on something ahead of her, her hands gathered in front of her chest.

Tamma came out of the door. She could not see what he was seeing because her view was blocked by the kitchen island.

"What?" she said. "Dan! What is it?"

"Dad!" he yelled. "*Lawrence!*"

Tamma staggered along the wall until she came to the living room lights and these she turned on.

He knelt down beside his mother. She lay on her side, chest heaving, staring at a point beneath the cupboards, her mouth opening reflexively. Slacking shut and opening wide again. Tamma came around the side of the counter and stopped and brought a hand to her mouth.

"She's dying," Dan said. It was like reaching for a tooth and finding just an empty, painful socket, so bad it was nauseous. He said it again, "She's dying," and it hurt so much to say it that he couldn't believe he was still there in the wake of having spoken the words aloud.

Tamma lifted the phone off the hook, punched 911, pinned it between shoulder and jaw.

"Alexandra," Dan said, and she turned her head to the side. He grabbed her by the shoulders and dragged her up against the cabinets. She started to slide back down. He seized her shirt and hauled her back up.

They heard the door to the bedroom creak open and Lawrence stood in the doorway, looking at them for one long, blinking, dazzled moment. He was wearing gray sweatpants and a ratted-out white henley. He passed his hand down his face, shook his head, and looked first at Dan. Then Dan saw him look aside, and all the color went out of his face. He took one step back and then another and fell against the doorjamb. He was holding one hand over his heart and with the other he gripped his thigh.

Through the phone, Dan could hear the tinny, distant voice of the dispatcher.

"Nine-one-one," she said. "What is your emergency?"

"We found my friend's mom on the floor. She's having trouble breathing. We need help. We need an ambulance."

"Mom, can you hear me?"

Alexandra blinked, her gaze swung toward him, and then she looked right through him into some darkness beyond. Her eyebrows up. Her mouth slack.

Lawrence stood and walked across the room toward them. He came tentatively, disbelieving, bent a little at the knees. His expression anguished. His mouth open. Holding his brow with one hand. He went down onto his knees, took Alexandra's pale wrist. "Oh, my love," he said. Her hand was small in his grasp. Her fingers pale, with dark tips.

"Dan."

"Dan."

"Dan."

"*Dan*," Tamma said.

"Yeah?"

"This chick wants to know, how old is she?"

"Like thirty-eight?" Dan said.

"Thirty-eight," Lawrence agreed. He was staring into her face. He loves her, Dan thought. He loves her more than he loves anything else. His entire life has been about her.

"Alexandra," Lawrence said. She turned fractionally toward him, and no recognition played there. She lay gasping. Dan had to hold her upright against the cabinets because she could not hold herself. He thought, Come back to us. Alexandra could not tear her eyes off the dark. They were wide and staring and her brow flexed as if having seen something she knew, something she recognized. Someone spoke, and spoke, and spoke again.

"Guys," Tamma said. "*Guys*."

"What?"

"This chick wants to know, does she have preexisting conditions? Like she does, right? Some heart thing, right?"

"Yes," Dan said. "Nine years ago she had an AVR. Aortic valve replacement. The valve is bioprosthetic. And it's failing."

"It must've just—gone," Lawrence said.

"Does she have any allergies?"

"Strawberries."

Alexandra lay against the cupboards. She turned her head as if she had heard something and opened her mouth as if she might speak, but did not speak, looking about as if she could not see, turning left and right and blinking and the blinks coming as if they were doll's eyes with weighted eyelids. The four of them stayed on the floor like that for twenty minutes, Lawrence holding her swollen, pale hand in his own dark, scarred, enormous one.

"Where are you?" Dan said to the dispatcher. "Where is that ambulance?"

"We're having a little problem," the dispatcher said. "You do not appear to be in our system. Can you describe where your house is, to me? My ambulance is—" and she gave an address that was far to the south of them.

"Tamma," Dan said, because Tamma could give you house by house descriptions of everything for miles. She started speaking to the dispatcher. Alexandra stared at the cabinets beneath the sink.

"How long?" Dan said.

"They're coming."

"How long?" Dan said again.

"They're close."

There was a moment of silence, then, and they listened to Alexandra's labored, panting breaths.

III.

ISOLATION

One

The paramedic tied off the tourniquet and, with one blue-gloved hand, searched her forearm, dimpling the skin, working his finger pad in small, circular motions. He found the vein and, with the other hand, tore open the backing on the IV kit.

Alexandra lay on the concrete floor. Her bare feet were cocked at different angles. Close beside the paramedic was an EMT holding a bag valve mask, slowly releasing and compressing the bag. It was coupled to a chipped green tank and Dan could hear the hiss of oxygen in the line. Another EMT was sorting through a duffel of gear. The gurney stood beside the stove. They'd tracked in a swath of sand. The red light throbbed through the door, laid a neon track across the concrete, shadowed the grit, lit the cabinets, then combed across the desert, and came wheeling back. Lawrence stood braced against the wall.

In one motion the paramedic tucked the catheter into the vein and triggered the safety button to retract the needle. He taped the hub in place and began mating tubing to the port.

He hooked his thumb over Alexandra's lower jaw and worried it side to side. She did not react. Her jaw was clenched. He picked out a glass bottle, upended it, drew liquid into the bore of a syringe.

"Two milligrams etomidate," he said.

He shucked the needle into a sharps container, screwed the syringe into the port of the IV, and depressed the plunger. "Seventy mikes rocuronium," he said, piercing a bottle's rubber stopper.

They waited. The EMT depressed and released the bag valve mask. Her chest rose and fell. Alexandra began to tremble all over. It looked like shivering. Then she lay still.

"Fasciculations," the paramedic said. The EMT lifted the mask and they waited to see if she would breathe. There was a hushed moment where she lay on the concrete not breathing. Then the EMT gave her a breath and her chest rose. He gave her another. They went on like that, watching her oxygen saturation come up on the pulse ox clipped to her finger. Then the EMT lifted the mask again and the paramedic hooked his blue-gloved thumb over her jaw and wagged it easily up and down, side to side.

"Okay," he said. He exhaled. "*Okay.*"

He tore a stainless-steel hook out of sterile packaging, slid it down into her mouth, and pulled her tongue out of the way. The blade was tipped with a flashlight. It lit the pink ribbed cathedral arch of her palate. He pried back her jaw, held out his hand, and was given a flexible blue stylet. He slid it down into her airway.

"What's that?" Tamma said.

"The bougie," an EMT said. "It's a kind of guide. Shhh."

"How about the seven-five?"

The EMT rifled through the toolbox, came up with a clear plastic hose, tore open the packaging, dispensed lubricating jelly onto it, and handed it to the paramedic, who began to thread it over the bougie. It made a wet noise as it went down. "There," he said. "We're in." He leaned back and passed his arm over his forehead. The EMT coupled the tube to the bag valve. The paramedic unyoked the stethoscope from around his neck and, fitting the earpieces to his ears, placed the diaphragm on her chest.

"Give me a breath," he said, and the EMT compressed the bag.

"Breath sounds on the left."

"Give me another."

"Breath sounds strong and equal."

The paramedic secured the tube with cloth tape, then he and the two EMTs grabbed on to her and said, "One, two, three!" and they lifted her straight up onto the gurney.

"We'll be going to the medical center," he said. "Off the 62."

The ambulance crew wheeled her out the door. Lawrence came up behind him, gripped his shoulder, and said, "I'm going to the hospital after them."

"I know."

Lawrence was out the door. He was starting up the truck even as the ambulance was pulling out.

Dan turned to Tamma and Tamma went right into him, crushing her face to his chest.

"I'm going to the hospital," he said. "You don't have to come."

"'You don't have to come' is your dad's catchphrase," she said.

They packed a duffel of clothes and locked up the house. Dan started the old green subaru and went roaring down the drive and out onto the road. They drove with the wash on their left. On their right, cutaways of mountains. It was dark in the car, the dust from the ambulance's passage sifting back down into the headlights.

He met Lawrence at the medical center, and they were greeted by the ER doc. They had done an echocardiogram, he said. Alexandra was in severe heart failure and would be going to San Bernardino by helicopter. Dan left Lawrence still in conversation and walked back out of the emergency room, the doors swishing open before him, and he could see the wide black parking lot, empty, with the lights at intervals, Tamma leaning against the hood, watching him come.

"I'm going to San Bernardino."

"I've never seen San Bernardino. Supposed to be beautiful."

"It is?"

"The Paris of the West, they call it."

"Really?"

"All young girls yearn, someday, to see the streets of San Bernardino."

"Okay," he said. "Okay, I can drop you off at your house."

"Suck my dick."

"You don't need to be here for this."

"Suck—my—*dick*," she said again.

The road came yard by yard into the headlights, dead and gray and shivered with cracks like the belly of a snake. Creosote, tamarisk, and smokebrush grew in the ditches. They reached the sprawl just after midnight, everything seeming to loom up into the headlights from out an oceanic murk: strip malls and car lots; hurricane fencing and overhanging green exit signs; swales of dead grass; travelodges, sizzlers, and palm trees; ten lanes of freeway climbing a rise to a gray-black, never-dark horizon.

The hospital was a glass tower annexed to a concrete box annexed to a multilevel concrete parking structure. They parked in the overflow lot and walked along a blind stucco cliff five stories high.

At the head of the waiting room was a large, empty, counter-height reception desk. Someone's knitting and yarn shears had been set down as if they had just left and were about to return. Beyond the desk, large double doors were paneled in stainless steel. In the corner there was a Christmas tree, hung in lights and ornaments and hand-painted wooden gingerbread men with iced-on stethoscopes. The windows made a wide black wall.

Dan called back using the phone at the desk and was told to wait and so he waited, while Tamma sat, legs akimbo, feet supinated on the floor, texting her mom to let her know where she was, getting up every so often to lean face-first and smush-nosed against the vending machine, looking mournfully inside, dredging her pockets with long, witchy fingers and finding nothing but fifteen cents and a nail and the shell of a great-great-great-grandfather snail.

Finally, the elevator doors dinged open, and Lawrence came into the waiting room. The weatheredness of his profession, which had always seemed to Dan to possess its own dignity and authority, looked misplaced. He looked poor. He looked uneducated and dirty and unprepared for all that would come next. He glanced around from the empty reception desk to the decorations and then to Dan and Tamma. He took a seat beside them.

"Got a little lost finding the place," he said.

Tamma nodded. Dan looked down at his own hands.

They waited just less than an hour. Then they heard the bolts go in the door and a girl not much older than Dan came out, blond, pale, dressed in blue scrubs and an oversized red velvet Santa hat with white trim.

"Hi, I'm Sophie," she said. "Alexandra's nurse. Are you here for Alexandra Redburn?"

"Yes."

"Tell me your name?"

"I'm Lawrence, Alexandra's husband."

"And who's this?"

"Dan. Her son. And this is Tamma."

"I'm sorry that you guys have to be here tonight," Sophie said. "I'm very sorry that this has happened. We're going to do everything we can to help. Now, please follow me. We're going to go back to Alexandra's room. Just to prepare you, she's intubated, meaning she has a breathing tube in. She's not sedated, but she's not responding right now. We're doing what we can to manage her blood pressure, but she's very sick. Both the surgeon, Dr. Todd, and the intensivist, Dr. Vagy, are waiting in her room and ready to talk to you."

She brought them back to the room. Alexandra was on the bed, her face obscured by tubes and cotton tape. Urine hung in a graduated plastic bag at the foot of the bed.

"Hi, I'm Dr. Todd," said a doctor, wearing mint-green hospital scrubs and a lab coat. "I'm a cardiovascular surgeon. I'm sorry to be meeting you under these circumstances, I'm sorry that you're here. Tell me your name?"

"Lawrence, her husband."

"Dan," Dan said.

"Lawrence, very nice to meet you. As they may have told you at the medical center, Alexandra's bioprosthetic valve is failing. We've done an echo and it shows severe aortic regurgitation, meaning the valve isn't closing properly and so blood is flowing backward into the heart. For this reason, her heart isn't able to supply blood to her whole body. Her organs are going to start to fail if we don't fix this problem, and the only way to fix it is a surgical replacement. As you know, this would mean a second sternotomy, and given that she is coming to us so sick, the surgery will likely be very difficult. We usually like to try and tune people up a little bit before a surgery like this, but it's not possible in this case. She's much too sick. Our only option moving forward is to proceed with a surgical repair, and the surgery will not be easy. Were you together for her first valve replacement?"

"Yes," Lawrence said.

Dan was finding it hard to look at the surgeon—his gaze would skitter away, down to the hems of scrubs, dansko clogs, noticing strange things. The line of staples welting the leather upper to the midsole. A large brown paper coffee filter on the counter, filled with coffee grounds. The outlets in the room came in pairs: one faced with stainless steel, the other red plastic. Stanchions hung from tracks in the ceiling, with pendant IV bags. A droning buzz filled his ears. He was having trouble following. The surgeon was still talking but the voice came in and out of focus, gaining, sometimes, a distorted, underwater quality. Then Dan would bear down and try to follow and it would come back. "Complications," he was saying, "will include bleeding, infection, failure to wean from the bypass machine, organ failure, and death. I'm particularly worried that we might have trouble weaning her off bypass, in which case we would have to run the machine at the bedside, something we call ECMO, or extracorporeal membrane oxygenation. That could potentially mean several days of sedation and intubation, which increases all postoperative complications. How long has she been sick for? And has she been getting her normal follow-up?"

"She's seemed sort of down lately," Lawrence said. The surgeon waited to see if there was more. The intensivist, standing to the side, also waited. With a great effort of attention, Dan dragged his gaze up to his father and looked at the man. Each breath was an effort of will. He thought for a moment he might be about to go down, and then Tamma grasped his upper arm and held him upright. How could we let this happen, he kept thinking. When he looked at Sophie, her expression was restrained. She was biting her lip. Dan had felt somehow that they were a family like any other. Just folks fallen on hard times. But in the bright light of the hospital room, the dysfunction and failure that had led to this moment were gruesome.

Dan took a step backward, and then another. He had the eerie, otherworldly sense he might backstep into some other reality in which this had never happened, in which everyone was still okay. Tamma steered him down into a chair and he sat with his elbows on his knees, his gaze pulled down, away from Sophie's concealed horror, away from his old man, hunting along the floor, following the black joints between vinyl tiles.

"Well, because we're catching this all so late," Dr. Todd was saying, "the surgery is much higher risk than we'd want it to be. But Alex is still young and our general assumption is that with a patient of this age, the patient and the family would want everything to be done. I want to be very clear, and make sure that we're all on the same page with our goals of care. The risks are enormous, and the surgery and subsequent recovery will be long, arduous, and full of complications. I cannot guarantee a good outcome or a return to her previous quality of life. Do you know what Alex's wishes are? Does she have an advance directive? Because this is the juncture where we consider how far we want to go, and what decisions Alex would like us to make." A weird, cold, tingling sensation started at the base of Dan's neck and spread outward into his jaw and across his scalp. They are suggesting, Dan thought, that we let her die.

"I can't imagine a life without her," Lawrence said.

"Dad," Dan said.

"Yeah?" Lawrence said.

"*Dad*," Dan said again. He was staring at his old man. What he meant to say was, She wanted us to let her die. But he couldn't look his father in the face and say it. He said instead, "Did you two discuss this?"

Lawrence clasped his hands and hung his head for a very long time. Dan wanted to cease to exist. He wanted to stop thinking, stop being alive. She had gone out to get herself a glass of water. You were in your room, stoned out of your mind, talking with Tamma, pissing your life and your promise away, and your mother was drowning in her own lungs on the concrete floor, terrified and alone.

Lawrence raised his head back up. "I think we should try for it," he said. "I think she would want to try, to be there for you, Danny, to see you grow up. I think she would rather anything than miss that. I think that would be worth any risk."

"Well then," the surgeon said. "We will start getting her prepped for surgery. The OR will be ready in an hour. I will have my PA come in and walk you through the surgery and have you sign consent. What questions can I answer for you at this time?"

Dan looked back at his father and thought, None of that is true. She wanted to never go through this again. Don't put her through it, Dad.

Two

The waiting room looked out onto the roof of another building: a flat gravel expanse strewn with HVAC units. Beyond, a parking lot, health strips, a four-lane road, more parking lots, strip malls, box stores, and an open, excavated foundation pit, where Christmas was dawning cobwebby and gray. Men and women with nowhere else to go were helping each other from out the pit, handing up the luggage and plastic bags that held their things. The reception desk reposed unattended, the knitting and shears abandoned.

They had been moved out to the waiting room and told that the circulating nurse would reach out for an update. Because neither Dan nor Lawrence had a phone, she had been given Tamma's number. Alexandra had been in surgery for more than seven hours. Lawrence slept in a chair and Tamma on the floor, pillowed on the duffel.

The phone vibrated and Dan stepped out into the stairwell and thumbed it on. "They're closing now," the nurse said. "And should be out in an hour or so."

"How did it go?"

"Are you in the waiting room?"

"Yes."

"The surgeon will be out shortly."

The surgeon came out much later. The elevator doors dinged and there he stood in the same green hospital scrubs and black leather dansko clogs, looking tired but also relaxed. He shook hands all around.

"So," Dan said. "How did it go?"

"Not well, *not well*," the surgeon said. "As we discussed, her heart failure was quite progressed. We successfully replaced the valve but failed to wean her off the pump so she's on ECMO now. And for the moment, we are not able to close her."

"What does that mean?" Lawrence said.

"Well, as you know, we cut through the sternum to perform the surgery. Sometimes, there is too much internal swelling for the sternum to be re-closed, so in this case we cover the sternotomy with a plastic membrane called ioban and wait for the swelling to go down. In the meantime, she has to be kept flat and sedated. Now she will be moved from the OR to the thoracic ICU and in an hour or so your nurse will come back out to the waiting room to get you."

"Okay," Dan said.

"Merry Christmas," Dr. Todd said.

"Merry Christmas," Dan said.

More waiting, the three of them in the waiting room for two more hours. Then a nurse brought them back to a different room and they found Alexandra intubated and draped in cords. She wore a gown, and through the neck, Dan could see the top of what looked like a dressing of sticky orange saran wrap. The ECMO machine loomed at the bedside, the cords gently swaying in rhythm with her heartbeat. They all waited in the interminable near-quiet of that room. Later that day,

Tamma's phone rang and she walked out into the hall to take it and then came back in and looked at them.

"I have to go," she said. "They had three sick calls. Sierra's got to work." She lifted her hands and let them fall. "Somebody still has to watch the kids."

Dan drove her the two hours back home and for the first time in all the years that he had known her, she had little to say. When he let her off at Sierra's, she got out, and then holding the door open, stooped back down, and, crimping the top edge of the doorframe, said, "Figures will still be there." Then she slammed the door and Dan turned the car around and drove right back to the hospital.

He was thinking of all those falls off the Princess. They had hurt like hell, every time, and the hurting had been part of the glory and aliveness of the undertaking. But now, all he could see was Alexandra lying on the concrete floor, when they had lifted the bag valve mask off her face. They had waited for her to breathe and she had not breathed. If there was anything good in all the world, it was a person, alive and brimful of their own hopes and dreams. And yet, those hopes and dreams could be extinguished.

The thing about the highstep crux on the Princess was that you could stand beneath the move, looking at it, almost forever. She asked that you discriminate between the deeply *felt* danger of committing and the *real* danger of hesitation. That had once been intelligible to him as a test of courage. But now that he'd been in the presence of death, he couldn't shake a sick feeling. They had not understood what they were risking. Not really. Some people thought that climbers were dim-witted adrenaline junkies who did not understand consequences. And that had been true.

Actually, he was thinking, it was only true of himself. In his heart of hearts, he had believed that Alexandra would write another book, that Tamma would send the Princess, and that he, whatever happened, would find his way to a life of meaning and purpose. But Tamma was not like him. She had no illusions of her own invincibility. Dan had been so sure that everything would be all right that he had used to tease Tamma about what she would do if he died in her arms. Buddy that she was, she had taken the teasing pretty well, but now Dan could barely keep the bile down for having said such things.

You grew up hand in hand with her, he was thinking, and so you thought there was parity. You believed that both of you saw the world the same way. But if the Princess did not go, you had another future laid out before you. Tamma had nothing. You grew up with security and material wealth. If bank accounts had dwindled, the feeling was still always that the Redburns were ready to return to their station upon the completion of a third novel. Alexandra was just procrastinating, as difficult geniuses were wont to do. Your folks were readers, and hers were not. Tamma lived in a trailer, and you in a handmade little house. Even just the way the families talked, the language they used, bore these differences. It was all that, and it was something more—your parents fundamentally believed that it was possible for you to go out into the world and succeed. That belief was built into your worldview. No one had ever believed that about Tamma. Tamma believed it about herself, against all evidence, contrary to everything she had ever been told, believed it provisionally, desperately, and it was an enormous psychological labor to keep that belief alive. You two walked out together—you, hoping to escape a mild feeling of aimlessness with which you were sometimes afflicted, and Tamma, fighting for her life. She had known the stakes and done it anyway—done it with an enthusiasm and panache that now appeared impossible, maybe immoral. Riven right through the center of the friendship, and invisible to him, had been a divide of class, privilege, and opportunity across which certain understandings had been lost.

Dan was driving back toward San Bernardino with the gray highway coming yard by yard and mile by mile into his headlights, and he understood for the first time, in a way he had never understood before. He was shaking his head and beating the steering wheel with the heel of his palm. God fucking damnit, he was thinking. God fucking damnit. He had never seen the world clearly before today. Alexandra had been right. Other people were not real to him. Out on the rocks, he had been searching for glory, for a feeling of ecstatic aliveness, but all of that had been merely trying to put off the fundamental recognition of what the world really was. He had clung to his childish dream of searching out, in the waste places, at the extreme limit of human endeavor, a luminous never neverland, soaked through with meaning, in which he could steal himself away. He knew now, none of that was real. There was no glory, nor any such thing as meaning. The world lay before him as a butchery, as a vast waste of meat and things and ruin and suffering, of lost and hopeless people, of blinding horror, a place blanched of hope, and there was nowhere else to go. I see now, Dan was thinking. This place has no numinous edge. The world is the world is the world.

Three

Tamma went up on tiptoe and made a short hop for the cereal box and pulled it down off the cabinet, heelhooked the fridge open, slung the milk out on two fingers, poured, let the fridge fall shut, swaggered back to the table, sat with one foot hanging off the chair, and Hyrum watched her the while from the couch.

"Hyrum," Tamma said. "We gotta stop meeting like this, Hyrum. Hyrum, we're almost out of cereal, Hyrum."

"I'll . . . ahhhhh . . . put it on my uh, grocery list."

"Hilarious, Hyrum. *Truly*. Oh, *Hyrum*, so funny."

"When I next . . . ahhhh . . . go to safeway."

She sat, eating, shaking her head, swinging one bruisy shank, her foot black and mottled green at the heel.

"Hmmmm . . . what's your ahhh . . . plan, anyway?"

"What plan, Hyrum?"

"For, ahh . . . after school."

"*Hyrum*, it's winter break, Hyrum."

"No, hmmm . . . I mean, after graduation."

"Hyrum, Hyrum," she said, tskingly, distractedly, headshakingly, spooning up cereal and making hard work of it, chewing carefully with the right side, her jaw crackling. On her phone was a video of Paisley doing one-arm pull-ups holding a ten-pound plate in the other hand. Tamma wanted to bite savagely into her armpit.

"Ahhh... hmmm... Tamma?"

"Ahh... hmmmmm... Hyrum?"

"Do you ever ahhh... think about ahhhh... making a plan?"

"No, Hyrum, I do not, Hyrum."

This girl was out there, living a life of maximal self-actualization, shaved smooth, creamy with moisturizers, wearing comp shorts and expensive sports bras, waking up in the morning in her beautiful house, going downstairs to her breakfast of blended green algae, beet juice, frozen kale, and organic protein powder. Tamma was waking up here.

"You could go to Humboldt and pick weed," he said. "I know people."

"Yeah, Hyrum, I bet you do," she said. In the video, Paisley was showing viewers around her home gym in Santa Cruz, Tamma incandescent with hatred.

"Good people," Hyrum said.

"Hyrum, you're just trying to get rid of me, Hyrum," Tamma said, watching Paisley casually jump onto her moon board and start up a V8 without putting on her shoes, just campusing the moves.

"Guys don't ahhh... try and get rid of their girlfriend's pretty daughters."

Tamma looked up from her phone. Rose to a stand. Braced both hands on the table. Opened her mouth. Gacked. Choked it down. Ralphed it back up. Held it caged in her jaws, her eyes watery with disgust. Then, bug-eyed, she stooped and poured cereal from her mouth back down into the bowl. She threw her head up in the air and swung side to side like a brontosaurus in its death throes, mouth open in a silent wail, squelching her eyes almost closed, drawing her chin into her neck, quivering all over, hanging her mouth open, and then she arched out her tongue and licked the air with electric disgust.

"Nice," he said.

She hacked strings of mucus down into her bowl.

"Classy," he said.

She walked to the sink.

"Don't pour that down the—" he said, and Tamma tripped the garbage disposal and poured everything down the sink, leaning over to suck water from the tap and spit it back into the basin.

"Turn that off."

She leaned against the counter with the water running and food fountaining back up out of the drain and the disposal rattling, and she slowly raised her middle finger. Brought up the other hand to make a pair.

"I said turn that off! People are sleeping!"

She tripped the switch. They both listened to it wind down. There was maybe a spoon in there.

"Dude," she said.

He looked away from her. He had a slow, smooth, affectless face and hooded, sleepy eyes. Twenty-three years old, the same age as Tamma's sister. His stubble was blond. He'd been left out on the side of the road near Cedar City, Utah, when he was eleven years old, and he'd been years hitchhiking around the West ever since. He had never been to high school, had no GED, no birth certificate, no driver's license, no social security card, was supposed to have an IQ of 140, drank all day, held his own intelligence in high regard, and sold just enough weed, flunitrazepam, and oxy to get by living with a woman who bought all his groceries. He was sitting on the couch with his arm over the back, knuckling up his fingers one at a time, touching the orange and brown twill with his fingertips thoughtfully.

"A job is ahhh . . . something to, ah, think about, anyway."

"Why don't you ahhhhh . . . *suck a dick?*"

"You're a uhhhhh . . . gross little person, you know that?"

"Oh, *I'm* gross?"

"It was a, *uhhhhhh*, joke."

"You better believe it was a joke."

"Some people might be ahhh . . . flattered."

"Duuuuuuuuuuuuuuuude."

"Some peo—"

"Duuuuuuuuuuuuuuuuuuuuuuuuuuuude," she said, cutting him off.

"Ta—"

"—Dude," she said, stopping him.

"I only—"

"—*Dude!*"

"It's six in the morning!" Kendra said, coming down the hall from the bedroom. "Do we really need to be running the garbage disposal, Tamma? Do we? And Jesus Christ. Did you eat all the cereal?"

"There was hardly any left."

"I just bought some. It's like feeding an army. Are you trying to drive me to bankruptcy?"

"Just trying to stay alive."

"Really? Because it looks like you poured it down the sink."

"There were extenuating circumstances."

"You're such a goddamn little brat, it's unbelievable."

"Mom!" Colin said, coming down the hall. "I'm taking a shower!"

"Go put a towel in the dryer for your brother," Kendra said.

"He can get his own towel."

"Tamarisk Jonesy Callahan!"

"Okay, fine," Tamma said, and walked down the hall to the laundry room, took down a towel from the cabinets, and dropped it into the dryer. She turned the dryer on and stood, leaning against it, hanging her head. She set her phone down and scrolled through the competitor list again, regretting having signed up. There were bound to be other serious climbers coming out of those Los Angeles gyms. There was no way in which Tamma was ready for that kind of competition.

"You better not be sitting on it in there!" Kendra called.

"Fuck, Mom!" Tamma said. She walked back into the kitchen and stood with her arms splayed. "What the hell?"

"Ask this nasty little person what she said to me, hmmmmm?" Hyrum said.

"I don't want to know."

"Go ahhh . . . suck a dick, Hyrum," Tamma said.

"Tamma!"

"Eat a *butthole*."

"*Tamma!*" her mother yelled.

"You too, you bag."

"Oh, really?" Kendra said, drawing herself up. "Oh, really. That *is just great*. What a way to talk to your own mother. Good job, Tamma. Well. Do you get a prize? Is there some kind of award? For being the most ungrateful, brattiest girl in California? What do you get?"

Kendra stood, looking at her daughter. Tamma could not look back at her.

"Your sister," she said, "picked up a 19L tomorrow and I told her that you could watch the kiddos."

"But I can't," Tamma said. A 19L was a twelve-hour shift starting at 7:00 p.m. "I already told her I can't. I've *just* been with them three nights!"

"Oh yeah? Well, I told her you could."

"I told Dan I'd go back to the hospital to be with him!"

"Well, give him a call and say you can't."

"Mooooom!"

"Sierra needs the money. Not everyone's lives revolve around you, you know."

Tamma planted her elbows and went down with her face against the counter, scissoring her fingers through her hair, gathering up handfuls, and wrapping a hank of it around her face to chew on.

"Does this really mean she called *you*, and asked *you* to watch them?"

"I know this may come as news to you, Tamma, but some of us work for a living. Because otherwise our children would eat us out of house and home, just throwing cereal down the drain. Some of us pay for the cell phones that their daughters can't ever seem to use to call us back, is how some of us spend our lives."

"Tell her about the ahhh . . . data," Hyrum said.

"Oh," Kendra said. "You're over on your data again."

"Tell her it's all that stepsister porn she's watching."

"Fuck you, you *creep*!"

"Tamma!" Kendra said.

Above the counter was a window, and cradled in the aluminum tracks were dead spiders, their legs tightly curled about their jointed abdomens. One of the panes was gone and they'd put in cardboard to replace it.

"Mom!" Colin yelled from the shower.

"Go get your brother's towel," Kendra said.

Tamma went down the hall, opened the dryer, and dragged out the warm towel. She cracked the bathroom door and pitched it in: "There's your towel, dickweed!" she yelled. Then she walked back down the hallway, opened the side door, dropped down into the sand. Flat and sere desert on every side, mountains on her left and mountains on her right and before her, low blue hills growing no closer.

It was the twenty-eighth of December. The comp was the twelfth of February. Something like six weeks away. Dan was gone and without her buddy, she was outflanked by life, and it was a kind of daily work, to keep hope alive. Bad thoughts kept creeping up along the edges. No one was going to give her a break and no one was going to give her permission and if she didn't make her own luck she wouldn't ever get her chance to hatefuck Paisley Cuthers entirely out of the sport of climbing.

She found a guy online that was trying to sell his bouldering pad for sixty dollars. *Cat peed on it but smell not bad*, he'd written. Tamma reached out and they agreed to meet in the parking lot behind the gear shop.

She sat cross-legged on the floor beside her mother's bed, considering it. She didn't have long to think. She had to get over to her sister's house by the afternoon. Dan was gone—so no rope climbing, no spotter. She didn't want to take the money. There were no words for how badly she did not want to take it. She sat there, thinking, This is one of those moments, where you could just stop trying. Tell yourself that you couldn't do it. Never go to the comp. Your whole life could be a ruin, but you'd be able to look back on things and say: You never had the chance. You were a failure, but it had been out of your hands.

Or, Tamma thought, you could do some scary shit. She'd never been to Los Angeles. She didn't know if she'd be safe, if she'd be able to get around, if she'd be okay without money, if she'd get raped to death. She didn't know, either, if she had the guts to walk into the comp alone, as just a short, ugly, big-eared desert rat lost in a gym full of city girls who were all stronger and prettier and better mannered. Didn't know if she could step out onto the mats and take her chance. Find out, under bright lights, if she was the real thing or not. She knew she should have the courage for that. But she didn't know if she actually did.

She took the bus into town and found the bouldering pad guy reading *Dune* in his sprinter van with the hatch open. She walked up and said, "Yo, dude," and he looked at her and said, "What is happening?" and then he leaned out of his van and looked side to side as if for cameras.

"You're a child. You didn't mention that you were *a child*. And what are you wearing? I can't sell you the pad," he said, and leapt down, out of the van.

"Dudebro," she said.

"Climbing is dangerous!" he said, waving his hands at her as if he could scare her off.

"Your mom is dangerous!"

"What?"

"What?"

"Are you a local?"

She shrugged. She wasn't not-local but she wasn't from town.

"The locals don't climb," he said. "They're rednecks. Yahoos. They just want to cook meth, fix up shitty cars, and vote against their own economic interests. They don't want to climb—the closest they come to exercise is dirt biking."

"Oh yeah?" Tamma said.

"Everybody says that, it's not just me."

"I heard that guys with sprinter vans aren't real climbers; they're rich, entitled *douche*bags pretending to be *dirt*bags while living off the money their parents made pillaging both the working class and the world."

She leered, cracking her knuckles.

"But," she added, apologetically, "everybody says that, it's not just me."

"Show me your hands," he said.

Tamma held up her hands, her smile zippering wide to reveal the whole chipped, crooked, shining-white sierra.

"Okay," he said. "Wow. Those are some gobies you have."

"Well, your mom's bush stubble is like steel wool."

"Where do you climb?"

"Here, in the park." Then she flung her hand out north. "Sometimes at some boulders out there. But I'm not a real climber, I just cook meth and fix up shitty cars." She reached into her back pocket, came out with the wad of bills. Could these bills have been found underneath her mother's bed in a rifle case keeping company with an AK-47 and oxy? Possibly, they might have. Would there be repercussions? Probably not. Hopefully not. Definitely not. Nah, it was fine. For sure, this was going to be okay.

"What've you climbed?" he said.

"I sent Fingerbang Princess." This was still her proudest send. Her trad climbs were not going to impress anybody. You did not just roll up to guys in sprinter vans and tell them that you'd climbed White Lightning.

"Never heard of it."

"Will you sell me the pad or not?"

"What if something happens to you?"

"Dude. I climb without a pad right now."

"You're not serious."

"No, yeah, I am serious."

"You climb *without a pad*? That's so dope! I mean—that's so fucked up!"

"Not as dope as giving John Long an HJ on the Thank God Ledge of Half Dome."

"What?" he said.

"What?" she said, looking around and furrowing her brow at the inappropriateness of this troubling, overheard comment of mysterious provenance. Why am I such a creep, she thought. Why can't I just be normal?

"What did you say?" he said.

"What did *you* say?" she shot back, drawing herself up with indignation that he'd slander John Long in this way.

He seated himself, drew out his phone, scrolled. His eyebrows went up.

"Fingerbang Princess is a highball." In mounting tones of alarm he read on. "*This horrific, rarely repeated highball boulder has put three or four good climbers in the hospital and has seen at least one fatality. Climb through an overhang on positive micro-edges, throw an enormous dyno to a shallow, greasy two-finger pocket, and turn the roof with a committing heel-hook mantle. Then challenge the cryptic slab, pinching outsloped crystal dikes which become sequential hand-foot matches leading to a bowel-loosening, butthole-puckering, heart-stopping, brain-melting, kidney-shriveling, mind-shattering highstep crux. If you top this thing out, call your mom and tell her you love her.*"

He looked up at her.

"You *climbed* this?"

"That description is overcooked, bro, it's only V4."

"It says here, *Although originally graded V4, the boulder has consequential and sustained V6 climbing, a low-percentage V7 dyno, and a send-or-splatter V8 crux.*"

"That's new," she said. "Somebody must've updated it after that chick died on it."

"What?"

"Yeah, some chick died while we were working it. We had to roll over an old tire so we didn't get her blood on our shoes and my buddy Dan sent it that night, actually."

"What in the holy fuck?" he said. "Where are your parents, tiny child?"

"Does it really say that—that the crux is V8?"

"Yes."

"*Dang.*"

"Dang, what?"

"We never would've even attempted it if we thought it was V8."

"You didn't notice that it seemed *pretty hard* for V4?"

"We just thought we sucked at climbing honestly."

"Jane Sasaki used to put up first ascents and then sit around the campfire, doing mushrooms and drinking whiskey, naming easier and easier grades until everyone was laughing at the idea of the route being V4 and that's what she'd call it. That's how she graded things. I climbed a route in Little Cottonwood that she graded 5.8+ but now it goes at *solid* 5.11d. I'm talking overhanging mono-digit locks in a crack full of shrieking bats, and Jane thought, 'Sure, that seems like stout 5.8 to me.' Jane saying that a boulder problem is V4 doesn't mean it's really *V4*."

"That would explain a lot, actually," Tamma said. "In fact that casts my entire life in a new light. All this time we've been thinking the Princess was a moderate and we sucked. But if it's V6 with V7/V8 cruxes, then we're solid climbers, actually."

"Solid climbers?" he said. "I *guess*. Y'all sound like savages. If I was climbing highball V8 without pads, it would be the crowning achievement of my climbing career. I'd consider my entire life a success."

"I could show you the beta, if you like."

"No, thank you. As much as I'd like to attempt a mind-blowing, send-or-splatter V8 while some baby lesbian spews sketchy beta from the deck, I would much rather *live*."

"We did take some screamers," Tamma admitted. "And my buddy, Dan, he pissed blood for like two weeks, but that might've just been our cycles syncing up."

"Fuck it," he said. "You can buy the pad. Just don't hurt yourself, tiny child."

On the third of January, Tamma went back to school. She walked two miles from Sierra's place to the park-and-ride, then she caught a city bus into town, and from town caught the school bus. She didn't know if he would be at class. But there he was when she came in. Stooped over his notebook, reviewing his homework, wearing one of his baseball shirts with the rough cotton pilling up. She hung her arms around him and he reached up to squeeze her elbow and Mrs. Mawry said, "Ms. Callahan, would you mind returning to your seat so class can begin?"

After school, she took the bus into town, from town caught the city bus to the park-and-ride, then walked two miles to Sierra's. When she let herself inside, she found Sierra asleep on the couch. River was in his pack-and-play and Samantha was at the cabinets with a chef's knife in one hand, clinging to the cupboard door. Tamma said very quietly "Op! Op! Op!" while hurrying across the room, trying to beam out: *You are safe! You are loved!* Then she carried Samantha into the next room, nuzzling and remonstrating in a whispering undertone, "Knives are not for babies!"

Tamma took River to his two-month appointment. River had diarrhea. His butt was covered in sores. When the pediatrician came in, she was beautiful and clean and slender in branded grey's anatomy scrubs. She ran marathons and wore expensive, deep-cushion ultramarathon shoes. She seated herself in a rustic children's chair. No one ever looked as clean as the pediatrician looked. The chair was tiny, and she sat with one leg hooked over the other to show her expensive socks. Tamma explained their concerns, that they had nine or ten poopy diapers a day, that they were worried that he was not tolerating the formula or perhaps had a yeast infection, that the poop was a concerning near-black, that the diaper rash was severe and they were trying to do everything they could and should they change formulas?

The doctor nodded, listening quietly.

"Should we be worried?" Tamma asked.

"Ehhhhhhhhh . . ." the pediatrician said. She smiled and shrugged and put her hands up in the air and waved them side to side. "Babies poop!" she said. "They poop *a lot*! Are the stools bloody?"

"No."

"Then I'm not worried!" She gestured conjuringly in the air. "You just have to be *a little more* disciplined with diaper cream."

Tamma hazarded, "I *feel* like we're pretty disciplined."

I mean, she thought. River's mom is a *nurse*. She applies barrier cream *professionally*.

"I know it sounds like a lot of work, but you have to use the diaper cream *every time*."

"I think we *do* use diaper cream every time?"

"Uh-huh. Well, I'm sure it will clear up!"

"I'm worried it's the formula. It just seems like a lot of diarrhea and it's not letting up and I'm incredibly scared about doing the right thing and he's already so vulnerable."

The pediatrician shook her head side to side and said, "Totally normal! Like I said: *Babies poop!*" Jazz hands. "Their skin is sensitive!" More jazz hands. "They're *babies*. If you can, breastfeed. Breastfeeding has all kinds of benefits! And among them is gut health. Breastfeeding *supports* the immune health of the gut. But since Sierra has made the decision not to breastfeed, I'm here to tell you that all those formulas are basically the same, by which I mean they're *fiiiiiiiiiiiine*."

Dismissive wave. Dismissive frowning facial expression. Tamma sat there, aware that if Dan were here, this whole conversation would go differently.

The pediatrician said, "What's happening is that your baby is *acclimating* to the formula. And if you change formulas in an attempt to help him, you will just interrupt your baby's *acclimation*, and he will just have gut health problems for that much longer! Parents sometimes—I mean. Sure. Okay. Some parents *report* that changing formulas helped. But *how do they know*? How do they know the issue didn't just *happen to clear up in time*—? *Have these parents done a double-blind study on changing formula*—?" The pediatrician chuckled, gestured in the air, broadly, with her outflung palm, like a Roman orator. "It's *never the formula*. The *formula* is fiiiiine."

"Okay," Tamma said, looking doubtfully down at River.

That night, Tamma sat at the table, having a bowl of cheerios for dinner, watching Paisley climb Iron Resolution on her phone. In the video, Paisley's mom stood below her, holding her hands up, spotting her daughter. The movie included cut scenes of Paisley talking to her mom about the process. Paisley's mom said, "When Paisley came to me with this idea, I said, 'Okay, dear,' and then I got on the phone with the guys from our gear shop and I was like, 'I would like to buy all of your bouldering pads, please.' And they were like 'Haha, but not *all* of them, right?' and I was like, 'No, all of them, please.'" In the video, Paisley laughed and shook her head, like *Oh, Mom!* And then said to the camera, "We had so many pads we had to drive out in a u-haul!" Tamma paused it with a fingertip and looked up. "Mom?" she said. Her mom was watching *IT* on VHS.

She said, "Yes, honey?"

Tamma said, "Mom, River has diaper rash. You don't . . . know any tricks do you?"

"Have you tried diaper cream?"

". . . Yes."

"So, what tricks would I have, honey?"

"Well, I don't think he's tolerating the formula."

"That's easy," Hyrum said. "Breastfeed. It's natural. It's safe. It's nature's way. Boom: fixed."

"Hyrum," Tamma said. "Hyrum, thank you for that, Hyrum. Hyrum, Sierra can't breastfeed, Hyrum, because she works twelve-hour shifts with one thirty-minute break that she never, in her whole entire working life, has actually gotten to take. So she can't, Hyrum."

"If they were my babies, I'd ahhhhh . . . find time," Hyrum said. "Just sayin'."

"Mom," Tamma said.

Her mom looked over.

"I just want to know if I'm doing everything right. He's so vulnerable."

"Vulnerable how?" Kendra said.

"Well, you know," Tamma said. "His head injury."

"Why don't *you* breastfeed?" Hyrum said.

"You're a dickwad," Tamma said.

"Oh, *I'm* a dickwad?"

"What do you mean, *his head injury*?" Kendra said.

"If I'm such a dickwad, how come I'm the only guy trying to come up with solutions for this kiddo? Huh? Tell me that? I'm just going to point out that Sierra has a lot of financial problems right now, and breastfeeding is *free*."

"Well we're worried about his milestones and—"

"His milestones?" Kendra said. "Listen to me. That kid is fine. Don't you *dare* tell me there's something wrong, because I'm telling you, there isn't. You may want to live in your own sick little world but I'm telling you my *truth*, what *I* believe, with all of *my heart*."

"I read that when women really care, they *can actually* breastfeed babies that aren't theirs, you know?"

"All right, Mom," Tamma said. "I hear you."

"Tell her ahhhhh . . . about the job," Hyrum said.

"And you're going to go get a job," Kendra said.

"What?" Tamma said.

"You're seventeen, you're an adult, it's time you contributed to this household," Kendra said. "You'll go out to target, to stater bros., to mcdonalds, I don't care where, and you'll get a job. And don't you ever tell me again that there is anything wrong with River. Don't you ever say it to me."

Four

Long, cold, quiet, empty days in the hospital with his old man. The water droplets in her endotracheal tube trembled. Sometimes, alarms would sound and Sophie would come clicking into the room and shut them off. But for desolate tracks of time the only sound was of the central air and the hiss and suction of the ventilator. It smelled mostly of coffee. Dan and his old man sometimes rode the elevator down to the cafeteria and ate burgers side by side at a wood-look laminate table. The burgers cost two fifty apiece and the fries seventy-five cents and when Dan asked if they could afford it, his old man just shrugged, not seeming to know. Sophie asked if they'd tried the tater tots and Dan said they had not, and Sophie said that the tater tots were her favorite. Later, Dan rode the elevator down to the cafeteria alone. It was empty save for the staff and a tech eating fries at a table while staring out into space. Dan brought the tray back up with him. He and his old man sat side by side, dredging tater tots through ketchup, and his old man looked at him and said, "They *are* good."

For more than a week, Dan was at the hospital all day, every day. Then, on the first day of spring semester, he drove back to school. He left a little before six to get to class by eight. After class he drove straight back. He did his homework. His old man read a book. At night Dan walked the quiet halls and passed a room where a machine went *puss-in-boots in puss-in-boots in puss-in-boots* very fast. The patient lay awake with all the lights on and watched TV very loud to cover the sound.

The hospital was kept cold. Night shift turned the lights down as dim as they would go. After nine, the rooms were dark save for the monitor screens. Sometimes a janitor rode through on a mop like a tractor mower, leaving the grime disordered into watercolorish streaks. Walking the halls, he found Sophie at the nurses' station, leaning against the counter, eating a plate of cold tater tots. She fetched up straight when she saw him and thumbed out her eyes, one and then the other. He asked her about the guy in E905. She said, "Oh, the artificial heart."

"It goes fast."

"A hundred and twenty-five beats per minute."

"Will he make it?"

"You want a tater tot?"

"Yes," he said, and leaned over and took one off the plate.

"What about my mom?"

She hung her head and stirred idly among the tots with one hand. She said, "I don't know."

"I don't feel like anybody is being honest with us."

She knocked the toe of her clog against the tiles. She said, "That's because nobody knows. The docs are soft-pedaling the idea that she's not gonna make it. I don't know why they do that. The family never gets it."

"Oh," he said. "That's what Dr. Vagy has been trying to communicate to us?"

She swallowed, nodded.

"Yeah. But they're not soft-pedaling it because of your feelings, they're soft-pedaling it because there's no knowing. No one wants to be the guy who says she's dead and then it turns out she's fine. It's just, she's very sick. And a lot of times when they're found down, like your mom, if they finally do wake up, they're not all there. They want you to take the hint and withdraw care."

"What are the odds?"

"Have another tater tot," she said, chewing.

Dan paced the halls at night. The artificial heart watched fox news. When the artificial heart went on walks, a nurse rolled the pump and a tech followed with a wheelchair.

His old man waited, day in and day out, a book in his lap, the pages folded back in his scarred mitt, looking at her. When she had a bowel movement and had to be changed, Dan rode the elevator down to the emergency room and left the hospital. He strolled out through the parking lot, took the stairs down into an overflow lot, walked across the cobbled strip to the sidewalk, then a seven-lane street, through another parking lot, up over a health strip, and through the smoked-glass doors into a bookstore. When he came inside, it was so carpeted, quiet, and air-conditioned that it did not feel like his life. He browsed down the aisles and was surprised to find her books there upon the shelves. He drew *Ephedra* forward, let it fall into his hand. He stood, holding it. A softcover novel, nine hundred pages. A bookseller about his age was coming down the aisle. She stopped and said, "If you're considering it, you should try it."

"Oh?" Dan said.

"That's the book that made me a reader," she said.

"Really?"

She nodded. "I think about it every day. She only has the two. I always keep them in stock. I don't know what happened to her. But there are some books you read that you never forget; they make you a book lover forever, even if you don't often find anything quite like it."

"Yes," Dan said. "I know that feeling."

He returned to the hospital empty-handed. He waited in silence, watching serosanguineous fluid moving down the lines, dripping into the graduated columns of the chest tube canister, the aqua-blue water seal tidaling up and down with the action of her ventilator.

"We should go to the bank," Dan said.

His old man looked up from some reverie, his eyebrows slowly rising, his eyes seeming to come into focus, his head turning on toward Dan.

"Before all this," Dan said, "I had a conversation with Mom. She wanted to move the funds into an account with my name on it so that the hospital wouldn't take it."

His old man nodded as if he understood. But Dan could tell he did not understand, had no attention for anything save Alexandra.

"And Dad."

"Yes, Danny?"

"I still need your help with FAFSA."

"Ah, Danny. I don't think I can help with that."

"But Dad, things like your social security number, income, tax returns. I don't know where any of that stuff is, or how to do any of that."

"Can this wait?" his old man said.

Dan was wringing his fist in his other hand. If I let it go, he thought, the hospital will take the money, we'll miss the application deadline, and I'll be free. It was Tuesday, January 10. Applications were due on the fifteenth and the first. All he had to do was stay quiet. And then drive out to Moab with Tamma, to seek his fortune in the great American West. The life he wanted. Right there.

They sat side by side and at last his old man nodded and hauled himself up and out of the chair. Dan had to ask one of the nurses where the bank branch was, and they went in together through the double doors, past the ATM, and in through another set of doors to the hushed interior. Then they waited at a manufactured wood desk. Dan looked at the printed-plastic veneer, thinking how his old man was a carpenter at a time and place where nothing was made of wood. Dan sat there, trying to think if he'd ever seen a real wooden table. They had one in their house. But anywhere else? He couldn't think. Everything was fake, everything plastic, everything was a printed-on veneer over glue and wood-pulp composite, nothing was real. When Dan looked up, he could see the bank's name on the wall, and beneath it, a huge banner showing mountains, for what reason Dan did not know. They were the Wasatch Mountains. Not mountains in California at all. He guessed he knew why that was. Those looked like "real" mountains. The desert rocks here looked like god had tried to make drop biscuits but it hadn't gone well, and so, embarrassed, he'd set the whole baking sheet aside in a corner. Then, 1.7 billion years later, people wandered through going, "What the fuck is all this?"

They did all the paperwork for Dan to open an account. Dan used his driver's license and SAT test results as proof of address. Then Lawrence had to initiate the wire transfer of thirteen thousand dollars from the savings account. The associate wore a clean white dress shirt and a black and pink collegiate-striped tie with a blue knit blazer. His thick brown hair was coifed up. He spoke with Lawrence and then typed and they spoke again. "Do you have your account number?" the associate asked, and Lawrence pursed his lips and blew out raggedly, shaking his head.

"That's okay, that's okay," the associate said. "Do you have a debit card? If it's attached to your account we can find it." And Lawrence lurched up from the seat and drew out his wallet, brown leather, overstuffed, enormous, glassy from use. He shucked it open and started sorting through it. "Jeepers," he said. "Let me see here. Jeepers. These things all look the same." Lawrence had not graduated high school, had never been so far east as Colorado, nor any farther north than Salt Lake City, had never flown in an airplane. Dan watched his old man and wondered how many problems had been put off not because they had been impossible but because they had been terrifying.

"This is it!" the associate said cheerfully, setting his fingers on the debit card and thumbing it up off the desktop. Then they walked back out and stood in the cold sunlight and his old man exhaled raggedly. He drove them back the hospital and Dan said, "I still need you to fill out the FAFSA, Dad," and Lawrence looked up at the glass tower of the hospital and shrugged. "That's about all the paperwork I can face today," he said. "And besides, Danny, I can't leave her. Just . . . fake my signature, or whatever. I don't have any doubts you can do it. You'll be fine. You always are." Then he reached into his pocket and drew out his wallet and opened it and passed Dan a hundred dollars. "For gas," he said.

Dan walked across the parking lot, the intersection, and another parking lot to the best buy and went inside. He picked out a scanner and carried it to the front and set it on the rubber belt and paid cash. Then the long walk back to the car and the two-hour drive home in the near-dark. He parked before his house. It looked small. A horny toad was waiting out on the porch.

Dan went inside. There were blue nitrile gloves and packaging on the concrete floor. He set his pack on the table. He opened the cabinet beneath the sink and took out the garbage can and collected all the trash. He swept up the sand. Then he put the can away.

He walked to the master bedroom and swung open the door and stood leaning in the jamb. It had a close smell. Blankets were tacked up over the windows. The sheets were yellow. The floor strewn with clothes. There was a plate of dried, half-eaten ramen noodles on the dresser. On the wall, there was a framed cutout from the *New York Times* profile, timed to the release of the second novel. A full-color portrait of Alexandra standing upon the desert in tailored jeans and ankle boots. Joshua trees behind and contrails above. She had once described walking down the aisle of her flight from LaGuardia to LAX, seeing people folding open their newspapers to that page. Dan walked to where it hung on the wall. *AMERICAN COLOSSUS*, it said. He stood with one hand clasped over the back of his neck, reading.

He had a memory then, of walking the brightly lit dairy aisle of the stater bros. with his mom. Alexandra had hefted down the organic gallon, knelt beside him, and said, "The cheap stuff is full of growth hormones and antibiotics, Danny. We don't need that." Kneeling beside him in her clean white tee and creakingly tight raw denim, her ankle boots lined with golden, black-spotted fur, she had seemed to be entertaining, for one bright, fluorescent-lighted moment, the dream that everything would be okay.

Dan backstepped to the bed and sat down. He felt sick. Then he leaned over, lifted up the bed skirts. Trampled, soiled sweatpants and dust. Straggled blond hair. A plate of buttered toast, long dead. Nothing else. He walked to the closet, slid open the door. Silk jackets. Western shirts. Japanese denim and European motorcycle jackets. Maybe fifty pairs of heels and ankle boots. Most of them never worn. Exquisite custom jobs in acrylic display boxes. At least a hundred thousand dollars in shoes, stored up against the tour of her forthcoming third novel.

He went into his room for a flashlight, took the keys off the hook by the door, walked barefoot through the graveled yard to the portable shed, unlocked it, and panned the flashlight over the grim interior. A farmhouse sink. Spare doors propped against the wall. Drills. Mason jars of screws and rusted nails. A table saw. Ghostly spider castings and widows' webs. Sawhorses. A half-eaten tarantula. A pink hula hoop. And several standard-duty white bankers boxes, unlabeled. He carried them one by one out into the yard, unlidded the first, and found a nest of fiberglass insulation and a trove of mouse shit. He went inside for yellow rubber dishwashing gloves, a trash can, and the shop-vac, tied a bandana over his face, and set to work vacuuming up insulation and scat, which went rattling away down the corrugated hose. He lifted the papers and carried them inside, stack by stack and folder by folder, setting them in wrinkled, piss-soaked piles on the concrete floor, rolling back the Navajo rug to make room. At the bottom of the first box he found a great stack of pages, good, weighty cotton stock, watermarked, rubber-banded together. He cut the rubber bands away and paged through the stack. Sand and crushed centipedes and his mother's own line annotations, as well as those he took to be the work of Kendra Callahan.

It was a great deal from Kendra. Whole paragraphs at the chapter ends, in minute, slanting cursive, alike to that of her daughter. Lots of dialogue penciled in margins. *No*, Kendra wrote. *You don't say sumbitch. That's wrong. People would think you were saying "some bitch." If you're listening they say sonofabitch. They just kind of swallow it.*

Deep in a box full of mouse shit, in a sealed legal envelope, he found last year's tax returns reporting a combined yearly income of $37,000. Deeper in, his own birth certificate and social security card. He worked on the floor, with the scanner and laptop beside him. The scanner ticked and whirred, the light passing side to side along the plastic edges.

He brewed coffee and sat at the counter, drinking, keying his essay into textedit. He pasted it into his online application. Then rose and walked to the coffee machine and poured himself another cup and walked back to the laptop and sat there drinking it. The work of more than a year. Every word considered.

He selected the title. "Better Bold Than Pretty." He deleted it. The route belonged to Jane Sasaki. To rename it was a lie. He typed *Fingerbang Princess*. He hit shift and tabbed down and down and down, selecting line after line, and deleted the entire essay. He considered it for two minutes, drumming his fingers. Then started typing. *My best friend and I came of age on a boulder problem called Fingerbang Princess, put up by Jane Sasaki in 1987. Now, my college counselor has advised me that the name is inappropriate and has suggested we retitle the route Girl Power. But the name isn't mine to change, and this raises a question of which is more important: integrity, or the appearance thereof.* He took a long draft of coffee. Then back to typing. The clock on the oven read 12:41. Then 1:00. Then 3:00. Then 4:50. He proofed it once and scrolled down to the bottom and submitted his application.

Then he rose and set his coffee cup down on the counter and walked across the room, past the couch, among the stacked, piss-soaked papers, and then out to the yard strewn with boxes and insulation. He stood beside the shop-vac, holding the back of his neck with one big hand. Don't worry, he was thinking. There's no way they let you into college with that personal statement. He spat and looked out at the dark. Scattered lights of other houses, cold bright stars, and the black silhouettes of joshua trees. Tamma thinks the world belongs to the strong, he was thinking. But that's not what he thought. His heart was breaking for all of them.

Five

Tamma sat in an office overlooking the checkout lanes. She had on a muscle shirt and a pair of Dan's jeans rolled at the waist and hems. The manager was making a study of Tamma, smiling very slightly over her desk, which was crowded with pictures, mugs of pens, and a grove of plastic joshua trees.

"What's with your hands?"

"Oh," Tamma said. "I tear them up climbing."

"Yeah?" She had a calm, relaxed, smiling manner. "Do you climb a lot?"

"I wouldn't say a lot, no."

"How often?"

"Well, I help watch my sister's kids, so I'm with them pretty often. I get like four hours on weekends, a few hours here and there before or after school. Plus I usually wake up around four thirty to hangboard. That's about it."

"That sounds like a lot to me."

"Well, it's my dream. To be a climber."

"A professional climber? People do that?"

"It's bigger in Europe. In the States, it's like ten people. Most folks have to do something like scrub toilets in a national park to support their habit."

"Oh, so not a viable career, then."

Tamma chewed on that. "Why wouldn't that be viable? I'd be thrilled to scrub toilets and climb."

The woman laughed. "You're not deterred by that?"

"Oh, no—you get one shot at life, right? You might as well have, like, *dreams*."

"And your dream is to scrub toilets so you can climb?"

"I mean . . . *yeah*," Tamma said, marveling at how great it sounded, when you put it like that.

From behind her desk, the manager smiled, clicking her pen open and closed. She said, "Okay, I'll give you a call, let you know."

Two days later, Tamma got the call. The after-school job left only scraps of time for climbing, but Tuesdays and Thursdays she had a study hall first period from 8:15 to 9:45 followed by a ten-minute "brunch" and five-minute "passing," so her first class didn't start until 10:00. She would set her alarm for 4:00, walk to the bus stop, and catch the 5:00 a.m. to the park entrance, slumped in her seat, her forehead against the seat ahead of her, texting in her lap.

> u up?
> hospital?
> well probs ur at the hospital
> and not on your computer
> which is good
> u should be there of course
> and ur reading or whatever
> anyway

CRUX

    i wus just wondering . . .
    like . . .
    you okay?
    you dont seem okay
    of course ur not
    that's dumb
    dumb
    sorry
    anyway. . . .
    im headed to town
    on the bus
    to try and climb
    boulders
    before class
    sending all my love
    your way
    so if you feel a great
    searching beam of
    sweaty climber girl love
    coming from out east
    like the eye of sauron
    but less homosexual
    . . . well
    equally homosexual
    a great beam of
    throbbingly
    homosexual
    climbergirl
    love
    thats me
    thinking that ur
    just the best guy

She would get off the bus and stroll backward along the boulevard with a sign that said INTERSECTION ROCK and a smile that said PLEASE DON'T RAPE ME, wearing ripped-up jeans and barn coat over tiger-striped tights and American flag bodysuit, composing the interviews she imagined she would do once she was famous.

> **CHRIS KALOUS [THE RUGGEDLY HANDSOME HOST OF *THE ENORMOCAST*]:** Have you always been a bonfire of sexual charisma, or is this something you've grown into?
>
> **TAMMA:** I've grown into it, Chris. In high school I was considered weird and awkward if you can believe that.
>
> **KALOUS:** Astonishing!
>
> **TAMMA:** I was wildly underfed and sleep deprived, with bad acne, a crooked jaw, ears that stood straight out from the sides of my face, and chipped teeth.
>
> **KALOUS:** I greatly admire a woman with chipped teeth. It gives me the feeling that she has been trying to get at the marrow of life, and life is a crusty moose femur laying out in the frozen tundra that is the endless, godless void of our meaningless existence, circling as it does a single supermassive black hole, swinging wide in its millennia-long trajectory that will finally take it down the galactic garbage disposal.
>
> **TAMMA:** Just so, Kalous.
>
> **KALOUS:** I also enjoy yoga pants.

If she did catch a ride, she'd dig out her stashed pad and climb boulders. The dude in the sprinter van had been right. The Princess had not been V4. Tamma crushed everything she touched, sprinting rock to rock, dragging the bouldering pad behind her with her kit piled atop it, filming herself with her phone propped in a shoe. It was not the time to tell Dan, but she was keeping the news in her back pocket for when he was ready. She'd climb, stash the pad, hitch out to school, go sprinting down the squeaky halls, open the door to Mr. Jeremiah saying, "You're late, Callahan," and Tamma would stand propped against the jamb, sweaty, sucking air, garbed in black-and-electric-pink bodysuit and cutoffs, holding her aching, swollen hands clamped in her armpits, nodding to acknowledge the general disaster that was her life.

The point of the bodysuit and tights, if you didn't know, was that they were awesome. The point of wearing skanky jeans over them was to keep her from ripping out the seat of her tights when she had to scoot around atop a boulder, looking for the way down.

In class, she propped her phone inside her textbook and rewatched videos of herself climbing, penning notes in her lab book. Nights, she turned the guidebook pages with chapped and bloody fingers. She'd set the book down on her chest, look over at the baby monitors, and miss Dan so desperately it felt like she might die. Everything she thought, everything that happened to her, it was all pent up inside, with no one to tell. There was a version of Tamma, in which Dan believed, that was competent, fearless, even a little psycho, but gifted. That was not what anyone else thought of her. Without him there, she felt lost, stupid, exhausted, and scared. It made those 4:00 a.m. wake-ups very hard. Her alarm would start cricketing and she'd thumb it off and think: *nope*. Then she'd roll out of bed and pull on her sweats anyway. Thinking: You can't let that blond slut Paisley Cuthers win.

Wednesdays and Thursdays she worked 5:00 p.m. till close. Her mom would pick her up and Tamma would spend the night at the trailer. Eating pizza around the couch one of those nights, Hyrum said, "Well, so, ahhhhh. How's the job going?"

"It's okay," Tamma said.

"Well, uh, here's the thing. I . . . uh . . . started ahhh . . . weighing bags coming in and going out of the house. And this ummmm . . . *someone* has been uh . . . stealing weed. It's twenty ounces last year that I know of, and uhhhhhh, some of it was ummmmm . . . pricy stuff. About five grand, all in. I'm willing to consider a family discount. But you know she's stealing out of Colin's college fund."

Tamma sat on the couch and everyone stared at her. Like a fucking idiot she could think of nothing to say except "Colin has a college fund?"

"Tamma?" Kendra said. "Is that true?"

"And uh . . . I thought that now she has a job she might be able to . . . ahh . . . pay some of that back."

"It's not true," Tamma said. "Think about it. *Twenty ounces*. How could I smoke *twenty ounces*."

"Not just uhhhh . . . weed but money. I had a hundred dollars go missing. Then the next day she turns up with this shiny new pad thingamabob."

"No, it's a lie," Tamma said, shaking her head.

"Let's see about that," Hyrum said, and rose to a stand.

Tamma vaulted over the back of the couch and Hyrum went sprinting after her. At the door to her room, he caught her and pushed her up against the wall, yelling, "Colin! Get her pants!" and Tamma said, "No! Colin! Don't!" and Colin swung her jeans up into the air by the leg and the film canister fell out and rolled across the floor. He stooped and picked it up and passed it to Hyrum, who popped it open, holding his hands out of Tamma's reach.

"Oooooh," he said. "This looks like *very fancy* weed for a girl who didn't have a job two weeks ago." He poured the buds from hand to hand. They were crusted in resin. "Looks *expensive*. It looks *familiar*. You think this is something out of Humboldt? Smells amazing—but does it have a, uhhhhh . . . strange smell, distinctive?—pretty skunky, wouldn't you say?—could it be the Sour Diesel I just got?"

Kendra clutched the doorframe, mouthing open and closed. Then staggered back down the hall, stiff-arming the wall. *"Mom!"* Tamma said, but Kendra didn't turn around. She ducked into her bedroom and Tamma, coming after her, stopped the door with her foot. Her mom swung the door back open. She was weeping. Her chest was splotchy with red blush. She pointed at Tamma.

"Don't you say *anything*," she said, and slammed the door. Tamma could hear her crying inside.

"Don't ever grow up to be like your big sis, kiddo," Hyrum said, and ruffled Colin's hair.

Weekends, Sierra would come home at eight in the morning, have a glass of wine, sleep until eleven, and drop Tamma off in the park at noon. Tamma would climb all day, then hike back out to the ranger station, and Sierra would say, "I can't keep coming into the park to pick you up, I don't get it; you hitch into the park, just hitch back," and Tamma, clambering over the consul into the backseat to look at the babies, would say, "Your mother can suck a dick, can't she? Because I hitch into the park, with families taking their kids to see joshua trees, but if I hitchhike on the 62, then I'll get raped to death and left in a rest stop dumpster! So she can suck a dick, can't she?" and at her voice,

River crinkled up his eyes and hung his mouth open in a jolly little smile.

They hadn't known if the smile would ever come and now it moved something deep inside her just to see it. Sierra said, "Don't flatter yourself, nobody's gonna rape some flat-chested tomboy." And Tamma, beaming down at River, said, "Excuse me, I am a *beacon* of sensuality. Any psychocreep would be lucky to have this." And Sierra said, "When are you gonna let go of this climbing thing? I don't get it. We're so overextended we're dying and you have to be out in the park all the time? For *what*? I hate to break it to you, Tams, but you *will never* be a climber, you have *zero chance*," and Tamma said, "Do you ever think that your husband is probably in Vegas, fucking some other girl like, *right now*, and forgetting all about you and your baggy puss and your ravaged tits and your mom jeans?" and her sister drove in silence for a long time and then said, "You're a real bitch, you know that?"

Lying in bed, holding the sleeping baby after a bad night, Tamma texted Dan.

---

u up

. . .

no i guess not
will you drive me to la?
not now obvi
later
wut are u thinking i wonder
r u ever there
looking at that ad on pornhub
that's all like
there are hot single moms
within 10 miles of ur location
and ur lying there

CRUX

> in bed thinking WHO
> like going thru
> all the neighbors in ur head
> what is it with those ads
> is it because single moms are
> trying to help their kids
> but are one ER visit
> away from homelessness???
> and people are just like
> i want to get my dick
> sucked by THAT
> is that why republicans
> hate healthcare
> do u think?
> passing each other in the halls
> of congress
> reminding each other
> hos suck harder
> when they're scared
> ooooop
> baby crying
> gotta go
> XOXOXO

At 4:30 a.m. she carried the baby into the kitchen. She got the bottle out from the fridge and set it under hot water and walked back and forth, from one side of the kitchen to the other, and then she carried the baby to the couch and sat, holding him, staring into the dark.

Six

His old man made a noise to himself, touched his thumb pad to his mouth, and said, "Well, darn, Danny. Well, shoot."

"What?"

"Well, I'll be. I've read this one before."

"Yeah?"

"Yeah, came to me just now. I thought—danged, all this stuff about euthanizing babies seems pretty familiar."

"You're halfway in."

"It's too bad, it was just getting good."

"I'll go on and get you another. Have any cash?"

"Sure, Danny," his old man said, hitching himself up and leaning to one side to get at his wallet.

Dan rose and let himself out. He took the elevator down to the emergency room, looking at his blanched and warped reflection standing in the brushed aluminum. He would've given anything, just then, to be walking out through the wash to the Princess Boulder with Tamma. He understood, in a distant and obscure way, that he needed to be reaching out to her, that he ought to be seeing her, that he had better be texting her back, but his grief, and something other than grief, this world-annihilating numbness to things, this profound sense of dislocation, it felt like something he had to carry around, everywhere he went, in every waking moment, and it took everything he had just to keep ahold of it.

There was a way that the biggest moves in climbing whited out all thought. A one-arm pull-up, or a big throw to a micro-edge, moves like this had a way of wringing everything else out of your brain, so that only single-minded effort remained. And the suffering was like that; every faculty, any capacity he had to notice, understand, think, or feel, was recruited into his enormous, mind-annihilating grief, if it was grief at all.

And he *knew*. He was *acutely aware* that it was stupid. He had walked out through the wash with Tamma however many times wondering why Alexandra could not just get the fuck out of bed, and how unfathomable it had seemed, how alien, how sure he had been that he would never, in his own life, come to such a pass. But now, on the other side of it, when he thought of reaching out to her, it seemed like so much work.

Sometimes, if he were on his laptop at the hospital, he might see her messages spooling in, and he would watch them come, and find that he didn't know what to say, didn't know where to start, couldn't imagine how he might respond.

> Dan!
> dude i miss you
> do you ever think
> what it would be like
> to make it with
> that sexy bratty english slut
> john oliver

> from the daily show
> u could just be like
> going to town on him
> and it would be like
> fucking all of america's problems
> but making love
> to all the possible solutions
> you know?
> and then
> he'd do a special
> like
> breaking news
> american girls:
> more nubile than u thought

Tamma, and Tamma's friendship, these were half-remembered things from some long ago dream, and he could recall that there had been a joy to them, and an importance, but he could not now make the joy and importance real to himself, not at all, and he could not attach any urgency to their recovery. It was all beyond him, and besides, he did not care, could not care, his suffering was all that was real and the work of suffering, the terrible labor of carrying it around, was all he could manage.

He let himself into the bookstore and walked down the mystery aisle, putting his finger to the spines and trying to remember what his old man had read. He took down another. Then he continued to the general fiction section, pulled one out, carried them both to the cash register. The cashier turned the novel over in her hand and frowned. She said, "Never heard of this one. Is it good?" She looked up at Dan and Dan could not find the wherewithal to answer, nor to form any expression. He just stood there until she rang it up and then he paid.

Dan and his old man sat side by side in the hospital room, reading. Dan went to school. He took notes, walked down hallways, dialed open his locker and stared inside with no memory of what he had come for nor any feeling that it mattered. Sat in class, the lecture sieving through his brain. He drove back, sat reading beside his old man. Sophie came clicking in for night shift, started checking her lines, and stole a look at the two men. To no one in particular she said, "Look at these two dorks," shaking her head. "Just look at these nerds."

Late into the night of the next day, Dan finished *Ephedra*. He closed it and set it down on the windowsill. His old man was asleep. Dan sat looking at it. If she could do this, he thought, then why hadn't she done it again?

Sometime later, maybe days, maybe weeks, Dan walked down Lifted Lorax Lane, on toward Tamma's place. The pink trailer, up on cinderblocks. He climbed the steps to a porch that had sunk away from the threshold. He wasn't thinking things through, didn't quite know why he was there; all that would take a sustained attention he couldn't muster; he was filled with a terrible aching that drowned out all thought. He knocked at the sliding glass door. He could see inside to where Hyrum was watching TV, Kendra at the table, smoking a cigarette. She got up and opened the door for him.

"Tamma's not here."

"I came to see you."

Kendra slid the door closed behind him, stirring the dust-caked vertical blinds. There was wall-to-wall orange shag carpeting, faded, and glinting with mica deep in the pile.

"How are you holding up?"

"I'm okay."

"It's fucked," Hyrum said. He swung a handgun around generously. "Ever ahhh . . . happens to me—" and he put the gun to his temple. "*Pow*," he said, blowing his lips out.

Dan dragged out the chair and sat. The table's printed veneer was curling up.

"What do you need, honey?"

"I came to ask you about Mom."

Her hand was upon her cigarette—turning it, ashing it, catching it between her knuckles and closing her fist so that she might examine her acrylics.

"What was she like?"

"Well, you know what she was like."

"Not really, no."

"What do you mean, no?"

"You were best friends."

"Well, she was like any pretty girl, I guess. She drank tequila and cheap whiskey. Enjoyed attention. Would wear her levi's so tight she had to lie on the bed and put her feet up in the air to pull them on. She liked to hang out with other pretty girls. She just had this one thing, this love, this thing she did, of writing little stories, which didn't seem to anyone like it meant anything at all, until it did."

Kendra crushed out her cigarette and picked a fresh one out of the pack and lit it. She drew on it and took it out of her mouth, stained with lipstick. She stared at it and then she issued the smoke in a tight plume. If someone, he thought, came to him in twenty years and asked what Tamma had been like, what would he say? More than that, he hoped. He was touching the table's edge. His hands were shaking. He set them down in his lap to still them, toying with Kendra's answer, turning it over in his mind. There was so much wrong, so many missed opportunities, so much casual selfishness in it that it beggared any reply. You read her novel, he thought. You helped her with it. You must have had some sense that the two of you were embarked upon something spectacular. In fact, I have seen, in your own handwriting, that you were aware of it. Where is that sensibility now? Was that, he thought, the best account she would give, of the woman who had been her closest friend? What did that mean, of your life, if it amounted to something like that story?

"Alexandra said you guys had some kind of fight."

"That's right."

"What about?"

"It was dumb. It was nothing."

"But what about?"

"I can hardly remember."

Dan could see a straight shot down the barrel of the kitchen, through the narrow hallway, past the bathroom, through the open door, and into Tamma and Colin's bedroom beyond. He could see Colin's unmade bed against the wall. Tamma's clothes on the floor. Tamma's bunk bed, which was lofted above her dresser and desk, was against the other wall and out of sight.

Kendra saw him looking. "That was Alex's room, you know? Before it was Tamma's."

He hadn't thought of that.

"Okay, okay," she said, tapping out her cigarette. "She came back from some trip and she was telling me about it; we were at the saloon;

everyone was there, we were having a party in her honor; welcome-home sort of thing. I asked her how you were, and she said, 'Oh you know, Daniel is the *perfect* child.'"

Kendra made a sour expression.

"I always hated the way she talked about you. Dan is the kindest. The gentlest. Dan puts away all his toys. Dan is *so sensitive*. Perfect Dan. Well, good for fucking her. Tamma was a shitweasel. I mean, the absolute fucking worst. So yeah. Great. I'm so happy for you, Alexandra, that Dan is a little angel."

"Uh-huh," Dan said. He touched again the curling-up veneer with shaking fingers. He did not know where to begin. Of course he had not been the kindest or gentlest anything. He had not put away all his toys. He had just been a kid. Alexandra was saying those things for reasons that had nothing to do with Dan. And Tamma, he was thinking. Tamma had also just been a kid. And here Kendra was, complaining about grievances a decade and more gone. Her daughter, however colicky or difficult, had grown up into the brightest, most talented, and most extraordinary young woman he had ever met, and Kendra had just no idea. What a thing, Dan thought. To be given this one life. For the troubled and brilliant friend with whom you had come of age to be lying, even now, in a hospital bed with a machine pumping her blood across an oxygenated mesh, and to find nothing to say about it. Imagine having such a daughter as Tamma, and all you thought about her, when you thought about her at all, was that she was a shitweasel, whatever that was. It was all just a heartbreaking waste.

"Fucking Alex," Kendra went on. "She'd be touring the world and I'd be turning tables at a scummy Mexican place. Then she'd come back and complain to me that the reception hadn't been kind enough at the bookstore in Whereverthefuck. The interviewer in Such-and-such-a-place hadn't read the book. The publicist wasn't behind her. Not enough people at the event. And so on. 'I'm so sorry,' I'd have to say, 'that your publicist has other clients, that just doesn't seem fair.' And then there we were, having beers out on the dance floor, and she said, 'This tour was hard, Kendra.' Kind of secretive, the way she said it. She even started to tear up. And I thought, Oh yeah? Was it, Alex? Her standing there in designer jeans and calvin klein tee. Telling me how rough she'd had it.

"You know, I used to wonder, with those T-shirts she wore, How is she keeping those suckers clean? What is it, bleach? You know. *How?* The woman has got a kid. And she's wearing a white tee every day. Well, she wasn't. Is the thing. She was throwing them away. A new T-shirt, every day. And she was so goddamn thin. Traveling the world, meeting people, drinking wine, eating quail at dinners with publishers, red-carpet parties, thousand-dollar sunglasses, and there I was. A single mom with three kids, getting fat, in my ancient, dirty trailer. My whole life was just *shit*, nothing turned out the way I wanted, and I said—I said, 'I could've been a writer if I'd had the chance.' I just wanted her to know I wasn't nothing. That she wasn't the only person who had dreams and things. And she turned and she gave me this *look*."

Dan watched her. Two friends, he thought, way out here in the desert; they have very little if not each other.

"That was the fight?" he said.

"That was the fight," she said, and drew on her cigarette.

He'd heard this same story from Alexandra. He'd just thought there had to be something more. He'd been hearing about this since he was a child. How her friend could not tolerate her success and turned against her. The great betrayal of Alexandra's life. Kendra was letting the cigarette smolder, studying the tweedy ash.

"Stupid," Kendra said.

You could just smell her self-hatred. You could very nearly taste it in the air. She gave a bitter little chuckle, shook her head. This was a woman of enormous personal charisma, but though she may not have been willing to own it, her rage and hostility were real; they were palpable to everyone around her. They had never been the flickering annoyances she was now making them out to be, and there had been a reason Alexandra had given her a look. You wanted a chance, he thought. Look around. You had one of the greatest literary minds of a generation living in your spare bedroom. What more chance did you want than that? Dan thought Kendra had been hard done by the world. But she was also an abusive and self-destructive asshole, who had been taking her rage and frustration out on Tamma for as long as Dan could remember. You had to see in Kendra the chance at another life. Just to be here, in her presence, was to feel her charm, her intelligence, her enormous promise. No person was all one thing, and in Kendra, you could see it both ways. You could see that somewhere or other, two paths had diverged.

He spent the night alone at his house, lying atop the covers. Turning things over in his mind. Fear ruins people, he thought. It just rots them. In the morning, he drove west, walked the parking lot, rode the elevator up, and exited into a waiting room with the recessed overhead lights laying glary archipelagos upon the tile. He stood at the window and looked out upon the soapy wastewater dawn backing up out of the eastern horizon, spilling across the world, and the world was highways and parking lots and strip malls as far as the eye could see.

Dan walked down hospital corridors, carrying a homemade picnic breakfast past rooms glassed in like museum exhibits. He and Lawrence ate breakfast burritos on their laps, lifting and setting down their coffee cups on the windowsill like a conversation. Long clear plastic tubes fell from bandages on her sunken flanks. Those tubes were tunneled up under her ribs to her heart. They were big as garden hoses. Her hands were secured with restraints about the wrists, the fingers curling up, lavender, edematous. Within the depths of her face there showed tangled dark piping like the leavings of bacon in the hardening white grease. There was a low thrum of the ECMO machine pushing blood across an oxygenated membrane, and the hiss and suction of the ventilator, to which noise the waxen reproduction of her lifted and sank.

He sat there long after his old man had returned to reading and long after his old man fell asleep. The window above her bed showed only the reflection of the window behind him, which looked back onto a lighted, white-walled hallway where the nurses trafficked back and forth beside the darkened room.

Dan was playing it over and over in his mind. He was trying to understand. Alexandra is back from some tour abroad for her second book. It is the fall of what? Of 2002, perhaps. Dan and Tamma are seven or eight years old. It would've been a few years after Tamma's dad broke her jaw. So Kendra is a single mom, living in a trailer with three kids, like she said. Perhaps Sierra is watching Tamma and Colin so that Kendra can be out for the night.

Kendra stands there and says, "I could've been a writer if I'd had the chance." Alexandra says, "Oh, Kendra, of course you could've!" And Kendra says, "Who am I kidding? Of course I couldn't."

That's not what happened. But why not? Dan went searching inside of himself for an answer.

Her best friend since high school, the woman who took her in when her parents disowned her, the slutty best friend who made line notes on the manuscript when Alexandra was a nobody, Kendra says, "I could've been a writer if I'd had the chance." And Alexandra gives her this *look*.

Dan was thinking it was like the exit-move crux on the Princess Boulder.

Kendra says, "I could've been a writer if I'd had the chance." And there is this moment where Alexandra can admit to her friend that she is afraid, that she herself fears that she is not a writer, where she can speak out loud all the things that are eating her from the inside out.

They are alike in this. Kendra too is full of rage at the smallness of her life. Full of rage that though she is as bright, as talented, as insightful as her best friend, success has come to one of them and not the other. Full of rage that her husband has broken her daughter's jaw. Full of rage at Tamma, because if not for Tamma, Patrick might still be around. The success that was his, later on, might have been Kendra's. But that was not how things went, and it was all because of Tamma. But Kendra is too beautiful to be full of rage. That is not a girl who can be angry, because an angry girl will never have the things Kendra wants, and so it is not that Kendra is angry. It is that Tamma is a shit-weasel. It is not that Kendra is angry. It is that Alexandra cannot accept her. And this anger, it's really fear. It's fear all the way down. It is a blank terror at the life that stretches before her. And this thing she says, "I could've been a writer if I'd had the chance," is a bid for comfort. Tell me I am not nothing, she is saying. Tell me I am worthwhile.

Tell me I can do this. Tell me there is some chance in all this hopeless hell. Tell me I am not just fucking doomed. Tell me my life isn't useless, the way it feels useless to me, every day. Tell me I have some dignity left. Tell me that we can still be friends. Tell me that I am not alone.

Kendra says, "I could've been a writer if I'd had the chance." And Alexandra, the Mojave-born Hemingway, the rising star of American literature, stands and looks at this chubby, sweating, angry diner waitress in knockoff walmart jeans, dirty sneakers, and wifebeater and sees what—a vision of herself, from which she recoils?

Kendra says, "I could've been a writer if I'd had the chance," and with this one word, *chance*, she elides all the work that Alexandra has done, elides those thousands of nights spent penning stories into the early morning, elides those marathon sessions typing in a windswept campsite after work, drinking black coffee and cheap whiskey, working by the light of a coleman lantern; with this one word, *chance*, Kendra seems to suggest that Alexandra does not deserve what she has, and because this is exactly what Alexandra fears to be true, she cannot speak, she can find no generosity, instead, all she can do is stand there, on the dance floor of the saloon, and give her closest friend in the world *this look*, a look of total contempt, a look that is really masked and stifled terror, a look that says, *I would rather be totally alone than extend any generosity to you, in this moment, when I myself am so scared and imperiled.*

Dan guessed that if you could talk to Alexandra, if you could ask her about it, there would be no contingency at all. Her life was made up of things she had to do, and things she could not do, and things done to her. No such cruxes were legible as moments in which you could've gone either way. But was that how things were? Were there choices that you made, or was your life just a doom you carried out? Could she have dredged herself for the courage to take that desperate step-out into an insecure friendship?

Kendra stands there, on the dance floor of the saloon, holding a beer, and she says, "I could've been a writer if I'd had the chance." And Alexandra reaches out and touches her friend's elbow and says, "Of course you could've! This shit is wild. I don't deserve any of this, Kendra! What is this? What am I doing? I'm touring the world! Why—I'm just a diner waitress from Buttfuck Nowhere, California. Of *course* you could've done it. I think you'd be a *great* writer. A better one than me—I live in fucking terror that I can't get the third book done, because I'm not the real thing!" And Kendra says, "Oh, Alex! Of course you'll get the third one done." And what comes next, they face together.

Lawrence is at work building box stores in Palm Springs. But Alex, just back from her tour, is not alone. It's the two of them, smoking cigarettes around the kitchen island, just like old times, Alexandra talking, gesturing with the hand that holds her cigarette, a story taking shape, the way two climbers might break down a problem together. And yet, Alexandra is tired. She has trouble breathing. And Kendra goes, "You know what, girl? I don't like this. We're taking you to the ER." They find the failing valve months earlier. And when Alexandra is in the ICU, it isn't just Daniel and Lawrence driving out on Friday nights after work, the way it was the first time, when Dan was small. Alexandra isn't alone. It's Kendra and Tamma and Sierra and Colin and Kendra's parade of deadbeat boyfriends. Alexandra says, "Kendra, they have me stitched up like a spiral notebook. I'm afraid my heart is going to fall out into my lap," and Kendra says, "So what? Having your heart fall out of your chest into your lap should be old hat for a novelist," and Alexandra lies in bed, stifling her laughter, shaking her head in mock rage. Alexandra is released from the hospital, and Kendra asks if she is writing again, and Alexandra says that she is. "It's all about," she says, "this high school girl who can't stop giving guys HJs on the bus to school. What's wrong with this girl?" And Kendra says, "Maybe her heart fell out of her chest into somebody else's lap, but she can't remember who, and now she's looking all over for it," and they both laugh and Kendra goes to the fridge to get herself a beer. Alexandra would've stepped out into darkness and it would've been like the darkness held; the whole world would've felt a little less lonely.

But that's not what happened.

In Alexandra's hospital room, the monitors showed their wave forms and when the waves reached the edge of the monitor they refreshed and the waves started again. Beside the lines, numbers showed the moving averages. A brassy shine came from the streetlights. It lay upon the drop ceiling, upon the floor tiles, the aluminum piping of the chair legs, and scant traces of it touched Alexandra herself. He waited, watching, in the window across from himself, the reflection of the nurses going up and down the lighted hallway behind him. Alexandra lay, breathing, slowly, terribly, mechanically through the plastic endotracheal tube. And for the first time, he saw her eye open: slowly, unlidding absent any other expression. Lawrence asleep beside him. Dan put his hand on his old man's knee, but Lawrence did not wake. *Mom!* he wanted to say, but kept quiet, choking it back, waiting to see what came, full of hope. She will come back to us, he thought. She will see that we love her and she will come back to us and everything will be all right.

Seven

Tamma woke and lifted her phone to see the time and lay back, holding it clasped in one hand to thumb off the alarm when it should start. She thought about all her mistakes and everything she'd done wrong. She thought about how much easier it would be if she just gave up. She thought of the way everyone hated her for what she wanted. Mostly, she thought about how scared she was to do this alone.

She'd texted Dan the day before, looking for a ride. For once, he'd answered.

> hey buddy
> how you holding up

> Alex is awake!
> Opened her eyes
> 3 days ago
> And has been
> Slowly
> Coming back

> she is?
> screaming
> screaming

CRUX

> screaming
> that's fantastic!!!

I think she's going
To make it!!!

> HUZZAH!
> callooh callay
> oh frabjous day
> oh dan!
> im so happy for you
> and for her
> its been a long road

I think this
Is going to turn things
Around.
She will come home
And it'll be a new chance!

> me too buddy
> sending love

Did you need anything

She'd stared at those words. *Did you need anything?* She'd gotten up and walked back and forth in Sierra's living room. Yes, she wanted to scream. Yes, I need *you*, you dickhole! Come to the comp. Better yet—compete! But she'd hunkered down, with her head on her knees, miserably typing:

> no no! im great!
> say hi to alex for me
> xoxo

XOXOX

The comp was today, in Los Angeles. Isolation opened at 7:30. It was 3:30 a.m. now. She lay tightening and relaxing her fingers, so heavy with callus they felt shellacked. If she didn't go, she could say, all her life, that it had been impossible.

She sat up. Groped around in her dirty clothes for her bag and picked it up. Found her tights and stepped into them. Found her jeans, stepped into them, reached deep inside the leg and drew out wadded underwear. Shrugged into a hoodie and barn coat. Snugged down a black beanie. Reached back and pulled her hair from out the neck of the hoodie. She went into the kitchen, uncapped a sharpie, wrote her sister a note.

Sis—

Gone climbing as discussed! Kiss the kiddos for me.
Give life the BIG DICK! Be back tonight or tomorrow.

Love,

T

Then she went out the front door and struck north by moonlight, following the dusty silver of the dirt lane. Every two hundred yards she would stop, prop herself on her knees, and dig for the strength to keep going. She tried to spit and could not. Hit the highway and started west, following the white line. A car crested the rise and she put out her thumb, mustering the best smile she could, the brights firing up the desert around her.

She walked almost an hour, nearly hoping no one would come. Then she heard a distant car and turned and walked backward, thinking,

Look, here comes the guy who's gonna drive me out to Nowhere, Arizona, and zip-tie me to his bumper. Headlights crested a rise to the east and swept down, picking up the brush and illuminating the blacktop. It pulled onto the shoulder, a VW bug. Tamma walked on toward it, shading her eyes, and the lights did not cut. She came around the side and the window rolled down and she stared in. It was a priest in black robes with clerical collar, lit by the dash lights.

"Hello, miss," he said.

Tamma looked back down the long, dark highway ahead of her and then leaned into the passenger-side window. They spoke and she got in.

"I'm Tamma," she said.

"Father McNamara."

"Nice to meet you, Father. Do I call you that? I don't know that I've ever met a Catholic before. I don't know what the protocol is. You're Catholic, right—that's what the litt—the white—the bow tie—are you Catholic?"

"Yes, of course, Tamara." He was calling her Tamara because he hadn't anticipated that she would be named after an invasive roadside weed.

"Rad," Tamma said.

"Yes," he said. "It is rad."

Father McNamara dropped her off among warehouses and broad empty roads in the pale dawn. She continued on toward the gym, found the parking lot already full, and went around back, where they had a card table set up. She had to surrender her cell phone. She wrote her name on painter's tape and stuck it to the back of the case. Then she put her phone into the box and saw others that had collected dozens of tape strips from comps all over the country.

Because it was onsight style, all the competitors waited in isolation so they could not preview the problems. She was given bib #69, and a volunteer took her back into a dusty room set behind the bouldering walls. The steel scaffolding was exposed and bolted to the cantilevered plywood panels. The backs of the panels were bare plywood studded with T-nuts. You could see daylight pinpointed through the unused sleeves. Everything was covered in chalk dust. One wall was taken up with staff lockers. Crates were stacked in the corner, filled with climbing holds. Chalk dust had settled above the lockers like snow. It was razored up on the struts and lay thick on the girders. Other girls were sitting in chairs, some of them listening to music, some not, most with their kit piled about their chair legs. There was a printout listing the athletes, their hometowns, and their ranks. In qualifiers, athletes went out in a randomized order. There were ninety women and one hundred men. She found her name. *Tamarisk Callahan.* She'd listed her hometown as 73 Coyotes, California, as a joke. She was unranked. There was a matted area for stretching, a power rack set up in the corner, and a bouldering area for warming up. All of it was curtained off from the rest of the gym and volunteers stood at the doors.

Tamma sat eating her breakfast of dry honey nut cheerios. Competitors climbed on alternating rotations—that is, you climbed women's #1, rested for four minutes, then climbed women's #2 while the next competitor started on #1. Tamma was the sixty-ninth climber, so it would take almost five hours for her turn to come. She waited in her plastic chair, her whole brain locked in a single thought that sparked and sparked again, coming in so crackling-hot that it hurt each time: *I can't do it. I can't do this alone.* Over and over again. Shaking so badly she kept dropping cheerios.

All the other girls looked beautiful, strong, and clean. In their brand-new tights, their volleyball shorts and racerback tanks, their aggressively sculpted comp shoes, they looked like they belonged here. Their skin was clear. Their hair glossy. Their teeth straight, or else in braces. Among them, Tamma had a crushing sense of unbelonging, with her acne-covered face, her snaggleteeth, her greasy hair, her ragged levi's over a trashy American flag leotard, a blown-out pair of TC pros on the floor beside her.

The girl sitting across from Tamma was filing her finger pads. She had a pink tank top over a black racerback sports bra. What the hell muscle is that in her arm, Tamma was thinking. Tamma didn't even have that muscle. On this chick, it was enormous, and tensed into view as she passed the emery board back and forth. Then, with a queasy, hair-raising, icewater-in-her-guts feeling, it dawned on Tamma: That was Paisley Cuthers. Sitting in a chair. Right across from her. On screen, she mostly looked pretty. But in person, she was enormous, almost a foot taller than Tamma: a blond, bone-crushing surfer chick with eight-pack abs.

Tamma's heart was hammering. She kept looking down at her own ravaged hands, with gobies and broken calluses shelving away in layers, her chipped nails and dying cuticles, and then up at Paisley, thinking, Look at this bitch. Just *look* at her. Everything that you have fought for, tooth and nail, risking your life, has been handed to her. She didn't fight for any of this, not like you did, not crawling out of windows, not taking screamers to the deck. Must be nice, to be born to it, to have a coach and a home gym. Look at her there in her hundred-and-twenty-dollar leggings and ninety-dollar sports bra, just look at her. That is the girl you have come here to disprove. You have come here to show that the American dream is still alive, that scraping and bootstrapping matter, that money alone cannot buy access to the highest echelons of this sport. And that is why you are going to beat her. Because you want it more than she does. Because you have grit.

Tamma said, "I like your nail polish."

Paisley looked up, took off her headphones, said, "What?"

"Nothing, nothing, sorry."

"No, that's okay. What did you say, I missed it."

"I said, I like your nail polish."

"Oh my gosh, thanks!" she said. "You know, it's what made me want to be a climber."

"What is?"

"Well, I went to a birthday party at a climbing gym when I was like seven and Sasha DiGiulian was there—"

"That's *crazy*!" Tamma said. "I would die! She's a *goddess*. You know, I saw Tommy Caldwell once and I kissed his hand."

"You did what?"

"He was in safeway, just walking around with a basket, like they just let TOMMY CALDWELL buy his own groceries, right? I was there getting milk and I was like: Oh my god. So I walk up to him. And I am like. Mr. Caldwell, sir. And he looks at me. And I like, I'm all, 'I've always wanted to'—but I was hyperventilating and sort of, like, *fanning* myself with one hand, all like, 'I've always wanted to'— but I ran out of breath, like, '*Heeeeeeeeeze*,' and he smiled at me, and held out his hand, you know, to shake, and instead, I took it and knelt on the floor and kissed it. Like he was the pope. And then I was so embarrassed I just put my gallon in the crook of my arm like a football and made my break for the doors. I could've died from embarrassment. I had to go back later and pay for it."

"That's amazing!" Paisley said. "Well, when I saw Sasha, I was like: Oh my god. She's a girl. You know. Like a *girl*. Like, she's got a cute top and pink nail polish and perfect skin and I was like, Wuuuuuuut, girls can be rad? Like, you don't have be some hobo, living in a cave, eating dog food with John Long. You can be like, *a girl*. You know, like a *freshly showered girl*! Like a *girly* girl, and be *sweet* and *kind* and do your hair and your nails and dress cute and still *crush*! Like, I was like, *Chicks can be chicks, and still be STRONG!*"

"That's amazing!" Tamma said. "I'm the opposite!"

"You're the opposite?"

"Like, I want to be living in a cave, taking tequila shots out of Dean Fidelman's belly button! And John Long—his book *Climbing Anchors* is my bible! I climbed his route Dung Fu on the Hemingway Wall. Oh! And I climbed his route Bird of Fire! And yeah of course Bird of Fire is 'better' than Dung Fu but, somehow, it's *too good*. It's too *perfect* to be *great*, you know: I love it, I think of it every night before I go to bed, but it has no edge to it, every *great* trad route should have something that would make your mom go, 'Umm—?'; On Bird of Fire there's just *fundamentally* not enough rat shit to be worth your time. It's like dating a girl who is flawless and successful and doesn't have emotional problems. *Sure*, in theory, that's better than dating a girl *with* emotional problems but: *Is it really???*"

"*Haha* what?"

"Right? Like Bird of Fire is flawless climbing on bulletproof patina edges going to an overhanging hand crack with gear never below your waist, so cool, if you *like* that sort of thing, but I'm here to grunge my way up a terrifying, awkward dihedral-chimney-thing full of bat shit!"

"*You are?*"

"*Oh yeah!* Dung Fu changed my life! It's like: *Wake up and smell the hantavirus, BITCHES!* And so I was all like: I want to shake the man's hand, who climbed it first; I want to play saxophone duets with him out in the desert late at night while on peyote, wearing tiny red track shorts and gym socks pulled *all the way up*; I want to hear his tales; I want to climb hard and dangerous routes that make you shit your pants! I want to live in caves and eat dog food!"

"You *do?*"

"Not *voluntarily*," Tamma said. "That would be weird! No—I want to be *made* to eat dog food because I am broke and starving and *desperate!*"

"Oh my god! *Who are you?*"

"I'm Tamma! And I love you! I follow you on youtube! And on instagram! I've seen all your videos! You're my HERO!" Tamma said, all in a rush, and if a yawning chasm to hell had broken open in the gym floor, just then, Tamma would've unhesitatingly taken the plunge down into eternal damnation just to escape the shame.

"So you trad climb?" Paisley said. "You climbed Hemingway Wall? That's, like, a, like, gnarly trad area with routes like Smashing Poodles and White Lightning, right?"

"No such route," Tamma said. "You're thinking of Poodles Are People Too."

"I made up a route called *Smashing Poodles?*"

"There's the Poodle Smasher, which is in the Wonderland. And there's Such a Poodle, Poodlesby, Scary Poodles, Tails of Poodles, Astropoodle, A Farewell to Poodles, For Whom the Poodle Tolls, the Old Man and the Poodle, Poodle-Oids from the Deep, Poodle in Shining Armor, Poodle Jive, and Poodle Skirt, but I don't know of a Smashing Poodles."

"*Who are you?*" Paisley said.

"Who are *you?*" Tamma said. "What climber doesn't know Hemingway Wall?"

"I've never climbed outside!"

"You *have*! You sent Iron Resolution!"

"*How did you know that?* Yeah, well, okay—I've never climbed on gear. I'd be too afraid! But you're, like, a *real* climber. You have a rack of cams and all that?"

"That I found in the trash," Tamma agreed. "And not cams, because cams are expensive. I only have chocks—you know, hexes and nuts. And no micros, no peanuts, nothing like that. Only old-school stuff. Which is okay because mostly in Josh you don't need micros, and the rock is too coarse for them anyway, but actually that route you were thinking about, Poodles Are People Too, is rather sporty without small gear."

"I'm sorry—that you found in the *trash?*"

"Yes!"

"*Whaaaaat?*" Paisley wailed. "That sounds sooooo dangerous!"

"It is!"

"No, I mean, that sounds *dangerous*. Like, not, funny haha dangerous. Like, *literally* dangerous!"

"No: yeah! *Literally!*"

"Like, I'm not kidding!"

"Like: I'm not either!" Tamma said. "*Literally* the rope has a core-shot in it."

"No!"

"No, yeah! It does! The rope is *suuuuuuper* coreshot."

"You can't climb on a coreshot rope!"

"Well we make sure the leader climbs on the un-coreshot side. Then the person who follows tries really hard not to fall."

"That's not safe!"

"No it's not!"

"LIKE: OH EM GEE! BUY ANOTHER ROPE!"

"I can't!" Tamma said.

"No, like, *Haha! you* 'can't'! *Haha!* but literally *you could die*—lit-er-al-ly DIE! So just, like: *Buy another rope!*"

"It's like: I *can't* though."

"But like, sure you 'can't' but just, like, *spend the money.*"

"I don't have the money!"

"Haha but *seriously.*"

"*No seriously!*" Tamma said.

"But just like, don't be cheap or whatever. Spend the two hundred dollars."

"I'm not being cheap! *I don't have the money,*" Tamma said. "I stole a hundred dollars from underneath my mom's bed one time, to buy a bouldering pad? But my mom's boyfriend noticed it was missing and he outed me to my mom for stealing like hella weed from him because he's a drug dealer, and actually, I smoke but *not that much*, not the twenty ounces or whatever he said I stole, so I figure it was my brother actually who stole most of it, but they love him, and they blame me for everything, and I'm worried that if he catches me stealing again he'll blackmail me for creepy sex or something, so I don't feel like I should risk it, or I'm gonna end up as one of those pornhub videos called like 'Stealing Whore Stepdaughter Blackmailed for Hard Anal Fucking' which, obviously . . . I've never seen, but I've, you know . . . heard about, from guys at school, or whatever."

"What? I'm just—wait!—*what?*"

"I know, right!"

"So, like," Paisley said, "why are you here? If you're like some crusty trad climber, who's, like, getting gear out of the trash and climbing on, like, dangerous, like, coreshot ropes, and eating dog food with John Long and trying not to be blackmailed for I-don't-even-want-to-say-what? Like, if you don't even have money to buy a rope?"

"I love comp climbing! I spent all my birthday money to get into this comp! I've always wanted to try! I've watched every comp I can find! I study Akiyo Noguchi like her movements hold the secrets of the universe! I know every comp boulder she's ever been filmed climbing move by move! It's my dream! It's like the biggest dream of my life to be here and podium and get sponsored and change my life! Okay, not my biggest dream because my biggest dream is to send Cobra Crack and in the one-finger undercling lockoff crux, I want to stop, light a spliff, blow out an ENORMOUS plume of smoke, look directly into the camera, and say, 'The jams are sooooooo good, *dude*,' and then SEND, still, this is *a* dream. I get up at four a.m. to get my hangboard workouts in! But I'm not gonna win! I suck and there isn't a gym near me and I want it but I'm noooooo good! Like I love it and I want to do it but I'm just totally fucking doomed!"

"No!"

"Yeah: No! Yeah! I'm the weakest girl here. I've never climbed in a gym!"

"What! But Tamma, that's insane! You couldn't just . . . come to the gym . . . and try some V6s with a girlfriend, or whatever?"

"No, yeah! That would've been a better idea! But it's really hard for me to get out here. And I've watched like *lots* of youtube videos of people comp climbing, so I feel like I'll be okay?"

"I can't tell if you're for serious? Like, I've seen some really inexperienced climbers sign up. There'd be girls who came to open nationals but only climbed like, V4—which, right, hahaha!—and they'd like, almost die on lead climbs, or whatever? I feel like most people know that just watching youtube videos is *not* preparation for a national cup, but I don't know if you know that?"

"Oh no! Paisley! That's me! I'm the girl who only climbs, like, V4! Though, one time I worked a V6 with a like, pretty, like, *stout* V7/V8 crux."

"Nooooo, Tamma! I'm so scared for you!"

"I told you! I'm just some dipshit who is gonna lose like, so hard!"

"Oh my god, now that I know who you are, I want you to win."

"I want you to win!" Tamma said. "You're so freaking strong! You're so kind! You're so beautiful! You're my hero!"

"I just met you and you're my hero!" Paisley said. "You deserve it more than I do! Like, I want your dreams to come true. Like: You're amazing!"

"You're a goddess!" Tamma said.

"No, you're a goddess!" Paisley said. "Like: very unsafe! But also: a goddess. And uh . . . this is awkward. But I have to go warm up now!"

"Okay!" Tamma screamed.

"Okay!" Paisley screamed back. She rose and dashed away into the bouldering area.

Eight

Hours into qualifiers it started to get quiet out there. Most of the spectators were parents and left after their children completed the rotation. She could hear the emcee calling for support. She got up, went to the bathroom, sat on the toilet, sweating, hot all over, knocking her knees together, filled with a sense of impending doom.

After a while she went into the bouldering area just to distract herself. A room bigger than Tamma's house was paneled in fifteen-foot-high spray-textured plywood walls gridded with plastic climbing holds. A few girls were climbing. Another was sitting on a bench in the middle of the room, her hands overturned in her lap. Tamma started just doing easy traverses on the wall to warm up. After watching thousands of hours of climbers on artificial walls, she had expected it to feel natural, but the texture of the holds, and the shape of them, took a lot of getting used to. The first thing she noticed was that the holds were better, but the routes were steeper. Isolation thinned out around her. More and more athletes were called out through the curtained doorway, onto the mats.

At last, a volunteer came to the door and said, "Tamma Callahan?

Eight minutes." Tamma picked her chalk bag off the bench and followed out to a chair beside the curtained doorway that led out onto the mats. The volunteer squatted next to her and explained what would happen next. Then she said, "Hey. You're gonna be fine."

They waited for the rotation to end, then Tamma walked out through the curtained doorway and along the mats to where a sympathetic-looking volunteer pointed her down into another folding chair, facing away from the wall. There, Tamma waited, making a deliberate, moment-by-moment effort not to throw up. Then the buzzer sounded and the emcee said, "Tamarisk Callahan, please welcome her from the town of 73 Coyotes!" and Tamma turned around and got her first look.

The competition wall spanned one side of the gym, styled with swirled bands of gray and blue. Beneath the wall were gymnastic mats and just beyond the mats were the judges and brushers. Behind the judges, a dozen onlookers. The route was twenty degrees overhanging, going on big orange slopers. She stood, taking her time, reading the route, miming each movement with her hands, letting it play in her imagination.

The boulders were scored on tops and zones. The zone was a single hold, halfway through, indicated with a gray plaque. Number of tops determined scoring. Ties were settled by zones, then attempts.

She dipped her hands in chalk, slapped them off on the butt of her jeans, and mounted up on the climb. Two hands on an angling fin. Feet on a sloping rail. Then boost up and right, snag an orange volume and sidepull it, go up left and sidepull a second volume—like bear-hugging your way up a fridge. She shuffled up, then she slung for a pinch, high up and dead on between the volumes. She hit it with fingers atop and thumb below, like pinching a copy of *War and Peace*. That was the zone.

The next move was out right—a far away, barely there crimp rail. Tamma bid for it—and stuck it. The next move was to breast it and then reach right for the finish, which was a round sloper like half a basketball. But there were no footholds—so she had to smear on the wall, her feet pedaling out beneath her, leaving black streaks of rubber.

She peeled off in exhaustion and then sat on her shins, chalking her hands, replaying the route in her mind. There seemed no way around it. It was a pull-up off a crimp. She threw herself at the route twice more. Then the buzzer sounded, signaling that she had a minute left and she rose and tried again, straining with everything she had, gritting her teeth, making little noises of effort, her feet skittering out from underneath her, pulling up to ninety degrees, reaching out with one desperate hand. She touched the finish hold. She had a hand on it, but she could not get her fingers atop it. She gave it everything she had and the final buzzer sounded and she pitched down to the mats, defeated.

She walked to women's #2 and sat in the folding chair, facing away from the wall. Then looked over at the volunteer beside her and said, "I have to go to the bathroom." They walked halfway there and then Tamma shucked off her shoes, ran barefoot down the tiled hallway, kicked open a stall, leaned over the toilet, and puked. She fetched hard against the beige aluminum divider, gacking up honey nut cheerios. The volunteer came in behind her.

"Are you okay?" she said.

"I'm great!" Tamma said, and then leaned forward and choked up bile. Then she rose. Spat. Got her feet under herself. Walked to the sink, running the faucet and raking puke out of her hair.

She dried her hands, then walked back beside the volunteer and sat down. She started lacing her shoes. The buzzer sounded, signaling the end of the rotation. Tamma stood up, turned around, stepped up onto the mats, and got her first look at women's #2.

The wall was dead vertical. The start hold was a pink, slopey boob as big as her head. The feet were near-edgeless screw-ons black with shoe rubber. Tamma picked up a brush and started to clean the start hold. She took that time to look at the route. Tiny crimps and slopers up a slab.

She started with two hands wrapped over the boob, toeing down on the slippery footholds. Boosted up off the start hold—and fell back onto the mats.

She got up, dusted her hands off. Mounted onto the problem and greased right off. She started to cry and choked it down. Mounted back onto the wall, weighted the foothold, and it skittered out from underneath her.

She had nine attempts and then lay on the mats and covered her face with her chalky hands. A buzzer sounded, signaling that she had a minute left.

"You can do it, Tamma!" Paisley called from the crowd, and then she whistled.

> **CHRIS KALOUS:** Can you tell our *Enormocast* listeners what it was like to go all the way out to Los Angeles for that competition and then to just completely and utterly shit the bed?
>
> All those nights you were up until two a.m., rewatching comps on your phone, dreaming of one day being in a comp yourself. Risking death on Fingerbang Princess. Getting up at four a.m.

to hitch into the park. All that work has culminated here, in this moment.

And it turns out, you can't even get on the wall.

TAMMA: Watch me, Kalous.

Tamma sat back up—wrapped her hands on the start hold, placed her feet, and boosted up onto the wall. She stuck the mantle, spanned out right, and caught the next hold—shockingly thin and sharp, sickeningly insecure, biting into her pads, but she held it. She matched her left hand and right foot on the boob—and then she simply rose to a stand on the start hold.

Left of her was a huge fiberglass half-globe, far out of reach. She took a deep breath, let herself fall leftward, hit the globe with her right hand, and smacked around left in a bear hug to try to catch a micro-crimp screw-on. It was like tackling a beach ball. That was the zone.

Her feet cut and she had a desperate moment, throwing her elbow up over the top of the beach ball, crimping it with her left hand, her feet hanging. She scrabbled, thrutched, clawed, and humped her way up the volume, then threw out right to a bowling-ball sloper, cut her feet, pendulumed out beneath it, and matched it. A second sloper out left, full extension of her arms. Five seconds remaining, and the sound effect of a ticking clock counting down. Tamma boosted up and hit the final sloper, the finish hold. One hand over the top and then the other. She turned and gave the judge an embarrassed look and the judge gave her the thumbs-up. Tamma beat the finish hold with her palm in victory and dropped to the mats.

Women's #3 went down in two attempts. Then women's #4 was thin climbing on desperate crimps with a tenuous step-out onto a foot jib and she didn't have enough rubber on her shoes to hold the jib. She left the mats with just a zone.

She sat, looking out toward the thinned-out audience, waiting for women's #5. She could hear the climber on the boulder behind her, hear her brushing holds, putting off her first moves, footsteps sinking into the vinyl mats, and then the sound of her climbing shoes on the wall as she pulled on. Ten seconds later the girl was off. Then she was off again. Then off a third time. Three moves in. Tamma listened as the climber took repeated, low-down pitches back into the mats. The crowd was somber and unimpressed—looking out at them, Tamma thought that there had been very few tops on women's #5. Oh no, she thought. Women's #5 is something fucked up, and no one can send it. It ends here.

The final buzzer sounded and Tamma stood up, and then the chime sounded and she turned around, stepped up onto the mats, and looked at the wall. She hesitated there, sure that she must be misunderstanding the beta. She could not believe what she was seeing.

It started off the ground with fingerpockets and ran left to two volumes, bolted together, forming a gap between them. Tamma knew what it was. It was a hand-crack problem. From the hand crack—a sloper and then the finish hold, a big outsloped pyramid. But the thing was, the hand crack looked casual.

She didn't know if she was missing something. Hand cracks were never set in competition. There were very few people out on the floor, perhaps a dozen. The judges and brushers watched her and Tamma turned back to the wall. She set herself on the start hold and boosted up for a two-finger pocket and stuck it with the second team, middle and ring. Then up with a left foot to a jib and left-hand two-finger pocket, first team. It was a rose move. She arched her left arm above her head like a ballerina in fourth position, the right hand threading beneath the arch, her left flank turned out to the audience. Tamma was short and she had to extend for the volumes with her right hand. She touched the right-hand volume with her fingertips. Then her knuckles. Then her palm. She set her hand and cut loose and hung from the hand jam, facing outward toward the audience. That was the zone. One guy started clapping and someone else whistled. She could tell from the response that she was the first person to make the move. But it didn't make sense. The hand crack was juicy. It was outrageously casual for crack climbing. Not even a boulder problem. Maybe 5.9.

She completed the turn and reached up and sank the second jam. They were steep, thin hands and Tamma held them effortlessly, and walked her way up the overhanging volumes. She boosted right and caught the sloper. And then went up to the finish hold and stuck it. Looked back at the judge. The judge gave her the thumbs-up. Tamma banged the hold in victory and everyone in the audience whistled and *ow-ow!*-ed and clapped and she plunged to the mats. Women's #5 on-sight.

She put her hands up and the crowd roared for her. All fourteen of them.

Nine

Tamma stepped down off the mats, picked up her kit, and walked directly out into the thinning crowd. She was working her way to the front desk when Paisley grabbed her by the shoulders.

"Oh, the *treachery*!" she said.

"I got lucky," Tamma said.

"You did, kind of!" Paisley admitted. "Like—do you remember when you went to your first comp and there was a hand crack? And out of the first sixty-nine girls you were the only trad climber? And you were the only girl who climbed it?"

"Seriously?"

"*Seriously!* That flash on number five saved your butt! You're thirteenth! So, maybe, *probably*, semifinals tomorrow morning!"

"What?" Tamma yelled. She started to leap up and down and Paisley started to leap up and down with her and there they were, hands on each other's shoulders, jumping like idiots.

"You're a comp climber now, girl!"

"Oh my god."

"You *outrageous* sandbagger! I am *sooooo mad* at you except I love you of course! I was in the audience watching and I was like, 'Oooooh, Mom, she's a lady trad climber,' and then I was just like, 'I know that girl, oooooh, Mom, look at her go! I talked to her!' I will never believe anything you say ever again. I mean remember when you were like: 'Oh, I can't even climb. Oh, I'm out of my depth. Oh, Paisley, I'm so scared!' Slash: I'm a hard-sending trad lady from the desert with a plus fourteen ape index and impeccable movement! My grandmother crimps harder than you do, and you can't seem to do a pull-up, but your style is sooooooooo goooooooooooood it's mind-bloooooowing! Come meet my mom. And my dad. Forgive him, he's a dentist, he doesn't know what's going on. He's the one over there who looks like a dentist. Mom! Møm! Maaaaawwwwwwwwwwwm!" Paisley said, leading Tamma away through the crowd and calling out for her mom, who turned around to look.

"This is the girl I was telling you about! Did you see her on number five?"

"I saw her," Paisley's mom said.

"You saw her?!"

"I did, sweetie, you were right there. You were standing next to me."

"She was just like THAT'S HOW YOU CRACK CLIMB, LAAA-DIEEEEZE!"

"Language, sweetie. Yes, I was right beside you, I saw that. And she is right here, she can hear you."

"Language?" Paisley said. "What's wrong with LAAADIEEE-EZE?"

"I won't have it from you, but I did very much admire your friend on women's number five, which you already know, because you were standing right beside me, and I said, I admire that young woman's quality of movement."

"Women's number five," Paisley's father said, "featured a move out of *traditional* climbing, is that correct? Climbers utilizing an artificial crevice-feature?"

He was wearing pleated khakis with a blue plaid shirt. He had taken his glasses off to inspect Tamma and was rolling the stem jauntily between thumb and forefinger. Paisley gestured to him with her outflung, open hand, looking back at Tamma and rolling her eyes.

"Honestly!" she said. "I mean *honestly!*"

Tamma went out for dinner with the Cutherses. What happened was Paisley said, "Do you want to come out to dinner with us?" and Tamma said, "No, I couldn't," and then Paisley seized her hand and somehow Tamma was walking out to the car with them. They went to a Mexican restaurant where Mr. and Mrs. Cuthers drank margaritas and shared a wooden bowl of chips. Stella Cuthers had a clean and professional tan and a clean and professional facelift, and her hair was a clean and professional blond. She was the sort of person Tamma was supposed to hate, but Tamma had never before met an adult who seemed so interested in her. She set her tablet out on the table and played through each of the boulders for Tamma, narrating every beat, telling Tamma everything she'd done right. Tamma was learning more at dinner, from Stella, than she had learned in entire years of her climbing life. The while, Paisley was slinging back tacos with careless panache. Oh, duh, Tamma thought, glancing over. Oh duh: I don't eat enough.

Kerry Cuthers sipped from his margarita and took off his glasses and stooped over the screen and said in tones of great knowingness,

"Well I think you did *very* well on that one, nugget," and Paisley rolled her eyes and said, "Honestly, Dad, it took me *nine* attempts."

"What happened was, you didn't read the toe catch, honey," Stella said.

"*Yeah*, Mom," Paisley said. "I see that *now*."

"I think you did magnificently, nugget," Kerry put in. "I'd be danged if I could've read that toe catch myself. And getting it after nine attempts, that shows perseverance and determination, which may not be rewarded by points, but is rewarded in my heart."

"*Yeah*, Dad: *We know*," Paisley said.

"Here's Tamma on the number four crimp problem," Stella said. They watched.

"You can't keep your foot on that jib," Stella said. "Is that a core engagement problem or what?"

"Core engagement?" Paisley said in rising tones of outrage. She paused to pitch back another taco, chewed furiously, then went on, "Mom, she has the core of a soviet gymnast! *Core engagement?!* Mom— have you seen her *shooooooooooooes?*"

"No," Stella said. "What's wrong with her shoes?"

Nothing would suffice, then, but that Tamma should produce her climbing shoes, and that Paisley should wave them around, shouting at her mom, and that Kerry should observe to everyone in tones of great knowingness, "I can see the high ankle designed to protect the wearer from rock *crevices*," and that Paisley should say, "Gah! *Honestly, Dad!*" and that Stella should say, "Kerry, Tamma cannot wear these shoes to semifinals," and that Kerry should hang the stem of his glasses from his teeth and remark, "Well, Tamma is a brilliant climber, *I* shouldn't want to second-guess her, and if she is pleased with them—" and that Paisley should say, "Dad! She's not *pleased with them*! She *can't afford better shoes!*" and that Tamma should put up her hands and begin to defend herself, and that Kerry should say, "Ah, well, oh, I see," with an air of having read about these sorts of things in *The New York Times*, and that after dinner they should all go, over Tamma's protests, to the local climbing shop, and that Tamma should be forced to try on shoes in front of all of them, Paisley (eating an enormous purple carrot she had found somewhere, scrunching up her face mulishly with every bite) saying, "Do you have any shoes that would fit a SANDBAGGING GNOME?" and that the employee should appear puzzled, and that Kerry should say, "Well, now, *that* looks like a good shoe; what matters, I think, Tamma, is that you should be comfortable, that's the most important thing," and that Paisley should take an enormous crunching bite of carrot and say, "Look at her, Dad!—[*crunch!*]—Does she look like she came here to be comfortable?! No!!!—[*crunching authoritatively*]—She wants to win!—[*crunching thoughtfully*]—She wants them sooooo tight she bleeeeeeeeeeeeeds!—[*gesturing with the gnawed-off shank of carrot*]—Tamma is a meat eater!—[*heroic chewing: certain attendant nose-crinkling facial expressions*]—She's a born competitor!" and that Kerry should stand polishing his glasses and remark, "I should say, nugget, that I think just making it into semifinals is a very big win, and that we should all maybe go get some ice cream to celebrate everyone's having had fun," and that it should be discovered that the only shoes in stock in her size should be a pair of la sportiva solutions, and that Tamma's vociferous protests should be overruled and the matter decided, and that they should all proceed to the register, whereupon Paisley should reappear with a beautiful, red, 9.4 mm dynamic sterling rope slung over her shoulder, and that her mother should protest and her father remove his glasses and hang the stem from his teeth, and that Paisley should shout, "*She needs a new rope or SHE'S GONNA DIE.*"

Everyone looked at Tamma to see if this was true, and Tamma said, "That is absolutely not true," and Paisley, still holding a stub of carrot, waved her arms as if signaling a helicopter for help, saying, "It's already established that she is a tricksy hobbitses! Don't listen to her! She needs a rope, guys! Please please please *please*!"

Panic was glug-glugging up from Tamma's guts into her throat. To have grubby trad shoes was one thing. But the rope reached back into the rest of her life; if Tamma didn't have a rope, then she wasn't climbing safely; she wasn't a responsible young woman at all; if she admitted that she was climbing on a bad rope, the Cutherses would see that she was poor, ADHD trash; that she had weird, enormous ears; that her mother was a fat, chain-smoking, verbally abusive diner waitress; that her mom's boyfriend was an illiterate, undocumented, alcoholic drug dealer; she wasn't like them; she was a desperate, doomed, pathetic hanger-on—scraping and begging for any chance at a sport to which she didn't belong. So, in a rush, she put her hands up and said, "I cannot accept this," and Kerry turned back to Paisley and said, "If she says she cannot accept it, nugget, then that suffices," and Paisley said, "But Dad, she's being *an idiot*! She's being *proud*! Who are you going to believe, your very own daughter, or a sandbagging minx of a person even if we do like her!" And Kerry said, "I would *happily* buy Tamma a rope, which I believe Tamma understands, but we have made the offer, she has refused, and that's the end of the matter. Unless she should relent—Tamma? I should say that I am happy to buy you a rope, if you only consent to come out to ice cream with us to celebrate your very big win?"

"No," Tamma said.

"Then we love and admire your passion, nugget, but it is also important to listen and to be accommodating to the concerns and thoughts of others."

To which, Paisley said, "But Dad—*her concerns and thoughts are dumb!*" and Kerry said, "That is how other people very often appear to us, nugget, and I should say that as a spirited young woman whose apprehension moves in leaps and bounds, that is a frustration you will carry with you your entire life."

So, the Cutherses bought Tamma a new pair of shoes, and the rope was left behind.

After that, Tamma excused herself and walked back to the climbing gym alone, carrying her brand-new shoes. The gym was in a strip mall and Tamma slept on a folded-up cardboard box out back, near the loading docks, hiding between a dumpster and the wall. She pillowed her head on her rolled-up barn coat and watched moths come in and out of the streetlights. She had ninety-four missed calls and her voicemail box was full. She opened and closed her aching hands, massaging the finger pulleys between thumb and forefinger. She sanded down the broken edges of blisters and coated the thin places with chapstick. Then she took a deep breath, opened the texts from her mother, and scrolled through. It must've been Sierra who told her.

> Tamma call me back!!!
> This isn't funny.
> Where are you?
> I have been scared for hours
> This isn't fair to do to me

Tamma was stooped over her phone, holding her brow with her hand. She didn't know why Kendra cared. Tamma only slept at the trailer Wednesday and Thursday. It was Sunday, and Sierra had gotten the Sunday and Monday shifts covered. Tamma sat, cross-legged, holding her hand over her mouth. Then she scrolled down farther.

> I can't believe you would do this to me
> You don't care about me
> You don't love me

Tamma paused the scroll with her finger and sat looking at that. There was more but she thumbed the phone off. Then she turned it back on and texted Dan.

> u up?

> TAMMA!
> How goes it!

> im at the comp

> Oh shit I was supposed to drive you!

> Sierra drove me

> That was cool of her
> Kind of unexpected tbh

> oh well she owes me

> How are you doing!

> dude I'm into semis!

> That's so great!

> I'm so scared!
> The plastic is so rough dude

CRUX

> It's killing my skin
> and all the holds are enormous
> but awkward and its VERY steep
> and it's weird because they
> stick OUT of the wall

whoa yeah that makes sense
but not your style

> no not at all

I'm so impressed with you

> hows our girl???

She had icechips today!
Which is huge
Semis on your first comp ever!
Whatever happens next
I think this is big
You're the best comp climber
In my heart

> thanks dude
> im pretty nervous

don't be nervous
failure is just your
awkward meetcute
with success

She pitched herself down onto the cardboard and lay on her back, staring at that, holding the phone very close her face. He doesn't care, she thought, if I win or lose. He doesn't care how well I do. He's gonna love me just as much whatever happens.

Ten

Tamma turned her phone in at the front desk and went back into isolation. She sat, raking her knuckles down her forearms, eating a fig bar, listening to the gym getting louder and louder as it filled up with people. She had lain awake all night, stretched out on her sheet of cardboard, staring at the streetlights. When she had started to sleep, she had dreamed about the comp and woken sweating, her heart hammering, and she'd had to wait herself out, propped against the stucco wall, knocking on her sternum, telling herself over and over again, You have to relax, Tams. You have to sleep.

Paisley came into the gym, gave Tamma a wave, put on her headphones, and went into the bouldering area to warm up. Tamma herself started on the mats. She was so sore she felt like she'd been beaten with a meat tenderizer. Later, she found Paisley sitting on the benches, listening to music.

"Pin my bib on?" Tamma said.

"Of course."

"Nervous?" Tamma said.

"Dying," Paisley said, pinning the bib in place. "You?"

"Dead, pretty much."

"You sleep at all?"

"Not a lot. You?"

"No. Not at all."

"Does it get easier?"

"Not for me," Paisley said. "For me, it's always so many nerves I can't think about anything else."

They sat side by side, watching other climbers on the wall. Girls were taking turns with a laser pointer, constructing awkward and gymnastic sequences for one another. Tamma could never have pulled those moves.

"Hey," Paisley said. "I kinda need to be quiet for a bit and psych myself up."

"Of course."

The semifinals round had the same setup as qualifiers, but there were only twenty girls, and they ran the male and female rotations concurrently, with eight problems on the wall, the strongest athletes out first. Tamma had placed thirteenth and Paisley third. So Tamma watched as a volunteer walked Paisley out to the mats.

As before, Tamma waited in a folding chair beside the curtained doorway. Across from her sat the male climber who was also coming out thirteenth. He appeared totally calm. He was already in laces. Tamma opened her kit. She had her old TC pros, and the new pair the Cutherses had bought her. Aggressive, downturned bouldering shoes with cutting edges, designed for just this type of climbing. By far the best piece of equipment she'd ever owned. She started pulling them on, but they were so tight, the rubber so new and stiff, that for a good minute she thought she would not be able to get into them. She hooked her pointer fingers through the pull tabs and extended with her leg, feeling like she might dislocate her index fingers. "Fuck! Shit! Balls!" she was saying under her breath. Her feet had swollen overnight. Her hands too felt enormous: meaty and creaky.

"You uh . . . want help?" the guy said, pretty gently.

"Yes!" Tamma said, and he came over, grasped the sole of the shoe, and eased it back over her heel, cheating it left and right. Together, the two of them got the shoe on.

"Did we do it?" he said, helping her with the other.

"We did it," Tamma said. "Do we have to get married now?"

"We'd better," he said.

Then she waited, the large digital clock by the doorway counting down. The gym was busier and louder than before. She could hear the *whump* of climbers taking falls. The rotation ended and she walked out to the folding chair in front of women's #1. The gym was packed shoulder to shoulder with grungy dirtbags, manicured gym rats, competitors done with their rotations, parents, curious bystanders, and a few beef-jerky-looking old guys who probably knew more about Tamma's home crag than she did herself.

The emcee was saying, "A surprising competitor from the town of 73 Coyotes. Never before seen in competition! Ladies and gentlemen. Please welcome Tamarisk Callahan! Show her some love, so she knows we want her back!"

Right then, Tamma realized that she had not peed and that this was a terrible mistake and she had to pee right now, desperately. Then the buzzer sounded, and she slogged up onto the mats, kegeling an entire fish tank of urine back up into her sloshing loins, each foot sinking into the vinyl mats, holding her chalk bag and digging into it with one hand, looking up at the boulder, afraid that if she relaxed, she would go rocketing away over the crowd, carried on a jet of fear-urine.

The route was a slab, just less than vertical. The holds traveled up and right, delicate work on micro-crimp underclings and outsloped volumes. It was like a gift from the route setters to Tamma. She pounced onto a starting volume like a pedestal and stood, face to the wall, her cheek pressed to the paint job. She had to stoop down and touch the pedestal with both hands for it to be a legal start. Then she rose up, her hands flush to the wall, and started the climb, flexing every muscle to hold tension, breathing slowly so as not to goose herself off the volume. She'd never felt so wrecked in all her life, tiptoeing from one precarious stance to the next. She came to the crux move. It was a barely there screw-on pinch she had to hold through a disastrous series of sidesteps on jibs.

Tamma reached for it, wringing all the doubt from her mind, vise-gripping the outsloped pinch, sidestepping up through 5 mm and 8 mm screw-ons, holds too small for Tamma ever to have stuck in her TC pros. Every step she took now, she owed to the Cutherses and to the sharp inside edges of her new comp shoes.

She worked up and right, alighting from one improbable hold to another, revising every gesture to minimalist perfection, smoothing away every eccentricity, the rubber of the new shoes biting into the edges, until finally she reached out and caught the finish hold.

She turned and looked at the judges and they gave her the thumbs-up, so she banged the wall in triumph and then dropped to the mats, unable to believe it. She could do this. And not in a small way—she belonged here, in competition. She had never before climbed in a gym, and here she was, flashing problems in semifinals. She walked off the mats, grabbed a volunteer, and sprinted for the bathrooms.

Women's #2 was a fifty-five-degree cave that went with bicycle holds, heel hooks, and drop knees. In four attempts, she got nowhere, and walked off the mats empty-handed.

Then she waited for women's #3, staring at her hands, willing the skin to grow back. Her pads were pink and weeping blood in dewy pinpoints. She dabbed superglue onto her pads and then taped them up. Then the buzzer sounded and she turned and started studying the route. It was gently overhung, on blue wall panels. Enormous start holds but bad starting feet on outsloped volumes. A big dynamic pounce up and right for an incut rail with a blocker hold. The blocker was a second hold, screwed onto the wall above the rail, leaving a gap of about an inch. Often, when you leapt for a hold, you hit the wall above it and dragged down onto it, but in this case, the blocker meant that you had to be accurate when you hit the rail. If you weren't exact, you'd hit the blocker hold and bounce off. The move was enormous.

Tamma walked to the start hold, dipping her hands one after another in the chalk bag, and then clapping them off on her butt. Someone in the crowd hooted encouragingly and Tamma turned and acknowledged it with an embarrassed wave.

The start hold was a blue elephant's ear. She got established, smearing rubber against the outsloped footholds, waggling her butt like a cat, settling deep into a crouch from which to spring up and right. She looked out at the rail, stripping everything else from her mind. The crowd, gone. The mats, gone. The music and the emcee, gone. She could hear her own breathing. Her fingers felt sloppy in their cuffs of athletic tape. The plastic burned her untaped pads.

She swung left, then right, and leapt for it: came entirely off the wall, hands outstretched, and struck, caught the rail with her right hand, felt her fingertips bite onto the edge. Her left hand hammered the blocker and rebounded. The rail was incut and she dug into it painfully, lifting the knuckles up so she could bear down onto the pads, her nails crunching against the wall.

She struck again with her left hand and again missed. Her feet swung out beneath her and she hung the rail one-handed, her sternum making a series of crackling and aligning noises, rib heads unseating from their joinings, her lips peeled back with effort, the strain braiding from her shoulder, across her back, into her hips.

She held the pendulum, her feet swung back left beneath her, and then her pinkie popped off the hold. All of the tension came onto her ring finger and her ring finger came loose with a wet, explosive popping noise. She was sucked out into the air and swatted down onto the mats, chalk dust effervescing around her.

She rolled facedown into the vinyl, holding her hand to her chest, breathing through the pain, not wanting this to be real. The crowd was silent. She gritted her teeth and tried to close her ring finger. It moved, but very little. She braced her fingertip with her thumb and pulled against it. The pain was mind-annihilating. Tamma closed her eyes and pressed her face down into the chalky mats. The emcee was talking about her.

Get up, Tamma, she thought to herself. You need to get up. She could hear the click of the camera shutters. She put out her good hand, levered herself off the mats, and stood up. She held her finger in her other hand to show that she was hurt. Then she shrugged in defeat and waved her thanks to the crowd.

"Tamma Callahan, everyone!" the emcee said. "Looks like she's hurt! Wish her well! Come back soon, Tamma!" and Tamma stepped off the mats. She spoke to the volunteer at women's #4, told her she was done, and then simply started threading her way back toward the front desk.

That was when Paisley found her, saying, "Tamma! Tamma! You did amazing!" and pulled her away by her arm. They found a secluded area among the top ropes and sat down together. Tamma held out her hand and Paisley palpated it with the pads of her thumbs, eyes closed. When she got to the first joint of the ring finger, Tamma sucked air. Paisley raised her eyebrows. "That hurt?" she said, and Tamma nodded.

"How's this?" and she tried the finger side to side.

"That's fine," Tamma said. "It's trying to close it that hurts."

Paisley pinned the damaged ligament beneath her finger pad, her brow furrowed.

"Partial tear of the A2 pulley," she said. "Most common injury in all of climbing."

"What should I do?" Tamma said.

"Well, there's a PT back in iso. We can find him. But he's gonna tell you the same thing. I've had lots of pulley injuries. Ice and compression. Then light duty work on a hangboard."

"Why not just rest it and wait for it to heal?"

"No injury heals through rest," Paisley said. "If you rest a pulley injury, the pulley just scars over, and the scar is never as strong or elastic. You could rest for a year, you'd never regain full mobility, and if you started again, it'd still be painful."

"How bad is this?"

"Oh, not bad! I've had lots of pulley injuries! If you're not getting hurt, you're not going hard enough! If you went out there, you'd rupture it, and then it would require a surgical repair, and the finger would never again be as strong and mobile as it was. But you rehab this, as it is, then in eight weeks you can climb moderates, and in twelve weeks, you can crimp hard without risk of blowing it. I can text you my hangboard protocol, if you like! All this is, if you think about it, is a great time to work on your conditioning."

"I've never had a pulley injury before."

"That's just lucky genetics."

"How did you do?" Tamma said.

"Eh," Paisley said. "I did pretty good, but I'm not gonna make it to finals. I definitely didn't send number one, you tramp! You're *leagues* better at slab!"

"I bet you sent the cave though."

"Of course I did! What am I, a *weakling*? I ate that cave for breakfast!"

"Paisley."

"Yeah?"

"I failed!"

"*What?*"

"I failed, Paisley! I can't hack it!"

Tamma was starting to cry, but holding it back, biting her lip, trying to smooth her crumpling face.

"Don't you start crying, Tamma," Paisley said. "You'll make me cry!" She grabbed Tamma by the shoulder and said, "Tamma, what are you *talking about*! You never saw a climbing gym until yesterday, and here you are, flashing bouldering problems in semifinals! Do you have any idea how *mind-blowingly* talented you are?"

Paisley pulled back, looking over Tamma's shoulder, and Tamma turned around and saw Paisley's parents walking along the top-rope wall. Kerry said, "Oh there you are, girls! Do you feel like any lunch? What's wrong?" and Paisley leapt up and said, "Mom! She thinks she's not good! Tell her! Talk to her, Mom!"

"Tamma does? Tamma thinks that?" Stella said.

"Yes! Mom!" Paisley leapt up and down. "She feels like she's a bad climber!"

"She's the most gifted slab climber I've ever seen," Stella said. "Wouldn't you say, honey?"

"Oh, I wouldn't know about that," Kerry said, with great amiableness. "Saying so-and-so is better than so-and-so feels silly—I'm just amazed *any of these girls* can hold on to those little doodads! Isn't the best slab climber the girl that is having the most fun?"

"Kerry, sweetheart, I was talking to your daughter."

"Oh," Kerry said. "Well then!"

"Don't listen to him, Tamma!" Paisley said. "What he doesn't know is that no slab climber is ever having fun. So what if you didn't make finals? Everybody comes out to a comp and gets walloped from time to time. I've been in *hundreds of comps* where I never made semis at all! It's an *outrage* that you've done as well as you have. Could I come out to your desert and expect to onsight whatever horrifying thing you're working on?"

"Probably," Tamma said.

"No! Tamma! Probably not!"

"Yeah, if you can't climb thin hands, then probably not," Tamma admitted.

Stella sat down on Tamma's other side.

"What did you want?" Stella said.

"I wanted to be Tommy Caldwell at Snowbird!" Tamma said. "This is my dream. Being a climber is my life's purpose. My buddy and I—we're talking about skipping college and going to Indian Creek to climb full time. But I don't know if I have what it takes. I thought that if I came here, and stood on the podium, I'd know, for sure, that I was going to *make it*. But instead, I came here and I got wrecked!"

"Oh, honey," Stella said very warmly. "Tommy Caldwell competed at Snowbird before you were even born, when climbing was a young sport, and there were enormous advancements to be made, simply by doing things like *training* and *not starting the day with a gallon of wine*. It's not that sport any more. Now everyone trains. I'll tell you a secret. You *weren't* ever going to make finals. As far as quality of movement, you've got an extraordinary gift, but you're good at just one style: slab. You don't know how to climb steep terrain, you can't crimp, and your fitness isn't quite there. To get into finals, you need to be superb in *all* disciplines of climbing. You can certainly do that, but you're not there *yet*."

"You don't understand," Tamma said. "I spend every spare minute of my life climbing, or else thinking about climbing. If I need to do more, then it's impossible."

"Tamma," Stella said. "You're competing against girls who train forty hours a week. That's not your life. If you want that to be your life, make it so. It's not a reasonable expectation to outperform girls who have out-trained, out-practiced, and out-worked you. I understand that you wanted to come here and finish on a podium and get a medal. But that can't be why you do this. When Paisley was young, it was clear, immediately, that she was a strong climber. And we pushed her very hard. And do you know what happened?"

"She lost hella weight and started winning hella comps," Tamma said. "She was unstoppable."

"That's right," Stella said, looking over at her daughter. "And how was that, Paisley? Was that everything you dreamed it would be?"

"It was the worst time of my life," Paisley said.

"I think sometimes, in our lives, for whatever reason, we go looking for podiums to stand on," Stella said. "But the podiums are never enough. Is how I remember it."

"Yup," Paisley said.

"Then she dropped out of the scene," Tamma said. "She was gone. She put on weight."

"Do we need to put it like that?" Paisley said.

"And then she climbed Iron Resolution," Tamma said. "Her biggest send ever. V12+. She floated it. And everyone thought: Oh, this is a climber to watch."

"Yes," Stella said, with some surprise. "The point is, Paisley's climbing has only ever been a joy to her when it has been her own. With any boulder, whether it's on a World Cup stage, or in J Tree, the Buttermilks, Font, or wherever, we have the privilege of working the problem. But all you are given is the attempt. You aren't entitled to the top. All it is—is if you solve enough problems in qualis, then you have the chance to solve problems in semis. But you don't own those tops. It's never certain and you can destroy your bone density, stomach lining, and life trying to make it certain, and if you got there, I think you'd find it wasn't even the point. You should climb because you love solving problems, Tamma. And watching you out there—I believe you *do*. Don't climb because you love tops or podiums or medals, those things come or they don't. Sweetheart, do you think Tamma needs any kind of awards or medals or sponsorship?"

"Oh, no!" Kerry put in. "No one needs any of that. Nugget here could fail every boulder she ever touched and watching her come down the stairs in the morning would still be among the greatest joys of my life, next to waking up beside her mother."

"Daaaaaaaaaaad!" Paisley said, clasping her hands over her eyes and swooning backward in agony.

"Kerry, my love, I was, once again, talking to your daughter," Stella said.

Later, Tamma asked them if they would stay for finals and Stella said they would. "First and foremost," she said, "we love the sport. Second, we're competitors." So they stayed for finals and afterward went out for pizza. Tamma watched Paisley eat in flat amazement and then Stella insisted on giving Tamma a ride home, even though it was hours out of their way.

In the back of the Cutherses' minivan, Paisley was asleep almost before they left the parking lot, with her head thrown back. Stella and Kerry talked quietly in the front. And Tamma sat, thinking about it all. It was dark in the van and dark out in the desert save for the lights upon the road. Hitchhike out to Los Angeles, she thought, hoping to rout Paisley Cuthers and sweep the competition. Instead, get crushed in semis, tear a finger pulley, end up ugly-crying on Paisley's shoulder, neither of them progressing to finals, and love it. Sounds about right, she thought.

It had all been a foolish dream, that she was Cinderella and the comp was her ball, that she would stand on a podium and have a gold medal dropped over her head and with that gesture, the judges would crown her the Queen of Sending: She'd no longer be some dirty, ashy urchin, scrubbing down hearthstones.

Tamma was looking at her hands, stained with blood and chalk, her nails chipped, the joints ringed in white athletic tape, her injured finger enormously swollen. Up in the front seat, she could hear Stella telling Kerry that she wanted some little botox shots *right here*, just for *these lines*, and Kerry was saying, "But honey, I *love* those lines," and Stella saying, "Sweetheart, *babe*, you're supposed to say, 'What lines?' No woman wants lines, hon." There were no words for how much these were not Tamma's people. And yet, she'd been wrong about that.

Her entire vision of the world was breaking apart and being remade in the back of a minivan heading east through the desert. She had expected these people to hate her. Tamma had wanted to be great, as if greatness were something one discovered about oneself in the crucible of competition, as if it were the only possible answer to her monstrous inadequacy. And then, the thing of which she had been most afraid had happened. She wasn't great. She might never be great. But the thing she most wanted, to belong here, was hers already.

Paisley teetered over and laid her head on Tamma's shoulder, snoozing, her mouth open. This close to her, Tamma could smell her, and she smelled like oxiclean and coconut and Justice. Tamma was filled with a wondrous breaking-open feeling. She and Dan, like fucking idiots, had been desperately looking for permission, trying to answer the question *Will we make it?* Setting benchmarks. If they could send the Princess. If they could climb Figures on a Landscape. But Botox Stella was right. There was no answer to that question, except in the terrifying, day-in, day-out work of the attempt. The doubt and suffering and pain—all that was the point. Without the doubt and suffering and pain, the tops were nothing.

IV.

WONDERLAND

One

Forty-eight days in the ICU, twelve on the floor, and on the twenty-second of February, Alexandra was wheeled out of the hospital. At the curb, Lawrence held open the door and she made the last few steps from wheelchair to car. She grimaced and cast sidelong glances and leaned back, her hand held over her closed sternotomy, breathing deliberately.

She was returned to them and she had a chance, it seemed to Dan, to make good on the dream of this family, in its snug little house in the desert. She had written *Ephedra* in eight months while living in a tent and working full time at a diner. If she could get out of bed, then she could fix this. Dan hung on her next move as if it prefigured his own.

In the cold, dark mornings, he would rise with his heart beating heavily in his chest, kneel on the concrete floor, grasp the kettlebell, and find he could not lift it. If he could, it would make him feel a little less sick. But he couldn't. He just couldn't. He'd walk out into the kitchen. The door to the master bedroom closed. Lawrence asleep on the couch, a book on his chest. Dan would break the suction seal with a thumb, hold the fridge door open, pour cold coffee. Return to his room and sit before his open textbook, working within the small golden province of the desk light, bounded on all sides by darkness. Reach the end of the page and dredge himself for the will to turn it. Telling himself: I *will* turn the page. I am *about* to turn the page.

On an afternoon that felt as if it had been years since Alexandra's discharge, but which must've been only days later, he ate lunch with Tamma. It was his first time seeing her except in passing. They had messaged each other, but Dan had not often been on his computer. The picnic bench was a brown, rubber-coated lattice. Behind them lay the low, rowlike buildings of the high school. Before them: charcoal-colored tarmac; hurricane fencing; a scrubby field of crabgrass and cranesbill; a cinder track, partially flooded by sprinklers; and a horizon gauzy with clouds.

"I'm sorry I missed the comp," he said. "I fucked up."

"Nah, dude." She was eating a quesadilla leftover from Hunter's snack, chewing with difficulty. "I'm running away to Los Angeles when I should've been there with you, and for what?"

"Well, let's see this A2 pulley I've heard so much about."

She displayed her hand, the finger enormous, swollen up sausage-like, almost immobile. "That's my full range of motion. Twenty degrees."

"Shit, dude."

"It hurts to lift up a glass, open the fridge, turn a doorknob. It's only a partial but every night I dream that it's ruptured and then it wakes me up with the aching. Paisley says to train through it once the swelling goes down, but I'm too scared to actually try."

"How is she in person?"

"Hanging out with her, I had this idea."

"What idea?"

"You know how people say friendships don't matter?"

"Yeah?"

"Those people are assholes."

Dan sat laughing, holding his book flat on the tabletop, marveling somewhat that he could sit here talking like old times, when inside, he was just a suckhole of emptiness and hurt. But to one extent or another, he had been pretending all his life. He had been forever the scared, hurting, and lost child standing beside and slightly behind the cardboard cutout of what others imagined him to be; only, it was the first time he'd ever been this way with her. Tamma finished her quesadilla and sat uneasily at the bench. Then she nodded to his sandwich. "You . . . uh, gonna eat that?" she said.

He slid the bag over.

"The comp," he said, still surprised that he could talk as if he cared, as if he were okay. "Were you—I mean, were you stronger than the other girls?"

Tamma shook her head. "Weaker," she said. "Much weaker. Turns out all this sandbagged granite, it doesn't make you strong. It makes you *good*. But not all that powerful, really. And also, climbing just one type of stone all the time—we're only solid at crack and slab. But these girls? They can climb anything. I mean, the experience you get climbing at different crags? It shows."

Dan was trying to get a sense of their promise, of their chances.

"So, we're just podunks," he said. "These other climbers really are better than us. More talented, more experienced, better conditioned, and with access to coaching."

Tamma shrugged. "Not more talented. They're basically just like us. They're our people—dorks and misfits. They're physically stronger, and they have techniques we don't, but their footwork is sloppy, their balance sucks, and they don't keep core tension. They rely on their strong fingers, which works, because plastic is excellent compared to the rock out here. They're better at gym climbing. We're better at granite."

"But we're not great, unstoppable geniuses who have gone undiscovered because of our low station in life?"

"No," Tamma said. Shaking her head. "Not exactly."

"Once upon a time," Dan said. "We agreed. We set a benchmark. We said—if we could send Figures on a Landscape, then we would know, for sure, that we could do this thing. You maybe thought the comp would prove that, but it didn't."

She wrapped her left hand around her injured right ring finger and sat thinking about it. Dan could see that she still wanted to get Figures. And too that she had stacked up reasons in her head against it. That surprised him. It was unlike her, to be scared of anything, no matter how fucked up it was, no matter how unprepared they might be. It felt like it should be easy, talking Tamma into another climb, but her reluctance and hesitation were palpable.

"We're dipshits," Dan said. "We've never done anything of consequence. It's total madness, it's *insane*, to bet our entire lives on becoming climbers, when we've never, not once, showed any promise. We've climbed a bunch of 5.7s, a few 8s and 9s, a couple 10s. That's all we've done, when other kids our age are sending 5.13 and 14. I want to do something cool, something ambitious, for once in our goddamn lives."

"We sent the Princess," Tamma said.

"A choss heap in a parking lot," Dan said.

"It turns out, though, that she was V8 the whole time."

"So what?" Dan said. "We've climbed one V8, and we had to work it for ninety-seven days—What has Paisley climbed?"

"V12+," Tamma said, with heavy reluctance. "Multiple V12s."

He could see that he was convincing her.

"I can lead it," Dan said. "We'll go at dawn; it'll be fifty degrees." As he was speaking, he knew who he sounded like. This toggling between withdrawal and overreach, between despair and manic, fixated excitement—this was Alexandra. Tamma was giving him a strange look. He knew that feeling, he had worn that very expression. *You've been gone for weeks—and now you want to send the biggest, most dangerous thing on our list, when I'm injured, you're deconditioned, and the climb is out of season?* He could see that, given her druthers, Tamma would keep on working through her ticklist of safe, classic moderates. Maybe even go back to bouldering, since the rope was coreshot. And she couldn't understand why he wasn't satisfied with that. But now, he saw it from the other side. In depression, the looming threat was that you were garbage, that the world was meaningless, and against that backdrop, small changes and half measures were offensive in their futility and hopelessness. He got it now; he understood his mother's on-again, off-again presence in his life. Your next step had to answer your extremity; otherwise, your hopes were as much garbage as you were garbage, were as stupid and small and foolish as you were stupid and small and foolish. That is why Dan wanted Figures. The only problem was that they had sent cool things before. Dan had led Rubicon, which was 10c, and Tamma had sent Illusion Dweller, which was 10b, and she'd only used three pieces of gear. It nagged him, that the logic didn't quite hold up. If you'd onsighted Rubicon with a rack of gear from the seventies, and it hadn't changed your sense of worthiness or belonging in the sport, then why would Figures matter? But it just seemed to him that it would. He would climb Figures and feel, finally, like a climber. He would feel *sure*. It would answer all his doubts.

"But it's R rated," Tamma said, half tempted and half flummoxed.

"The book doesn't give it an R," Dan said.

"No," Tamma said. "The book gives it 5.10b, and so good, so clean, so scary, so perfect, that your dick will lift up to the vast and empty night, open its jaws wide, and sing haunting operatic notes of otherworldly loveliness, like those worms in *Dune*."

"The book doesn't say that."

"HHHHHEEEEEEERRRRRG!"

"What?"

"AAAAYYYYYYYYYUUUUURRRRRR!"

"Oh my god, stop!"

"*EEEEEEAAAAAAHHHHHHHHHHHHRRRRRR!*"

"Tamma, please!"

"Swaying side to side, crying out to the empty places among the stars, singing its song of meaning in emptiness, of loneliness and glory in a vast and uncaring universe where no glory seems truly possible."

"You *do* want it."

"Of course I want it! But look around, Dan. I don't get everything I want."

"We can't leave it behind."

"Of course we can! We just nut up and go: one scary highstep crux into the rest of our lives."

"I want it," Dan said.

"Please don't do this."

"I'm determined."

"I'm begging you, Dan."

"I might get into a good school," Dan said. He had understood depression to be a staggered, speechless despair, but now this desire to convince her of Figures was on him like a panic, and in the convincing, he felt he had a vast store of things he could say, the lines of argumentation seemed to lay out before him. He could out-talk and out-reason her. And yet, he was sundered from anything like truth, anything approaching what he really felt or believed, he was all elocution without fundament, dizzied and amazed in all the things he could say without having any certain bearing on what was inside of him, so that even trying to persuade her, he wondered if this idea of Figures wasn't a phantasm, if it wasn't sickness. It was a spike in his guts, this twisting worry that he was carried along in an evanescent enthusiasm the way he had seen his mother carried along, so many times before, and yet, he had to convince her, he had to shut that worry away, he couldn't pay full attention to his own doubts because he *had nothing fucking else*. Without Figures, he was out on the slabs of his life without a single next move, with nothing, just blank and hopeless stone stretching in all directions. And so he had to go for it, right or wrong. "I might get into a good school," he said again, just to remind her what she was asking from him. "I haven't heard back, but I might. I'd be the first in my family. And my folks—they don't have any retirement, they don't have anything set aside, they need someone to take care of them, it's their dream for me. And if that dream doesn't come true, what has become of their lives, and how will they live, you know? If I'm going to turn all that down, I need some proof, I need some concrete thing I can point to, some evidence, that when push comes to shove, we really can send the gnar. Because right now, we don't have it, and it looks like we're venturing an awful lot for maybe nothing gained. We have sent classic moderates. Tourist climbs. The sorts of things dentists from Denver come here to send. Plus a few soft tens that take gear the whole way. I need this. Before I commit, I want to know that I'm doing the right thing."

She put her head in her hands. Then she raked the hair out of her face, scissoring her fingers back through the tangled locks and sweeping them behind her ears, raising her face up from the table like a girl coming up from a pool, and she said, "You're really doubting that much?"

"I'm really doubting that much."

She was silent for a long time. Gently testing the partially torn pulley with the thumb and forefinger of her left hand. To Tamma, this seemed to be contravening every hard-earned lesson of the last year. It was like the Princess's highstep crux. You could take the risky, top-out move, which felt uncertain every time, or you could hold on, at the last good stance, waiting until you felt ready, waiting for the moment the move would feel certain, waiting until you felt strong enough, waiting for some sign, waiting for something to rescue you. But it was a trap, it was a desperate lie your brain was telling you, because certainty never came. What had Stella told her? Stella had said, "I think sometimes, in our lives, for whatever reason, we go looking for podiums to stand on, but the podiums are never enough." To Dan, Figures was a trophy, it would mean he was the real thing, but he didn't need it, he already was the real thing. To Tamma, it was obvious that if Alexandra's life proved anything it was that you could have every accolade, every success, all the renown, and it might not be enough: No accomplishment, not in climbing, not in writing, not anywhere, could save you. Tamma seemed always to be trying to persuade Dan of this. She had already told him as much, that night she sent Fingerbang Princess. They had something extraordinary, but that thing wasn't climbing, that thing was each other. If he still couldn't see that, she didn't know what to say.

"Okay," she said. "So be it. Figures on a Fucking Landscape. But I need time, Dan. I need to rehab my finger. It's two or three pitches, depending how you break it up, and because it traverses, you can't do it alone. You need me to be able to climb it with you."

"How long do you need?"

"Twelve weeks," Tamma said.

"Twelve weeks?"

"These little tendons—they're not very vascular. They heal slowly. And if I try for Figures, and fully rupture the tendon, that's it, that's my entire career. And Figures isn't some line I can cheat through. Figures is hard and consequential crimping on thin edges, even for the follower. So, I need to do this carefully."

Dan was counting it off on his fingers. It was the twenty-seventh of February. Twelve weeks took them to May 21.

"It'll be too hot," he said.

"We can go very early in the morning that Tuesday. Sierra doesn't work Mondays. So I can spend the night at the trailer, we can leave at two a.m. We'll get there at four. It'll be cool enough. We can send this thing at dawn and be back at town in time for you to go to class."

"Twelve weeks," Dan said, agreeing to it. "One last climb in the park."

"Don't call it that!"

"Why?"

"A climb is never the last of anything. Not the last before lunch, not the last of the day, not the last of the season, and never the last in J Tree. It's bad luck."

Then he came home from school and found the door to the master bedroom closed. No sign of her. Save perhaps the remains of some lunch on the counter. A bowl of half-eaten ramen. The flavor packet left carelessly in the sink.

The last two days of February, just like that. March, the same.

Walking the halls, Tamma relayed how Sierra had worked three shifts at the medical center, flown out to a nursing strike in Idaho, worked eight shifts, flown back home, and worked three more. "I don't know how," she said, sauntering past banks of lockers, "she's still alive. We're in hella medical debt. The bills are still coming in, if you can believe that. And she's trying to claw her way back out. At this rate, she'll get there too, if we survive. But actually my mom did help. Although: I got home from class the other day? and walked in? and she was giving River coke in a baby bottle. I was like, 'Mommmmmmm! What are you doing?' and she said, 'Don't worry, it's *diet*.' And I was all, like, '*So?*' and she was all, like, 'It won't make him a fatty,' and I was all, like, '... ?' And she was all, like, 'Whaaaaat? He *loooooooooves it*!'"

"How's your finger?" he said.

"Rehab on the hangboard," she said. "Twice a day. It aches, but it's a *good ache*, I think."

"Will it be ready?"

"It'll have to be."

CRUX

Wake in the dark, heart pounding. Some feeling of needing to tell someone something. The panicked remains of a dream, slipping away as he came to consciousness. Then he'd sit on the edge of the bed, trying to hold on to it, finding it insubstantial, like chasing about for cobwebs, unsure quite what the urgency had been. Whatever was sick in Alexandra, it was sick in him too, but knowing did not seem to be enough. Some entangled strain of intelligence and madness both passed down generation to generation, his mormon forebears going west in search of godly purpose, until they had found themselves here, impoverished and abandoned. Through all that it had come down to Dan, who now sat upon the edge of the bed and fought with it as others had fought. He knew in theory that it was a fight for his life. Maybe more than his life. But he couldn't make it real to himself. Besides, there was nothing to do. The meaningfulness was going out of the world, and for all that he wanted to keep it, it drained out through his hands just the same, and the most he could feel was, Oh, there it goes.

There was a children's song he had learned in kindergarten.

> *There's a hole in my bucket, dear Liza, dear Liza*
> *There's a hole in my bucket, dear Liza, a hole.*

> *Then mend it, dear Henry, dear Henry, dear Henry*
> *Then mend it, dear Henry, dear Henry, mend it.*

Liza chides Henry to fix the bucket, and at first, it sounds possible, but everything she suggests requires, in the end, the use of a bucket, and Henry tells Liza the bucket has a hole, and around and around they go, the sick person and the well. As a child he had taken the side of Liza. Fix the goddamn bucket, Henry. Now he took both parts, turn and turn again, a fevered merry-go-round of hope and despair. There was a hole in his bucket, and to fix it, he only needed to care, but he couldn't care, couldn't remember what it had been like to care, couldn't even pretend, it was all hopeless, it was all fucked, and yet, maybe with something big, maybe if he could just send Figures on a Landscape, then maybe he could fix it all, after all, there *had* to be a solution, and yet, any solution you could come up with, it would run out through the bucket too. The hole in his bucket took everything and drained it away, and there was no solution. Sometimes, he would sit on the edge of the bed, and think, I will be okay, I *have* to be okay, but the truth was, some people never patched their buckets and their entire lives drained out and that would probably be him. He didn't see any reason why not.

Toast in the toaster. Coffee from the carafe. The golden glow thrown by the desk light. What meaning had the world? No meaning. He should call Tamma. Text her. Would he? No. And why not? He didn't know. It was just that any intention to call her drained out through the bucket like everything else and was lost to him. The shadow of the pencil across the paper. Tamma strolling down the hall, stained muscle shirt silk-screened with juicy lemon wedge, borrowed levi's rolled up to show the redline selvedge, the girl making a ring of thumb and forefinger, reciprocating her index through this aperture with a smirk, meaning something like: I am alive and ridiculous. Nobody, not anyone, ever, more beautiful to him.

Turn off the highway on the way home. Stop at the mailbox, key it open, and take out the heavy, full-sized envelopes. Lie at length atop the Mexican blanket, one arm behind his head, slowly opening and closing one hand in silence. The problem was that he didn't trust himself. He didn't know what he wanted.

Rise and cross the room, passing through the shafts of moonlight. Take a seat at the desk and turn the light back on. Snap open the clasp knife, slit the envelope, and spill bright confetti across the desktop. Pink and gold and blue. Read the letter. The reply date May 1.

Wake as if never having slept. Open his computer. See a message from Tamma coming in.

> Dude!

He checked the time. It was 3:27 a.m. He sat at the desk. Holding his head in his hands. He just waited, watching messages come in:

> dude i had a wet dream
> about a manatee
> no embrace has ever been
> so soft
> no nuzzles
> so sweet
> do i need therapy
> also
> how r u

He looked at the texts again. *How r u?* Well—how to start. In some boulderfields, there were gaps that went down to a hollowing and mineral-smelling darkness among the tumbled stones. In the warming of the day, those pits exhaled a cold, cryptlike air. His heart was like that. There came no sign. So that there was no possible answer to the dumb fucking question *how r u*. The sky was falling, it seemed to Dan, the world was hopeless and brutal and awful, and no one, not anyone, could prove that it wasn't, and yet, here he was, surrounded by hopeful and myopic morons, all asking things like *how r u*. He was filled with rage at everybody and at her, and in his rage, he felt more voluble, more discursive than ever. He had always known that depressed people hated themselves. But now he understood that even more than that, they hated everybody around them, in part because everyone was always wondering why they didn't just try *not being* depressed. He was surrounded by Lizas—blithely asking him to just fix the bucket when if they stopped and thought about it for one goddamn moment, they would see the futility of it. And Dan was the Henry, able to see, before Liza could see it herself, that any solution she might suggest required, in the end, the use of a bucket, when the bucket was the one thing they didn't have, and her failure to anticipate this problem, her repeated, poorly considered rejoinders to just fix the bucket, they were callous, they were irresponsible and self-involved, given that the bucket could not be fixed. In the end, they weren't about Henry or Henry's bucket at all, they were about discharging the unease most people felt in the presence of hopelessness and nihilism. Here Dan was, living through the onset of a major and life-destroying mental illness—and in all this, Tamma was telling him about a wet dream she had about a manatee, and asking *how r u*. Really, he was angry at Tamma, who thought they should just go out to Canyonlands, and start climbing, and pretend they weren't doomed, pretend they weren't absolutely hosed, pretend that Tamma herself hadn't just gone out to LA, intending to prove that she had what it took, and instead gotten stomped, and not only stomped, but nearly crippled. The frolicking audacity of that was an outrage to him, and it left Dan alone in wrestling with the seriousness and hopelessness of what she proposed they do, and she wasn't reckoning with it, because she was preoccupied by some wet dream she had about a manatee.

Sit in the subaru, watching sprinklers arching colorless gray water over a colorless gray horizon, a glary shine off the track's flooded far turn. Walk the halls, sit in desks, take notes, his backpack at his feet. Sierra working another strike; Tamarisk in the wind. No way homegirl was passing any of her classes. A high school dropout, then. Monday, April 9. Figures on a Landscape forty-three days away.

He let himself into the windowless, dropceilinged guidance office and pitched the envelopes onto the desk. After a while, and without looking up, the counselor motioned that he should sit, and Dan took a seat. The counselor dropped the letter to the desktop, said, "Congratulations!" and with a great effort heaved himself to a stand. In the tight confines behind his desk, he labored about, trying to keep from knocking into stacked books and papers. Groaning, he opened a mini fridge, and then planted one enormous hand atop it and pressed himself back to a stand, holding out, by the neck, a bottle of what looked like champagne.

"What's this?" Dan said.

The counselor forked up two plastic wineglasses and set them on the desk. "Sparkling apple cider!" he said. He unwound the choker on the muselet, caught the cork in his fist. "This is a *big day*. Whooboy I have been waiting for this."

"You have?"

"I stayed up many nights writing your letter. I showed it to my girlfriend."

The girlfriend was news to Dan.

"She's a great writer. *Great* writer. Self-publishes this series about giant otters living in the postapocalyptic upper Midwest, where all the humans have been wiped out thousands of years ago, and then one of these otters, Tah'queelie, finds a human child? And there is one evil otter who wants to put the child to death, so they have to wrestle for dominance."

"Wait," Dan said. "What?"

"Anyway, she has a good ear. *She* could tell you that I had some sleepless nights over this. I just want to say. Wow, Dan! Bravo. This school, they give out one of these scholarship packages a year. Only one. Drink that!"

Dan picked up his wineglass. Say it, he thought. Just dyno for it.

"Usually," the counselor said. "People react, they tell me about their hopes, sketch in the direction they imagine for their lives. They permit themselves to be a little excited. The world opens up for graduates of a school like this."

He motioned with one hand to indicate that Dan should talk.

Dan said, "I guess I've been doubting if I want to go."

The counselor looked up at the corner of the room, over Dan's head, his mouth slacking open. Sometimes, in moments of reflection, his eyes tracked left to right repeatedly as if he were reading out of the air. Dan liked this enormously, it gave some sense of the vast experience and learning stored up in the man.

"And by doubting," Dan said, "I mean, I go back and forth. I'm scared to pass up this opportunity. But I don't want to go."

"You don't want to go?"

"That's right."

"What else would you do?"

"I have this buddy. She and I want to set off into Canyonlands and be dirtbag climbers."

"*Dirtbag*, what do you mean by *dirtbag*?"

"It means opting out of the valorized status economy. Live in a vehicle. Sleep in the wilderness. Work, but only to save up enough money to keep climbing. Own little, buy less, and see wild, beautiful places while there are wild, beautiful places left. I love climbing. It's all that's kept me alive these last few years, it's the only thing that's important to me. That, and this friendship I have. My mom is not a stable person, and sometimes I think I may not be that stable, either. All my life people have called me gifted and I sometimes wonder if really what I have is anxiety and depression, if my giftedness isn't really a terror, which I carry around, all the time, and which spurs me to perform at high levels. Terror that the world is fundamentally insecure. That the bottom could drop out of it, at any time. That if I am not brilliant and high performing, my parents will stop loving me. But also, terror at myself, at who I may become. So maybe my *giftedness* is not going to a translate to a great life, after high school. Maybe the ordinary thing, the normal college-and-a-career thing, it's not gonna work for me. So, maybe I need to turn back and face it. The terror, I mean. When I look around, it's everyone living these purposeless lives they don't understand, lives they don't enjoy, forced from one thing to the next, broke and afraid of being broke, working jobs they hate for a life in which they find no meaning, and it looks like there's *nothing else*, no hope or beauty anywhere, in anyone's lives, no one knows how to find it, no one knows where it went, or why it's gone, everywhere you turn there's no chance, no hope, no way forward, no one I've ever met sees any point in it, no one thinks anything is possible, and at the same time, they can't stop grinding for money, and I don't want that for myself, I don't want to go to school and have people tell me what things mean so that I will be content and effective working whatever job comes after. I am suspicious of the well-accepted answers. I want to go out there into the desert and see for myself; I want to stay up nights in the back of a truck reading Plato, George Eliot, Melville, Toni Morrison, Thomas Hardy, Mavis Gallant; I want to reread Proust, because I didn't understand it; they kept bringing up the Dreyfus Affair, and I didn't look it up, because I thought surely that would pass, but the Dreyfus stuff just kept going, and I never understood that entire part of the book. And when I look at who's going to college, I see mostly kids who want to get a degree and be credentialed so they can get jobs and have *things* and *security*. I don't want that; I want to go out onto the White Rim with my friend and climb sandstone towers at the peril of our lives, swim in the Colorado River, wander slot canyons, and search out Anasazi ruins hidden in hanging valleys. It is one of the last places, maybe the very last place, where you can still dirtbag in America like the old-school climbers did. You can sleep in canyons and washes at night with other climbers, all with campfires and beer and weed, frying up tacos beneath cottonwood trees while people play guitars and read poetry. There are risk-takers, misfits, and weirdos out there. People searching for meaning, measuring their lives not by how insulated they are from the vicissitudes of fortune, but by their incandescent proximity to the real. And my buddy and I, we could do something great, something extraordinary, we could forge a life glorious and risky, honorable, even: Full of beauty, every moment, no matter how scary, how painful, how difficult, full, at least, of the gorgeousness of real places and real people, totally unlike the skid mark I see stretched out before me—if we get this chance, I think we could go to the very ends of the earth and stare off the side and come back with a story to tell. My buddy, she believes that such a story might change this nation for the better, at least a little bit, and I'm not at all sure that she's wrong."

The counselor picked up his pen, cued it up in his hands, and spun it about his thumb. Picked it up again. The cup of golden cider stood on the desk, fizzing. Then he raised his eyebrows and said, with heavy reluctance, "Daniel, I have to tell you. This is the opportunity of a lifetime. You cannot give this up for some friendship you had in high school." He spun the pen around his thumb again. He seemed to want to be careful. As if his primary wish were to do no harm. He seemed to consider the possibility of a friendship for which you might forsake an opportunity such as this, and then, at last, to find it incumbent upon himself to continue. He said, "Daniel. You will forgive me for saying so, but I have never in my life had the privilege of working with a young person as promising as yourself. You have a *great* mind, and you need to be among other people who, like you, are excited about learning. You're wrong about the type of kids going to college. People are going to be reading Foucault and Derrida in French and Aeschylus in the original Greek. It is going to be exciting. These are the brilliant young people who are going to shape the course of human events over the next five decades. It is the reason I do what I do—to usher people like yourself into those opportunities."

"I think Tamma *is* a brilliant young person, who really might do great things," Dan said, and the counselor's eyebrows went up. At the name, he registered gentle confusion: a furrowing of the brow and a searching of the eyes side to side as he racked his brains for any reason that Dan might spend time with this individual. Smiling and incredulous, seeming to expect some punch line, some correction or misunderstanding, seeming to think he might be being pranked, he said, "The burnout girl with the jaw thing?"

When Dan did not correct him, the counselor hesitated there. He brought himself up short and searched for any error he might make. He seemed to take this job seriously; he seemed to want, in a considered way, to give the best possible advice as to Dan's future. At last he tossed aside the pen and leaned forward, out of his chair, breasted upon the desk with his great forearms among the papers. His bulk lent to him a gentle imposingness. "Daniel," he said, looking at the kid very seriously. "I have to tell you. With the wisdom of experience. Friends come and go—they are just people you are thrown close to by circumstance, and incidentally spend time with for a while. This scholarship is worth two hundred thousand dollars. But more than that—it is an opportunity to change your financial circumstances, and the financial circumstances of your entire family. Measured against that—a friendship with a person from whom you will almost certainly grow apart, in time? She is not as promising as you are. She isn't driven like you. Her future is not as bright, and you cannot let her hold you back. You have to consider that you have your whole career ahead of you. If you really want to accomplish something, you should be at college."

Dan stared across the wood laminate desk at the counselor. At last he picked up his backpack and collected his papers. The counselor watched him with canny, deep-set eyes.

"Have a good day," he said, as Dan was letting himself out the door.

"Thanks," Dan said. "You too."

Two

Three weeks later, Alexandra came into his room and sat on the chair beside the bed where Dan was reading atop the covers. She clasped her hands and unclasped them and touched her lips together and parted them with a dry click. Dan set the book facedown on his lap.

She said, "Daniel, I am going to go away for a time."

"What?"

"I'm sorry."

He looked down at the book. He had trouble looking her in the face.

"Where will you go?"

"I've been offered a teaching position at a school in Texas."

"In April?" he said.

She made an awkward expression.

"Fall quarter doesn't start until September. But I've agreed to teach a summer extension starting in June. It's not glamorous, Danny. It's academic drudgery, nothing like being a full professor. That summer cohort will be mostly kids who failed their regular-term classes, and I'll be something less than an adjunct. I wouldn't do it if I wasn't desperate. And I will need some time. To study the texts again. To get myself up to speed."

She was wringing her hands and then pulling them apart, the fingers interlocked so that they dragged against each other without cleaving free. It was a surprise to him, that he could keep on breathing. The moment seemed impossible, like the world must break open around him, like she must be joking, like something must give, like it must change, like she must react, say more than she was saying, feel differently than she felt, but nothing gave. She sat beside him, gently insistent. Nine weeks since discharge. Friday the twenty-seventh of April. The reply date for Reed less than a week away, twenty-five days until Figures. She did not even really need to leave. The job did not start for months. She was just giving up. She did not care about him. How could she? She was Emma Bovary, a glamorous woman trapped in the unglamorous hinterlands, bereft of all that she deserved, married to a plodding imbecile, and he was Bovary's little daughter, who no one remembered or cared about, not Emma, not Charles, not the reader. He did not ask if she would come back for graduation. He already knew that she would not. He sat there in bed with no idea what he would do with his life.

"I read *Ephedra* when you were in the hospital," he said.

She watched him. Her head canted slightly forward. Her bright blue eyes searching from out her dark blond eyebrows.

"The bookseller, she said that was the book that made her a reader. You touched lives with that book. You spoke kindness and humanity to people."

When she did not respond, he went on.

"I know you had heart surgery. But lots of people do. So why couldn't you write another? Why do you have to leave?"

She cast her gaze straight up, her ankle boots side by side, elbows on her thighs, hands clasped. If there was any expression on her calm, high-cheekboned face, it was a moue of unhappiness. She said, "You must understand, Danny. These things you mention, they were my life's purpose. To be a novelist. To write a book that would mean something to some girl out there in the world. I gave it everything I had, I worked as hard on that book as I could, to fill it with such compassion and beauty that it could not be ignored. But when I attained all those things about which I had dreamed, when I finally arrived, after all that work, what I found was"—she gestured about herself in the air, turning side to side, pantomiming her encounter with something insubstantial, catching at effervescent fluff and nothingness with her fingertips, like cottonwood blooms in the wind—"there was nothing there. Nothing in all of that success except more success, if you wanted it, more money, more recognition, if you could even stomach it, but it didn't *mean* anything, it was totally hollow and insubstantial. The meaning I thought I would find there, at the end, didn't come."

"It was all, what—pointless?" Dan said.

"What happened, Danny, is that I chased a dream, and when I caught it, I discovered what maybe everyone else already knew: That meaning and purpose are not real things; that there was no secret to be discovered in life; nothing beyond the reality we see. The rugs, coffee cups, and typewriters with which we furnish our everyday lives, that's life. There is nothing more to it. And believe you me, I have gone looking. Any hope of Walden Pond, of a version of oneself other than the self one already finds oneself to be, those are like the lines of trees planted along highways to give the pleasing sensation of wilderness on either side, where no wilderness remains. These are the mirrors in the elevator meant to allay claustrophobia. Myths and lies, meant to make our world seem more capacious than it is. Thoreau's mother was doing his laundry the entire time. This is what I have been trying to tell you. Go to school. Make money. Live a good life, Danny—a life with central air, health insurance, and a dishwasher, a life without ever having to worry about the cost of a gallon of milk. To eschew security may seem romantic now, but it will not seem romantic when you have a screaming baby in your arms and the blood in your heart begins to eddy and run backward."

Dan could barely speak. At first he thought he would not be able to.

"I'm sorry," he said, at very long last.

"That's okay," she said. "You're going to be all right?" she said.

"Sure, yeah," he said. "You know me, I'll be fine. Look—" he said. "Look here." He crawled out across the bed, slung his legs off the side, crossed to the desk, and came back with the full-sized white envelopes. He did not know why he did it, except that there existed in him the mad hope that she might see how hard he had worked, how much he had accomplished, how far he had come, and seeing that, she might turn and see him, beside her; that there might be a moment where she became aware of who he was; he was willing to throw away all his bold dreams of meaning in the wastelands, and walk instead down this well-trodden path, at the end of which he saw only ruin, so that he might have this one chance, for Alexandra to see what he had done and love him for it, however briefly.

"What?" she said. "What's this?"

Dan seated himself cross-legged on the bed and opened the envelope. He found the cover letter and passed it to her. She took it in one shaking hand, and sat, arrested.

"But Danny," she said. "You're going to school. A good school."

"Yes," he said, again.

She blew out a shuddering breath. "This is everything I wanted," she said. Then she rose, leaned forward, kissed him on the forehead, and let herself out of the room.

Lawrence came home later. She was not supposed to lift things and Dan heard Lawrence talk to her, and then heard him carrying her things out to the car. After that Lawrence came into Dan's room. He sat in the chair by the bed.

"Well, Danny," he said. "You want to come say goodbye to your mom?"

"Yes," Dan said, and got up. He followed his old man. The front door was open and the two of them walked out. Dan leaned against the split rail fence. The subaru was packed with boxes. She moved to close the hatchback and stopped, because she was not supposed to reach above her head, and Lawrence came forward and slammed it closed.

"Are you going to be okay?" he said. "Will you make it?"

"I'll make it," she said.

She was crying. She had her hair up in a ponytail. Tight denim, ankle boots, white tee, black suit jacket. She stood and looked at them and they stood and looked at her. Then she came forward and hugged Lawrence. She hugged Dan. She felt slender and fragile. She touched him with her shoulder and hand only.

"Good luck, Mom," he said, and she walked to the still-running car, got in, and pulled out through the drive. They watched the plume of dust going on toward the 62, the two of them leaning on the split rail fence.

His old man looked over at him.

"Well, Danny," he said. "You want to go into town and get burgers?"

That night, he lay atop the flat-woven blanket with his thoughts going and going and going. He could not still them and they were much the same thought. He knew he had to stop but he could not stop. He got up and paced back and forth in his room. At last, he crossed to the computer and sat down at the desk. He opened his laptop, waited for the internet to connect. He had received, after his admissions letter, an email that included a student portal. He signed in to it now and looked at his pending admissions decision. Clicked *respond* and waited, cracking his knuckles. There was a way he wished he felt; that was not the way he did feel.

He looked at his student portal. Then he clicked *accept*. The next page required his bank account information for the $500 nonrefundable acceptance deposit.

He finished entering his bank account information and submitted it. The next page just said: *Congratulations!* He stared at it, hating himself with a profundity akin to pain, a visceral recoiling from himself so strong, so gut-churning, that it was a private, drawn-out, interior suffering.

He rose, backing away from the computer, running his hand up the back of his neck. He backstepped and backstepped again until his calves met the bed and he sat down. He wished he had the strength to just go with Tamma. But he didn't have it. He was going to have to let something other than himself decide.

Three

He woke to his alarm, silenced it, and then lay facedown in his bed. The room not quite black. Some faint, bruisy light beyond those windows. He thought of getting up and could not. He thought of going into the kitchen, imagined opening the fridge to pour coffee for himself, and it sounded like just too much work, and for what, he didn't know. He lay, hanging his head off the edge to stare at the floor. One arm dangling to touch the concrete slab. Maybe your life was your life. And it didn't matter if you got up in the morning and got yourself coffee and toast or not. It was worse, without coffee, but maybe if you got up every morning and worked hard, if you had your coffee, and your toast, and you did your kettlebell get-ups and your pull-ups and your homework and you went to class, then maybe your life was a meaningless suckhole just the same, only with different detailing. It was all still your life.

It was Saturday, April 28. Alexandra gone only the night before. Maybe he could go to college, and just pretend that he was all right. Maybe he could pretend his whole entire life. Not care for any of it. Feel nothing. No, guys, this world we've all made, it's great. I love all these highways and strip malls and box stores you've built. The parking lots are a big part of it, and they live up to the hype. Truly. And this thing we're doing, where there are hardly bookstores anymore? The chain restaurants bear mentioning. Why would we let people run their own restaurants, when we could turn everyone into a minor functionary in a vast corporate hierarchy? That's clearly the way. Also healthcare? The way the bills are indecipherable, and can come at any time, that really gives a certain *je ne sais quoi* to a life otherwise spent mostly riding elevators up and down, walking back and forth through blank featureless hallways beneath fluorescent lighting, looking at the world from out the bland, air-conditioned interiors of cars, offices, hospital rooms, waiting rooms, classrooms, grocery stores. It's a great world we have here, and I am thrilled to be a part of it.

Daniel Redburn could maybe pretend the whole way through. Have children and not love them. No, better not to have children. He could take this strain of madness and major depression to the grave as his only good work in life. Let Tamma have children. Snaggle-toothed, bat-eared children, ravaged with learning disorders, and manically alive just the same, children he would never know, because his life would be full of normal people, who spoke and thought and behaved like normal human beings. He could work at goldman sachs and have the hell out of some rugs, coffee cups, and typewriters, maybe coffee tables too, coffee table books, even, a life appointed with beautiful things as a stand-in for everything he had really wanted to do. Maybe from time to time he would remember her and then remind himself that friendships didn't mean anything. Friends were just people you were thrown in with by circumstance. Unlike coffee cups. You'd purchased the coffee cup, so it represented a choice: a gorgeous, shining act of self-actualization. There was a cleanness to that. He could work a job and feel nothing about it and pretend until he died all so the intervening years could be full of good furniture and nice clothes. That would be okay. What was happening inside him was that his heart was like that cold gap among the stones. But maybe that wouldn't bother him, so long as he never looked at it, never thought of the possibility that more was down there, beyond the veil of the visible.

He was lying that way when a tap, tap, tapping sounded on the window. He looked up to see Tamma slide the sash up from the outside and duck inside, swinging each leg in turn over the sill while smoking a hand-rolled spliff. She wore very small cutoffs and a very large, acid-washed purple tee that said I ♥ HOT MOMS. Speaking around the spliff clamped in her teeth, she said, "Put your big-girl panties on, Dan, and pull them *all the way up*: We're going climbing!"

"I can't," he said. He didn't understand how she had gotten here. Sierra worked night shift Friday, Saturday, and Sunday, which had to mean that Sierra had gotten home and Tamma had cut out immediately. If she'd run up the lane from Sierra's house to the bus stop, caught the bus into town, and sprinted up Lifted Lorax Lane, then she could just barely have made it. To do something like that spoke to tremendous personal fitness.

"How are you even here?" he said.

"I flew here," she said, "on wings of Courage and Destiny, basting the land below with tears of exhaustion."

"Shouldn't you sleep?"

"Sleep is for the weak, Dan."

She went into the living room, came back a little while later with mason jars of coffee and a tinfoil packet of buttered toast, and found

Dan still upon the bed. She set her things on the desk, quenched the joint between thumb and forefinger, stuck it behind her ear, then leapt up onto the bedframe and kicked him twice, saying, "Get up, get up!" and Dan said, "I can't," and Tamma exclaimed, "Cast down your buckets from where you stand!" and Dan said, "That's racist, that's racist appropriation to say that," and Tamma said, "The rocks are waiting for you, Dan!" and then something occurred to her and she leapt down and crossed back out of the room and Dan could hear her beating on the door to the master with her shoe and she said, "I'm taking the truck, old man!" He heard something from Lawrence, and Tamma shouted back, "Thieves! Vagabonds! Marauders! Burglars, rapists, and robbers! Hark and alarum! Ring the bells! Circle the wagons! I am here to abscond with your vehicles, disparage the virginity of your children, and nut into your coffee cups! Hark and alarum!" She came back into the room and said, "He seemed confused but what he meant was, sure, you can take the truck, get up, get up! It's Saturday and the rocks are a-warming! The boulders lie lonely upon the plain, pining for want of your strong, thick, decisive fingers! Arise and go! Arise and go now, to a park I know, that sits upon the joining of three deserts, each more blighted and lonely than the last! Arise and go!"

Dan levered himself up out of bed and said, "You mean *despoil*. To disparage someone's virginity would be to impugn it, to represent it as being of little worth."

"Even better!" Tamma cried, and leapt back onto the bed, seized his hair, and dragged Dan complaining to the floor, hurrying him along with kicks, shouting, "Get thee hence, pathetic virgin!"

"I'm going, I'm going," he said.

"I'll start the truck!" she said.

She came back in and found him dressing.

"Come on, come on, if you want to send Figures, you gotta *climb*." She grabbed him by the front of the shirt and dragged him through the house to the truck, where he got in the driver side as she ran back for the toast and coffees and then hopped in the passenger seat. He pulled out, headed toward the 62.

They got to the park late and found a line at the fee station. Tamma did her best. She leaned across Dan to leer snaggletoothedly out the window and said, "Naomi, will you please, please, *please* let us into the park for free in exchange for sexytimes?"

"*Tempting*," Naomi said dryly. "But no."

They parked at Intersection Rock and Tamma toured him boulder to boulder, chasing shade. Dan was creaky, weak, and out of practice, but Tamma didn't seem to care. She'd stand close in beside him and cheer him through every attempt saying, "Everyone acts like—'*Oooooh*, your V-card! Such a big deal!' You're a little girl, coming up in the world, and everyone's all like, 'Protect it all costs!' you know? But you grow up and come to find you can't give it away for love or money." Then, after Dan had greased off some foothold a dozen times, she would say patiently, "Not that, *this*," and, digging out a nugget of chalk, she'd tick some nothing-bullshit crystal and he'd say, "Sure, dude," meaning *no way*, but he would try it, and that small adjustment would unlock the whole problem, and he'd send, and she seemed to enjoy it as much as he did, warmly and patiently walking him to the next problem, dragging the bouldering pad behind with their stuff heaped upon it, saying, "Do you think every girl has that problem, or is it just the *very sexiest* among us?" And Dan would say, "I think it's that you intimidate people," and Tamma would say, "RIGHT?!" And Dan would say, "Is it this line here?" and Tamma would nod, and Dan would make a study of the route, testing out the holds with his fingertips, before getting down on the pad, pulling on his shoes, saying, "I think really what it was, is she didn't want to be ruined for all other women."

"That's it," Tamma said. "Because that's what I would've done."

"Totally. You'd've wrecked her for all time: her life ever after a dwindling pale afterglow."

"Awfully wise of her, to steer clear. Highstep here. Like you mean it. Then just stem through. Wider than that. Way out left there is a scabby sloper like Josh Brolin's chin, you're smearing for that."

"The other consideration," Dan said, stepping far out left, and stemming up, "is that maybe Naomi *would* go for you, except that she deplores prostitution as inimical to human freedom and dignity."

"You're there! Just go big for the top!"

She had each of these boulders sketched in the giant lab notebook she carried, but there was no need of it. She had them down by heart. And that was because, Dan thought, it was easy to remember the things you loved.

While Dan lay on the pad between attempts, lathered in sweat, Tamma would lap the slabs hands-free, holding her arms up by her head like she was being mugged, tiptoeing from hold to hold. She would pause, trembling, after each step, making subtle adjustments forward and back as she tightened through the core, and then she would make the next step, and the next. If she dabbed the rock with her hands, she'd leap down and try again.

Other times, she just watched him while he unlocked some problem or other. Saying, "Nice, nice," and not spotting him, because of the danger to her finger, but simply stepping away when he fell.

She walked him out to another problem that required a committing stand-up to a potato-chip undercling and Dan stalled, time after time, beneath the move, before dropping off.

"I can't do it," he said.

"Uh-huh."

"I can't."

"Hmmm."

"I *can't do it*," he said. "I just can't."

"This time," she said. "Instead of letting go, like a little bitch, commit through it, like Shauna Coxsey."

Dan climbed back to the stance.

"It's too high," he said.

"Nothing is too high for Shauna," she said.

"Shit shit shit shit," he said.

Tamma goosed him with two fingers of her left hand, driving them at a terrifying and steep upward angle. "Ack!" Dan said, and committed up, caught the potato chip, and held it. He got a foot up. Shaking all over with nerves, got another foot up, and then mantled over the top.

"You did it!" she said.

"You *menace*!"

"Amazing!" she said. "People don't talk enough about the motivating fear of anal sodomation. Somebody should write a book about that."

"Somebody did. It's called *Deliverance*."

"It's cuter though, when you sub in white trash climbing chicks for violent hillbillies. Isn't it?"

"So much cuter."

"We should add hard-sending climbers to everything," Tamma said. "*Jurassic Park*, say. Colonel Sanders is like, 'We've engineered the perfect climber.' The huge gates open, and there he is, pacing back and forth behind an electric fence, holding his climbing shoes—"

"*Adam Ondra*," Dan said.

"Yes!" Tamma said, "Resplendent, necky, and gorgeous, and Jeff Goldblum looks at him in awe, and says, 'Your scientists were so preoccupied with whether or not they could, they didn't stop to think if they *should*.'"

They lay on the pad, laughing, their backs to an overhanging boulder, shadowed by Intersection Rock, eating a lunch of cold roasted chicken thighs and biscuits with butter and jam.

"Alexandra left," he said, out of nowhere.

"What do you mean, left?"

"I mean, she accepted a teaching position at some school in Texas."

"I wondered why the subaru was gone."

"Yeah."

"When was this?"

"Yesterday."

"Shit, dude."

"She didn't even really need to go. The position doesn't start for months. Not really. She just wanted out."

"I'm so sorry."

"I'm glad you came."

"I always come."

"Oh!"

"I come faster and harder than anyone you know."

"Oh, lord!"

Dan climbed a half dozen more problems and then they drove back and met Sierra at the door. Dan could have left then. He could've gotten back in the truck and driven home, and maybe he should've, certainly he was stranding Lawrence without a vehicle, but he found himself carried along in Tamma's wake, up the stairs, past Sierra, who was adjusting her ponytail as she came down. Tamma let herself into the door, throwing out jazz hands, shrieking, "Babies!" and Hunter and Sam sat straight up, swung around to look at her, and lit with beaming smiles. Even River, lying on the floor, lit with joy. His eyes crinkled down and his tiny, wet mouth slacked open and he reached out for her. Hunter came galloping across the room into her arms, and Tamma, not much larger, spun him around and then set him back down and pointed her finger forward, into the room, into the future, and said, "Dinner!" After that she was ceaselessly in motion, carrying River on her hip as she took down plates, grabbed tupperware from the fridge, and heated leftovers; serving water when Samantha signed for it with an open-hand-to-chin gesture; and putting River into Dan's lap when Hunter wanted to sit in hers, but only after three or four insistent repetitions of "Hunter, you can sit down and eat or you can wash your hands, those are the options." And then Dan was helping her bus the table (Tamma putting any scrap, no matter how soggy and chewed, into her mouth), scrub the high chair, vacuum the rug, wash the dishes, and mop the floor. They finished just in time for another snack—bottle for River, cheerios and milk for Sam, graham crackers with peanut butter for Hunter—and then it was bedtime. Hunter had "quiet time" in his room, involving very many noises of crashes, explosions, and sirens, while Tamma bathed Samantha and River, first testing the water with an instant-read thermometer and seeming to know that if you let it run for three minutes at max temp and then seven minutes at 103 degrees, it would come out to be just about 102 degrees by the time everybody was in the tub. Soon she was toweling, lotioning, and diapering them together on the bathroom floor, applying ointment to River's eczema, and then reading to both babies, held together in her lap in a rocker, until one-handing River into his crib, singing Samantha to sleep, and returning to Hunter with a Magic School Bus book until the light was off and the sound machine on. Through all this, she was the same girl Dan had known all his life, and yet also the calm, confident leader of a small band of tiny, unruly humans.

Afterward, Dan and Tamma lay down on Sierra's bed, Dan half dead just from watching and helping.

"Is it always that much work?"

"Always."

"How are you?" Dan said.

"My heart is breaking, dude. I can't believe how hard this is, how much Sierra is working, how bad brain injuries are, I can't believe how many mistakes we find on the insurance bills and how hard they are to dispute. That could be a full-time job on its own. I mean, I'm glad *we have* insurance. Did Alex?"

"No."

"What about Obamacare?"

"She never signed up."

"Why not?"

"I don't know. Ignorance, anxiety, and major, life-ruining depression, I guess."

"Wouldn't it be pretty much free, and wouldn't you get fined, for not having insurance?"

"I didn't say it made sense."

"Our parents are such dipshits."

"*Such* dipshits."

"So, you guys are basically hosed, huh? Financially, I mean."

"Well, the hospital set my old man up with a social worker whose job it is to help. But yes—we're hosed."

"Well, I'm glad we do have insurance, but also, why do we support this multibillion-dollar insurance industry if it's going to suck, be impossible to navigate, and make constant, infuriating clerical errors? And also, River's accident was in December. And the deductible starts over in January. So if you think about it, his care would've cost twenty grand less if he'd fallen on January fifth rather than December fifth. Isn't that wild? Anyway. That's a mess. And also, River is supposed to start turning from his back to his belly any day now, and he's not! There's no sign! There's all this stuff you're supposed to do, to help him, but I don't have time to do it all! He started turning over belly to back a while ago. But I don't know if that's *real*—like, I think he just lifts his head up, and the weight *rolls him over* because he's so small. I don't think it's like, *coordinated* and *on purpose*. So really, I don't know if he's rolling at all. And he sees a PT who is this six-foot-eight ginger Christian guy with *Everything is going to be okay* eyes? And the PT can't get him to turn over, either. And by the way, insurance won't pay for the PT anymore, so there's that! They pay for a certain number of weeks and that's it. So, does Sierra work more, and not see her children, and pay for PT? Or does she come home and see him and let the PT go? These decisions are our life, right now. And every day I'm just like—! What if this is it—! What if that's the last milestone—! You know? Which is stupid, he probably will turn over eventually—! But

I'm just like—! What if he doesn't—! On the other hand, Sam is getting easier, so that's good, and her baby sign language is good, she knows about a hundred words, which is a lot. The baby sign language, if you didn't know, is because kids can sign more words than they can really say—so it's one way to start communicating with them before they can talk. So there are good things! If we die, Sierra and me, I mean, and River never really grows up, maybe Sam can take care of him—? That's awful to say but you have to think of these things! Every day feels about a week long but the weeks go by like nothing and every minute of every day, I'm terrified, just *terrified*, except when I'm out climbing, which is weird if you think about it, because that's the only time I could actually die, except no, that's when I'm calm, and everything else is scarier, because it's worse than death. Sierra made ninety an hour working that strike, plus a differential for nights and overtime. Twenty grand in two weeks. She's already pulled in close to seventy grand extra. If she can keep that up, then we can climb out of this hole we're in. And she's a Callahan so she *can* keep it up, if you know what I mean. But still!"

Dan lay on his back, listening to all this, and more, and speaking back to her or just making noises to show that he was listening, and thinking to himself, she is so much stronger than even I knew, and I always knew she was strong.

In the morning, Tamma fed the kiddos and Dan labored over the hot cast iron, frying whole-grain pancakes, which he had made off a much-amended recipe in her lab notebook. Nearby pages were full of dense notes on formula calculations. Tamma had River in a wrap and was gently quizzing Samantha on her words while feeding her pancakes in the high chair, saying, "Sammy, can you say 'Mom'?" Samantha touched her thumb to her chin. "Good!" Tamma said. "Good! Mom! That's right! And what sound does a bear make?" To which Samantha growled, tiny and ferocious. "That counts as a word," Tamma told Dan, and then Samantha gently touched her hands together, fingertip to fingertip, to sign for more pancakes, and Tamma obligingly added more pancakes to her tray.

That was how it was when Sierra came in the front door, letting down her hair, shucking off one clog then the other, pulling her scrub top over her head, and peeling off her compression stockings. "There's coffee," Dan said, and Sierra shambled over and poured herself a cup. She groaned with the pleasure of it, then reached a hand up inside her undershirt, and, setting down the coffee, pulled her bra out through the arm of her shirt with the other hand. "Pancakes in the oven," Dan said, and Sierra opened the oven and hooked out a pancake.

Tamma went into the living room and collected it all in the laundry basket and put the shoes away and then returned to Samantha's high chair.

"So," Sierra said, taking her seat at the table, leaning forward on her elbows. "Distract me from my exhaustion. Are you guys going to prom?"

Tamma laughed, nodded, and passed River to Sierra, who took him in her arms and began syruping her pancake.

Hunter rose, ran into the other room, and came back carrying a black cowboy hat. He put it on Sierra's head, seated himself, and then looked over at Dan and stage-whispered, "She looks better with the hat on."

Laughing, Sierra said, "I do, honey?"

To Dan, he whispered: "She's losing her hair."

"Jeepers," Sierra said. "It's brutal out here."

"How goes work?" Dan said. "How's the hospital?"

"So much walking," Sierra said.

"*Mom*," Hunter said.

"Yes, honey?"

Hunter leaned over and whispered: "You look *really tired*."

Sierra looked at Dan and shook her head slowly side to side.

You could tell that Hunter was excited to have Dan around the house. When Tamma had gone into his room to fetch him up, he had hidden under his blankets, shrieking that he wanted Dan, that he didn't want Tamma to get him, he didn't want to get up on his own, he wanted Dan. When Dan had obligingly gone into the room and said, "Time to get up, buddy," Hunter had cavalierly swept aside his blankets and arisen from his toddler bed like an English gentleman, walking out side by side with Dan.

When Dan had finished on the stove top, he joined the table and started buttering his own pancake. Hunter looked at Dan. Then reached out with a knife and shaved off a pat and passed it over his own pancake, the butter melting as it spread. Tamma and Sierra both went silent.

Dan took a bite, and beside him, in exactly the same way, Hunter bore down with the edge of his fork, sheared off a section, speared it, and ate it. He looked at Dan. Dan sheared off another bite. So did Hunter.

"So, uh," Tamma said, nonchalantly. "How you finding that pancake, cowboy?"

"It's good," Hunter said, nodding. "Yeah. It's good. *Yeah*."

"I've been," Tamma said, with some outrage, "T-R-Y-I-N-G to G-E-T H-I-M to E-A-T B-U-T-T-E-R for months."

"So," Sierra said, reminding them, "*prom?*"

"Oh, you're serious?" Tamma said.

"Yeah."

"I thought," Tamma said, looking down at herself and cleaning a dab of yogurt off her shirt with a spoon, "that was like, a tasteless but hilarious joke?"

"No joke."

"I'm not going to prom. Dan, are you going to prom?"

"Oh, you didn't hear?" Dan said. "Kendra's taking me."

"You're going to prom with Grandma?" Hunter asked, his brow furrowed seriously.

"No, no, a joke, buddy," Dan said quickly.

"You can't *not go* to prom," Sierra said, punching caffeine pills out from their tinfoil backing directly into her coffee.

"You're not going to sleep?" Dan said.

"Sleep when the baby sleeps, Dan," Sierra said.

"What do you mean," Tamma said, "I 'can't not go to prom'? *Of course* I'm not going."

"You guys *have* to go," Sierra said. "It's the greatest night of your life."

"I very much hope *that's* not true."

"Go," Sierra said. "You *guys*. You *must* go."

"Prom is May nineteenth. You're already scheduled the nineteenth."

"I'll switch out for dayshift. Sprint home at seven thirty and you can leave by eight."

"Why?"

"Because it's *prom*," Sierra said. "I'm not gonna be the reason you miss *prom*."

"Why is prom the thing?"

"I appreciate that you're here. I'm grateful. But we're needing your help less and less—because of you! We made a lot of money on that last strike. I guess I'm starting to see the light at the end of the tunnel. I'm starting to see the day when we won't need you anymore, at least not quite so badly, and I don't want to have been the reason you stayed, not when you have . . ." Sierra sighed. Put her head in her hands. Didn't want to say it but came out with it at last. ". . . dreams."

"Impossible dreams, I thought, stupid dreams," Tamma said.

River looked up at Sierra curiously and caught at her index finger with his hand, reeled it down to his mouth, and chewed upon it. "To be honest," Sierra said, letting River nom away, "I see you taking care of everybody all night and then getting up at four a.m. to do your little hanging-by-your-fingertips exercise thing and I think about what you might do, with a real chance. I don't want to ruin your life."

"You're not ruining my life, dude."

"Go," she said.

"You can't just go to prom. You need tickets."

Sierra went for her purse, dug in it, took out her wallet and brought out the bills. "You can't," she said again, "not go."

Tamma reached for the money and Sierra retracted it at the last moment.

"Now, don't just use this to buy D-I-L-D-Os or whatever."

"Oh," Tamma said. "I'm definitely using it to buy D-I-L-D-Os."

"And isn't there something you want to ask?" Sierra said to Tamma, finally handing off the money.

"Oh!" said Tamma. "Oh! Dan! Will you go to prom with me?"

"I don't have anything to wear," Dan said.

"You can borrow my American flag leotard."

"Then yes," Dan said.

"Okay, you kids," Sierra said. "I know what you really want. Go on. Get out of here."

Tamma had her apron off and was at the door like a shot. Dan looked after her.

"Don't let her die," Sierra said.

"I won't," Dan said.

"Don't you die, either," Sierra said, after a moment of thought.

Four

Dan sat at the table with his old man, eating enchiladas with green chile. They were silent for a very long time. It was the seventeenth of May. Dan had spent every spare moment bouldering with Tamma. Tamma warmed up slowly, had not recovered full range of motion, and her finger always ached afterward, but if she kept the aching to a two or three out of ten, it didn't seem to worry her. They'd been out weekends, on Tuesday and Thursday mornings, and there were nights when she shook him awake and Dan sat up, bewildered, to Tamma saying, "Come on, come on, come *on*."

"Shouldn't you be sleeping?" he'd say.

"I'll sleep when I'm dead," she'd say. It worried him, seeing how hard she was working, and she had the rawboned look of someone pushed to the limit of human endurance. They'd go out with flashlights and slay moderates. It made, for Tamma, a monstrously long day, up at four and crawling back into bed at three. These were days when Tamma would crash at the trailer, and so would sleep in the next morning, but this was still a girl running on too much life and too little sleep, though if she must've felt half dead, she seemed ecstatically alive, holding the flashlight, telling him the name of the climb, and who had sent it first, and what moves she had first tried, saying of two side-by-side granite crystals, "I call these two Nibsie and Nubsie, and I love them!" and after he dragged himself home he would sleep in a way he had not slept for months, deeply and untroubled. Sometimes, when he woke, he'd think of Tamma climbing across his lap to lean out the driver's-side window and say, "My V-card, Naomi, my *V-card*," and how Naomi had just shaken her head tiredly and waved them into the park without making them pay, and it would be almost as if his bucket were not punched at all.

Now at the dinner table, across from his old man, Dan could find nothing to say. He kept stopping and looking at Lawrence, who was wearing sweatpants and a work shirt turned up at the sleeves, staring down into his own dinner as he ate. A scene Dan had beheld a thousand times before. More. And yet a scene new and important to him each time.

Finally, Lawrence asked, "So, are you going to go to the dance?"

"Well," Dan said. Tilted his head to the side. "Tamma asked me but, you know, I'm not sure."

"What aren't you sure about?"

"Well," Dan said. "I don't have anything to wear. And tickets, renting a tux, flowers, it all costs money. Sierra gave Tamma money for tickets, but she might've used it to buy anything, we haven't talked about it since, and honestly, I bet she kind of forgot."

"What do you talk about?"

"Climbing. Just climbing. And a hot park ranger named Naomi."

"Oh, well," his old man said. "Lucky for you, I have an answer."

He rose and walked away into the master bedroom. He came back, unzipping a garment bag. He dropped the bag to the floor and held up a black suit and a white dress shirt. He turned and looked down at it, with some emotion.

"See? See!" his old man said. "I was married in this suit."

"Didn't you elope?"

"Well, I wore this suit."

"You bought a suit to elope?"

"I had it for church. 1988 I got this suit, I think. A good year for men's fashion, Dan."

"Oh, well, I don't know about this, Dad."

"What's wrong with it?"

"... Nothing!" Dan said.

"You get her a corsage?"

"She doesn't want a corsage."

"Every girl likes a corsage."

"She's not a girl-girl though," Dan said. "She is a thirteen-year-old Viking with the soul of a beatnik, the hands of an orangutan, and a day job as Mrs. Doubtfire."

"I don't see why," his old man said, "a Viking shouldn't like a corsage, if he-she was going to prom."

Dan sat shaking his head. Lawrence let him sit for a while. Then he said, "Come on, Danny, I don't get to do that many dad things for you."

The next day, his old man took him to the florist. They went in together and his old man took corsages out of an industrial refrigerator one by one. They were in clamshells, on beds of shredded paper, with tags stickered to the lids. Holding them out, his hands shook very slightly.

"Can't go wrong with white roses," he said.

"I feel like we ought to get her thistles and blackberry flowers or something."

"She's a tough little biscuit for sure. But nobody wants to be tough all the time."

"You better let me buy it," Dan said. "I have the money Mom left."

"Better be me, Danny," Lawrence said. "That money is for school. Besides, we're up to our eyeballs in medical bills. A guy'd have to build a lot of concrete molds to pay it all off. We'll lose the house anyway, I bet. It's good you had us transfer the funds to you. You keep it safe. That was your mom's life work. This one is on me."

"Maybe Mom will write another book."

"Maybe, Danny. Maybe."

That was on Friday. On Saturday, Dan picked Tamma up at eight. She'd been with the kids all day and came out of Sierra's house alone, laughing and saying something to Sierra over her shoulder, and climbed down the steps. She was wearing a black dress and chuck taylors, carrying the bouldering pad. Her smile showed all of her teeth and she had a high blush in her freckled cheeks. Dan walked around the hood and flourished her door open. She said, "Fuck yeah! What is this suit?"

"It's my dad's," he said. "He got married in it."

"You look ready to dip your hand in cocaine and fist Fleetwood Mac!"

"Good," said Dan, "because that's how I feel."

He thought of asking Tamma if she knew that Lawrence Redburn wasn't really that old, but he decided against it.

Tamma curtsied herself inside, saying, "Why thank you, sir!" and Dan climbed back into the truck and held out the corsage, all wrapped and tied with a bow.

"What's this?"

She shucked open the paper and lifted out the clamshell.

"A *corsage*," she said, clutching her pearls.

"Sorry," he said.

"It's the greatest!" She slid it onto her wrist and held it out. "No one's ever gotten me flowers," she said. Her lips parted and closed. Parted and closed again. She scooted herself back against the door, drew her knees up, hooked one arm in front of her shins, by turns waving her other hand and by turns reaching to touch her eye, remembering her mascara, and fanning it in a thwarted gesture.

"Is everything okay?" Dan said.

"Fuck," she said. "You're gonna ruin my makeup."

She was looking fixedly upward to hold the tears puddled in her eyes.

"The *one* time I wear mascara," she said.

"Nobody cares about your mascara."

"I care."

"Do you really?"

"Yes! I'm a hot girl, Dan!"

"Of course," Dan said.

"I don't get to everything, all the time, but *still*, you know!"

"I do know."

"It's just—you think River is going to have this? Go to the prom? Bring some chick a corsage? Or get a corsage? Or whateverthefuck?"

"Yes," Dan said.

"You think so?" she said.

"I don't *know* that he will," Dan said. "But I think so. He's a pretty cool, smiley, chill little guy."

"The cooooolest!" Tamma said. "He's my little dude!"

She had him drive to the gas station and Dan stayed in the rig and watched as his date solicited a straw man whiskey purchase. From there they drove on toward school and got out together and stood side by side, Dan in his borrowed suit and Tamma in her borrowed dress. They could see the open doors of the gymnasium where Mrs. Davidson was accepting tickets. There was an arch of gold, white, and blue balloons over the door.

"So, duuuuuuuude," Tamma said. "I have a confession."

"What?"

"I spent the ticket money on dildos."

"Right," Dan said. "Naturally. I mean, what else would you spend it on?"

"Exactly," Tamma said. "I mean, when a girl comes into forty dollars, there is but *one* thing on her mind."

"Dildos," Dan said.

"You get it," Tamma said, and gave him finger guns, clicking her tongue to indicate the cocking of the hammers.

"I do. I totally get it. You really spent it on whiskey, didn't you?"

"No, I really gave it back to her, because I didn't think we were going. And then you texted, and I thought, well, let's drive around, because I sort of wished I *had* bought tickets, and then I spent my own, hard-earned, target-checkout-girl money on whiskey."

"You didn't think to tell me this?"

"What I thought was: Why don't we skip this, go into the park, and have our own prom?"

"Yes," Dan said. "Let's."

They walked back to the truck and drove on toward the park. It was dark. They found the ranger station closed and kept on out into the desert with the plain falling away from them and the joshua trees going on toward distant cliffs. Dan parked and they walked out together with a flashlight. Chuckwallas watched them, fat bellied, cleaving to the rocks which still held the heat of the day. They hiked into the boulders and Tamma laid the pad out and scraped her shoes clean and sat. Dan uncorked the whiskey and passed it to her. She took the handle and drank, exhaling in ragged disgust.

"How does your finger feel?"

"Paisley was right," Tamma said. "Rest is bullshit."

"Will it be strong enough?"

"Yes."

Dan undid his tie, unbuttoned the shirt, and shucked it off. Sat there in his dress pants and undershirt. She passed the whiskey, and he drank and sat holding it.

"Remember when we used to walk out together?"

"To the Princess Boulder?" she said. "Of course."

"Those were the happiest nights of my life."

"Mine too."

"Can you believe the falls we took?"

"We were young and dumb and made out of rubber."

"That was less than a year ago."

"Ah the good old days."

"I want that all my life."

"Then I have a proposal."

"What?"

"Leave Figures behind. Pour that hope out into the sand like an offering to the gods and set off for Indian Creek with no proof at all. Just two total, one hundred percent dipshits who believe, impossibly, they can make it against all odds with no evidence whatsoever that that is the case."

"I thought you said your A2 pulley was good?"

"It is, but this business of Figures—I don't like it. I think we're undertaking it for the wrong reasons. No climb really means anything, they're something we do for love, and when you start making them into more than they really are, that's when people get hurt. This proof you want, it's not possible. Let's go to Indian Creek without it."

"You make it sound so easy," Dan said. "Just bet your entire life on a dream."

"Yes," Tamma said. "That's it exactly. Bet your whole entire life on a dream."

They sat in silence, beneath some monolith unknown to him. It loomed into the shine of the flashlight, cinnamon-gold, the holds, deep, wind-hollowed huecos cut into the overhang, the chalk phosphorescent in the dark.

"I can't do that," he said. "That's too much exposure for me."

"You *can* do it though."

"Have you climbed this thing?" he asked, lifting the whiskey bottle to indicate the boulder looming over them.

"Yeah, it's good."

She collapsed onto her back and mimed the moves, smiling the way certain problems made her smile.

"She's both intensely physical and technically demanding, like your mom."

"My mom is so technically demanding that she left."

"Fuck. I'm sorry. I didn't mean anything."

"It doesn't matter. I'm just teasing you back."

"I apologize."

Dan was sitting up, his legs stretched at length, crossed at the ankle, wearing normal socks and creased slacks. Out here, with Tamma, he felt the warmth of the world.

She stiff-armed herself up, groped around in the dark, came up with the whiskey, and drank. Set it down so hard it made a wonderful sloshing noise. "You know how I used to talk about meeting the devil out here?"

"Yes."

"What if you really did?"

"Really met the devil?"

"Fuck yeah, dude. What if we came upon him one dark night. And he said, 'Ho, Daniel Redburn. Hail and well met! I am the Lord of Darkness. I am the Invisible Hand, the Hakken-Krak of Hakken-Kraks. I wait upon the crossroads, preside upon the runouts, wiggle hexes from their placements, tear babies from their fathers' arms, cut ropes, sever friendships, purvey oxycontin and rohypnol. When Alexandra Redburn faced her typewriter, I was there; when the young fiancée reached the Princess's exit-move highstep crux, I was there; when Kendra met Hyrum, I whispered that she couldn't make it on her own; I have been with you every step of the way.'"

"Jesus Christ," Dan said. "It's impossible to remember how voluble you are."

"I'm immensely valuable."

"You're not wrong."

"You know what I'd ask for?"

"To be the best climber in the world?"

"Do you remember, before the Princess, when we were climbing that cryptic V3 slab called Pet My Hamster? And there were those two guys drinking beer on their tailgate?"

"Yeah," Dan said.

"One of these guys comes over, and says, 'Do you kids know that you can crawl up the back of this thing?' and you go, 'What?' and rip off your hat, throw it to the ground, and stomp on it. 'You're fucking with me!' you say. And he's all, 'No, I'm not fucking with you.' So all three of us walk around the back side, and sure enough, it's a ramp. And you're all, 'Jesus fucking shitballs!' And this guy is all, 'Out of curiosity, how long have you been trying to get up this thing?' and you're all, 'Three hours,' and he's all, like, '*Three hours?!*'"

"I remember it," Dan said, very quietly.

"It's funny, because what *we* knew, and what the guy didn't know, is that walking to the top is meaningless. And Dan. If you met the devil and sold your soul to be the best climber in the world, then all your climbing would be a lie, and somewhere out there would be a girl risking her neck on 5.7 and *she'd* be the beating heart of the sport, because it's really only *climbing* when you get up into the empty, gut-coiling, unprotected places, high up, lonely, and out of sight, and you think *I can't do it*, and then you do it anyway. I went out to LA hoping that if someone would just crown me the Queen-Bitch of Unstoppable Sendage, then I'd have the courage to chase this dream. I wanted to know, for sure, that I could do it, before I made that dicey step-out into darkness. I wanted a guarantee. But that's not how it works. You find out by trying. And for sure, whatever is out there for us, it's gonna be scary, but *scary* is part of it. Think about it. You had the best nights of your life projecting the Princess, but if you ever started to believe that the summit of Fingerbang Princess actually *meant something*, you'd die unhappy, because the top was a barren, godforsaken, useless stretch of rock. You'd get there and think—What the fuck? All that for *this*? What have I done with my life? Right? That guy, sitting on his tailgate, drinking his beer, he walked over and handed you the summit of Pet My Hamster. And we laughed. Because why?"

"Because tops are bullshit," Dan said.

"That's right. It's cruxes that matter. The top is only a symbol, and without the crux, it refers to nothing. The crux is the heart of the boulder."

"*Fuuuuuuckkk*," said Dan, wonderingly.

"So that's my answer. Of what I'd ask from the devil: *nothing*."

"You'd just be like, 'No thanks, Mr. Devil.'"

"Yes, and that'd be the true story of how Tamma Callahan gave the devil an HJ one night in Joshua Tree."

"Wait, what?"

"And then spent her whole entire life climbing and nobody ever heard of her, and she probably died with nothing to show for it and only a couple people remembered her and all she was was a little unremarked obit in the back of *Rock and Ice* that no one noticed."

"Because somebody else took the deal."

"That's right."

"Is that true? You wouldn't ask for anything?"

"Of course it's true. But I'm going to try anyway—I'm going to go out into the dangerous, beautiful, empty places of the world and make of that wasteland a church and a home. And maybe, possibly, have a shot at being that hard-sending chick on the poster in the bedroom of every little girl in the world. But only that: a shot. I will consider it my very great privilege to make the attempt."

"This is your second argument."

"Yeah."

"Your second try to talk me out of Figures."

"Yes. You want some sort of promise that everything will be okay. You think Figures can give that to you. But there can be no such promise. This is how people fuck up and die."

The joshua trees leaned out over them and they could see bats passing between the branches, cut dark against the blue-black vault, blotting out the stars with their passage. There upon the horizon were distant lights from campgrounds where firelight and headlights shone against the granite domes and lit up their flanks. They lay in silence, looking up at the looming face of the boulder, eaten by huecos.

"Have another drink," he said.

"Sure. Pass the gentleman over."

Dan peeled off his socks, and walked a ways away, going gingerly on his bare feet.

"Are you running away?"

"Pissing."

"Oh man, wait for me."

Tamma got herself up, walked out of the circle of light, hitched up her black dress, unburdened herself of her panties, and hunkered down. He heard her peeing and looked over.

"Watch out," he said.

"Oh jesus," she said, crabwalking away, laughing as she went.

She leaned forward and with great difficulty picked her panties up out of the sand and walked back to the bouldering pad and didn't know what to do with them. She hooked them over a fingertip and stretched the elastic tight and shot them away out into the dark. Immediately regretted it. Had the presence of mind not to go after them. Stood knock-kneed beside the flashlight peering out into the desert.

He was leaning back on his elbow. He took a drink. Then set the whiskey down hard, watched it toss and settle. Dapples of light thrown into the interior from the flashlight.

"I don't want to leave Figures behind."

"Okay," she said.

"You're not going to try a third time?"

"No," she said. "I guess not. I guess if you want to go down and knock on the gates of hell, then I'll come with and ring the bell. Then we'll see, I guess, if the devil meets us at the door, and what he says."

"You really think it's that much of a mistake?"

"Yes."

They lay together, there in the dark.

Five

Dan stopped the truck and Tamma popped the latch and staggered out into the sand shielding her eyes in the crook of her elbow. Her teeth felt like the baked dry ends of chicken bones. A slant of morning glare broke along the trailer's roofline and right-hand edge. She reeled toward the stairs and had to wait at every step, dry heaving and white-knuckling the railing. Colin was sitting at the table with Hyrum and Kendra. He was slouched in his chair, wearing jeans, a polo shirt, high-top sneakers, and a baseball cap. She trudged to the sink, opened a cabinet, and with a heroic effort, took down a tumbler. Began filling it from the faucet.

"Glad you could uh . . . join us," Hyrum said, and at the sound of his voice, Tamma closed her eyes and braced against the counter, feeling a vein going in her forehead. She shut off the sink and turned around.

"Where were you last night?" Kendra said.

"In the park."

"Very nice, Tamma."

"What?"

"Where were you before that?"

"Dan picked me up. We went to the dance, but we didn't have tickets, so we went into Josh."

Her mother braced her elbow on the surface of the table and covered her brow with the edge of her hand in distress.

"Tamma," she said. "Why do you do this?"

"Do what?"

"You need to look out for your brother."

"Why, what happened?"

"Do you remember," Kendra said, "that you have a little brother?"

Tamma stood leaning back against the sink, holding her oversized plastic tumbler, looking at them all. No one said anything so she said, "Yes."

"Do you know that you might look after him, keep him out of trouble?"

Tamma glanced around the kitchen. Suspended motes of dust circling in the light. Open, unwashed cans on the counter. Small plastic figures of aliens. Scales. Kitchen shears covered in resin. A box of powdered milk.

"Can you please tell me what happened?" Tamma said.

Kendra covered her mouth with her hand and sat grimacing into her palm, shaking her head and racking her cigarette with her thumb, ashing onto the tabletop and then scraping it onto the floor with the edge of her hand, too overcome to speak.

Hyrum broke in. "Your brother is in trouble," he said. "You could've been looking out for him."

"Will somebody," Tamma said, and then stopped. She swallowed with difficulty. She wanted to calm her voice down. "Will somebody please explain what happened? Because I don't know what you're talking about."

"He got caught with his girlfriend and, ahhhhh . . . the girl is passing it off like it's, uhhhhhhh . . . rape," Hyrum said.

Kendra rose with her hands cupped over the sides of her head and walked down the hall saying, "I can't, I just *can't*, *I just*—*I can't*."

"With Katie?" Tamma said.

"The girl's name is Jenny Armstrong. Apparently, she ahhh . . . told her dad that Colin ahhh . . . forced her into it."

"What?" Tamma said. "The ball shed girl?"

"The, mmmmm . . . what?" Hyrum said.

"Your—ah—girlfriend?" Tamma asked.

"She's not my girlfriend!" Colin said.

"Same girl, right?"

He nodded.

"What is she saying?" Tamma said.

Kendra came back down the hallway. She plucked her cigarette out of her mouth and stood hunched forward, toward Tamma, with her hand outflung, and said, "Much as this may come as a surprise to you, you're not the only person in this family. This happened when you should've been *here*. You have responsibilities to *us*. You're letting down the people who love you when we need you most, but you don't *care*, do you?, you don't *care about other people*, all that matters to you is your stupid little *sport*."

"Jenny Armstrong," Tamma said, turning to Colin. "What does she say happened?"

"She's saying I grabbed her head and made her give me a blowjob," Colin said.

"Did you?"

"Well—no," Colin said.

"Except there is video that appears to uh, show, pretty much, uh . . . exactly that," Hyrum said.

"Colin!"

"But she'd done it before! I didn't think it was a big deal! It *wasn't* a big deal. It was only a big deal because Bryce took a video and it uploaded to the cloud and Bryce's mom saw it and sent it to Jenny's dad and her dad got mad, so she said it was rape. But she only said it was rape after he got mad."

"He could be in real trouble," Kendra said. "He may not be allowed back to school."

Tamma turned and walked down the hall.

"Come back here!" Kendra yelled after her. Tamma kicked the bathroom door open and fell inside and grabbed the toilet and spilled her guts down into the bowl.

"Aw Jesus Christ!" Kendra said, standing in the hall behind her.

Tamma was on her knees, breathing hard. She turned and looked at her mom, cuffing at her mouth. Kendra said, "This is your fault, Tamma. You could have prevented this if only you'd been there. If only you cared. You know that?" Tamma was holding her heart with her clawed hand, panting, taking looks at her mom and then back at the floor. She nodded and got slowly back to her feet, braced against the wall. Hanks of sweaty hair were falling into her face and she did not have the strength to move them aside. She flushed the toilet and watched it churn and go down.

"Mom," Tamma said. She had to stop. She closed her eyes. The darkness swam with expanding whorls of green and orange. She opened her eyes, took another breath. "You don't mean that."

"I do."

"What could I have done?"

"You could've been there with him when he needed you. Instead you are always sneaking out. Running away. You don't want to be part of this family. You don't love us. You're trying to escape us. Because you think you're somehow better than the only people who love you."

Tamma shook her head.

"Mom, I couldn't've gone to a middle school dance. Think about it. They wouldn't let me."

"You're supposed to talk to your little brother! See how he's doing! Find out about things like this before they happen. It's more than the dance, Tamma, you're never around. You're not *here*."

"Mom," Tamma said. Choked down dry heaving. Took a difficult, shuddering breath. "Tell me how I can help."

Her mom didn't reply and so Tamma looked up at her. Kendra was shaking all over. She clasped her hand over her mouth to keep herself from speaking. She turned on her heel and walked away down the hall. Tamma shuffled her hands along the wall until she came to the sink and she opened the mirror and took down the bottle of ibuprofen and shook five of them into her hand and she tossed them back and sucked water straight from the tap. Then she let herself back down onto the floor and sat propped against the wall, holding her temples tight with the heels of her hands.

Six

Tamma was nowhere that Monday. Not in class. Not in the halls. Not waiting at her locker. They had picked Tuesday for their attempt on Figures, and Dan had long, lonely class periods to think about it.

He knew he could send it. Figures on a Landscape was only 5.10b. It was at least two number grades easier than Princess, and three grades easier than the highstep. Sure, Figures was longer, and there would be no chance to work the moves, as they had done on Princess, but it was drastically less intimidating, and with a rope, it was safer.

And *yet*, he thought, sitting there in class, was there something wrong, deeply wrong with that way of thinking?

Dan drove home and shared a silent dinner across from his old man, who ate with his head hung, his big forearms braced on the table's edge, shaking his head at times. Is that what it did to a person, to spend twenty years trying to drag a depressed person out of their depression? I can't do that to Tamma, he thought. Even if she would consent to it, I cannot undertake this thing with her unless I can stand on my own two feet.

Dan went into his room and sat with his chin upon his fist and he stared down into the concrete and round and round he went in his mind.

With Figures, one way or the other, the decision would be made. Maybe that meant glory. Or maybe he would go away to college, easy in soul, knowing that he could never have made it.

If he couldn't send Figures, then he wasn't ever really going to be a climber anyway.

He did not sleep that night. He lay in bed and when he closed his eyes, he saw the sere desert at dawn, with North Astrodome standing before him, a band of golden light upon the horizon's far edge, and he felt the twinned horror and wanting of it. He could do it. He would send death and sickness. He would climb his way out of whatever was wrong with him. Figures would be his marker. And then he would go with Tamma, and never fear a climb again.

He was still awake when he heard the click before his alarm would sound, and he put his hand upon the clock to silence it. Then he dressed in the dark. Eighty-two degrees and forecasted above a hundred. He shouldered the rope, let himself out the front door, pitched the pack into the bed, and pushed the truck backward down the drive. He waited, looking to the north. When she did not come, he sat on a fallen joshua tree and read *Daniel Deronda* by flashlight. A sickle moon rose yellow over distant hills. There were night geckos in the yuccas and he could hear their chirping barks.

At last he saw a tiny figure sprinting down the road, her laces untied, holding up her unbuttoned cutoffs with one hand, and with the other, pulling a singlet over her head. He rose up to a stand and she ran past him.

Dan got into the truck and looked over at her.

"What happened?"

She was breathless from the run. She sucked air, nodding to indicate that she would talk when she could, and then talking through it, anyway, "I slept through my alarm."

"You slept through your alarm?" he said. "You never sleep through an alarm. You go weeks without getting a full night of sleep."

"Yeah, well," she said, raking her straggled and disordered hair out of her face and then putting it up into a ponytail, thumb-hooking the hair tie off her wrist. "It caught up with me, didn't it?"

Dan started back down the lane, on toward the 62. He hit the highway, found it empty, and struck east. Tamma was still breathing hard beside him. They were both quiet, one taking in the other, and Dan had the unbearable yet wondrous feeling that driving toward a climb always brought him. It was always scary, whatever they were going to climb, but everything he had told the counselor was true: For all the fear, it was the greatest, most wide-open, breaking-apart feeling in all the world, there in the quiet truck with his best friend.

He turned into the park and passed the unmanned toll station. They had been supposed to leave at two and it was almost six now, the sun slanting up over eastern hills, the sky banded pale green and riesling-gold, the desert gray and open with blue shadows of granite on the horizon and the road overhung with stooping desert lilies, tarantulas braving the tarmac in places, running full out upon their knuckly shadows, the headlights smoking with windblown sand.

They parked at an empty pullout and Dan walked around back. He had the rope coiled there and the bag with their shoes and gear and three liters of water. What is that moment? There were, in Dan's experiences of climbing, very many epic fights and desperate circumstances. But there was also this, two climbers standing close beside one another, shouldering the pack from out the truck bed, Dan passing his thumbs up and down the straps to seat them evenly, the rope hanging over his shoulders like a stole. A small, poised moment of preparation, in which neither of them needed to talk, before they set out on the approach.

It was bright enough that they did not need the flashlight. They followed trails out through scrub oak tangled with mistletoe. They passed a pink-painted ruin on the banks of a dry pond and followed washes hemmed with decaying palisades, choking down to narrow alleys spanned in boulders, a hard-mineral smell on the morning air. Sprawling, trumpetlike blooms of sacred datura shone white upon the buggy golden stone.

Walking close beside her, he cast a look over and caught her looking back at him, her teeth denting her lower lip, her eyes crinkling down with a smile, brimming with such contained mischief that he knew she felt it too, that for all her reservations, she could not but love the long walk in, leaving behind her family, her failing grades, her obligations, venturing from out some world in which they did not belong into the only place that was finally theirs. Dan remembered and understood their separation after winter break to be a kind of foretaste of what their lives could be, without one another. Tamma, trapped here by her family, working in box stores, taking care of her sister's children, her soul burning with thwarted dreams, and Dan sunk into an isolated depression-world, sick in his head, his life abounding with privileges and opportunities about which he did not and could not care, whiling away his time in a daze. But here they were, walking into the Wonderland, side by side, to undertake something utterly wild. It was a coming-back-alive sort of feeling.

They came from out a maze of granite and before them lay a wide prospect strewn with ruined castles, North and South Astrodome shouldering together in the distance. They were stark in the gray light of dawn, a kind of latte-gold color, with black and red water stains painted down their flanks.

They worked among shelves of rock and low, fissured barricades where mound cactuses grew in the cracks and they came at last to South Astrodome, and when they hit it, they walked along the shelves, past the saddle, to North Astrodome beside a shaggy blue pinyon. There Tamma stopped and stood, looking up at the shaded wall limned in golden light. Beside her, tall, narrow waisted, and broad shouldered, shirt sweated to his stomach and showing the muscle, jeans rolled up over his calves and suntouched hair in disarray, Dan made a study of the route.

Seven

North Astrodome rose into the sky like a headstone, hashed with shorn and shallow roofs from which hung rust-red and lead-white stains. Embossed upon the face was a shield of black and gold eschar, the landscape that gave the route Figures on a Landscape its name. Below, an exfoliated granite pillar leaned against the wall. Dan clambered up the backside of the pillar, unshouldered the bag, and looked up, assessing the clipping positions, and so racking the gear on his right or left hip. Tamma climbed up after him. The pillar was a chunk of stone cast off from the wall sometime in the distant past. It was of a height with the big pinyon that grew beside it. Standing atop the pillar, she began to flake the creaky blue rope down into a rope stack. This was the first rope into which they'd ever tied in, and she sorted it so that she would climb on the coreshot and Dan would lead on the undamaged length. Both of them were sweating, even in the shade.

Dan tied his figure eight, threaded the bitter end up through his harness, and retraced the knot. His heart like a thing caged in his chest and trying to get out. His mouth dry. His hands sweating. Tamma unpocketed a roll of tape, split the end with her teeth, peeled off a strip, and bound it tightly about her injured pulley to support it. Then she fitted a bite of rope down into the mouth of the ATC, clipped it with the carabiner, and screwed the locking sleeve tight. The ritual of it like a little prayer to their friendship. Dan looked over at her. She looked up at him and smiled. Years and years together, thousands of nights, all the good, hard moments that had unfolded this way. And here, another climb, another chance. It was an open question, like a coin lofted into the air, and he could make it true, one way or the other. He would write his fate in the next pitch.

Dan dipped in his chalk bag, breaking curds apart in his fist. There were treacherous gaps between the pillar and the wall, of which they were mindful. Tamma glanced at his knot—saw it was good.

"Are you clicky?" he said.

"Sooooo clicky," she said, and demonstrated that the belay carabiner was locked by clicking the threaded aluminum sleeve against the nose.

"I love you, buddy," he said.

"I love you too, dude."

The first pitch was shaped roughly like an S, drawn from the bottom up. It started with a long traverse to the right. Then it climbed straight up, to where it met the great, shield-shaped patina landscape, and then diagonaled up and left, in what would be the spine of the S, following the left-hand edge of the shield, to the high left-hand corner. Then, for the final, rightward stroke of the S, it traversed thirty feet to chain anchors.

Because the route started on a pillar that leaned against the wall, as soon as he stepped off the pillar for the first rightward traverse, he was above the crown of the pinyon, edging out through terra-cotta streaks on a foot rail. Twenty feet and the last step was a single move of friction to a stance in a scoop, from which Dan clipped the bolt.

The ground below was strewn with boulders, exfoliated flakes, and cubbies of rocky soil folded into the flaring skirts of North Astrodome. There wasn't anywhere good to hit the deck down there.

Dan fastened a flake scar beside the bolt and matched it. This was where a scale of granite had broken away, leaving an edge the same texture and depth as a pottery plate broken in half. He sank onto the sharp, half-pad edge, his knuckles crimping up.

Right of him, there was a shallow crack system nooked among patina plates, like the fissuring that might form atop a loaf of cooling banana bread. He bumped right to a triangular notch in that crack, rocked up onto a high left foot, then to a right foot on a patina edge, put his helmet to the wall, and breathed. Thin, committing moves on granite that was warm to the touch. He matched feet on the right patina edge and crossed with his left hand to a gaston, hooked three fingers into the crack, single pad, thumb down, and pulled himself up and right, counterbalancing off the foot.

He edged up through scars and relief, following what would be the first upward stroke of the S. He crossed his left foot through his right on tiptoes in blown-out shoes, then unwound the right foot onto a smeary edge in the porcelain streak out right. He spanned right and caught an outsloped, three-finger groove, his last bolt far below. He bumped his left hand from the gaston up to a half-pad wrinkle. From there he reached right for a left-slanting eroded dike. He followed the dike down and to the right, hand over hand through nooks like the sultry, gently parted lips of damsels baring their teeth. He still couldn't see the second bolt but had to trust it was there.

Every move was right at the limit of what he could do. He extended right and caught the lapped, ladle-like edge where the patina scooped away to soft white stone. He pulled up, found the bolt hiding in a recess, locked off, and clipped. From there he climbed into unvarnished granite, choppy as pond water in a storm, and clipped the third bolt with the second bolt almost at his feet.

Above him lay the slanting, left-hand edge of the patina shield. It was formed by a shallow, undercut flake stained black from seepage. He extended for it and caught it in a tenuous, thumbhook undercling and worked his feet up, only the trembling of his extended arm showing the strain of his position. Then he threw with the left for a chalky sidepull edge, caught it, and worked up on laybacks, underclings, and high feet. Clipped the fourth bolt and continued along the left-hand edge of the shield, following what would be the spine of the S, until he could reach right for an incut edge. The next was a hero jug. He rested there, cherishing the enormous hold, taking turns shaking out each hand. Then he climbed to the fifth bolt on buckets in a rusty umber water stain. He clipped it and stood on stone rails like ladder rungs at the high left shoulder of the shield. One final traverse lay ahead of him. Seeing the route as a capital S, this was the summit of the spine, just before the horizonal, rightward stroke to the finish. He could look over, thirty feet to chain anchors. A single two-bolt anchor, placed by mistake, broke the traverse into two stages of fifteen feet each. He would clip that anchor and keep climbing to the next, true belay stance. He was maybe ninety feet off the ground. Hard to be sure of the distances.

Sweat was greasy down his flanks, he was sucking air, and he stank of terror, but for the moment, he was at his bolt, with time to breathe and consider what lay ahead of him. He chalked and clapped off his hands on his thighs. Then he downclimbed three moves on bucket holds. From the last good hold, he bumped right to a positive crystal. He breathed, crimped down, hearing his fingertips bite creakingly into the granite, every crease and whorl grained with chalk. Then a rose-pink crystal rail, gently outsloped. Match, shuffle over, and bump right to an outsloped edge, toeing on little patina knobs like fingertips. Drops of sweat glittered in his eyelashes, which made a wet clicking noise when he blinked. Above that came his own breathing, the ring of aluminum carabiners sounding against the granite, and the scraping of shoe rubber. To his right, a raised patina horseshoe in soft white stone, with outsloped, single-pad edges along the inside margin.

He reached right, caught the leg of the horseshoe, sidepulled it, crossed through with his left and hooked the basin, everything greasy to the touch, the edges good so long as he could keep his weight low, so he skulked rightward, dropping into stances, the footholds like umber and burnt umber pigments on an oil painting when the paint has mudded up and made keeled edges around sunken brushstrokes. The work of keeping tension was like the absorbed, intuitive state of someone walking across a balance beam.

He matched hands at the bottom of the horseshoe and took a breath. He was deep in the runout, but he had the wonderous feeling that though committing, and though he was afraid, this was the best and most technical climbing he had ever done, and he was reminded of the way your life took on color and depth when you worked right at the edge of what was possible.

From the match, he went up to the right arm of the horseshoe, matched again, and leaned rightward, sidepulling it, freed his right hand, reached back to his harness, unclipped a sling. Shaking all over, the carabiners rattling, he extended out right and clipped the bolt, reached down to his hip, grabbed the rope, spanned out with it, and dropped it through the gate into the draw. He was halfway through the traverse and, for the moment, right at his bolt and safe. Only the last, unprotected, fifteen-foot stretch from this bolt to the anchor remained. Then he would be done.

Standing on the granite pillar below, Tamma was by turns watching Dan and passing the crunchy blue rope through her hands. Oh, rope, she thought. You have held through a thousand adventures. And now I need you to hold for one more great send. One last push.

It had just come to her that they had fucked up in a huge way but that it was probably going to be fine. The problem was that she was standing on a stone pillar and Dan had traversed twenty feet to the right before clipping the first bolt, which was level with Tamma's head. So if he fell, Tamma was going to be dragged, ripped off the pillar, and swung out into open space.

She should've belayed from the ground, below the first bolt. That way, if he fell, she would be pulled harmlessly up the wall. Now she was thinking that if Dan fell, the situation was going to get somewhat-to-moderately fucked up very quickly.

North Astrodome curved away above her, Dan at the limit of that horizon, a figure she could've covered with her thumb, partially cut against the pale blue sky, and partially against the patina, which was marled umber, terra-cotta, and white.

She paid out slack, sometimes looking up at him, sometimes minding her rope coil. She could not believe she'd made the mistake. It was the sort of mistake you made when you got to the parking lot too late and you were in a hurry. Accidents in climbing were rarely the result of a single error. They were usually the result of a cascading series of fuckups. But it would all be fine if Dan didn't fall. If Dan just hung on to the wall, everything would hold together. She paid rope up off the rope stack with her right hand, feeding it into the mouth of the belay tube, around the locking carabiner, and with her left hand she passed it to where Dan was climbing above her. Because of the S-shaped zigzagging route, there was a hell of a lot of slack in the system. Tamma didn't like that, either, and yet couldn't keep him any tighter without short-roping him. And, again, if he didn't fall, the slack didn't matter. If he did fall, though, it was gonna be big.

There were other mistakes, going further back. When she'd been at the checkout counter, with Paisley Cuthers holding up that beautiful coil of brand-new rope, she should've accepted it. Paisley had been trying to help, and Tamma had been too scared and too ashamed to just say yes.

But it was all going to be fine because Dan was not going to fall.

Above, Dan had committed into the second stage of the traverse, shuffling and sidestepping, coming to places where the patina was cloven away, leaving only edgeless, sand-colored recesses like dried lake beds. He matched hands on the last jug, his bolt already behind him, and reached up and right for a patina feature shaped like a bat in flight. He hit the bat's left wing and bumped again to the right wing. Good, clean, shallow edges. There was a blond, sandy pigeonhole by his right hip, but he could find no use for it.

Ahead of him it was blank, sand-colored stone. The next move was for the right foot to extend out, locating the only good edge, three inches long, shallow, and canted forward so that it threatened to spill you off. The sequence was going to be utterly wild and insecure.

The rubber of his shoes was as greasy and soft as frying bacon. The leather was black with sweat and the slipper squelched when he weighted the hold. He backed off and took a moment.

The rope ran from his harness in a great slack catenary to the bolt fifteen feet behind him. Eighty, ninety feet above the ground. Slowly, he rocked his foot onto the hold, trying to squelch the rubber into the inside corner. He scummed a cluster of crystals with his right hand. His left foot was a solid rail, but he would have to leave it behind. He was shaking all over. He started to weight the right, tipped-out foothold, but the feeling of insecurity grew and grew until he could take it no longer and he recoiled from the hold once again.

He crushed his helmet to the wall, and huddled, sucking air, blinking sweat out of his eyelashes, muscles in his shoulders jumping, the strength of his hands draining like sand out of an hourglass. When he opened his eyes, he saw the defocused, watercolorish gray, ocher, and mahogany of the wall. His heels were jittering and his breath came ragged. He was at the end of a long and technical traverse, and two or three moves away from the chains. Sweat clung to the helmet's flared white rim, and in each droplet hung a trembling mote of light, an inverted reduplication of the sun where it crested North Astrodome's shoulder, the light breaking across the granite edge into brilliant fan blades.

If I stay here, he thought, I fall. For certain, I fall. If I make the move, maybe it holds or maybe it doesn't. But still, he hung on, unmoving. Some recoiling part of him could not bear to take that step. When he looked up, he could see the granite sweeping away from him, a vast ivory pyramid, islanded in ruin and dust, curtained with water stains, piebald with cinnamon and amber patina.

He looked down at his own sweat-soaked climbing shoe jittering and scraping against the wall, and then he turned and looked left, a dangerous thing to do, a movement that might barn-door him off the wall, but there far below him, standing atop a stone pillar, was Tamma, barefoot, in cutoffs and a singlet, tending the ancient blue rope, stirring the brake strand to sort one coil away from another.

Then Dan looked on ahead, at the foothold. He was tucked close into the stone, breathing its hot mineral scent and his own fear stink and the chemical smell of the heat-activated glue in his shoes, which was foaming along the seam where the sole met the rand.

Then he reached out with his right foot and sank the hot rubber onto that tipped-forward edge. Just hold on, he thought. He leaned out onto it, feeling every moment that his world was about to go out from under him. Hold, he thought, sinking down into that foothold. Just two moves to the chains. Oh, god, he thought. Hold on. Just *hold on*. Then the hold greased out from under him, he was wrenched forward, his left hand blew off the crimp, and he took flight, out into the air.

Eight

Tamma watched Dan laboring at the margin of the bright blue sky and the tobacco-colored granite. There were no clouds. Birds passed over the top of the dome, calling, flickering in and out of sight above them. She watched Dan creeping through the traverse, the rope trailing down to her, a narrow, twisting blue umbilicus. The draw behind him, in the middle of the traverse, swung in the wind and tinked again and again against the wall, a high, aluminum note. Tiny spiders floated by in the air, suspended on gossamer nets. High up on the wall, Dan had stopped. He was searching among the possible holds. She didn't like him to pause but he had to take his time. He was very close to the anchors now. Which meant he was very far away from his last bolt. She looked down to pay rope from the stack and when she looked up, Dan was off the wall. He came backward, curled slightly, the gear on his harness not quite rising but growing slack and weightless on the gearloops. He came silently, but he was off.

Oh my god, Tamma thought.

She began hand-over-handing slack back down through the ATC, the pattern familiar to all climbers. The rope was starting to lash and the carabiners were racking and clinking as plunging waves reflected up and down the tightening line. Then Tamma white-knuckled the rope and brought it hard down to her hip and she was ripped off her feet and dragged across the top of the pillar, kicking all the way, and then her foot snagged a block, and she was flung out into open space, spinning around backward off the pillar, holding the rope down by her hip.

It was a complicated fall because Dan was falling, and Tamma was falling, and they were connected by the lead rope. As the rope started to catch, turning her fall into a plunging, backward swing that would suck her up into the bolt, she could hear this weird noise, a strange, eerie crackling, utterly beyond her experience. She looked down at her ATC and as she watched, the bright blue sheath split open and began to yawn up away from her, exposing the cream-colored core strands, which were attenuating and counter rotating as they extended under tension, stretching to absorb the fall. But where the rope bent over the lip of the ATC, the core strands were splitting apart and peeling away. Then the rope split and the burst white end of the lead strand sprang out of her ATC and Tamma felt the bottom drop out of her world.

She was out in open air. The split rope end was rising away from her and she was falling away from it. That was Dan's end; he was tied into the other end of that rope. It looked like a flower of ruptured blue sheath strands and daisy white core strands flaring wide and dancing in the air like a live thing, whiplashing back and forth as it was sucked upward. She looked at it and she thought to herself: *I can catch that.* She thought, *I have to catch that. There goes my world.*

She swam her left hand up to it. She was moving with honeyed slowness and yet, dreamlike, she could move no faster. Noises had a strange, underwater quality. She saw her hand flare open. Saw the long, slender fingers and chipped, pink-painted nails as clearly as if it were someone else's hand. She struck out and caught the lashing whip-like strand six inches from the end. She thought, *I can hold it.* Her fingers blanched white with effort and the meat of her palm pursed up around the cord with her crushing grasp. She throttled the death out of that line, already bringing the other hand up toward it. Once she had it in two hands, it was done, nothing could shake her off. She gave it everything she had, and it didn't matter. The rope squirted out of her fist so fast it sucked the skin off her palm and freckled the wall with blood. There was no feeling of effort, nor of any pain. The line simply eeled up out of her grasp and Tamma pursued it, bringing her right hand up toward it, thinking—*My world!* but she was falling backward and the rope was retreating from her, slurped through the draws, and then gone, writhing up the wall, and she saw Dan framed above her against open blue sky, his back to her, his hands extended. *Oh,* she thought.

It seemed somehow like everything happened very slowly and then very fast. An angle of granite came into view out of the upper left-hand corner of her vision as swift and hard and flat as a swung frying pan and Tamma took the blow on the face and it spiked her backward, tipping sideways, pirouetting as she fell, and she caught a flash of the ground and she thought *No—stop!* and put her hands out and then she struck facedown among exfoliated granite and pinyon cones. Dead needles were stuck to her face. Slowly she propped herself up. *No,* she thought. *No no no no*—but yes: A figure plummeted into her field of view and cratered into the ground with a *whump* that lofted dust and pollen into the air all about them. Into the long, smoking silence that came after, the cut rope piled beside him with a pouring sound.

Nine

Dan lay on his side, the helmet spiderwebbed with cracks like a struck egg. Tamma wallowed toward him on her elbows. Pine needles and twigs were in her hair and blood kept dripping through her field of view and the loudest sound was of her own gasping which came to her distorted and overloud. She searched his neck for any pulse, sucking air, leaving bloody dabs wherever she touched him, and when she looked at the insides of her hands, she found that the rope had cut her left palm down to matted white flesh.

"Dan," she said.

He did not stir and for a moment she did not know what to do. Then she found a heartbeat. Hard and heavy and fast. She grasped him by the shoulder and rolled him onto his back. He lay breathing for a moment and then his eyes opened and she stared down into them.

"Dan!" she said.

"Fuuuuuuuuuuuuuuuuuck me," he said.

"You're alive!"

He started to sit up and then eased back down and stared up at the boughs of the pinyon. There was blood on his face and blood clung to the points of his eyelashes. He reached up, unbuckled his helmet, and shucked it away.

"Tamma," he said.

"Yeah?"

There was a silence.

"I forgot," he said.

Tamma patted her pockets, found nothing. The pack was above them, atop the pillar. She knew she needed to go get it, but she had a hard time imagining standing up. It was hot. The air was scintillant with pollen. Both of them were gasping. Tamma propped herself up and stood. She did not think she could walk and then she thought, Up and at 'em, Tams!

"Stay here," she said.

"If you say so," he said, with grimacing humor.

She limped to the top of the pillar, holding her hip like an old lady. She dug in the bag, leaving bloody handprints, mopping blood off her brow with her shirt. Her hands were shaking so badly she could hardly work the zippers. But she found the clasp knife, slung the bag, and scrambled down to him. Dan had dragged himself up. He sat with his back to the wall. One leg was extended. The right leg bent.

"I remember—I remember, I *remember* a noise," he said.

"Yeah?"

"I remember hearing this noise and you know what I think it was?"

"What?"

"I think it was my leg."

He was making a little hitching grimace of pain with every breath.

Tamma tried and tried again to open the clasp knife but her hands were too weak and slippery. She caught the blade's notch in her teeth, snapped it open, and passed the point up along the leg of his jeans with a smooth tearing noise. The blood that had been bagged up in the denim spread across the sand in a crackling wash, sweeping across the rock, lifting up pinyon needles and pollen. She didn't get up in time and it spread out across her knees and bare feet. She could smell it.

There was a gash in his shin like pursed lips. She'd seen similar injuries in accident reports. It happened when your shinbones punched out through the skin. She couldn't see the bones themselves, but she wasn't about to go looking. Above the break, his kneecap was gone and where it should've been she could see the skin cleaving to the lobed shapes of the joint. She put her hands on his leg and felt around, found the lens-shaped lump of kneecap on the outside of the knee.

Tamma cut his shoe off and revealed his foot, huge, shapeless, bruisy purple. She bore down on the nails and it was like they were full of ink and the ink blanched away and did not return.

"Dan?" she said.

"Yeah?"

"I've got to go get help."

"Don't leave me here, dude."

"*Dan.*"

"Promise me."

"Think about it," she said. "I can haul ass out to the road, flag down a car, and be back here with help in less than an hour."

"I don't want to die alone."

"You're not going to die."

"I'm hit on the head," he said. "And if I'm gonna die, I want to die with you."

"If you have a broken back, and try and come with, you're gonna total it."

"My back's not done."

"You don't know that."

She squatted in the sand and looked out across the hot, golden desert, on toward where she knew the truck waited.

"Do you feel like you've got a concussion?"

"The world is kind of going with my heartbeat?"

"Going?"

"It's like the world is on a screen and when my heart goes, someone hits it with a hammer."

There were girls who would know what to do in this situation. She wanted to grow up to be one of them, but she wasn't that girl now.

"Okay," she said.

She stood and started feeling her way with her fingers through his hair. He was leaning against the wall breathing hard and holding the injured leg, bent at the knee. She felt gruesomely ignorant and out of her depth.

"What hurts?"

"Everything hurts."

She found a broken rib along his right side. Found the place where it hinged. Before the break it was firm and beyond the break it sank to compression.

"Broken rib," she said.

"Several?"

"All I feel is the one."

"Feels like all of them to me."

"I don't doubt that all of them hurt. Plus your shinbones are broken and sticking out of your leg."

"Are they really?"

"Can you straighten your knee?"

She watched him try to extend the broken leg. The blood drained from his face and his neck took on an ugly green cast and then he exhaled raggedly and said, "Nope. Not at all."

"Okay. All right. Now, I have some bad news. I can't carry you a mile and a half. And you don't want me to go alone. Do you see what I'm getting at?"

"What?"

"You have to walk, Dan."

"Oh."

"It's not going to be a hell of a lot of fun but we'll get through it and afterward it will just be a cool thing we did one time. You'll tell girls all about it and they'll want to sit on my face. So remember, pain is temporary but glory is forever. Okay, dude?"

"Okay," he said.

She walked over to the backpack and began cutting the nylon free from the stays, thinking as hard and as fast as she could. She didn't want to make any mistakes if she could help it but nor did she have the time to think it through. It was an old backpack, framed with half-inch aluminum piping. She didn't have her cell phone. There was no service even if she did have the phone. In the spring and fall, and all through winter, there'd be climbers at these cliffs, but there weren't any now. She cut out the piping, walked back to him, framed it into a makeshift splint, tied it closed with cut lengths of cordura, and bound it tight with a roll of athletic tape. The while, Dan gripped his leg and grimaced, rocking back and forth.

She picked up the water bottles, clipped them to a sling and slung them. Then she braced and pulled him to his feet and there came a bad moment where Dan realized all over again, but more profoundly, that—Oh, shit!—*he could not extend the bent leg*, and Tamma realized that he was heavier than she thought, and he teetered out of her grasp and went to the ground. He screamed in a way that Tamma had never heard a human scream, in a way she had not thought he could scream, and he rolled over and sat in the dust, holding his straightened, extended leg.

"Ohhhhhhh—" he said. "Oooooooh fuck!"

"Are you all right?"

He had both hands on his upper thigh, white-knuckling it, sinking the fingertips deep into the denim, and for the first time she'd ever seen, he was crying. Tears were cutting runs through the pollen and dust on his face.

"Are you okay?"

"Actually . . . ?" he said.

"What?"

"It feels *better*."

"*What?*"

He shook his head. Then he tested the knee. He grimaced, brought his arm up to his face, and bit savagely down into his forearm, shaking his head, but he was able to fully extend the broken leg. Then bend it again.

"I think the fall popped my kneecap back into place?"

"Seriously?"

He reached down and clawed back the bloody denim. The knee was an ugly green and black. But the patella sat astride the joint.

"Well . . . that's good," she said.

They sat in the dust, panting, putting off the moment. Then Tamma said, "I hate to say it, buddy, but . . . ah . . ."

"Take two," Dan said.

Tamma stood up, slacked her knees, one foot forward, took Dan by the wrists, hauled him to his feet, and then cuddled in beneath his arm, keeping her stance wide. He leaned heavily on her, and they started out, Dan hissing through his teeth with every step.

"You all right?" she said.

"Yeah, I'm great."

They worked among rocks. Each was a delicate operation where Tamma would hop forward, to the next boulder, and then stand, holding his hand, while Dan came hopping after her, his arms reaching. It was slow progress. They dropped into the gully that would take them to the broad valley above Barker Dam. The stream was dry and they walked down the center of it.

When they came into the shade of pinyons, she helped him down, and they both sat, their legs stretched out ahead of them, panting. They finished their water. The quartz crystals in the sand flashed like mirrors. The heat seemed to come off the granite like a sound. The ground was hazed with lapping, rippled shadows cast down onto the desert floor by the boiling air rising off the stones.

"This isn't even that bad," Tamma said. "Hell, it's not even properly summer yet. This is sort of a springtime caper. You know. Some people have really had to haul ass out of painful and remote places. North

Astrodome is almost a roadside crag, and this is just a sort of a romp, if you think about it."

Dan didn't reply. She looked over at him. He was lying against a juniper with his legs out in front of him. The splint was soaked. Blood was leaching across the sand. Yellowjackets and tarantula hawks hung in the air. They were alighting on the splint, and where they walked across the fresh tape they left pinpoint footprints. Elsewhere they were chewing on the cloth and she could see their jointed bellies heaving with their respiration. His eyes were closed and he seemed to be asleep. A yellowjacket was drinking sweat from the tangled hairs of his eyebrow. She clapped her hands to get his attention and his eyes opened very slowly and he looked over at her and smiled.

"Put on your big-girl panties, Dan. It's not far but I need you to be a team player. Are you a team player?"

"Put me in the game, coach," he said.

She staggered to her feet. About them lay biscuity granite fins, yuccas, blue junipers, and buckwheat. She braced one hand on the rock and grabbed him by the shirtfront and hauled him up with single, one-arm row, dragged him out into the sunlight, and the heat fell on her like a weight. He would lean on her and then stop and stare. When they started going again, tarantula hawks would rise up off their shirts and hang about them, buzzing.

They came to the place where the gully was choked with boulders and Dan crawled rock to rock on hands and knees with the surfaces shining in the sun. He would lie in any pool of shade and go to sleep. In the lees of rocks. Beneath yuccas. Tamma would nudge him awake with her foot and say, "Up and at 'em," and he would say, "Yeehaw," with all the humor he had left.

The wash emptied them into a broad, rippled granite alley with swaths of sand, a meandering streambed, here and there low granite hurdles, and high, scalloping walls on either side. They limped along with the sun staring down at them and their shadows puddled at their feet and flies crawling on the barrel cactuses. After a while, Dan lay down in the shadow of a boulder. Tamma squatted beside him.

"Wake up," she said.

He lulled his head to the side but could not rouse.

"Dan," she said.

She slapped his face and he opened his eyes and she said, "Come on, get up," and reached down and took his forearm and pulled him to a stand and boosted him up onto her sweatslick back and carried him piggyback. She had to talk herself through every step. Thinking, Come on, Tamma. Standing there, willing herself to keep moving.

She started to pick out mileposts for herself, the shadows cast by junipers, or by shoulders of stone, walking shadow to shadow in a stumbling, heat-sick zigzag, and at each shadow she stood, getting her breath back. The ground came rolling on toward her like a great comforter shaken out to sort the ripples. Swells would rise out of the distance and she would stop and brace and it would fall away and then she would keep going. After a while, Dan peeled off and fell back into the sand and lay in the dust breathing but making no other sign. She sat down beside him, mopping grease-thick sweat off her brow. A yellowjacket walked across her hairline. More were feeding upon the splint.

"Dan," she said, and there was no answer. She seized the lobe of his ear and crushed it between her fingers and he opened his eyes slowly and looked at her sleepily and she stooped over him.

"Dan, buddy," she said, and his eyes met hers.

"You need to stay awake."

"I can't."

"Here's what we're gonna do. I'm gonna tell you a story. And you're gonna keep saying 'uh-huh,' and if you don't say 'uh-huh,' I'm gonna drop you to the ground and punch you in the balls until you wake up."

"Don't drop me."

"Then you just gotta keep saying 'uh-huh.'"

"Uh-huh."

"Can you walk?"

"Uh-huh."

But he couldn't get up. Tamma helped him stand against the rock and then she backed into him and hoisted him up piggyback and went staggering forward in the broad stone valley with golden walls on either side of them. When she turned and looked back, she'd left a long, wandering drizzle of blood behind her. Blood was dripping down the splint, which had swollen to enormous size, and the blood had run down onto her legs and into her shoes, which squished with it.

"So I went to the doctor," she said.

"Uh-huh."

"And do you know what this guy says to me?" Tamma was sucking air hard, but somehow still getting it all out, choking out gasps at every comma and talking off the top of her lungs like a stoner. "He looks at me and he's like, 'Whoooooa, would you like some help with that acne?' Which. First of all. *Rude*. And by the by, this is not, like, a handsome man? This is not like: My doctor is Ryan Gosling and Ryan Gosling thinks I need help with my skincare. This is like: My doctor is a horrifying, manky, republican-looking guy and *he* thinks my skincare isn't good? And I am thinking to myself, Do you need some help with your MOM?"

"Uh-huh."

"And without even asking he turns around and begins to write a prescription! He's all like, 'If we can get you on the pill it will help with your hormonal outbreaks and then later, if necessary, we can start accutane—and I was all like—'Hold up!—this wild stallion will not be tamed!' and he was all like, 'Mare,' and I was all like, 'Mayor what,' and he was all like, 'You mean *mare*,' and I was all like, 'Sure, *okay*, I, the Mayor of Poundtown, the Mayor of Sendville, the Mayor of Rocking-Your-Mother's-World—' and he was like, 'No, not mayor: *mare*, a lady stallion.'"

"Ah."

Tamma broke off, sucking air, and then she started again: "And I was like, 'Well, sir! This magnificent lady stallion will not be gelded; I will not take your little, like, hormonal therapies,' and then he was like, 'Now, a thing to consider is that these will help if you become sexually active,' and I was like, 'Oh yeah? Well not if I'm sexually active with YOUR MOM,' and he was like, 'What?' and I was like, 'Not if I'm sexually active with OLIVIA WILDE,' and he was like, 'Huh?' And I was like, 'Will these help me if I exhume the body of Mary Wollstonecraft from her cold, worm-ridden grave and bring her back to life with a lightning strike and the two of us have undead lesbian sex while wearing full-body latex catsuits?' And he was like, 'No, I suppose in that case, birth control would be the least of your very many extraordinary problems,' and I was all like, 'Right?' And he was all like, 'I see, forgive me, I made a mistake. Also, I recommend silicone lubricant or baby powder to aid in getting into and out of latex garments. Unfortunately, I no longer recommend baby powder for diapers, because I have concerns about infants inhaling the talcum. But I think that this is a good use case.' And I was a little, like, *surprised* because this guy, he's so old and pudgy? I thought for sure he wouldn't be cool? But he was cool? People can, like, *surprise* you, you know?"

"Uh-huh."

"And he was all like—he goes—'I hope you and Mary Wollstonecraft are very happy, and would you like me to write you a script in case you change your mind?' and I was like—'Change my mind, sir? *Change my mind!* THIS, sir, is not a choice; it is who I *am!*' I was all like: 'There is only, sir, one circumstance in which I would switch-hit. And that is if I could be a SEXUAL TYRANNOSAURUS waiting for the electric fences to short out so that I could be unleashed upon a tiny, terrified, rain-soaked, desperately-trying-to-escape Jeff Goldblum, and then crashing through the wires and pounding down the tarmac after him, waving my tiny arms, gnashing my teeth, just like, 'Come back, Jeff!' but then getting into it and coming after him like—'RAAAAAWWWWWRRRRRRR! FLEE, TINY MAMMAL! FLEE FOR MY DELIGHT! IT ONLY INCREASES THE SEXUAL TENSION.'"

"Ah-huh."

"But he was still cool, and he was like, 'I am sorry, I should clarify that I don't mean change your mind about your sexual orientation. I mean in case you change your mind about taking birth control to help with your hormonal acne. Lots of young women choose to take birth control, and not because they are sexually active, but in order to help regulate their periods.'"

"Uh-huh."

Tamma was making her way across the desert floor. The trail from North Astrodome ran mostly south and east toward the old pink ruin and the sun was ahead of her and she was lidding her eyes against it and looking out at the desert white with glare and her field of vision obscured by her eyelashes.

"And I was like: 'What bullshit is this! Would you take a medication that took the rough edge off your masculinity?' And he was like: 'I do take that medication. It's called old age. Do you find that you have heavy, painful, uncomfortable periods?' And I was like, 'Oh man! DO I EVER. I menstruate like it's the fucking battle of Khazad-dûm! Drums in the deep! Drums! *Doom doom* go the drums! They delved too deep! Something in the darkness wakes! The battle is pitched and all is turmoil and clangor and blood! And Gandalf is standing at the gates like 'ALAS FOR THE REALMS OF MEN! WHAT TIDE OF FIERY DARKNESS COMES FROM OUT THE DEEP FASTNESSES OF THE WORLD!' and *Doom doom!* go the drums, *Doomboom, doom-boom!* and Gandalf is like 'YOU SHALL NOT PASS!' and the fiery elder uterus is like 'WATCH ME,' and the hobbits are like 'FLEE! FLEE!'"

"Uh-huh."

"And he, the doctor, he seemed a little taken aback, but he was all like, 'Okay! Well . . . Huh! You *may* find that hormonal birth control would help with that . . . or you . . . may not, I'm not sure,' And I was like, '. . . Um . . . help? How much help are we talking about here?' And he was like, 'Well if you take these pills, you will only have a period four times a year, and they will be very mild.' And I was like, 'Four times a year?! What dark sorcery is this? Can you—um—tell me more about that? For purely hypothetical and/or informational purposes?' But then I was like, 'No! GET BEHIND ME, SATAN! I need my blazing sex drive to lead me through these dangerous run-outs!' And he was like: 'I understand and support your decision, and I agree that hormonal birth control has side effects and may not be the right choice for every young person, particularly athletes with strength training goals,' so he gave me this amoxicillin face wash instead. Because I guess he looked at my face and he was like, Home-girl still needs *hellllllllp*."

Tamma squatted down and laid him into the shade and Dan looked up at her and he said, "Are we stopping?" and Tamma said, "Yeah, because we're here." She dug in her pockets and unlocked the truck. "And Dreamy McGee," she said, "is going to the hospital!" She helped him back up, and into the open passenger-side door, and he said, "Who is Dreamy McGee?"

V.

EXPOSURE

One

Graduation was held in the auditorium. Dan sat in a folding metal chair in his cheap black robes. They let him sit at the end of a row. Tamma was not there. It was the first of June. Feedback kept coming through the speakers. He crutched himself across the stage with difficulty and the principal shook his hand, grasped his elbow, and said, "So proud. *So proud.*" Dan held up the diploma and then crutched himself down the stairs, out along the bleachers, and dropped into the wheelchair his old man was holding for him.

When it was all done, Dan wheeled himself through the crush and then his father helped him into the passenger seat and tossed the wheelchair into the bed. Dan sat on the rattling bench seat, hitching up his black gown to show his bare foot. The leg was enormous, mottled yellow and black, with neat rows of stitching from the original open fracture, from the surgical incisions, and from a prophylactic compartment release. The leg was haloed in circular, stainless-steel external fixators spanned apart by rods, and he had pins and wires tunneled in through drill holes, the flesh a little tented and red where it met the steel. There had been thirty bone fragments, some of which were pulverized. The surgeon had said, "It was kind of a puzzle!"

Care consisted mostly of washing it with soap and water and keeping it elevated. That meant staying in the wheelchair and off crutches. But Dan had been determined to walk. And was regretting it now. He could feel his heartbeat in his shin.

"How is it, Danny?" his old man said, looking over at him.

"It's fine."

"You made a noise."

"Just aches, is all."

Dan did not remember the accident. Nor did he remember the drive to the hospital. He knew that as soon as they hit the fee station, they'd picked up a ranger escort, and the ranger had called ahead. They'd gotten to the medical center, and there Dan had been packaged and taken to San Bernardino by helicopter, but he didn't remember that, either. Tamma had been taken in to do a debrief. Dan hoped that had been with Naomi, but he didn't know.

He'd kept asking the nurse about it. Her name was Quina. She was six foot two, broad shouldered, huge bellied, her skin pale white and freckled, with eczema on her upper arms, neck, and cheeks. When Quina found out that he was a climber, she'd had a lot of questions for him, none of which he could answer. She was in training for some kind of competition and deep in the weeds. He didn't quite understand what she did—whenever asked, she'd say, "I pick things up and then put them down again!"

His IV had gone bad and she'd had to put in another at the bedside, feeling up and down his veins, shaking her head the entire time, talking to him. "Ooooh, look at that one," she said, testing its pliancy with a gloved finger. "You're an easy stick, but still harder than you look. Because. Feel that?" Sinking her finger into the vein. "That's a valve. And here, another. You're valves up and down." Shaking her head. "Look at this one, this is a good one. Oooooooh. I don't think other humans have this vein. Climbing, huh?! Great for grip, climbing! You ever tried the rolling thunder?"

"No," Dan said. "What is that?"

"A rolling bar deadlift handle, two and three-quarter inches in diameter."

"What do you pull on that?"

"A hundred pounds."

"Sounds like a lot."

"It's not. I bet you'd pull one fifteen no problem. What do you deadlift?"

"I don't," Dan said. "But I can do a hundred one-arm thirty-six-kilo kettlebell swings in under three minutes."

"Ugh," Quina said with disgust. "Sounds like cardio." She shook her head. "Look at these veins. Just *look* at them. I'm gonna bring the nursing students in here and have them take turns."

"Do it," Dan said. "God knows I'm not being useful any other way."

She put in the IV. Effortlessly, first try.

"That was smooth."

"Yeah, well, I don't suck," she said. "I was a phleb tech for years before nursing school. So, you know. I got practice. Once you get that leg under you, we gotta start you deadlifting. You're built for it. I'd purely love to know what you could pull with a year of training."

"Why am I here," he said. "In San Bernardino? I mean, not that I'm not grateful. But why did I get flown here rather than staying at the medical center?"

"Any fall over a certain height gets called a trauma one and has to go to a trauma one hospital."

"How far did I fall?"

"In your notes, it says eighty feet."

Dan was silent. He was trying to remember it. He almost felt like he could. But he might've been just making things up.

"Do you know what happened?"

"In report, I heard your rope cut."

Dan was thinking about it. If he'd fallen on the final traverse, it had fifteen-foot spans between protection. He easily could've fallen thirty, thirty-five feet, been partially arrested by the rope, and then fallen forty feet to the deck. It was still a bad fall, but greatly mitigated.

"So, it's just protocol?" he said. "To take fall survivors to a trauma one?"

"Yeah. Over a certain height like I said. And the other reason is that your leg was in thirty pieces plus a comminuted patella fracture, closed head injury, three broken ribs, and punctured lung but luckily—no flail chest. They can't deal with that at your podunk little medical center. With these small hospitals, there is very little incentive to take a big trauma, and there are strong liability disincentives. They just don't have the experience. We do. You don't want to miss something in the initial trauma workup and then have someone die of a liver lac you didn't even know they had. Another major factor is the length of time between injury and treatment. In report, one of the nurses said that you were carried out of a wilderness area?"

"Was I?" Dan said. "By who?"

"By your climbing partner?"

"Tamma?" Dan said. "Tamma carried me?"

"Big girl, Tamma?" Quina asked, with the tremendous curiosity of an athlete hearing of an interesting feat of strength. Probably she wanted to know what Tamma could deadlift.

"No," Dan said. "Not a very big girl."

"Huh," Quina said. "She must like you, boy. Because I tell you what. If you fell eighty feet and landed next to me, I don't know that I'd wanna carry you out two miles. I'd be like: 'Stay here. Take spinal precautions. I'll go get help.' So, don't kid me. How big is this girl?"

"I'm telling you, not big," Dan said. "Five feet tall, very fit? I don't like to guess at weight."

"Not a chance," Quina said. "Not a *chance*. She must have some guts. That girl. Carrying a guy out? A guy your size? That's hard work. She must be pretty well used to the pain cave, your girl." Quina's sport, whatever it was, came with a whole other lexicon, which Dan couldn't quite follow.

"Pain cave?" he said.

"Tough," Quina said, still thinking of it. "Psychologically tough."

The next day, he'd asked Quina if she was going to let him go home for graduation and she said it was up to the intensivist but that they generally let people go home pretty early, even with the fixators. The tech had come in, and she was stocking the cabinets from a cart she towed in behind her.

"What do I wear over this thing?" Dan said, looking at the stainless-steel hoops.

"A kilt," Quina suggested.

"Tearaway pants," the tech said.

"A sundress."

"A sarong."

"But seriously," Dan said.

"Shorts," Quina said.

He'd waited for Tamma to come, but she had not come. He was tilted back in bed, his leg in a sling. Mostly, he spent time with his dad, who, practiced at this now, sat by the bedside reading a Dean Koontz novel. The surgeon was a small man, well-built and handsome, with thick, close-cut white hair, a neat, close-cut white mustache, and deeply tanned skin cut with smile lines at his eyes. He would draw up a stool beside the bed and talk. When Dan asked about the fixator, he said, "Well it depends upon the comminution of the bone and the disposition of fracture ends. But what really worried me was the length of time between injury and treatment. Those open fractures can be quite dirty, especially with wilderness evacs. And what you really don't want is to put in the plate and screws and have an infection take hold on the hardware and get into the bone. Because then you're in all kinds of trouble. The external fixator gives us a little more leeway to keep an eye on things. Although you still got to keep them clean, or you get infections in the pin track."

"Quina said I fell eighty feet."

"That's what I got in report," the surgeon said, nodding. "But if you fell eighty feet, then some angel was watching out for you."

"You don't think my injuries are serious?"

The surgeon beamed at him. He seemed to deliberate and then to allow himself an answer not entirely appropriate. "No," he said at last.

"Falls can be terrible. I treated a young gal hardly older than you who fell twenty-five feet and died."

"Was that on Fingerbang Princess?"

The surgeon seemed surprised. "I don't remember the name of the climb, and even if I did, I couldn't say. But you can have all kinds of trauma and die a pretty bad death at twenty feet. She had a TBI, flail chest, four broken vertebrae. At eighty? Mostly what we see is massive trauma and cause of death is multiple injuries, like a bug on a windshield."

"Oh," Dan said.

"You got a new lease on life, boy. Use it well, is my advice."

The night after graduation, he sat at the dinner table with his old man, and his old man ate hunching forward with his elbows on the tabletop, hanging his head, sometimes shaking it, sometimes sighing out through his broken nose, jawing thoughtfully, and from time to time he would look askance at Dan.

"How's the knee, Danny?" he said.

And Dan said, "Needs a little WD-40, Dad."

His old man nodded, thumb and forefinger ringing the water glass, saying, "Ah, that's funny."

That night, Dan lay in bed, his leg elevated on pillows and folded blankets, sweat dripping down his flanks. He couldn't read. Couldn't think. Couldn't stand to be himself. And when sleep came, it came with a lurching sensation of falling backward, some vast and dizzying outer darkness opening up around him, and then he jerked upright in bed, gasping. He maneuvered until he could prop himself against the wall, the bad leg and the fixator stretched out before him, steel shining in the moonlight. He sat there, working to calm his breathing. Wondering if he had the courage to try for sleep again.

After a while, he leaned over and felt around on the floor. Found his crutches, spidered painfully across the room to the desk, grimacing, picked up his wallet and checkbook. Crutched to the door, found the keys, and then through the living room. Stopped at the entryway, looking at his boots, and then went on without them, maneuvering with difficulty through the doorway, and then pivoting around and crutching to the truck. He unlocked it and opened the passenger-side door. Slung in the crutches one after another. Hauled himself up inside and then scooched sideways across the bench seat and started up the engine. He pulled out, drove south down Lifted Lorax toward the 62. He was working the pedals left-footed, and he had a tough time keeping his right foot out of the way. He stopped where the lane met the highway, vast and empty, unlighted in any direction. Then he pulled out, going west. He drove, clenching and unclenching the wheel. He turned off the highway on a lane going south and followed gravel roads. Cut the lights and eased down the last hundred yards to Sierra's place. And there, on the steps, was Tamma. A small, drab figure in dim blue moonlight, with the baby monitors propped on the steps.

She watched him impassively. He opened the door. Slung out one crutch, propped it against the quarter panel. Slung out the other, propped it in the lee of the door. Slid himself out, collected his crutches and then started swinging his way across the yard. He got to her, set the crutches against the house, and lowered himself to the steps.

"You're up late," he said.

"Samantha's teething. It's not supposed to affect their sleep. Hundreds of studies show that it does not. But I don't know. It seems to. She only does this when she's teething or has ear infections. She wakes up. I give her ibuprofen and send her back to bed. And it's cooler out here, than it is inside."

"Ah," Dan said.

"What about you?"

"Trouble sleeping."

"I can't imagine why."

"Maybe I'm teething."

Silence. The crackle of the monitors.

"Kind of missed you at the hospital."

"I'm sorry. I was too gutless."

"What do you mean?"

"I was terrified of what you'd say to me."

"Ah."

"I felt responsible."

"You told me that Figures was a bad idea from the start."

"Well, Paisley tried to give me a brand-new rope and I said no."

"You did?"

Dan sat on the steps. He felt rage, then. Rage that this girl, who had always wanted someone to just give her a rope, this girl who had always wanted a chance, had gotten it, and said no. But the rage passed, as quickly as it came, and he started to laugh, shaking his head. He laughed until he started coughing and then he left off, leaned forward, groaning with difficulty, and picked up a handful of rocks. Began pitching them out into the dark. Shaking his head. Still coughing at times.

"Why did you say no? All you've wanted, since you were eight years old, was for someone to just *give* you a rope and a rack."

"Because I'm a fucking idiot," Tamma said. He thought at first she'd said it with great and admirable toughness, but then she made an awful, wet, sucking gasp, and started to cry.

"This is not your fault," Dan said.

"I should've talked you out of it."

"Nah, I was like a moth to a fucking flame."

"I saw you crater, dude. You hit so hard, there was bloodsplatter on the rock fifteen feet away. I'm so sorry."

The ideal climber was a warrior, stone-faced, unstoppable, staring down death with inscrutable calm. They were both aware of that. But Tamma had never been that kind of a person, and she was crying hard now, muffling herself with the heel of her palm.

"No, Tams," Dan said. "You said we ought not to climb Figures. And I insisted we go. That's what happened."

"What's the last thing you remember?"

"The last thing I remember is getting up. And sitting on the edge of my bed in the dark. Thinking about climbing Figures."

"So, a pretty serious TBI then."

"Serious enough that I'm glad they already let me into college."

"That's not funny, Dan."

"I know it's not."

They sat side by side for a long time.

"I wonder about myself though," Dan said. "I wonder if I did something."

"If you blew the sequence on purpose."

"Yeah."

"That's how much you hate me," she said.

"I don't hate you. You're the only thing that has ever been good, in my entire life, you're the only thing that ever felt alive. I was just scared. I just got terribly scared, Tamma. There's something wrong with me. I'm scared all the time. And I'm scared most of the good things."

"So, what now?"

"I accepted a full ride to a liberal arts school in the Pacific Northwest."

He's going to do what he has to do, she thought. It's his life, and the only thing that matters is that he be as happy as he can be, and the only thing you want him to feel from you is your love and your support and your belief so don't say it. Don't say it, Tamma. Don't be some dumb, selfish bitch. Just keep your mouth shut and don't beg. Just let him do it without torturing him, if it's what he has to do.

"Look," she said. "I think you'll do amazing. And all those kids out there, they're lucky to have you. I think you will make something of yourself."

He was silent.

"I wanted to go with you," Dan said. "But I couldn't face it. And now—"

"Sure," Tamma said. "I understand. Your leg. Hey—don't worry about it. No sweat. Dirtbagging was always going to be a precarious life. You'd be giving up a lot. And for what? It was a pipe dream."

"Listen, Tams, I've thought a lot about this."

"What?"

"I want you to have Alex's money."

"I don't want it."

"Where I'm going, it's a full ride."

"I don't care. You keep it."

"It's yours," he said. "I don't need it."

"I don't need it, either, much less want it."

"Let me do this."

"No."

"I *want* to do this."

"Still no."

"Please."

"I can't accept it, Dan."

"You can, and you're going to. Because it's your chance. And me? I believe. Go out there and do it, Tamma. Be that hard-sending chick on the poster in the bedroom of every little girl in the world."

"What about you?" she said.

"Who cares?" he said. "Fuck the weak. The world belongs to the strong." He dragged himself up and drew out a check with flourish. It was made out to TAMARISK "THE FINGERBANG PRINCESS" CALLAHAN. It was for $12,500. All the money Dan had gotten from his parents, less the $500 acceptance deposit. Dan had signed it.

"What if the lady at the bank demands to see my credentials as 'The Fingerbang Princess'?"

"Take her into the ladies' room and rock her world."

"You fucking *asshole*," she said.

Two

The independent study packets arrived in the mail. Sierra had paid seventy-five dollars for each, in the hope that Tamma could still get her diploma, and Tamma carried them to the dumpster and dropped them inside with a hollow boom. Then she caught the bus into town and went to the bank. It was cold and dim inside, with islands of carpeting among wide stone walkways and burlap cubicles. Tamma was wearing a tiger-striped bodysuit, cutoffs, and a crop top with the bust of a bald eagle superimposed upon a rippled, flaking-away American flag. She picked up the pen chained to the desktop and filled out the slip. There were no other customers. The stand was manufactured wood printed with woodgrain. The agents at the counter watched her. Behind them, the vault door stood open. Tamma walked over and clicked her ID and debit card onto the granite.

The girl put two fingers on the check, drew it across the counter, lifted her keyboard, and set it atop the edge to pin it flat. She typed. Then she said, "All done! Would you like a receipt?"

Tamma killed an hour in town, worked her shift at target, caught the bus, and slept through the ride with her head against the window.

Got out, and walked the last two miles, every once in a while throwing down a cartwheel, handstand-walking short distances, and then kicking out into a walk. There was a strange car in the drive: a green subaru impreza with rusted undercarriage and a seedling juniper growing out of the rotted sealant around the moon roof. Tamma let herself in to Sierra's house and said, "Someone here?"

"No," Sierra said, grinning, holding Sam on her hip. Hunter was in his room and River was on his play gym, kicking his kickers.

"What's with the car?"

"In a sec!" Sierra said. "But first: guess what!"

"I don't want to guess!" Tamma said, thinking, *He turned over!* It was, of all the things she wanted, the thing she wanted most, but if she said it and she was wrong, she would beggar whatever good news her sister might have.

"*Guess!*"

"I'm scared!"

"River was lying there, farting away, and then he reached for his rattle and turned over, back to front. I held the rattle just out of reach, and ten minutes later, he did it again!"

"He *turned over?*" Tamma repeated.

"*He turned over!*" Sierra said. "He's been doing it all morning!"

Tamma leapt, and then Sierra leapt, and they leapt up and down, across from one another and then Tamma crawled over to where River was nomming on his whole entire slobbery wet hand and when she came near, he dimpled up and gave her a grin, drawing his shoulders up and wiggling all over in eye-crinkling delight, and she said, "Zoom zoom zooooom!" and kissed his little baby nose and then zoom-zoom-zoomed again and kissed his little baby cheek and River chuckled to himself and patted his chubby belly. When she was ready to come up for air, she turned over and said, "So does your tinder date drive a subaru?"

"No."

"Whose then?"

"Yours."

"My tinder date?"

"Your *car*."

"*No.*"

"I mean for tax reasons I have to sell it to you for a dollar but it's a gift."

"Does that work? Is that a real thing?"

"Who knows. Apparently the rich don't pay taxes at all so I'm just doing my best."

"I can't accept this. I don't think I'll stick around. One day Paisley Cuthers is going to call me and we're going to go away to France together to climb limestone."

"I know," Sierra said. She said it quietly and even if she did know, it must've been bad news. "It's not a car for sticking around. It's just thanks. *Thank you* for being here almost every day in the hardest, worst year of my life. Here, when nobody else was. Everybody abandoned us. Except you. You were in the thick of it, reading mommy blogs and buying sound machines and cleaning spit-up. And I was so scared, I was a bitch to you every day, and you bitched right back, but kept showing up. Then I woke up one day and realized that my filthy, bratty, geeky little sister, who never used to wear shoes, or wash her hair, grew up into just this caring, patient, incredible, tough-as-nails young woman with dirty hair. And because you showed up like you did, I got to fly out and work strikes, and we paid down all our medical bills. They even gave me a promotion."

"They did?"

"Nurse manager," Sierra said. "It's not much more money. But it's nine-to-five. Meaning, we can put River in daycare, when we're ready. So, with everything paid down, we've come out ever so slightly ahead. There will be more bills—PT and OT. But for the moment? We can take a breath. So, I thought. Well. I'd try and do something for you."

"That's terrific," Tamma said. "That's amazing."

"It is. I'm just sorry it's not a van. I know you wanted a van."

"No," Tamma said. "It's perfect. It turns out I won't need a van."

"I'm sorry. At least, Dan has the chance to go to school. That's big."

"That's true. He'll be magnificent."

Tamma lay on the floor. After a while she pressed herself up and crawled over to her sister and kissed her on the cheek.

"Get out of here," Sierra said. "You will never, ever be happy unless you at least try. We will figure it out. You've done enough. More than enough."

"Thanks," Tamma said. And she felt it, because while Sierra might truly want Tamma to take this chance, Tamma did not see how. Neither of them wanted to put River, who was seven months old, and still very vulnerable, in daycare. Maybe soon, but not yet. Besides, the expenses associated with River's ongoing PT and OT were enormous, and Tamma didn't see how Sierra could afford all that, plus full-time daycare for two babies, not to mention the time spent grocery shopping, cooking, cleaning, and navigating California's labyrinthine insurance system. The car was generous, but Tamma felt like she was holding this family together with two chalky hands.

"So, what's your plan?"

"I guess I'll stick around through the summer. Climbing is garbage everywhere in the summer, anyway. Except Squamish, but I don't have a passport. Maybe Index? But nah, I'll stay. Pick up more hours at target. Hang out with the cutest and best kids in the world. One of whom can turn over now. To be honest, I'm scared to set out on my own. I don't know what I'll find out there."

She worked four days a week at target, and when she wasn't at work, she kept house. June, July, and then August, Tamma played with the babies, did dishes, scrubbed floors, made meals, cleaned bathrooms, organized paperwork, paid bills, folded laundry, and kept a meticulous pen-and-paper budget in her lab notebook. She laid carpet and installed drywall. She painted the nursery walls to look like Indian Creek, with red sandstone buttresses and a valley of green cottonwoods. She baked sourdough biscuits and served them with chicken gravy, scrambled eggs, and wilted spinach. She reached out to a mom she'd met through facebook and, on her advice, changed River's formula, and in twenty-four hours River's diaper rash, his eczema, the dry places on his scalp that she used to rub down with cream, it was all gone. He stopped spitting up, and started pooping just once or twice a day, and Tamma cried for being an idiot, cried for wanting to make no mistakes at all with these babies, cried for making those mistakes anyway, and cried in thankfulness for highly motivated moms on the internet. At work, she scrubbed toilets and mopped floors and emptied trash cans. She worked checkout counters. When it was slow, she stocked the gum. People sometimes asked her what was wrong with her, and it was true, she stood in a daze beneath the fluorescent lighting, wearing pleated khaki pants and a red polo shirt, dreaming of the White Rim, passing items off the belt, across the scanner, and into the bags. Target was proud of their plastic bags. Her manager was proud of the plastic bags. Heavier gauge plastic than the competition, her manager used to tell her. Wonderful, durable bag. Uh-huh, Tamma would say. Use this bag for anything around the house, her manager said. Won't rip on the way to the car. Uh-huh, Tamma said. Tamma's manager introduced her to another employee as the girl who cleans the toilets. He was trying to be nice; he was trying to set Tamma up with the only other pleated-khaki and red-polo lesbian there, he was trying to make a joke. Tamma thought: Sure. Yes. I am actually the girl who cleans the toilets.

She had a break halfway through her shift and would go upstairs to sit on a plastic chair with her feet on a wood-laminate table in a vinyl-tiled, windowless room with a coat rack in the corner and she would read mommy blogs on her phone. Other women have solved these problems, Tamma thought. So can I. Give me your wisdom, mommies of the world. How do we raise these kids, how do we keep them fed, how do we put them all to bed, how do we handle their tantrums, how do we keep them in clothes and teach them how to say please, how do we potty train them, how do we keep them from raping somebody else's child in the bathroom while yet another child films it on their phone? How do we teach them to be generous and kind and yet guarded, and what is this hell, what is this hopeless place full of doomed and failed people, and why did we bring children here?

This summer could become her life. And it could be a pretty good one. She loved the kids; she loved her sister. It turned out, Tamma was a problem solver, and when you were keeping house, there were plenty of problems to solve. She was dialing in her buttermilk-brined roasted chicken; every week, her sourdough biscuits got better; nap schedules were on point. Cinnamon rolls were proving difficult, but every once in a while, she got them done. Maybe this could be enough. She sat and put her head against her steering wheel and when she could get herself together, she dabbed her eyes with the hem of her shirt and got out and climbed up the steps and swung the door open and surprised all three kids on the floor and Samantha boosted up and went toddling toward her crying, "Damma! Damma!" and Tamma said, "Honey! I'm home!" and hiked Samantha back between her legs, swung her up into the air, holding her aloft, pirouetting, exclaiming, "You're the cutest! The *cutest* of them all!" and Samantha gaped open her smiling mouth and crinkled closed her delighted eyes and with her small hands she signed, "More! More!"

Then her mother came to see her. The end of August. Almost September. Tamma opened the door to find them crowded on the front steps. Kendra, Hyrum, and Colin. She backed up, and they all came in.

"It's a shoeless household," Tamma said, and everyone stopped to look at her and then went on just as before. Both doorways were bounded with gates and the outlets were blocked. The dining table legs were covered in PVC insulation. Colin slunk to the end of the couch. Hyrum walked to the table and dragged back a chair. Then he seemed to think of something and rose and stepped over the kitchen gate and Tamma said, "There isn't any beer," and he said, "Tea?" and she said, "There's iced tea." He came back, dragged his chair out, seated himself with his elbow on the table and cracked open the can.

Tamma sat cross-legged on the floor with Samantha beside her.

River crawled into her lap and pulled at the front of her shirt. Tamma ran her palm over his fuzzy head, feeling the scars.

"What is this about?" she said.

Kendra sat down on the couch. She started to speak and then rose and shaded her eyes and walked back and forth in front of Tamma while Tamma tucked her hair back from River's grasping hands.

"He crawls now," Tamma said.

"What?"

"He's started crawling. Pretty much right on time. He can almost stand. He can prop himself on the coffee table. Sierra cried when he first did it. It's—I can't tell you how huge it is, for us. He's not babbling, but he pays attention and I have hopes. He may be all right."

"It's not news to me," Kendra said. "You were the only one with doubts. I said he was perfect. But do you listen to me? No, you do not. I'm *nothing* to you. You *never* listen to me. You *never* have. And here it is. You come to me saying, 'Oh, he crawls now.' Like I didn't believe from the start that he was a strong, beautiful, perfect baby. Like you had to ask anyone else. Like your own mother wasn't good enough to talk to you."

River looked up at Tamma and his face crumpled, his blue eyes crushed down, the corners of his mouth fell, his lip pouted out, and he started to cry with trembling sobs. Tamma swung him up into her arms and then squatted to a stand and walked back and forth shushing him while Samantha tracked her worriedly from the floor.

Kendra sat down and groped in her purse for her pack of cigarettes and took it out and uncapped it and Tamma said, "No," and Kendra said "Just—" and Tamma said, "No, dude, *no*," and Kendra flung up her hands in annoyance and then put the pack back in her purse and zipped it closed, shaking her head furiously.

"Ahhhhhhh," Hyrum said, "don't call your mother 'dude,' *dude*."

"Besides!" Kendra said. "It doesn't hurt them. I smoked every day with you. You're *spoiling* those kids. You don't know how to raise children, they shouldn't be with you."

"Why did you come, Mom?"

From the table, Hyrum said, "We need you to pay us back. We wouldn't ask except that Colin is in trouble and needs a lawyer. Things have gotten out of hand with this Jenny girl. Two other girls have come forward. And there are pictures that Colin has apparently circulated. They consider that he has been uh . . . trafficking in . . . uhhhhhhhhh, child pornography. Even though he is, of course, a child. You stole from us, and it was fine. We let it go. But now we need that money."

"I can't help you."

"We thought we'd give you this one opportunity to do the right thing."

"Have you tried using his college fund?"

No one said anything. Tamma understood that there had never been a college fund, except perhaps, in the sense that Kendra and Hyrum might have lain around some evening, talking about putting money away for Colin's education in a wishful and well-intentioned way. But really, it had only ever been a lie.

At last Hyrum said, "Colin could go to juvie."

"I doubt it."

"Oh *you doubt it*," Kendra said, shaking her head. "Easy for you to say. Oh—you *doubt* it?"

"Okay," Hyrum said. "All right." He rose and dusted off his thighs. "That's what we came here to say. Your brother needs help and we need you to pay us back the money you stole."

"Suck my dick," Tamma said.

"Right, okay. Do you ever consider that there is a reason no one likes you?" Hyrum lifted the can high, poured it across the table, and walked out. Kendra and Colin went after him. Colin looked back as he closed the door and Tamma waved and he did not wave back. After they left, Tamma held both babies in her arms and walked back and forth, shushing them while they cried.

"It's okay," she said, over and over again. "They're gone."

Three

Dan waited in his seat, watching the plane empty out, row by row. Then a flight attendant brought forward his crutches and he rose and crutched down the jetway and out into the terminal at PDX. Before him, well-dressed people towing roller bags, going their own crisscrossing ways. He leaned on the crutches, wearing jeans and a baseball shirt and one boot, chewing his chapped lips. He had never been this far from home before. He continued on to the baggage claim, and there he waited for his oversized olive drab duffel. Watched it go by once, and again, his armpits aching. A guy beside him lifted it off the carousel, said, "Do you need help, brother?" and Dan shook his head.

He stuffed his book into the duffel, slung it, went through the sliding glass doors, and caught a shuttle. Sat on the bench, jostled side to side, his crutches upright in the crook of his elbow, feeling lost and far from home. Other students on the bus were talking and meeting one another but Dan kept to himself. At the university he climbed laboriously down and stepped out onto the curb.

There was, before him, a stone fountain and brick walls opening onto a plaza, the colonnaded front of the student union building, the clock tower, the glass-walled library, a riffled blue stream, masonry bridges, brilliant green lawns, and plane trees with their leaves rustling in the wind. He let the others go on and then walked past the fountain alone. It was freshman orientation, two weeks ahead of term, and campus was nearly empty. Just beyond the fountain were volunteers in blue shirts with name tags on lanyards, but Dan crutched by with purpose, out onto the plaza, fronting a stream with grassy banks. He continued on, swinging forward and planting his crutches and swinging again, his armpits wet, his jeans cloying. The light was so heavy, it felt about like he could chew on it, the world much too green and close, with Gothic buildings on every side, the horizon nowhere. He crutched across a bridge and then out along a flagstone walkway, the river behind him, and before him the quad bordered in magnolias and brick buildings completely unlike any he'd ever seen. He dropped his duffel and stood, propped in the middle of the sidewalk. Everything he owned in that bag, save the thirty-six-kilo bell, which he couldn't lift anyway. The clock tower began to sound, behind him. He knew the name of the dorm he was in, but he didn't know how to find it. He pivoted slowly around, making a survey.

A woman crossing the quad the other way had stopped and was looking at him. He must've looked exactly like what he was, because she called out, "Enjoy it while it lasts! These'll be the best years of your life!" He looked back at her with a plunging lurch. A sickening moment of disorientation. A mistake, he thought. And then, like god had reached down and touched him on the forehead, his world was split with light and he saw then a vast and golden wilderness of granite, the horizon strewn with weathered and tumbled stone, amber palisades pleated with cracks, the sun reading over his shoulder, the heat like that of an open oven door, the bedrock riven with crystal dikes, barrel and hedgehog cactus grouted into cracks, all of it brindled in rippling shadows, as if they labored across the floor of a whiskey glass freshly set upon the bar top. Huddled in lees of rock grew rust-red buckwheat and junipers nested in their coppery duff and scaled, dusty-blue berries. Tarantula hawks hung all about in the air, their legs dangling like the loose ends of knots. Tamma was helping him along, powerful and unsteady, reeling as she walked, his arm slung across her, muscles flexing in the yoke of her shoulders. Sometimes she would reach across with her other hand to steady him and her grasp was iron-hard. She was taking him in a zigzag, shadow to shadow, talking the while, and he could smell his own fear-stink, the mineral tang of the stone in the heat, and he could smell her, her sweaty-girl scent, and it was as if he could recall exactly how her voice had felt, could almost catch its texture between thumb and forefinger, he was that close to it, the way it ran tilting and headlong with dashing cadences and sudden, emphatic haltings, but he could not call to mind what she was saying, not exactly, and when he turned to look at her, turned to speak, turned to say, "*Wait*," she was gone, the Wonderland gone, and he was standing there on campus, propped on his crutches, and before him lay the green quad lined in tall, leafy trees, high brick buildings, the bridge and the river behind him.

Four

It wasn't until the early hours of the morning that she thought of it. She sat up on the couch, alone, in the dark. Laddered moonlight came from blinded windows. She could not swallow. She pressed her elbows to her knees and held her forehead, quenched her mouth with her fist. She went to her phone and thumbed it on. No service. Yup, she thought. That's what I deserve. She padded down the hall, carrying the baby monitors, and let herself into Sierra's room. She woke her sister, crouched by the side of the bed, lit by the eerie glow of the screens.

"I need to head out," Tamma said.

"Everything all right?" Sierra said, sitting up.

"Everything is fine," Tamma said. "Everything is okay but I have to do something. Can I leave the monitors with you?"

"Sure," Sierra said, covering her forehead with her hand and falling back into bed. Tamma plugged the monitors in and set them up on the bedside table. She crept back out of the room and in the living room, she dressed out of the duffel bag. Cutoffs, bralette, Veruca Salt muscle shirt, chuck taylors. She went out the front door and started the car and drove on down the lane. It was a warren of gravel roads back here. She drove, compulsively checking her phone. It was disconnected. There was nothing to see.

She blew through town not even slowing. A roar of lights and engine and then she was out on open highway again with the headlights picking out creosote and smoketrees. To the right of her she could see the chossy low hills that bounded the northern edge of the park. Spur roads ran off to both sides. She passed Lifted Lorax Lane, eased up on the gas, and let the speedometer fall back down to sixty. She was having trouble breathing, knocking on her sternum with the knuckles of her right hand to help calm herself, wrapping and rewrapping her left on the wheel, the wind blustering plastic bags and tumbleweeds across the roadway. She turned off at the bank. Parked beside the drive-through and walked up to the ATM. Moths were swarming the overhead lights. It was warm in the dark. She pulled her wallet out of her back pocket, shucked it open, found her debit card, and waited for the machine to process. Punched in her pin and waited again. Then she keyed through screens to check account balance. She stood waiting as the machine ticked and printed. She tore off the receipt and looked at it. She had $0.00 in her account. They had cleaned her out of all of Dan's money, and what savings she had added to that.

Tamma folded the receipt and put it away in her pocket. She walked back and sat on the curb. Behind her, a cactus garden. Moths came in and out of the light. She had a full tank of gas and forty dollars cash. She had no education, nowhere to be, no friends, and no future. She looked at her open hands. Just climber hands, the pads callused, though not as callused as they'd once been. They were long fingers for her size, the nails cut clean and close, painted bright pink, the first two fingers notched with scars from finger cracks, and beneath the tanned skin, veins running tangled and blue. The ring finger of her right hand still could not touch her palm. If she made a project of it, she could get it within about an inch. The breeze picked up her hair and beat her shirt flutteringly against her back.

I'm so stupid, she thought. I can't believe I lost all that money. But that's just the latest. I can't believe I let Dan climb Figures. I can't believe I said no to Paisley's rope. I can't believe I didn't go into the park sooner. I can't believe I kept thinking my mom would love me. I can't believe. I can't believe. *I can't believe all the things I did wrong.*

Then she thought, Nope. It's like you're thirty feet above your bolt and trying to pull a hard move, now is not the time to start thinking bad things, and not because they're not true, but because they're not helpful. It was terror and exposure to start hoping. But girls had done it before her. Jane Sasaki had done it. And if Jane could do it, then Tamma could do it too. She sat there on the curb. And she wasn't alone. She had Hunter and River and Samantha. She had Sierra.

She crouched forward, her knees drawn up to her belly, and ran her hands up and down her stubbled shins. You haven't been acting like a girl with a dream, she thought, rocking a little. You've been depressed. You haven't been working for it. The truth is, you've been too scared to try without Dan. But that's not who you want to be. It'll be harder alone, but half the impossible things were only ever impossible in your head. That's why girls like Paisley do so well. They look at the world an entirely different way. They think they belong. You ought to try it.

Well played, Mom, she thought. You sure showed me.

Then she thought: Nope. Let's pick a different line.

She sat in her car until the bank opened, and then she went in. The agent came out, opened her desk, logged in to her computer, and looked at Tamma and Tamma explained what had happened. The agent pursed her lips and shook her head.

"You opened the account with your mom as a cosignatory. She's not doing anything illegal."

"Uh-huh," Tamma said.

"Why not go to your mom and ask her for the money back?"

"Mm-hmm," Tamma said.

She sat in the chair opening and closing her hands, feeling the heavy callus of her fingers flexing.

"I'd like to close the account," she said. She waited as the agent typed. At last the agent said, "Okay, all done!"

"Thank you," Tamma said. She rose up out of the chair and let herself out through the smoked glass doors, crossed the parking lot, got into the car. She turned onto the highway. It was ten thirty in the morning, the sky cut with white contrails, a shimmer of heat coming off the parking lots, which were the crackled gray-black of chuckwalla hide. Low hills to the left and low hills to right, a valley of dead galleta, creosote, and yucca between, a line of telephone poles scalloping into the distance, the road running to a vanishing, level horizon.

She took the highway east and turned off north again. She drove out through open desert with strange sandy piles scattered on either side, like the catch heaps of hourglasses. After three hours, she pulled the car hard off onto the shoulder, yarded up the parking brake, kicked open the door, and stood on the side of the road. She braced on the hood and then reeled back from it, looking at her palms, spat onto the sheet metal and watched it toss and caper about on tiptoe, hissing. She turned and leaned the seat of her jeans back against the car and she took a look to see what she could see.

Joshua trees stood out there on the desert plain and they seemed to raise their arms and come slowly on toward her in ecstatic, worshipful misery. The road ran north like a mirrory slick of smoking grease. In the dust about her feet, velvet ants and sidewinder tracks. The sand was floury and deep and she was not at all sure that she could get the car back onto the road. Behind her, train tracks spanned the washes with low iron bridges.

She dug in the pocket of her cutoffs, and there, at the very bottom, found a quarter. What are you gonna do, Tamma Callahan, she thought. Are you going strike out on your own to Canyonlands? Or are you out here, having a curry pizza and a thinky-thought before you go pick River up out of his crib and kiss his little baby head? Which is it, girl? Back south, you have a home, responsibilities, people who need you. Out there, it's just Indian Creek, campfire tacos, and freedom.

She stood there on the side of the road, the hood burning her through the seat of her cutoffs. Heads, I leave, she thought. Tails, I stay. She slapped the quarter down onto her fist and lofted it into the air. It hung, coruscating in the sun, her own shadow upon the gray tarmac, and the shadow of the coin beside her coming in and out of existence as it turned.

The image came to her then, of her dad. That had been however many years ago, to the day, and just this hot. The anniversary of the moment she realized she could be hurt, of the moment she'd spent waiting for him to come pick her up, sure that he would come back, and finding, at last, that he never would. There she had been, her mouth hung wide open, unable to close it, blood dammed up behind her teeth and syruping over her lip. He must've been scared gutless, she thought. He must've had his reasons. They must've been convincing. Probably, he could tell you all about it, and all of his choices would be necessities. There had been dreams and ambitions to which his difficult and colicky daughter had been a hindrance. She hoped it was a joy to him, his freedom and success. Great things had happened. She'd seen him on instagram, playing in his pool with his newer, prettier child. She'd seen him on *Oprah*, looking very comfortable in a grand, leather chair. She thought of Daniel Redburn, gone to college. Alexandra, gone away from her family so that she could make her art. In her heart of hearts, Tamma thought that no great things came from limpdick cowards. Maybe you make good enough art to be rich and famous, and that wasn't the same. In her heart of hearts, Tamma thought Patrick Callahan was done. Alexandra was done. Brad was gone away from his kids when they needed him most and there didn't need to be a hell in the next world because there was one here, and he was living in it. And for what—raising Sam, Hunter, and River was one of the most joyful things Tamma had ever done. She thought of her own mom, standing in the bathroom doorway, saying that it was Tamma's fault, that Colin had raped a girl at school.

Terror, Tamma thought. It was terror and exposure to love someone and here she was, staring down the highway, and all about her, people ruined, lost, alone, choked at the cruxes of their lives. Maybe Dan was right, and it wasn't anybody's fault. Maybe everybody was doing the best they could, maybe they all had their reasons, and those reasons were good. The exposure was real, and some days it took more than just courage to face it down. Some days it didn't seem possible. And what about Tamma Callahan, had she done the best she could? What kind of girl are you, Tamma?

She caught the quarter upon her arm and stood that way, covering it with her hand, looking down the highway, thinking, What if I uncover this coin and it says *Leave*, will I leave? Walk away from those kids, out through the sand, and never look back? She was starting to smile, starting to smile despite herself, overcome with it.

When Tamma had been young, there had been nerve damage in her cheek and jaw that hadn't yet healed, so her expressions had been palsied and asymmetrical. Mrs. Curry had used to ask her not to smile so as not to scare the other children and Tamma was ever after always more or less in the habit of smiling and then trying not to smile, faltering in embarrassment, sealing it over with her lips stretched tight over her snaggletooth, then cracking open nonetheless into a delight she was powerless to stem, her smile zippering open left to right to show the whole chipped and disorderly shebang, waiting there on the side of the road with the grove all around her.

Was there a risk, if she stayed, that she'd be stuck in 73 Coyotes forever, slowly becoming her mom? Sure, there was a risk. Whatever was coming down the pike, it was a gut-coiler for sure, if only judging by what it had done to others. But she already had the hot, good, boulder-solving feeling coming over her, she was already trying to find the footholds, already looking for the line, and as she looked, it started to fall into place. This desert had shaped some of the strongest and boldest climbers of a generation. It could shape one more. Am I going to run away from children who need me, she thought, because it's going to be hard, because my mom was mean to me, because my dude-friend let me down, because I lost money? Am I going to run off, or am I the fucking *Fingerbang Princess*, am I about to grab my adventure taco in one hand, and my life in the other, and do this thing—take care of those kids and send hard boulders and swallow my pride and call Paisley and ask for her help? Tell her, "Paisley—I want to get onto the competition circuit, how do I do it? Help me, Paisley." Am I too scared to face this? Fuck no, she thought, grinning, molar to molar, cuffing snot off her lip. There were risks. Where she stood now, at the base of this thing, others had stood, just as hopeful, and they hadn't made it. But Tamma had climbed from out gore-strewn landings before. All these people, they'd lost what mattered, they'd thought real life was something you had when all the risks and frustrations were through. They had wanted to be safe, when it turned out the world was never safe, the world was a dicey highball, full of tenuous and low-percentage moves, and it was your very great privilege to try. She thought, There's a way forward, not an easy line, but a line, and I can fucking find it. Because I'm a goddamn trad climber, and it's not supposed to be easy; I don't even want it to be easy; I want it to be a horrifying chimney full of rat shit and hantavirus and doubt. The world, she thought, in all of its glory and terror and vastness. Not some escape. Not running away. The world for me, bitches.

Acknowledgments

I owe a great debt to a great many people. First of all, my agent, Joy Harris. A person could never hope for a stauncher ally. My editor, Sarah McGrath, who has been invaluable. My moms, Gloria and Elizabeth, who always supported my dreams. My buddy Tom, from whom I pillaged many jokes, stories, and mantras. Danny Parker, one of the kindest and most inspirational people I've ever met. I also have to apologize to Danny, that he endured a fun but dehydrated and somewhat sketchy ascent of a world-class climb that did not, in the end, make it into this book. Shingo Ohkawa, the Lorax of the Wasatch. Or the Gandalf? It depends on who you ask. But also, as my son calls them, all the "old crotchety climber guys" at IME. In particular Merrill Bitter, who was wonderfully willing to talk about Joshua Tree back in the day. I expected to have the chance to ask Merrill more questions, and I will always regret that I did not. Dr. Steve Santora, for the beta on fractures. Dr. Ross Greenlee and Dr. Patricia Greenlee, for answering endless and eclectic medical questions. And Ross again, for letting us borrow his cool old climbing gear when Hattie and I were too poor for trad climbing but too stoked not to try. Jess Itoh, who is

ACKNOWLEDGMENTS

a smashingly great buddy, for whiling away the day, struggling up climbs. No one has ever made the topout on Bongeater look (or sound) cooler. Meg, who was going to help me straighten out my many anachronisms, and who is dearly missed. I think I should also register that Meg vociferously advocated that Dan and Tamma should be readers of old climbing magazines. But in the early stages of writing this book, I tore a finger pulley and watched many, many hours of climbing comps while doing slow and painful rehab. So, the comps are a nod to that experience. Andy, the rad guide I hung out with in Joshua Tree, who was willing to sit and go through the beta on a few climbs move by move. Jake Billitteri, who decks more and stokes harder than almost anyone. Jonathan Eig, who is a reader, friend, and fashion icon. Ruchika Tomar, whose diamond-hard intellect I fall back on in times of doubt. Emily Berg, the most hilariously funny writing buddy I've ever had. Kylie Szilagyi, who was willing to talk to me all about comp climbing, and who is a blazingly impressive young woman with, I think, a novel in her back pocket. Michael Chasar, my college creative writing instructor, very dear friend, and favorite writer of cozy mysteries. Matt Sumell, who waded through many early, excruciatingly bad pages of this book. Michelle Latiolais, who saved everybody a hundred more pages of bouldering. Finally, my wife, Harriet, who was rollicking and hilarious during a pregnancy, a pandemic, colic, reflux, motherhood, another pregnancy (twins!), liver failure, the NICU, and everything that came after. Through it all, she kicked butt so I could be down in the basement crack-dungeon, writing. Hattie, you're the best person with whom to go adventuring, be it thrutching up desert towers or staying up late and sleep-deprived with tiny, tiny babies.